THE STEEL ROSE

THE STEEL ROSE

BOOK 2 OF THE BOAR KING'S HONOR TRILOGY

NANCY NORTHCOTT

Charlotte, NC

FALSTAFF
BOOKS

WWW.FALSTAFFBOOKS.COM

For the Davidson Wild Women
because each of them is, in her own way,
a steel rose.
ILYS

CHAPTER 1

London, England
February 26, 1815

Y ou're thinking about murder again, aren't you?"
   The question jolted Amelia Basingstoke, Viscountess Buckton, out of her reverie and pulled her attention back to the
crowded ballroom.

Her closest friend in London, Sophie Barton, Viscountess Whitestone,
stood beside her. Concern glimmered in Sophie's blue eyes.

Amelia pulled a wry smile. "How could you tell?"

She had been thinking of murder—two of them, actually—that'd
happened more than three hundred years in the past.

"You looked distracted, and not in the way you do when you have a
vision."

"You know me too well." Indeed, even another magically Gifted
person couldn't tell the difference between a seer's vision and mere
preoccupation unless that person knew the seer well.

On the dance floor, young ladies in pastel gowns and gentlemen in
black-and-white evening dress of cutaway coats and knee breeches glided
and wove through a quadrille. Here and there, dresses in deeper, richer
colors marked out women who were married or, like Amelia, widowed.
Amelia's gown had the high waistline and round skirt of the current style,

1

but she could never have worn this warm green, the color of new leaves, and its silver lace trim before her marriage.

Amelia linked her arm with Sophie's. "Take a turn about the room with me, if you please."

They fell into step, skirting the dance floor and other guests standing on the perimeter. When they reached a relatively clear space, Sophie asked, "Have you spoken to anyone with useful information?"

"No, alas." Amelia sighed. She'd agreed to come to London in part so she could meet other Gifted, who were rare at her home in Yorkshire. Those with deeper knowledge of magic might have some idea how she could lift her family curse. Not that she was ever specific about her reasons for asking questions. Those were not for sharing with casual acquaintances. Sophie knew about it because her eldest brother, Robert Grayson—Viscount Yeavering to the world, but Robin to his friends and family—had been one of Amelia's brother Adam's closest friends.

Amelia added, "Mrs. Evanston professed to have a number of grimoires but hadn't read any of them. Mr. Carruthers described himself as 'the merest dabbler' and recommended I apply to the realm's foremost expert on magical Gifts, the Earl of Aysgarth."

"Which you already did," Sophie noted, her voice dry.

Amelia shrugged. Julian Winfield, Earl of Aysgarth, had also been one of Adam's most trusted friends. When Adam and Papa died in a magical accident sixteen months ago, Julian had come to the funeral. She'd asked him then if he would help her find a way to release their souls from this curse. He'd promised to try, with a caveat. The war against Napoleon Bonaparte had still been raging, and Julian had been heavily involved. He not only worked for the Home Office but ran the Merlin Club, a group of Gifted dedicated to covertly serving Britain's interests. Naturally that work had taken priority.

"I did hope, with the war over...but perhaps he has nothing and simply doesn't wish to say so. To disappoint me."

"Or to admit defeat. Julian hates to give up." Sophie paused as they walked past another knot of people. "Just the other day, I overheard Robin tell Papa he's worried about Julian, that the war and other things—he didn't say what, and it seemed Papa knew—had taken a toll on him."

"Adam said he liked to spend the winters either traveling in search of old books on magic or working with his horses. I suppose that's what he's doing. And honestly, Sophie, I can't resent anyone who was involved in that conflict for needing time to recover."

"Robin wrote to him, asking when he planned to come to London for the Season, but he's had no reply yet."

They paused by one of the long windows, open to allow the winter air to cool the crowded room. Lowering her voice, Amelia added, "I now need his help on a different matter, one that might concern the Merlin Club. Several nights this past week, I've had a recurring dream of an eagle attacking a lion. The two of them fighting."

Sophie frowned. "Bonaparte used the eagle as his emblem."

"While Britain uses the lion. I know. I've consulted the ghosts of my many-times-great-grandparents. Grandmother Miranda agrees it's a portent, but she and Grandfather Richard are no more certain than I am about its meaning. We do all agree it could presage renewed conflict between England and France."

"That's disturbing. Though I envy you being able to talk to them. One of my great aunts was shockingly scandalous in the reign of George I. I would love to talk to her."

Since Sophie knew Amelia could converse with the ghosts only because she was their descendant and they were in a shadowy afterworld between the realms of the living and the dead, she must have meant to lighten the mood. Unfortunately, the effort failed.

Amelia said, "I could write to Julian." They'd been friends, addressing each other by their given names for that reason as well as the custom of the Gifted, and she was no longer an unwed girl. A letter was entirely within social bounds. Even if it were not, he knew her well enough not to read anything untoward into it. "I've delayed, partly because I don't want to seem impatient about Adam and partly because I hoped Julian would soon come to Town for the Season."

She'd also delayed because he'd looked so weary when he came to the funeral, like a man carrying burdens that weighed on his soul. Sharing that with Sophie, though, felt wrong.

"This probably isn't the sort of thing you want to put in a letter anyway," Sophie pointed out. "Have you Seen him?"

In a seer's vision, she meant.

"A few times, and I've scried him once or twice. He's always riding through a town or the countryside or surrounded by books, never in the same place."

Sophie wrinkled her nose. "Robin says Julian thinks the Gifted in the days of Merlin and Morgan had abilities we've lost. That's partly why he seeks out antique books, especially old codices, grimoires, and monastic chronicles, anything that might contain lost magical lore. The older a book is, the fewer copies existed at all, let alone survived centuries passing. Such books must be extremely difficult to find."

Based on Amelia's conversations since coming to London, information on blood curses was also extremely difficult to find. More than three hundred years before, her ancestor Edmund Mainwaring, then Earl of Hawkstowe, had unwittingly helped murder Edward IV's young sons, who had come to be known as the Princes in the Tower. He'd magically helped agents of his liege lord, the Duke of Buckingham, sneak into and out of the Tower of London's royal apartments undetected. He'd had no idea that those agents would kill the two boys or that Buckingham intended to seize the throne and saw them as rival claimants.

When Edmund realized what he had done, he threw himself on the mercy of the boys' uncle, King Richard III, who had installed them in the Tower apartments for their safety. The king ordered him to stay silent until the political situation improved. Unfortunately, King Richard died at Bosworth Field before giving Edmund leave to speak.

The accession of the Tudors, who blamed Richard III for the boys' deaths and any other crime they could, had made revealing the truth dangerous. Any challenge to their version of events would've been punished as treason.

Unable to speak safely during his lifetime but tormented by guilt, Edmund had rashly cursed all his heirs to not rest in life or death until they proved the truth about the murders and cleared King Richard's name. Now he and all the Mainwaring heirs, most recently Papa and Adam, were trapped in a shadowy, wraith-infested realm. Adam was having particular problems dealing with that ghastly place. She simply had to free him.

"You're wool gathering," Sophie murmured. "Smile."

How incredibly tedious, but Sophie was right. It was never wise to give the *ton*, England's social elite, anything to speculate about. Curving her lips upward, Amelia couldn't help remembering Edmund had never summoned the courtesy—or perhaps the nerve—to face her. He could've. She was also his descendant, but he'd avoided her instead.

Amelia sighed. She had done what she could this evening. She should put her disappointment aside for now and enjoy herself. Sophie and her family were always good company, and Amelia could begin a new round of inquiries tomorrow. One never knew who might have a clue to the truth or information about other ways to lift family curses.

"Let's walk again," Sophie said.

The two women moved along. Amelia watched the dancing, smiling couples. They seemed to enjoy themselves, and why not? She and Crispin, her tall, dark-haired husband, had enjoyed flirting with each other from the moment they met until a few days before his death.

They'd shared everything about themselves, including her closeness to the family ghosts. She would've bet her pin money few of the dancers, if any, believed in ghosts.

Yet ghosts had been Amelia's main teachers in the use of her Gifts. Her mother opposed the use of magic, allowing training for Adam, Amelia's twin, only because he was the heir. Fortunately, Adam had shared what he'd learned, and their ghostly great-great-grandparents had offered further aid. Grandmother Miranda had taught her summoning and guided her in using her Gifts since she was small.

"Sophie, do you—"

The ballroom winked out of being. In its stead, faint, fuzzy images drifted over shadowy ground. Gradually they resolved into men in blue or red or green uniforms fighting on foot or horseback. She knew those uniforms, worn by Napoleon Bonaparte's armies and the Allies who opposed him.

A red-jacketed cavalryman charged at her, his sword high. Shrieking, she tried to dodge, only to have him ride through her in a rush of icy cold that made her shiver.

Out, she thought. *I need out of this vision. Out.*

She tried to put power behind the words, as her ghostly tutors had instructed, but nothing changed. Another rider charged. She scrambled out of his path—and through a red-coated infantryman's musket barrel. Gasping with cold and terror, she dived under a slashing blade to cower against a waist-high outcropping of rock.

The soldiers fired at each other through air already thick with gunpowder smoke. The din rang in her ears. Smoke and the acrid stench of blood stung her nostrils, and she coughed.

"Amelia!"

As suddenly as it had begun, the vision ended. She was back in the ballroom with Sophie peering at her anxiously. The scents of beeswax and perfumes supplanted those of gunpowder and blood. The musicians still played the same quadrille.

Yet her heart pounded, and her head felt light. Shivering, she clutched her shawl. Her seer Gift had never manifested so strongly on its own. Why now?

"Did I do or say anything odd?" she asked Sophie.

"No, but you looked dazed. What is it?"

"Not here. Let's find a private place."

The library or some other unoccupied room would have a fire. Amelia could use the flames to scry, to see if she could develop what she'd Seen.

Circling toward the door, Sophie stopped a footman and took two crystal glasses of lemonade from his tray. Amelia sipped the cool, tart liquid, a relief in the stuffy room. Not everyone could have lemonade in February, but their hosts, the Earl and Countess of Draven, had a conservatory at their country property. As Lady Draven liked to remind everyone.

Amelia and Sophie reached the corridor, and Amelia took a grateful breath of cooler air. They exchanged greetings with a passing matron in a russet silk gown and a russet-and-cream-striped turban.

The library lay a short distance down the corridor. Muffled by Axminster carpeting in a subtle, floral pattern, their footsteps made little noise.

"Isn't Whitestone coming tonight?" Amelia asked. "Should you leave word where he can find you?" Sophie's husband had been at their estate in Devonshire these past three weeks, and she'd made no secret of missing him. Fair-haired, sturdy Ned Barton, Viscount Whitestone, was Gifted and easygoing, a perfect match for his petite, brown-haired wife and her cheerful nature.

Amelia bit back a sigh. Sometimes she couldn't help envying her friends whose lives followed the courses they'd planned.

"He won't arrive until later," Sophie replied.

Voices came through the library's closed door. Frowning, she said, "Well, that's no good. Let's try this parlor."

It proved to be empty, though the plates and cups on the round tables flanking the blue-and-gold-striped sofa meant someone had been here earlier. A fire crackled on the hearth, and the room had a cozy feel. Still, whoever had been here should've had the fire banked when they departed. A lone spark on the carpet in an empty chamber could have the room ablaze before anyone discovered it.

"Sit down," Sophie said. "You look pale. Sip your lemonade and then have mine. I haven't touched it."

"Thank you, but mine will suffice." Amelia sat and took a long swallow.

"I've rarely had more than a brief flicker of awareness or a momentary mental image from a vision when I wasn't trying to summon one about something in particular. The intensity and clarity of this vision were as disturbing as the events it revealed." She described what she'd Seen for her friend. "It was like accounts I read of the war. Napoleon abdicated only last year. Perhaps I passed near a soldier, someone who remembered it or is haunted by it. Perhaps someone in that last battle. Leipzig, if I remember rightly."

"You know not one woman in ten in the ballroom would admit to remembering that all these months later. War being the province of men, you know."

"Men have sisters," Amelia said softly. Grief for Adam welled anew into her throat, though he hadn't died in the war. "And mothers and daughters and cousins. Those women, I wager, remember well enough."

"Yes, and we owe them all, the men and their families, a debt."

They sat in silence, watching the flames.

Amelia finished her lemonade and set the glass down. "I'm ready. You needn't stay if you want to return to the dancing."

Sophie shook her head. "I'll stay. I'm intrigued now."

"As you wish." Staring at the flames, Amelia extended her power until she could feel them crackle and flicker. The image formed between the andirons, steady despite the dancing fire behind it. Amelia reached, trying to draw out her viewing, but she managed to capture only a few more moments of the clash she'd Seen.

She let the vision go and took a deep breath. "Did you see?" Any Gifted person should be able to see a scrying with ordinary sight, but Sophie had said she wasn't good at that skill. All Gifted could do it to some extent, but, as with any talent, some were better at it than others.

"Yes, and it's puzzling. Why would you See something like that?"

"I don't know. I rarely See things I don't understand, perhaps because I live a fairly peaceful life."

If only she'd foreseen the dreadful illness that struck Crispin in India, could she have persuaded him not to go? But there was no use walking over that ground again.

"I'll try for the vision's past," Amelia said.

That served a little better. They watched armies take the field, infantry and cavalry charging. The Duke of Wellington sat on a chestnut horse on a ridge, barking orders as cannon balls fell all around, musket balls and canister shot flew, and gun smoke clouded the air. Before him stretched a line of British infantry in red and what must be Allied troops in blue and gray.

She released that image and reached farther back. In the flames, a rocky shore appeared. Sunlight sparkled on the waves and brightened the sides and seats of a small sailboat moored by a dock. Beyond it, in deeper water, a ship rode at anchor.

Smiling, blue-coated figures with red epaulets at the shoulders and white cross-belts over the chests of their coats marched in smart order toward the pier. The sunlight glinted off the brass eagle plates on the fronts of their tall, black bearskin hats and the silver cord draping them. A cockade of red, white, and blue circles around an eagle emblem anchored an upright red plume to the left side of each hat. In the midst of the group walked a short, stout man with neatly trimmed, receding brown hair. The man climbed into the boat. He turned to seat himself and looked directly at her—no, through her.

Ice rippled down her spine. She'd seen that face sketched in the news-papers. Why would Napoleon Bonaparte be climbing into a boat with such a large escort?

The men in the boat raised the sail and pushed off, apparently headed for the black-and-white ship in the background. Longboats by the shore filled with more blue-coated men. They slid oars into the locks and rowed after the sailboat.

Amelia's heart pounded. Was Bonaparte escaping his exile on Elba, possibly returning to France? Or was he merely going for a pleasure cruise? If Bonaparte returned to France, the vision she'd had earlier could make horrible sense.

Please let it be only a brief cruise.

Amelia let the scrying fade. She and Sophie looked at each other in shared worry.

"Robin should see this. I'll have someone summon him." Sophie hurried into the corridor.

Robin was Julian's second at the Merlin Club and worked with him at the Home Office. Perhaps he would know whether the last vision was benign. If it wasn't, the sooner he knew Bonaparte had left Elba, the sooner the government and the club's agents could act.

Sophie returned and closed the door. "A footman will bring him. This would be a superb moment for one of your ghostly however-many-great grandparents to appear. Can you...I don't know...call one of them?"

"I could if they were near, but I never know they are until they appear.

According to what Grandmother said, a scrying of the past should be clear. Detailed. The present also. As the scene with Bonaparte was. But the future…" A chill ran down Amelia's back.

"What is it?" Sophie asked.

"Grandmother said the future is constantly influenced by events, always changing. Scrying or Seeing more than a few weeks ahead thus often produces odd, symbolic visions or mere glimpses. Such as the vision I had of a battle. As events become more likely or more important, though, the future visions become clearer. Longer. Past or present events usually show clearly and with great detail." As this last one had been.

Sophie's expression turned grim.

The door opened, and her tall, dark-haired brother Robin entered. He took one look at their faces, and his smile faded. "What's happened?"

"You must see this," Sophie said.

Amelia directed her magic at the flames. "I had a brief vision of battle first. When I tried to scry more, this is all I could find, not much more than the original vision." When he nodded acknowledgement, she summoned the scrying of Wellington in battle. "Looking for the vision's past, I found this."

Robin's face became granite hard, his blue eyes icy as he watched the battle scenes.

When the scrying faded out, Amelia said, "This is the one that worries us the most, as we fear it explains the others." She summoned the fiery image of Bonaparte embarking in the sailboat and the ship lying at anchor beyond. This time, she didn't stop the scrying when the sailboat pulled away from the dock and the longboats launched after it.

Robin frowned. "That lead ship, the *Inconstant*, is painted in the Royal Navy pattern of black and white. Amelia, can we see who's on deck?"

She changed her angle, which also brought into view other ships lying at anchor and the group of longboats trailing Bonaparte's. The men in the longboats, like those along the ship's nearside railing, wore the same uniforms as those who had escorted Bonaparte to the water.

"Bloody hell," Robin breathed. "Those are Bonaparte's elite Imperial Guard. He wouldn't have so many along if he meant to return to Elba."

Bonaparte's boat reached the ship. As the men on deck cheered, he climbed a rope ladder and stepped through a gap in the railing. The crowd enveloped him, hiding him from sight. The ship weighed anchor and set sail.

"That's enough," Robin said.

Amelia let the vision fade and rubbed her brow.

Sophie squeezed her arm. "How are you, Amelia? That was a long scrying."

"I'm terrified. During that last scrying, I felt it already had happened or is happening, while the battle vision's vagueness implies it may not occur."

"We should all be terrified." Robin scowled. "Say nothing of this. I'll continue trying to scry Bonaparte."

"Will the Home Office do something?" Sophie asked. "Or the War Office?"

"No, blast it." Robin stared at the hearth. "Since I cannot say we magically learned the bast—scoundrel escaped, they won't believe he did. Even if I say I had word from a friend on Elba, that word couldn't reach here so quickly. Unless this was several days ago?"

Amelia shook her head. "I cannot be sure, but it feels like the very recent past, sometime in the last day or so."

Robin shook his head.

"There's nothing to be done?" Amelia asked.

"The Merlin Club can act without delay, and we will. As for the government, we must wait a few days before I can make any plausible claim of receiving word. By then, perhaps information will have come by official channels." He ran a hand through his hair. "Bonaparte had a tiny kingdom on Elba, even was allowed to use the title of Emperor. If he's leaving there, it can only be because he has his eye on something bigger."

"The French throne," Sophie guessed.

Robin nodded. "Under no circumstances can we allow him to rule France again. The Allies must stop him. Again, curse him."

Feeling faintly sick, Amelia said, "So we're back to war."

"I fear so." Robin added, "We need Julian. If the Merlin Club takes action, he should direct it. I'll send him word by one of our couriers, who'll track him down if necessary."

"You'll put that in a letter?" Sophie gaped at her brother.

"Of course not. I'll simply tell him the devil is loose, our standing code for Bonaparte on a new rampage, and we need him. He'll return as swiftly as he can."

Amelia said nothing as Robin took his leave. A courier's progress would depend on the state of the roads and the weather. There might be a faster way to summon Julian.

If she could manage it.

⌇

A seer need not scry to See what is, what was, and what will be.
Grandmother Miranda's words were etched into Amelia's memory. Over time, she'd come to regard that saying as overly simple. A seer could See, but not always what she—or he—wished to See, when it was wanted. That took not only power and practice but luck.

Miranda's and Richard's ghosts had instructed her in using her magical Gifts, but they didn't tell her everything she wondered about. She still didn't know precisely what they'd done to allow Grandfather Richard to move through time when the other Mainwaring men—except Edmund, because he'd started the curse—were trapped in the eras when they'd lived. Or why Miranda had been allowed to stay in the afterworld and move freely through time. She'd chosen to remain with Richard, but that didn't explain it. Every other Mainwaring woman who died passed into the afterworld at the final portal and through it for judgment.

Grandmother Miranda's ghostly form shimmered into view by the fireplace. The hearth and its crackling flame were visible through her figure.

"You look unhappy, Amelia. What troubles you?"

She had lived to be almost eighty but appeared to be in her mid-thirties, her dark brown hair in a style much like Amelia's, coiled in a knot at the crown of her head with ringlets framing her face. Her rose satin gown, conjured from the afterworld's magic, had the wide neckline, elongated waistline, and puffy, elbow-length sleeves of her favorite era. Frothy, white lace trimmed the neckline and sleeves.

Amelia told her about the evening's odd events. "Do you know what would explain that spontaneous vision of battle?"

"It sounds like a future Sight." Miranda frowned. "Magic comes from within, but we shape it with our intention and the force of our will. Of all the Gifts, the seer talent most resists that direction. Another possibility is that someone very nearby used magic and you felt it. But seers sense intent, not only action. It could be that you sensed the plan of someone who passed close to you."

"Perhaps someone who knew of Bonaparte's escape?"

"That man is clever to his bones, and he has a way of persuading people to his ends. Richard or I will verify your scrying, but I expect it was accurate."

Through the afterworld, they could travel anywhere except into structures warded by wizards who were not their kin. They also couldn't leave that realm to enter the living world, but they could observe what transpired there.

"We were at war with France for almost twenty years." Amelia had been a child when the war began. "Crispin's cousin died at Corunna, and Adam's friend Augustus, at Salamanca. Captain Alan Douglas, Lord Stornaway's son, lost an eye at Toulouse. Having war resume would be horrible."

"It may not come to that." Miranda laid a hand on Amelia's shoulder, conveying understanding and support even though she couldn't actually touch her.

She could help in another way, though. "Grandmother, when you summoned Grandfather to you, did you know where he was? Precisely, I mean."

A smile curved Miranda's lips and warmed her eyes. "I didn't even know who he was."

"Will you tell me again about summoning him?"

"You know that story well. Why do you want to discuss it again?"

Amelia explained about Julian. "The Merlin Club needs him. The sort of summons you sent will arrive faster than their courier."

"Surely." The answer was dry. "Yet you didn't summon him to gain his help with the curse?"

"My need was urgent only for our family, and I didn't know whether he perhaps wanted to be alone. He looked so weary when I saw him last. This is different."

"Of course. Your Gifts are better developed than mine were then—"

"Thanks to you and Grandfather."

"—so you may not need the elaborate ritual I used, but in case you do, write this down."

CHAPTER 2

"Amelia? I'm here."

Adam's mental voice broke through the haze of sleep. Amelia kept her eyes closed, the better to envision him. Even though ghosts could normally communicate only with direct descendants, her great-great grandparents had said she and Adam could reach each other because they were twins. Even then, with each ghost restricted to the years he'd lived in the spiral of time, he could only speak with her, not appear to her as Grandmother Miranda and Grandfather Richard did. Papa seldom spoke to her, perhaps because doing so seemed to distress him.

"It's so good to hear from you." Amelia imagined his familiar face, a squarer, more masculine version of hers. "How are you?"

"I'm growing accustomed. So is Papa." He sounded weary. "I should've listened to you about the curse. To Grandfather Richard. Papa should've."

Amelia's heart clenched. "You and Papa did what you thought best. It's useless to reproach yourself for it."

"I miss you," he said softly. "I miss my friends, especially Robin and Julian. I'm glad you and Sophie are close, despite her being two years younger. You need more friends."

He was her dearest friend, but saying that wouldn't help anything. "I'm trying to help you and Papa and all the rest. We hope Julian will uncover useful information."

"If anyone can, he will. He drives himself to forget that shrew he married. We tried to tell him, Robin and I, but he wouldn't listen. It's too bad she died, but he was well rid of her."

Perhaps that was the "other" matter Robin had mentioned to his father. Regardless, Julian probably would not appreciate these confidences.

Amelia said, "I plan to consult with Julian when he returns to London."

"Be patient with him. He's a good man. Clever. He wouldn't have been as stupid as I was."

Before she could reply, the sense of his presence vanished. "I'll do all I can to free you," she promised, even though he was no longer able to hear her.

The easiest way to do so was lost. According to Richard and Miranda, Edmund had written a full confession explaining how Buckingham had tricked him into unwittingly helping murder the Princes in the Tower. Omitting his use of magic from the document so there would be no bar to publishing it among the unGifted, he had assumed his descendants would wait until the Tudors no longer ruled and then publish his confession. When he realized his son cared little about the dead king's honor and reputation, Edmund had angrily cursed the line to ensure the confession was published when it was safe to do so. Unfortunately, that document had disappeared, as Richard and Miranda had discovered when they tried to retrieve it more than a century before. So had any trace of Edmund's ever having written it.

If Amelia could find and publish it, that would clear King Richard of his nephews' murders, as would proving the truth by any other means. That would free not only Papa and Adam but all the other doomed Mainwaring men.

If she could find the confession or other proof.

Amelia looked to the window. The faintest hint of light softened the darkness. She had best hurry. The household would be stirring soon, and having anyone spot her would lead to awkward questions.

"Grandmother?" she asked softly.

"Here." Miranda shimmered into view.

Amelia dressed quickly in an old frock she kept only for making jams and fruit preserves. The stains on it would conceal any dirt from the garden. An old reticule held the workings for the spell, assembled the night before.

She hurried downstairs, out the back door, and down the steps to the long, narrow lawn bounded by six-foot brick walls. Only from the upper floors would any neighbors be able to see her, and the windows in their houses remained dark. Good.

The sky was noticeably lightening now, but the sun was not yet up. The cold air bit through her clothes. She should've thought to bring a cloak, but going back for it would delay her. Every moment that passed brought her nearer to the time the maids and kitchen staff would start their day. Perhaps look out the window and see her.

There was no private outdoor space here at her aunt and uncle's house. The knot garden in the yard's rear corner, with its five-foot brick walls, would have to do. She walked into the garden and knelt by the bench to the left of the gate with her back to the house.

"You're certain no one will see the dragon avatar?" she asked the ghost at her side.

"Anyone Gifted will be able to see it, but no one else."

Amelia laid her reticule on the bench and drew out her workings. A scrap of green silk for color, twigs for bones, kindling from her bedchamber for fire, and a needle to prick her finger.

"This is no different from making the tiny beings you do so well," Grandmother assured her. "'Tis only larger."

Much larger. Amelia had never created anything so big or meant to travel so far. The tiny squirrels and mice she'd made had been for practice, and she'd sent them a few dozen yards at most. With no messages implanted.

Regardless, this must succeed. She'd always loved gryphons, dragons, and winged horses. In honor of Grandmother Miranda's summons to her future husband more than a century ago, Amelia would use a dragon for this. Besides, that summoning had succeeded in all respects. Perhaps imitating it would bring her luck.

She used her bare hands to scrape leaves and dead plants away from the withered flower beds and bare a square patch of earth a couple of feet across. "Is that large enough?"

"It will do."

She chose a pebble from the path and laid it in the center of the bare space. On top of it went the first piece of kindling with the silk wrapped around it. The second bit of kindling went on top of that. She used the needle to prick the fourth finger of her left hand, the one with the vein that led to her heart.

"An incantation might help," Miranda said, "even if you say it only to yourself. I couldn't do this without one, but you likely can if you practice it more often."

Watching blood drip onto the little stack, Amelia thought, *Twigs for bones, scales and talons from silk and stones.*

Closing her eyes, she imagined the different items fusing. She sent magic into the mental image and felt the kindling catch fire. Another flicker of magic sent air rushing over it all. *Wind and magic for power in flight, fire and blood to give vision life.*

The image of a dragon formed in her mind, and she pushed that into the construct along with her message for Julian. To guide the avatar, she summoned her memory of him, a tall man in his mid-twenties with the rugged Winfield features, including a strong nose, gray eyes, and brown hair.

The tiny fire crackled in the cold air. Around it, her magic swelled, growing into the creature she envisioned. A great, green head stretched skyward on a long neck. Leathery wings the same color glistened in the faint, predawn light.

"Oh, well done," Grandmother said softly, and Amelia opened her eyes.

A large, green dragon stood in the flowerbed, its folded wings brushing the garden wall and blocking the path.

Amelia smiled. To finish the spell, holding her message for Julian in her mind, she ordered, "Fly, my dragon, with wings unfurled and send me back this wayward earl."

With a surge of power, the dragon leaped skyward. Its great wings swept down, and it rose into the lightening sky.

Amelia's heart lifted with it. *Please, please let me have done it properly.* "What if it can't convey my message?"

"It will," her grandmother assured her. "The message is in your intent, your will. The magic will do the rest. By the by, I found young Aysgarth last night at an inn near his seat in Yorkshire. He'll likely be at home by the time your dragon reaches him. Whether or not he is, it will find him."

Amelia looked up at the sky. "It can't be too soon."

Near Hampstead, a carriage rolled through the wrought-iron gates of Wyndon House and across the courtyard to the stone Palladian house's front door. Silas de Vere, Earl of Wyndon, stepped down from the carriage. The night's gaming had been productive. He'd won several hundred pounds and come away with potentially useful secrets in hand. Secrets were power. Fortunately for him, few of the *ton* had the sense to realize that until it was too late.

He mounted the front steps. His efficient porter already had the door open, as expected.

When Silas reached the threshold, awareness brushed across his nape. Magic. Above?

He looked up. High overhead, a green dragon flapped its great wings and sped northward.

Well, well, someone either had learned summoning or possessed impressive illusion skills. This required investigation.

A footman took his greatcoat, and the earl strode through his house. The fire in his bedchamber should have been kept burning while he was out. Using that one would be faster than having another stoked.

His tall, thin valet, Ottersley, helped him out of his evening wear with silent efficiency. Only when Silas sat before the hearth in his nightshirt and a gray satin, crimson-embroidered banyan, or dressing gown, did the man speak. "Would my lord care for anything to eat?" he asked.

"No, that will be all." Silas was still sated from the beef sandwiches at Hazard House. For a gaming hell, it supplied excellent victuals. Of course, that helped bring the Quality back to the tables. That and the availability of choice wenches.

When the dressing room door closed behind Ottersley, Silas sent his magic into the flames. The dragon appeared, now well north of the city and still flying. Patiently, he traced it into the past, to its origins. A garden in Mayfair and a woman wizard.

His eyes narrowed. The woman looked up as her dragon took flight, and he recognized her. His heart leaped.

The widowed Viscountess Buckton, née Lady Amelia Mainwaring, obviously had powerful magic to recommend her. Could she also have the seer Gift? It often accompanied the summoning Gift, and both ran in her family lines.

He had suspected she might be a useful asset, but she'd shown no sign of any significant magical ability. At least not during his covert spying. If she did possess the seer Gift, she posed a danger to his plans. The wizards loyal to mad George III and his revolting son the Prince Regent, commonly known as Prinny, couldn't be allowed to recruit her to oppose his scheme.

In exchange for aiding the French wizards and their Scots dupes, he would rule the Isle of Man after the French conquered England. It would be his base to gather England's Gifted. After a decade or so of French rule, he and his Gifted allies would expel the French. Their fellow Englishmen would be so grateful that the Gifted would no longer have to hide what they were. They could rule, as they always should have.

Unless someone exposed his plan.

If Lady Buckton was a seer, she was a threat. One that must be neutralized.

Gossip said her mother, the Dowager Countess of Hawkstowe, aspired to a grand match for her widowed daughter. An unlikely prospect for most widows, especially those her age, but not among England's wizards, not for one superbly Gifted. What grander match could there be than one with an earl who possessed a vast fortune and bloodlines going back to the Conquest?

The dowager countess had cut her family off from the realm's Gifted even before her husband's and son's deaths. Her husband had been a fool to allow it. Now Silas could turn their isolation to his advantage. The best way to control a woman, after all, was by marrying her.

He would learn all he could about the viscountess, the better to weave a snare around her. If that failed, he had a trump card. He would hold that, though, for future leverage if he could win her without it.

Before she knew it, she would be saying vows with him. Then she would be his, bound to obey and serve him.

CHAPTER 3

Julian Winfield, Earl of Aysgarth and holder of assorted other titles, frowned at the bits of parchment spread across his library worktable. The ancient codex, supposedly the work of Viking wizards in the eighth century, had fallen apart, and a household fire—again, supposedly, though the damage didn't fit that explanation—had destroyed parts of the pages.

The Latin script was an odd choice for Viking wizards of that pagan era.

Standing just above six feet, he had to bend over the long table. Perhaps he should have a higher one made, but this one served well enough most of the time.

"Making progress?" his Aunt Augusta asked. She lounged back against the cushions of her chair, a decidedly unladylike pose. At fifty-one, a widow for a decade, his mother's sister wore her graying blond hair in a simple bun-and-ringlets style and chose her frocks for comfort with the barest nod to fashion.

Her lack of concern with propriety, at least in private, was one reason they got on so well. He rarely wore a cravat or coat or waistcoat at Aysgarth, in or out of the house, and bedamned to society.

"Some," he replied. "The more I look at this codex, the more I think the story old Fortescue told me was made up out of whole cloth. Though perhaps that's the story given to him. It doesn't matter now. I'll uncover the truth soon enough."

The writing had faded on the fragment in front of him, and singe marks obliterated some of the words. At the edge, though, the letters o-p-p were clear enough. Was that *oppidum*, for town? Or some form of *opprimere*, to oppress?

"Can't you sort all that magically?" his aunt asked.

"Where's the fun in that?" Scowling, he shifted the fragments, looking for one that continued the word. *Bloody hell*, the singed pages made matching things up difficult. Magic had failed to restore the damage, perhaps because it was so longstanding. At least he could magically bind fragments together once he determined how they fit.

Aunt Augusta added, "If you want puzzles, I'm certain the Home Office would welcome your return."

"I've had my fill of their sort of puzzles, thank you." Not to mention the way everyone wanted to put in his oar. If not for the secret help of the Merlin Club's Gifted members, well-meant Home Office interference would've made accomplishing anything difficult.

He turned his attention back to the fragments. His aunt devoted herself to her book.

Mounds of snow still blanketed the shady parts of the back lawn that were visible through the windows and the French doors to the terrace. Frost sparkled on the windowpanes. In here, though, the fire kept the room cozy. Only its crackling and the occasional whispery sound of his aunt turning a page broke the silence. He liked it that way. This room was his haven, the books like old friends. The crossed cavalry sabers and broadswords above the two mantels and the family portraits hanging above those were so familiar that he scarcely noticed them.

With the war over and that Corsican menace, Bonaparte, safely confined, he could go back to his horses and his books in peace. Perhaps even find something that would help lift the curse confining his friend Adam's soul.

"Julian?"

His aunt's voice sounded odd, but it sometimes did when she was distracted. "Yes, Aunt?"

Was that word *poena*, for punishment, or—

"My dear, there's a dragon landing on the lawn."

—no, perhaps it was *postulo*, for ask or demand. "I'm sure Hawes will tend to it," he told her. No, it wasn't *postulo*. It was...*wait. What?*

He lifted his head to look at his aunt. Sitting ramrod straight now, she stared out the windows. Her lips were slightly parted. As though suddenly aware her jaw had dropped, she snapped her mouth shut.

"What did you say?" he asked.

"You heard me perfectly well. Come and look."

He walked around the table to join her. Staring out the window, he blinked, rubbed his eyes, and looked again. "Yes," he said slowly, "I do believe that's a dragon." The creature's long neck, big, scaly body, and leathery wings could belong to nothing else.

The beast crouched on the dead grass next to the walled, Elizabethan garden, its head on its long neck three to four feet higher than the six-foot wall. Its green scales glinted in the morning sunlight, and its fiery gold eyes stared at the library window.

"Feel the magic crackling around it?" his aunt asked.

"Indeed. A bit much for Hawes to deal with. I'd best go and—"

Lord Aysgarth, said a deep, rusty voice in his head.

"I'm coming out," he told the creature, wheeling toward the terrace doors. He glanced at the crossed sabers above the mantel, but blades wouldn't do much against magical apparitions.

"I don't think that's wise," Aunt Augusta said. Wise or not, she fell into step with him as he hurried outside. "What is that thing?"

"It's likely an avatar," he replied, walking down the broad steps from the terrace, "such as were once used for summoning. Though nobody's done that regularly in centuries. Requires a great deal of power. Also a great deal of nerve, landing that thing on a fellow's lawn and demanding his time."

He could dispel it, of course, but then he would never know why it sought him out. When it had done whatever it had come for, perhaps he could study it. See how long it lasted. What effect, if any, its magic had on the grass.

His aunt kept pace with him. For once, he breached courtesy by stepping in front of her.

"Julian," she breathed, her tone a warning, as they neared the creature.

She had a point. Ten feet away, he stopped and stared up at the beast. "Well?"

It lowered its head, bringing its large, toothy snout uncomfortably close. Speaking aloud this time, it announced, "Adam Mainwaring's sister sent me."

Hearing Adam's name made his face flash into Julian's mind, and fresh grief threatened to choke him.

The beast continued, "She wants you to know the devil is loose."

That phrase chilled his blood. Amelia must've spoken with Robin. Even if she hadn't, she was a seer. She might know that phrase's meaning for him because of her Gift.

"The Merlin Club needs you," the creature finished.

If Bonaparte was loose, it certainly did.

Of course Amelia knew of the club. Its founders had been her ancestors Richard and Miranda Mainwaring and three of their friends, including Julian's forebears Cabot and Jeremy Winfield. She wouldn't evoke it lightly. Had Robin asked her to send this creature? It was likely faster than a courier.

"Julian," his aunt said, "I believe it's waiting for your answer."

He looked up at the dragon again. How in blazes had it warped its fierce countenance into an expectant look?

This time in Yorkshire had been his treat to himself, a chance to add to his collection of ancient books, to study them, visit his tenants, and tend his horses. To enjoy the life Bonaparte's antics had interrupted for so long. But he was Director of the Merlin Club. If danger threatened his country, he was sworn to meet it.

"I'll leave as soon as I can pack."

Surely the creature hadn't given him a look of approval. It nodded its great head, spread its vast, gleaming wings, and leaped skyward. One downstroke of those wings, then another, and yet another took it high above the trees that edged the lawn. Then it vanished.

"So much for studying that construct," he muttered.

Only now did he notice the bitter wind biting through his shirt sleeves and pantaloons. Still, he advanced to the spot the dragon had occupied and knelt. No sign of its presence remained. No depression in the frozen grass, no traces of remaining magic.

"Nothing," he said. "It's as though the blasted thing were never here."

"Then let us please go indoors."

When he turned, his aunt stood with her arms crossed and her shoulders hunched against the cold. "Sorry, Aunt," he said.

"Understandable," she replied. They walked toward the terrace steps together.

"What did it mean?" she asked. "About the devil being loose?"

"It means Napoleon Bonaparte has escaped Elba." Over her gasp, he added, "We'll verify it, but Amelia is not one to sound unnecessary alarms."

Even as a girl, she'd been level-headed, and nursing her husband through a fatal case of dysentery had required good sense and emotional control. When he'd seen her after Adam's funeral, she'd been supremely poised, if understandably sad. He'd meant to call on her this past summer, to let her know he hadn't forgotten his promise to help with the family curse, but he'd been busy with the aftermath of Bonaparte's abdication in April.

They crossed the terrace, and he opened the door for his aunt. Following her in, he added, "I promised Amelia I would seek a way to lift her family curse. Since I can do nothing about Bonaparte until I reach London, I'll take that new book on blood magic to check en route. Nothing I've found about such matters thus far was of use, but perhaps it will have something."

"If Bonaparte is running free, how much time does the government have to act?"

"That depends entirely on how long he has been running about. While I trust Amelia's word, I must verify that she's correct."

He walked to the hearth and stared into the crackling flames. Scrying wasn't the strongest of his magical Gifts, but he could generally access the recent past and the present. When he directed his power at the flames and thought of Bonaparte, a carriage appeared, one he couldn't see into. It must be warded. Other coaches and wagons trailed it, men in the blue uniforms of Napoleon's Imperial Guard filling them. When he pulled the scrying back, widening its scope, the size of the land mass confirmed it was not Elba or any other island. This must be the Continent. Likely France, since this was Bonaparte.

Damnation.

To be certain, he scried Bonaparte's house on Elba. It appeared empty but for servants. When he shifted to thinking of Bonaparte, the coach on its winding road replaced the island in the flames.

Shaking his head, he let the images fade. He turned to his aunt, whose worried expression confirmed that she'd seen his scrying.

"So you're bound for London," she said.

"Alas, yes." Julian grimaced. "I'll likely be forced to attend social events to see what I can learn in the gossip mill that is the *ton*." London during the Season, the months when the nobility flocked in to attend Parliament, was one constant irritant.

"My dear," Aunt Augusta said, "you do need an heir. Going about socially in London might not be a bad idea."

"Speak for yourself," he muttered. His late wife's infidelity, gambling, and recklessness had soured him on both marriage and spoiled young damsels, but his aunt was right.

He stalked to the corridor door and opened it. To the footman seated nearby, he said, "Toby, please have the travelling coach prepared and ask Baker to pack for an extended stay in London."

The man sprang away on his errand.

"I'll take some books about Richard III and his accession to the throne," Julian said, striding to his history shelves. "I've looked through them, of course, but I'm no seer. If Amelia reads them, perhaps one will spur a vision that could help us find proof of Buckingham's guilt in murdering the boys in the Tower."

"How well do you know her?" his aunt asked.

"I danced with her often. All of Adam's friends did. She was an amiable, clever girl. She's also quiet and bookish, which won't help her in London ballrooms. I rather liked her." In fact, he'd wished his then-wife had more of her quiet consideration.

"I saw her before I left Town. She seems not much interested in the social whirl. She has acquired a reputation as a bluestocking, which doesn't seem to bother her. Like you, I thought her pleasant and intelligent. She would be wasted on most of the young men there at the moment."

"It may be as well she isn't interested." Julian drew two volumes from the bookcase and set them on the table. In a dry voice, he noted, "She's the same age as Adam, so she'll have turned four-and-twenty in January. That puts her decidedly on the shelf." The *ton*'s belief that any woman much over twenty was beyond marriageable age was merely more proof of society's idiocy. "It's too bad Buckton contracted dysentery. Man goes to India to help his brother, only to lose his life for his troubles."

Skillful application of magic could heal most illnesses, but not those like dysentery and malaria that might appear vanquished, only to recur mysteriously months later. That must've been torment for Amelia.

"I'll come with you." Aunt Augusta held up a hand. "I'm not so old as to find swift travel a problem, and Cranshaw can pack for me quickly."

"Then I'll be glad of the company. The sooner we muster our resources against Bonaparte, the better."

~

Trailed by grooms, Amelia and Sophie slowly rode their mares along Rotten Row, the wide dirt track that ran from Hyde Park Corner to Kensington Gardens. Bright sunshine made the chilly afternoon tolerable. They had come before the fashionable hour, but the path was already choked with riders making the endless loop through the park for the *ton* to see and be seen. Other people strolled along the path beside the Row.

The muffled thuds of hooves on dirt mingled with the rattle of harnesses and the babble of voices. With so many people present, the park was anything but restful.

"Such a crush," Amelia murmured, giving a smiling nod to Miss Evaline Cooper, an attractive brunette with a sharp edge to her tongue.

"Times like this," Sophie said, "I miss the country. What I wouldn't give for a good gallop."

Amelia grinned at her. "If we left the path, perhaps raced to the end of the Serpentine…"

"We would scatter people like geese." Sophie glanced toward the long, manmade lake in question, her face alight with mischief. "If it wouldn't create the scandal of the month, I would say let's."

"The scandal and perhaps injuries if people don't move quickly enough." Amelia sighed but kept her expression cheerful. Four friends of her mother's approached in an open landau. They all exchanged smiles and greetings.

"I'll meet you in the morning if you like," Amelia offered. "No one will be in the way around eight."

"No, they'll be abed. I likely will be too, and so should you, since the Granthams' musicale tonight will likely run late. Robin obtained four tickets to a lecture next Saturday afternoon, a talk about Egypt at the British Museum. Would you like to go?"

"Of course. But we must present it to Mama in such a way that it doesn't sound like something for bluestockings."

Amelia had mainly come to London to investigate the family curse. But wanting to bolster her grieving mother had played a part too. Unfortunately, Amelia hadn't anticipated Mama's overly managing behavior or her insistence that Amelia entertain suitors.

Sophie said, "We can mention all the eligible men who—isn't that your mother?"

Amelia followed her friend's gaze. Her Uncle Harry's barouche came toward them, bearing Lady Hawkstowe and Amelia's Aunt Louisa, Lady Lifton. Mama and her sister looked younger than their forties, but Mama had more life in her face than Aunt Louisa.

The two women were beaming and giving coy looks to a man riding a big chestnut beside the barouche. His black riding coat and buckskin breeches hugged his body, revealing powerful shoulders and thighs. His topboots gleamed in the afternoon sunshine. He wore his black beaver hat at a jaunty angle atop artfully disordered blond curls. The intricate knot in his cravat, secured with a diamond stickpin that flashed in the sun, proclaimed him a man of fashion and wealth.

More important than all of that was the faint sense of familiarity about him, a sign that he was also Gifted.

"Who's that with Mama and Aunt Louisa?"

Sophie's face closed over. Resentment flashed in her eyes before she pulled a smiling expression over her face like a mask. "That's the Earl of Wyndon, Silas de Vere. Gifted, as I expect you see, ruthless, and no friend to the Mainwarings."

"Or the Graysons, I gather?"

"Indeed not. The Mainwarings, the Graysons, and the Winfields have ever opposed this branch of the de Veres. They serve themselves first and England second, if at all."

Out of the corner of her eye, Amelia watched the man, who appeared to be in his forties. He certainly seemed on friendly terms with Mama, but that was no surprise. Mama had been a diamond of the first water in her day, with a petite, curvy form, rich auburn curls, and a classically elegant face. And she was friendly.

Especially to anyone with a title—unless she had reason not to be.

"His finances?" Amelia asked.

"Thirty thousand a year," Sophie muttered.

Oh, lovely. Considering that fortune and his friendly manner, Mama would be flinging Amelia at his head. Unless, of course, he was already wed.

He sat his horse with ease, tall in the saddle, large hands in tan kid gloves light on the reins. In all, he seemed rather formidable.

Amelia's mother spotted her and waved. "We can't avoid pulling up, I'm afraid," Amelia said. "My apologies, Sophie."

"Unnecessary. Even if I could avoid it, I wouldn't leave you alone with that man. The way your mother's simpering up at him, she's no idea what he is."

"He's that bad?"

The two young women drew rein. Waiting for a chance to cross to the barouche, Sophie answered, "Worse. Robin acts the lordly older brother when I ask and says these things are *not fit for a lady's ears.*" Sophie had dropped her voice in a decent imitation of her brother's, and Amelia laughed.

"Seriously, Amelia, Robin told me never to be alone with him. He's said to be on the lookout for a wife since his young son's death last year. Your jointure might draw his attention."

"It's modest compared to many dowries."

Thanks to some ill-advised financial choices of Papa's, the Mainwarings were land rich and cash poor. Crispin had bequeathed her their manor, which had an income in rents and wasn't entailed. He'd bought it so they would have a home closer to their families than his seat at Buckton. He'd also left a fund established for her support and that of any children. She could live comfortably if she avoided extravagance.

Sophie shook her head. "Your estate and your funds, together, are rather better than modest. Besides, my friend, your Gifts are prodigious, a lure for any Gifted man. He may know seers run in your line."

"If our families are enemies, surely that renders me ineligible."

"No." Though Sophie still smiled, her eyes hardened. "That family loves power, whatever its source, and they never forget a slight. In the reign of Edward IV, our families helped prove Gervais de Vere a traitor, both to the king and to the Gifted Conclave. Both ordered his execution, though the king didn't know of the Conclave, of course. No one in that family will ever forget it. Having dominion of any sort over any one of us would be better than Twelfth Night revels to them."

The Gifted Conclave was the assembly of the Gifted in Britain. Its Council was their governing body. Amelia studied her friend. "You're not joking."

"No. Be on your guard with him, always."

The family ghosts hadn't shared that information, though she'd known they were at odds with the Wyndon of their era. Why? Since she wasn't acquainted with this Wyndon, had they assumed she didn't need to know?

One of the grooms signaled a lull in oncoming traffic. He blocked the way with his mount. Sophie and Amelia trotted over to her mother's barouche. The coachman pulled it over to the side, mostly out of traffic, and the grooms moved off the path.

Sophie's smile didn't waver, but her shoulders stiffened. Lady Hawkstowe beamed at the two young women. At her side, her thinner, more solemn sister smiled complacently.

"There you are, Amelia," Mama said.

Lord Wyndon looked up. He had the coldest eyes she had ever seen, deep brown and hard as frozen earth. A warning chill ran down Amelia's neck and arms. No wonder Robin cautioned his sister against this man.

The smile he flicked at Sophie did nothing to warm his expression. "Lady Whitestone, good day."

Mama said, "Lady Buckton, I don't believe you know Lord Wyndon."

"My lord." Unable to curtsey on horseback, Amelia nodded to the earl.

Although he smiled at her, the predatory keenness of his gaze was unsettling. "I understand you'll attend the Granthams' musicale this evening. I look forward to seeing you...both...there."

"Of course, my lord," Sophie answered swiftly. "I know my eldest brother, Lord Yeavering, will enjoy seeing you as well."

At the reference to Robin, a flash of displeasure lit Wyndon's eyes. He quickly masked it.

Aunt Louisa said, "So many popular singers lately come from Italy. Is it because only they are willing to travel here? The end of the war must have eased travel restrictions everywhere on the Continent, so it's odd that only Italians are so prominent."

"Italian singers have become fashionable," Lord Wyndon said, his tone wry, "and you ladies surely know how everyone scurries to follow the fashion in anything. I dare say there are many superb singers in London who haven't had the good fortune of their nations' coming into vogue."

"My daughter has a wonderful ear for music," Mama said as Amelia winced inwardly. "She's rather accomplished on the pianoforte, if I do say so."

"I look forward to hearing you play, Lady Buckton," Wyndon stated.

Could Mama not see the assessment in his gaze? She smiled up at him as though he were a king bestowing a compliment on a scullery maid.

Amelia made herself smile at the earl. If she didn't respond politely, Mama would go on about it for hours. "Though it's kind of you to say so, my lord, I fear you'll find me an unremarkable pianist. Are you enjoying the Season?"

"It has its charms," he replied, looking directly at her.

Amelia shivered, and Sophie leaned closer to her.

Aunt Louisa asked Wyndon about his horse, and the conversation turned to proper mounts for ladies.

"If you'll excuse us, everyone," Sophie said, "we're due at home for tea shortly."

Mama's face fell. Her mouth moved, as though to protest. Of course she wanted to, as she clearly considered Wyndon an eligible match and thus wanted Amelia to cultivate him. But she couldn't ask her daughter to break an engagement.

"A pity," Lord Wyndon said. "I was about to invite you all to Gunter's for ices, as my guests, of course. Perhaps another time."

"Of course," Sophie said.

Everyone offered polite farewells. Lord Wyndon looked directly at Amelia. "I look forward to seeing you this evening."

She nodded her thanks. Judging by Mama's disappointed expression, that cool response would have repercussions. Amelia and Sophie wheeled their mounts and joined the line of riders headed for the exit at Hyde Park Corner.

When they were safely distant from the barouche, with the sounds of horses and harnesses to cover their conversation, Amelia asked, "Did I forget we were to have tea?"

"No, but the way he was looking at you...I thought it best to offer an excuse."

"I'm glad you did. His calculating manner makes me uneasy. Even if you hadn't warned me, I wouldn't be comfortable around him."

"Nor should you be." Sophie's expression turned grim. "That one cares far less whether a woman is a beauty than he does about the power she can bring. I'd wager he suspects you possess rare Gifts. If so, he'll covet them and you. Be very wary, my friend."

～

Amelia's chamber at her aunt and uncle's house was comfortable enough, with pale yellow wallpaper and hangings, a desk, and a rocking chair set by the hearth. It wasn't truly hers, though. She missed the familiar chamber and furnishings she'd shared with Crispin at Leyburn Manor.

Scrying seemed so much easier there, but she couldn't let homesickness hinder her now. Grandfather always said information was the key to power. If there was even a possibility of Wyndon pursuing her, she needed to know about him. There was time before dinner for what she needed to do.

She curled up on the hearth, sent her power into the flames, and summoned images of Lord Wyndon. A large, Palladian house appeared, but she couldn't scry into it. Wyndon must have warded it. Well, then. He wasn't in his house all the time.

Seeking the past, she watched him in the park, at his club, at his boot-maker. Hoby, of course. Wyndon dressed in the first stare of fashion. Naturally he would want London's best bootmaker.

At the Cock and Woolpack Tavern in Finch Lane, he met a short, stout man whose dark hair was a jumble of wind-blown curls, perhaps due to fashion but possibly due to carelessness. The two shared coffee and a meal. Despite their relaxed postures, the way their gazes moved across the room from time to time implied a desire for secrecy.

Amelia directed her power at Wyndon's companion. Who was he?

The image in the flames shifted. Dressed in an elegant greatcoat with multiple capes at the shoulders, with a fine beaver hat on his head, the stout man strolled through the gates of the French embassy. That build-ing, too, blocked her magic. It must also be warded, which made sense for an embassy.

Probing farther back in the day, she found him in rooms in Maryle-bone. Nothing he did, however, seemed at all remarkable.

She ended the scrying and summoned her Gift, envisioning Wyndon and this mysterious man in the tavern. Unlike scrying, her seer visions included sound. Purple-gray fog that stank of rotten eggs rolled across her sight. When it cleared, she again saw the two men in the tavern.

Unfortunately, they spoke of nothing important. She learned only the other man's name, LeFebvre, and his status as an attaché at the French Embassy. Perhaps Robin knew of him and could give her more information.

Grandfather Richard shimmered into view and knelt beside her, his form translucent. Like his wife, he appeared to be in his thirties and wore clothing popular in his youth—in his case a blue doublet and knee breeches, hose, and buckled shoes. His blue eyes and strong features could've come out of any one of the family portraits. "Practicing your skills?"

"Without much luck." She told him what had happened in the park.

As she talked, his warm smile gradually shifted into a hard, thoughtful expression.

"It does sound as though he has developed a particular interest in you," he said.

"I feared so." She rubbed her hands along her arms in hopes of banishing the chill.

Richard curved an insubstantial arm around her shoulder. "We'll watch him. At the first sign of trouble, we'll warn you, and you can alert your friend Robin. He'll know what to do. Meanwhile, practice your defensive magics and your glamours and carry Miranda's dagger."

"I will, starting tomorrow. I've a thigh sheath to wear under my skirts." Inherited by the oldest daughter in the direct line in each generation, the weapon was a tangible reminder of her link to these beloved figures.

Depending on how much power Wyndon wielded, the normal magical tactics of creating fire or ice or using a magical push for distance might or might not be much help. The illusions known as glamours also had limited utility against a wizard, who could detect them at close range.

"Good. With a Wyndon, it's best to take no chances."

Amelia nodded. If only she could lean against Richard, draw comfort from the embrace of someone who not only loved her but understood her. Mama meant well, but her insistence that Amelia socialize had quickly grown tedious. Only understanding how desperately Mama sought to escape her grief for Adam and Papa enabled Amelia to tolerate it.

"I dislike London," Richard said, "but one benefit is that your mother cannot cut you off from other Gifted, as she did before your marriage."

Cocking her head, she peered at him. "I remember you had a problem with the Lord Wyndon of your era. What happened? You've always been rather vague about that."

"By design, I admit." He smiled. "The world is better for having certain sorts of knowledge pass out of it. Be careful of Wyndon, regardless. We should've realized your paths might cross and warned you about him. If he realizes how powerful you are, nothing will deter his pursuit. Alert your friends and stand fast. We'll watch out for you too."

"I know. Thank you."

Ghostly lips brushed her forehead. "I'll see what I can learn of this particular Wyndon. Courage, granddaughter. You have it in abundance if you only remember that."

Easier said than done, she thought as he faded from view. Clearly, she needed to devote more time to learning about Wyndon. Everyone had a weakness. If she could find his, she could make him leave her in peace.

CHAPTER 4

Every time Julian returned to London, he remembered how much he disliked the noise and the smell. Coal smoke tainted the air, mingling with the sweat of horses and people, dung in the streets, and the rare, clean whiff of grasses or greenery. Even here in St. James's, not far from the palace and the Prince Regent's showy Carlton House, there was a constant cacophony of the clatter of wheels and hooves, the jingle of harnesses, and the mingled shouts of raised voices. It made him long for the quiet of Aysgarth.

At least his aunt enjoyed London. He'd delivered her to his house and immediately traded the coach for the curricle he kept in Town. Robin had left a note asking to meet here as soon as possible. Perhaps he'd scried to see when Julian would arrive, or perhaps Lewis, the courier Julian had met halfway between London and York, had beaten him to the city.

After a wagon full of barrels passed, he turned his curricle off Haymarket and into Charles Street. Down a narrow lane stood his London haven, the Merlin Club.

He pulled up in front of the club, an unassuming house painted a nondescript grayish green with a black door. Its width, twice that of many London townhouses, was uncommon but not particularly remarkable. More distinct was the plaque by the door, bronze engraved with the image of a merlin looking over its shoulder and the words *The Merlin Club*. Like the house itself, which masqueraded as a modest gentlemen's club, the plaque was a blind. The club wasn't named for the bird but for King Arthur's Gifted advisor.

An icy wind blew off the Thames, ruffling the four capes on his blue greatcoat and whistling between the close-set buildings. With Adam on his mind so much, he couldn't help fearing the gloomy weather was an omen.

His groom, a sturdy, Gifted Welshman, jumped down and came forward.

Julian dropped from the high seat. Passing the reins over, he said, "I'll be a while, Hugh. Take them round to the mews, if you will, and have the kitchen fix you something."

"Wouldn't mind a warm bite in this weather."

Julian turned away before Hugh had settled on the seat. The informality of their exchange, given their disparate ranks, would have startled anyone not Gifted. But tradition dating to the days of Arthur, Merlin, and Morgan le Fay made magical Gifts a social equalizer. Only when unGifted were present did he and any of his Gifted staff stand on ceremony. It was the same among most of the Gifted. When he met Amelia again, the *ton* would assume they were on a first-name basis because of his friendship with Adam. In truth, however, their magical Gifts made them kindred of a sort and rendered the usual formalities unnecessary.

He mounted the steps and placed his palm against the merlin's image on the brass plate by the door. When he released a small pulse of magic, the lock clicked. The door swung open.

Julian stepped inside, onto the blue and gold carpet in the center of the foyer's gleaming parquet floor. Voices came from the morning room on his left but none from the lounge to his right. The stairs rose just past the lounge door and curved gracefully left to reach the first floor.

Josiah Dorton, the middle-aged former soldier who served as door warden, greeted him with a smile. Behind him came Harry Carter, the sturdy, cheerful footman.

Josiah said, "Robin told us to expect you today. So good to see you, Julian."

"You as well. How's Agnes?" Julian passed his cloak, hat, and gloves to Harry, who interjected, "Welcome back, Julian."

They established that all their families were doing well. Within these walls, everyone was Gifted. He was the club's director, responsible for choosing its course and devising strategies, but everyone here had a voice.

Harry said, "Robin's up in the library. He said to tell you."

"Alasdair MacGregor arrived yesterday," Josiah added. "Told me he'd something very important to talk to you about. He's out just now, though."

"Perhaps he'll return by the time Robin and I finish our discussion. Let me know, will you?"

Julian thanked the men and climbed the curving stair to the first floor, the polished wood creaking slightly under his weight. The scents of roasting beef and baking bread drifted up from the kitchen, a cozy, welcoming change from the city stink outside.

At the top, he nodded to the portrait of two of the club's founders, Richard and Miranda Mainwaring, once the Earl and Countess of Hawkstowe. Had Amelia and Adam's many-generations-back grandparents possessed any inkling of the important tasks the club's members would secretly perform for England as the years rolled forward? Miranda had been a seer, according to the archived correspondence at Aysgarth, so perhaps they'd had some idea. Regardless, their country owed them a greater debt than it would ever know.

Julian turned right. The library covered half of the first floor, with the remainder divided among several bedchambers, all comfortable but not luxurious. More such bedchambers occupied the second and third floors, with quarters at the top and in the cellar for staff who wanted them.

When Julian opened the library door, the scents of leather, old paper, and coffee welcomed him back. Was that cinnamon as well?

His second in directing the club, Robin Grayson, heir to ancient Havelock earldom, sat near the far end of the long table with his back to the hearth. The silver tray at his elbow held a silver Baroque coffee service, a blue Wedgewood platter piled with pastries, and a small stack of matching plates and teacups. At the room's far end, the lone window between the floor-to-ceiling bookshelves admitted little light on such a gray day. Beeswax candles burned in the sconces between shelving units and in the three candelabra on the table.

Smiling, his friend strode forward to welcome him. They embraced swiftly.

"Lewis returned this morning. He told us you would likely arrive today, so I've been scrying. Saw you enter the city." With a grin, Robin added, "I told Eloise, and she immediately set to baking your favorite cinnamon wheels."

"Very kind of Eloise." Julian dropped into the mahogany Hepplewhite chair next to Robin's. Nodding at the large, leather-bound volume open on the table, he asked, "Find anything useful?"

"Alas, no. While I waited for you, I read about seers. Everything I've seen so far repeats what we already knew, that seers have visions, that various things can cause them, and that their meaning isn't always clear."

"It's one of the rarest Gifts, so information is difficult to find and is usually in obscure sources."

Robin raised an eyebrow. "If you were already headed this way when Lewis found you, why did you set out?"

"Amelia sent a dragon avatar to tell me the devil was loose. I confirmed Bonaparte was not on Elba, though I couldn't actually find him, only a coach that appeared to be somewhere in France. Since I couldn't see inside because of wards, I assumed he was the passenger."

"A dragon visitor?" Robin's eyes widened. "You're serious."

"Entirely." Julian explained about the avatar's visit. "How is Amelia? I take it you didn't ask her to summon me."

"I had no idea she could." Robin shook his head. "She seems well enough, if a little shaken by her recent visions. She and Sophie have become close, so she's often at Havelock House." Quietly, he added, "Spending time with her makes me think of Adam. Some days, I miss him rather badly. I think of something I should tell him, and then I remember. Especially when I'm fencing at Angelo's. You know how fast he was with a blade. Any blade."

"Lightning fast. Better than me, certainly."

"Only a little. If you cared half as much about swordplay as you do about horses and books, you could stand against any man, any wizard, in the realm."

Julian said nothing. In their youth, they had joked that they would become highwaymen together for a lark—Adam with a rapier, Robin with pistols, and Julian taking charge of reconnaissance and their mounts. The world had seemed so much lighter then, even with the threat of Bonaparte hanging over their heads. Boney had ravaged the Continent, but he couldn't best the Royal Navy to reach England.

If he started another war, it would drag Julian back into intrigue, possibly including theft and even killing, a depressing thought. He'd done what he must to protect his country, but he'd hoped all that was over.

"Anyway," Robin said, "she had a vision that led her to scry Bonaparte's escape. She also reports odd dreams of an eagle and a lion fighting."

Robin described what she'd shown them in the fire, and Julian's unease deepened.

Robin finished, and Julian mulled over his report. The street noises outside, the crackle of fire in the hearth—wood supplied by members from their lands, rather than coal, so as to protect the books—and the ticking of the antique, ornate mantel clock barely registered with him.

Robin helped himself to a cinnamon wheel. "In your absence, I've set Wat Granger to frequent the taverns where French embassy servants drink, Paul Morton to do the same with the diplomats, and Harry Braswell to pry into where the embassy's money is going. So far, they've turned up nothing, but I left a report in your office."

"All that sounds good. Any word from France?"

The club currently had one agent there, a carpenter in Paris. Every morning at a set time, he wrote a report on the situation and sat with it on the table for ten minutes. Someone back at the Merlin Club scried that person during that time period. Then the agent burned the report with witchfire, leaving no trace.

"Harrison reports a great deal of tension there. The king and the royalists are in a bit of a panic. The common people seem divided."

"So nothing surprising." Julian rubbed his chin. "Does Amelia have any other unusual Gifts?"

"She talks to ghosts," Robin replied, his voice dry. As Julian gaped, Robin continued, "The spirits of our married founders visit her frequently. Or so she claims."

"Do you believe her?"

"She's too level-headed to harbor a delusion of that sort and too adept to be deceived. She told Sophie the ghosts taught her most of what she knows. Adam once said their mother allowed magical instruction for him only because he was the heir and forbade it for Amelia. He shared with his sister, but he was no seer. Yet someone taught her."

"If Bonaparte is truly heading for Paris, we need her seer Gift."

"We do. I scry the bastard daily. Sometimes, when he isn't in a warded coach or structure, I see him and not only those around him. He made landfall at Golfe-Juan on the French coast three days ago."

Julian's lips tightened. That news killed his tiny, unrealistic shard of hope Bonaparte would go into obscurity. "If he manages to win substantial support—which seems unlikely, given that the entire country was sick of his wars when he abdicated last year—we'll be at war. Then we'll need all the men the government demobilized after the abdication."

"Let's not forget all the experienced soldiers who're still in the Americas, dealing with that upstart new nation. We can't bring them all back quickly."

Hostilities had officially ceased when the American Senate ratified the Treaty of Ghent only a couple of weeks ago. That wasn't enough time even to begin wide-scale troop withdrawal.

Robin continued, "No official word of his escape has yet arrived, which is baffling. I tried to convince Liverpool I'd had word from a friend that Bonaparte was on the loose. Even faked a letter. Since I couldn't produce this nonexistent friend, however, the prime minster refused to believe me. Which I admit was no surprise."

"At least you tried."

"For all the good that did. The other bad news is, Wyndon has taken a marked interest in Amelia, who detests him but is under pressure from her mother. Sophie says Lady Hawkstowe is ecstatic over his thirty thousand a year and ancient name. At a dance a few days ago, he stood up with Amelia twice and lingered by her chair all evening."

That was cause for concern, as it was the most interest a man could show in a woman he wasn't betrothed to without causing a scandal.

Julian narrowed his eyes. "We must protect her."

"We will, but as I'm betrothed, much of the protection that involves the events of the Season may fall to you." As Julian grimaced, Robin continued, "Wyndon is ingratiating himself with Lady Hawkstowe. Since she isn't Gifted, she can't pick up on magical auras. Amelia can, of course. Although she doesn't like the man, they're to dine at Wyndon House before the Arbuthnot at-home tomorrow evening. Sophie and I are going, and I procured an invitation for you."

"To the dinner?" Julian teased, though he would rather fence verbally with Wyndon than dive into the perilous hunting ground of the Season. An at-home involved inviting scores of the *ton* to roam one's house, play games or cards, and generally poke into one another's affairs.

Robin gave him a stern look. "It's good to have our director back in Town, especially if there's any chance of war starting up again. I expect Amelia will be happy to use her Gifts and her ghosts to gather information, but it's up to you to determine what we need."

Shaking his head, Julian replied, "I wish I had a better knack for scrying."

"Not everyone is equally adept with every Gift." Robin glanced at the clock. "Amelia's having tea with Sophie this afternoon. If we hurry, you can talk to her before she returns home."

Julian hesitated. With street dust on his boots and outerwear, he wasn't dressed for a polite call. The situation, however, was urgent.

"Let's go," he said.

⁓

A fire crackling in the hearth warmed the upstairs parlor at Havelock House, Sophie's family home. With overstuffed furniture and chintz draperies, this room was decorated for comfort rather than to make a social impression. Amelia and Sophie shared the sofa facing the hearth.

"It's sad," Amelia said, staring down at her tea, "that I have no interest in the social concerns so dear to Mama's heart. I came to London in part to support her. I didn't realize she intended to make a project of me."

Mama's intense grief for her husband and son still lurked behind her social smiles. London's distractions helped, as Amelia had hoped, but Mama's insistence on treating her as an unmarried girl was a problem. Not wanting to distress her mother, Amelia had avoided confronting her about that thus far, but doing so indefinitely might not be possible.

"You have more important concerns just now."

"Yes, but she doesn't know that. Nor would she like it if she did. If the Merlin Club needs my Gifts, that must come before social frivolity. I'll reduce my social commitments accordingly. If I didn't hope to learn something that could help Papa and Adam, I would already have done so. As the weather warms, though, more Gifted I haven't yet spoken to come into London. I realize the chances of learning anything are minimal, but I must try unless I'm needed elsewhere."

The parlor door opened. Robin walked in with a tall, familiar man. The sight of him made Amelia's breath catch on a rush of hope. Julian Winfield had come at last.

"Don't get up," Robin said. "I hope we needn't stand on ceremony. I've ordered two more cups."

"It's good to see you both again," Julian said. "I beg you to pardon my dusty boots. I've only just arrived in the city, but I thought it best not to delay."

Assured by Sophie that no one minded, he and Robin took chairs flanking the sofa. At least Julian didn't seem angry.

Amelia thanked him for coming so quickly. "I apologize for my odd summons. I didn't know what else to do."

"So you planted a dragon on my lawn." Julian smiled at her.

She'd forgotten he had such a warm smile. His blue cutaway coat and buckskin breeches emphasized his wide shoulders and muscular build, which in turn supported his air of authority. He gave an impression of solid, dependable strength.

"Robin has told me of your unsettling visions," he said, "but I would like to hear your description. No detail is too small to include."

"Very well." Quietly, she explained about her visions. "I should probably also tell you I've scried Lord Wyndon, and my observations lead me to think he may be helping the French." She explained what she'd learned.

When she finished, Julian rubbed his chin. "I understand you speak with the ghosts of your great-great-grandparents Richard and Miranda." Amelia nodded, and Julian continued, "When you speak with them next, can you ask them to see what Bonaparte is up to? Is that within their abilities? He's in France. We fear he's headed to Paris, but we cannot yet be certain."

"They can go wherever they need to, save through wards not raised by our family. I'll ask them tonight." Amelia hesitated. "I know you've been very busy, but I wonder if you've run across anything that could help Adam."

"As yet I've found nothing that can solve the problem, but I have some ideas. While searching old correspondence for clues a few weeks back, I ran across an odd reference. Do you know the details of an adventure your great-great grandparents shared with my Winfield uncles of the same era?"

When she shook her head, he said, "There was an intriguing letter from Jeremy Winfield, who had recently retired from his post as Archbishop of York, to Admiral of the Blue Sir Cabot Winfield, in July 1712. Their friend Richard Mainwaring, Lord Hawkstowe, had just died, and Jeremy said he was 'comforted to know Richard and Miranda's valor won Richard release, even if he does not take it.'"

"Well, that's odd," Amelia said. "You think it's release from the family curse?"

"I don't see what else it could be. There was nothing specific about that. The only other interesting bit was in Cabot's reply. 'We accomplished that much, at least, or so Richard said. Alas that we've no memory of that grand adventure, but perhaps it's as well we don't. Some secrets are best lost, and some portals should never be opened.'"

"Stranger and stranger," Sophie commented.

The bit he quoted reminded Amelia of Grandfather Richard saying the world was better off without some forms of knowledge in it. "All I know," she said, "is that the shadow realm touches all places and all times. My grandparents can travel quickly from one place to another. Miranda thinks the seer Gift taps into that world to See other places and times."

"That's intriguing," Julian responded. "When you have the chance, please ask them what more they can tell you of that place. Perhaps something in its nature will help us break the curse if we cannot satisfy its terms. The more we know of it, the better."

Though she tried to hide her disappointment, it must've shown. His expression softened.

He said, "Robin, here, can tell you I'm so persistent as to be annoying when I've a mystery to solve. We need your help to keep track of Bonaparte, but that won't consume entire days. Or so I hope. When there is time, would you care to help me work on this puzzle?"

"Yes, very much." His belief that she might be able to help was flattering. Mama wouldn't like that, but it was too important to let social engagements interfere. "Grandfather Richard says knowledge is power."

Julian smiled again. "I would expect no less of the Merlin Club's founder."

A footman tapped on the door and entered with two teacups and two small plates on a tray. As Sophie poured tea, Amelia used the time to order her thoughts.

Julian had offered a tiny sliver of hope about Adam, but he'd confirmed her worst fears about these disturbing visions.

❧

Dinner at Wyndon House the next evening seemed interminable. Only the knowledge that everyone would eventually depart for the Arbuthnots' gathering helped Amelia bear it. She really needed to speak to Mama about accepting invitations without consulting her.

Lord Wyndon sat at one end of a long table set with snowy Irish linen and a heavy silver service. His aunt, Mrs. Hastings, presided over the table's other end. Her smile had the same predatory edge as her nephew's.

At last, the ladies left the men to their port. Amelia and her mother joined Mrs. Hastings and her daughter and daughter-in-law, along with two friends of the family, in a snug parlor hung with burgundy silk and decorated in the classical style. Amelia was the only unwed, eligible woman present, a clear and unsettling indication of Wyndon's interest.

The conversation idly touched on what everyone had enjoyed about the Season. Although the talk was unremarkable, Amelia couldn't relax. Perhaps it was her imagination, but she felt as though Mrs. Hastings was paying close attention to her without wishing it to be obvious.

After almost an hour by the delicate mantel clock, Mrs. Hastings's daughter asked, "Lady Hawkstowe, will you stay long in London?"

"Until summer. There's so little to do at Hawkstowe in the winter, and I should stay out of the new earl's way. Give the tenants time to grow accustomed, to learn they must turn to him now."

"Very wise." Wyndon's aunt nodded. "Lady Buckton, I understand you are bookish. Silas has a fine library at Wyndon. In Kent, you know. I'm sure he would be delighted to show it to you."

The gentlemen joined them in time to hear her comment.

"Indeed," Lord Wyndon replied, taking the spot on the sofa beside Amelia. He gave her a smile that did nothing to soften his eyes. "In addition, we have gardens that are famed throughout the region, though they aren't yet in bloom."

Mama looked pleased, and Amelia groaned inwardly.

Perhaps she could still salvage something out of this wretched evening. Her seer Gift had sensed nothing during dinner, but perhaps conversation could lead to a clue.

She turned to the young man in the armchair on her right, Lord Wyndon's cousin Algernon. "Have you visited the Continent, Mr. de Vere? I hear it's rather popular now that Bonaparte is gone."

"I have not, but I expect to take the Grand Tour next year, since that's again possible."

"The war changed so much," Amelia agreed. "Do you think Elba will hold Bonaparte? He's said to be dreadfully clever."

"He isn't as clever as those who guard him," Lord Wyndon assured her. "Now, however, we must leave if we're not to be late."

While that sounded reasonable, the long line of carriages sure to form in the Arbuthnots' street, each waiting to set its passengers down at the door, would ensure that many would arrive after the designated time. Did he care about that, or was he diverting the conversation?

Everyone filed out of the room. Lord Wyndon fell into step with

Amelia. "I've books on blood curses," he said under cover of the others' conversations. "I understand they're an interest of yours."

"I am curious," she replied, careful to keep her tone casual. "Have you studied them?"

"Extensively. We must make time to discuss them." With a meaningful glance, he added, "One in particular will interest you."

Did he know of the family curse? His ancestor had, so perhaps he did. His having any deep knowledge of her family could not be a good thing. Amelia forced her lips into a light smile. "La, my lord, I don't know what you mean."

"Yes, you do," he replied softly. In a louder voice, he said, "Lady Buckton, the Arbuthnots have an extensive portrait gallery. May I have the honor of visiting it with you?"

Only a rude guest would refuse after the elegant dinner he'd provided. Amelia nodded but kept her voice cool. "Of course, my lord."

Then she would find Sophie and devise a way to avoid him for the remainder of the evening.

He took her cloak from the footman and laid it around her shoulders, his fingers lingering and making her skin crawl. When he squeezed gently, the entry hall blanked out. Instead, Lord Wyndon stood in a stone chamber—underground, she knew through the vision—with a candelabrum in his hand. On the table before him lay a sheet of parchment encased in glass. The writing was old, the lettering unfamiliar. Why would she See this now, after he'd hinted he knew of the Mainwaring curse? Did the vision have to do with that?

"Lady Buckton?" The scene vanished like a soap bubble. Lord Wyndon now stood in front of her. Despite his solicitous expression, his eyes probed hers.

He might suspect she'd had a vision. If what she'd Seen had anything to do with the family curse, she needed to understand it as well as learn what he and his French friends planned.

"Are you well?" he asked. Definite suspicion in his eyes now.

"Of course, my lord." She managed a flicker of a smile. "Thank you."

If she had to spend time with him, perhaps she could use his presence to summon visions of what she wanted to see. Learn his plans. Then, somehow, whether Mama liked it or not, she would end this acquaintance.

CHAPTER 5

Half an hour after they arrived at the Arbuthnots', Amelia was heartily sick of Wyndon. She'd learned nothing useful, and his proprietary air was becoming more and more alarming. Once they finished this interminable stroll among the portraits, she would avoid him for the rest of the evening.

"Have I told you how lovely you look?" he asked.

"You are too kind, my lord."

"Not at all." He gave her a doting look that made her gorge rise.

Portraits of women, men, or families in the stiff garments of earlier ages lined the paneled walls. Amelia and Wyndon made their way through the throng of others walking down the thick, blue carpet and gawking at the artwork.

"I prefer landscapes," Wyndon said, "though many of these are well done. I do believe that's a Holbein."

"The clothing is of the right era," Amelia noted.

Wyndon nodded to a stout, dark-haired man coming the other way, the Frenchman she'd seen with him when she scried.

Without thought, she opened to her Gift. The usual smelly fog flickered across her sight. It gave way to a dark, rainy night that obscured the gallery. Mounds on the ground, in the mud, were soldiers under sodden blankets. One wore the tricolor of France on the hat set over his face.

Amelia shuddered.

"Is something the matter?" Wyndon asked.

"No, thank you, merely a draft." Amelia clutched her shawl around her with both hands. "I'd like to sit down for a bit."

They turned a corner, and the couple coming toward them smiled at her. Amelia smiled back. Crispin's parents, the Earl and Countess of Bainbridge, had always been dear to her. Crispin had gotten his green eyes and his wry sense of humor from his mother, with his black hair and ruggedly handsome looks coming from his father and his Gifts from them both. Gray streaked his father's hair now, and the loss of Crispin and the brother he'd gone to find, Adrian, shadowed both his parents' faces.

"Amelia, my dear." Mama Bainbridge leaned in so she and Amelia could kiss the air over each other's cheeks. "It's so good to see you."

"Indeed," her husband said. In a cooler tone, he added, "Good evening, Lord Wyndon."

"Lord Bainbridge, my lady. Lady Buckton is unwell. I'm escorting her to her mother, if you'll excuse us."

Papa Bainbridge's eyes held a question. Amelia answered him with a smile and a slight headshake. The two couples said their farewells, and Amelia walked back to the parlor with Wyndon. The musicians at the room's far end played a light, cheerful tune she scarcely noticed. Her chair beside Mama, near the open window, was still vacant. Amelia settled into it. The fresh air, though chilly, helped her shake off the vision's effects.

"May I bring you anything?" Wyndon asked.

"Thank you, no, my lord." She would feel considerably better if he would only go away.

Captain Alan Douglas emerged from the crowd and bowed to Amelia and her mother. With his ruddy complexion, tousled brown hair, and Black Watch regimentals of blue, black, and green tartan kilt and red jacket, he cut a dashing figure despite the patch over his right eye.

"Good evening, Lady Hawkstowe," he said. "Lady Buckton, Lord Wyndon."

Mama favored him with a slight nod. As a fourth son of limited means, he didn't meet her requirements for a suitable match. Wyndon also nodded briefly.

Amelia smiled at the captain. The eye patch covered an injury incurred in Wellington's army at Toulouse. He was a hero who not only cut a fine figure in his uniform but had an amiable disposition. His warmth provided an antidote to Lord Wyndon's calculation.

Surveying the parlor, Douglas commented, "Quite a mob this evening. I'm glad to stay near the windows for a bit."

"Indeed," Amelia answered. "Have you enjoyed your stay in London, Captain?"

"It's good to see old friends." He paused, smiling at her, before adding, "And make new ones."

"Lady Buckton," Wyndon cut in, "would you join me to tour the conservatory? It's a riot of flowers, even this time of year."

If she couldn't avoid Wyndon, perhaps she could outmaneuver him. "How kind of you," she replied, smiling. "Perhaps after supper? Lady Whitestone expressed a wish to see the conservatory as well, and I would so hate to enjoy the treat without her. If we wait, I'll have time to find her."

Mama's face stiffened. Amelia braced inwardly.

Wyndon's gaze chilled, but he bowed. "I am at your service, Lady Buckton." He stalked away.

Mama shot Amelia a stern look, but she would say nothing in front of other people.

Another man in Black Watch regimentals hailed Douglas. The captain made his excuses and walked away.

Sophie emerged from the crowd. Amelia jumped up and hurried to her friend. "Take a turn about the room with me, Sophie, will you?"

They linked arms as they skirted the clumps of gossiping people. "I see Wyndon has been plaguing you," Sophie said. "When Robin and Julian arrive, they'll give you some relief."

"I hope that will be soon."

Sophie squeezed her arm. "It's dreadful, your having to deal with him when you've so much else on your mind."

"It would be dreadful regardless." Amelia flashed her friend a wry grin.

She and Sophie walked between the twin pillars separating the refreshment tables from the rest of the long room, as matching pillars did for the musicians at the far end. In a low voice, Amelia warned Sophie they might have to tour the conservatory with Wyndon if he pressed the matter.

Petite, blond Corisande Wilton joined them at the refreshment table with two gentlemen trailing her. The calculation in her eyes did not bode well.

Everyone exchanged greetings.

Over the lilt of the music, Miss Wilton said, "Lady Buckton, I was trying to tell Lord Amury what you said at Lady Harwood's tea about Richard III and the Wars of the Roses. I can never remember the details." She trilled a self-deprecating laugh. "Do, please, remind me."

Her sweet glance held a hint of malice. Little did the girl realize Amelia actually wanted to be thought bookish. Because few of the *ton's* dandies wanted wives who read extensively, they left such women in peace.

Amelia nodded. "If everyone cares to hear it, of course I will." Ignoring the satisfaction on Miss Wilton's face, she began, "Historians have wronged Richard III, in part due to Shakespeare's depiction. One cannot take drama as history."

At least her bluestocking pose let her discuss matters more interesting than dowries and titles. Besides, someone knowledgeable about Richard III's nephews might overhear her and offer useful information.

~

Next door, in the morning room, Julian watched the strolling gossips and brooded. No confirmation of Bonaparte's escape had yet reached London. What in hell were the people on Elba doing?

Meanwhile, the Merlin Club's agent in Paris wrote daily reports about the rising tensions there. Members in London kept up surveillance of Bonaparte via scrying when he wasn't in warded areas. He was marching toward Grenoble with about a thousand of his Imperial Guard. There were army units in his path. They had the numbers to stop him, but would they?

Their actions might determine whether Europe went back to war.

Yet here Julian was, preparing to spend the evening as the quarry for young misses who might or might not care as much about his opinions as they did his title. Granted, he could do little about Bonaparte at this point, but his knowledge of events made this evening less appealing than usual.

The only bright spot was that Amelia was here somewhere with Sophie. Talking to her was easy. She had no apparent social expectations of him and never put on airs.

A friend of his mother's minced past on the arm of her son, and he exchanged nods with her. He knew his manners. If only he could avoid practicing them so often. Still, he couldn't resent being dragged away from his Yorkshire winter with war looming again.

"Oh, Lord Aysgarth! How lovely to see you."

Pasting a smile on his face, he turned to the speaker. "Mrs. Harcourt, good evening."

A wide-eyed blonde in the pale pink of a girl in her first season regarded him nervously. Bloody hell, he'd been targeted. How soon could he escape?

The lady gave him a wide smile. "Dora, my dear, allow me to introduce the Earl of Aysgarth. My lord, this is my daughter, Miss Harcourt."

The two women curtsied, and he bowed.

In a slightly breathless voice, the girl said, "I understand you breed horses, my lord. Do tell me about your stable."

The desperation in her eyes pierced his irritation. She'd doubtless been told her future depended on making a good match. He would not be that match, though. She was too anxious and far too eager for him.

"I work with a trainer in Middleham," he answered. "We'll have an entrant in the Derby this spring."

"I love the Derby. It's so exciting," Miss Harcourt answered, again a bit breathlessly. "What's your horse's name?"

"Athelstan. He's a bay." He'd been polite. Now he needed an escape.

Movement to his left caught his eye, and he exchanged nods of greeting with Robin.

"Ladies, I must beg you to excuse me. I've business with Lord Yeavering, and I see him over there. If I lose him, I may not find him again in this crush. Very nice to meet you, Miss Harcourt."

The women curtsied, he bowed, and he walked over to Robin. His friend's blue eyes glinted with amusement. It was all very well for him to be smug. The announcement of his betrothal had ended his status as prey.

"Not a word," Julian told him as they walked away.

"Amelia and Sophie are in the long parlor, where there are refreshments. Let's go greet them." They walked into the corridor and, skirting people gawking at the bric-a-brac on tables, turned toward the rear of the house.

"By the way," Robin said, "I forgot to ask about your mother. Is she still in Brussels?"

"Oh, yes. Everyone there still revels in Bonaparte's absence, with no idea of the trouble that could be brewing. Of course, she could tire of that and return home any day." If she did, the house would fill with people, each of them requiring his polite attention, according to her, every day and many evenings.

Julian grimaced. His mother and aunt had the best of intentions,

47

believing an affectionate wife would undo the damage Charlotte had caused, but they weren't the ones who had to endure the ordeal of courtship.

He and Robin turned into the green-papered long parlor and headed for the refreshment tables. Amelia's low, pleasant voice penetrated the babble of conversation. "Richard III," she said, "had great courage. Not even Shakespeare and Sir Thomas More could deny that."

With a little jolt of pleasure, Julian turned toward her. This was the first chance he'd had to observe her without her noticing.

Her fine, even features held a lively intelligence that would age well. The sparkle of her debut years, however, had vanished after her husband's death.

Well, loss would do that to a person, just as betrayal might.

Yet her manner wasn't what most struck him. Her resemblance to her brother, her eyes identical to his and the shape of her mouth much like Adam's, only fuller, grabbed Julian's heart and squeezed. For Adam's sake, he would do whatever he could to aid her in any matter that concerned her.

"He was his brother Edward IV's ablest commander," she continued.

Two of the six men in the group around her looked interested. A couple appeared bored. The women, except for Sophie, wore cats-finding-cream expressions.

No wonder. Every word out of Amelia's mouth painted her a bluestocking. Not the sort most noblemen wanted to wed.

Pitching his voice for Robin's ears only, he noted, "She's shoving all these dandies away as effectively as if she'd used an oar." Without the enhanced hearing of the Gifted, no one around them could possibly grasp what he said.

"She lets the tabbies bait her," Robin murmured. "According to Sophie, Amelia knows precisely what she's doing."

"Of course she does." Julian smiled. "Let's join them and confound the tabbies' expectations."

CHAPTER 6

"Assuming King Richard slew his nephews is silly," Amelia continued.

Judging by the men's bored expressions, most of them would soon drift away, and the young women would, again, dismiss her as not a threat. The fewer insincere conversations eating into her time, the more she could devote herself to important matters.

"He held the throne. His right to it was confirmed by Parliament. He had no motive to kill them."

"La, Lady Buckton," Miss Wilton tittered.

At Amelia's side, Sophie stiffened as the young woman added, "With this talk of motives, you sound like a Bow Street runner. Perhaps you should instruct them how to go on?"

A deep voice to Amelia's right said, "I'm sure Bow Street would welcome such a charming and astute visitor." She turned, surprised, and met Julian's level, gray eyes.

Standing at his shoulder, Robin Grayson added, "I've no doubt they would."

The rest of the little group looked stunned. Dismay rippled across several women's faces, but Amelia saw that only from the corner of her eye. Her gaze remained locked with Julian's. He'd defended her, even complimented her, and that was a pleasant surprise.

He smiled and inclined his head. "Your servant, Lady Buckton. I hope your evening is going well. Would you care to visit the library?"

"Yes, thank you."

They made their excuses to Miss Wilton and her friends and departed.

Walking beside Julian brought no disturbing visions or awareness. His easy movements had not changed. He was probably still a very good dancer.

"Thank you," she said again as they walked away with Sophie and Robin, "for speaking up for me. That was kind of you."

"Even though you wish I hadn't done it?" His lips quirked up in a crooked smile. "You chose an excellent way to discourage any overtures from that lot."

His admiration warmed her far more than any empty compliment on the dance floor. "You saw that. Adam always said you were clever." She hesitated. "I hope it's not too forward to say we need your cleverness now."

"It's certainly less forward than landing a dragon on my lawn." Because of his dry tone, she looked up quickly, but amusement warmed his eyes.

"My aunt," he continued as they strolled through the crowded room, "is a good friend of Mrs. Drummond-Burrell and is confident she can convince that lady to grant you vouchers for Almack's. I hope that will make your working with Robin and me easier by undercutting your mother's concerns about your spending so much time with us Gifted reprobates."

Amelia's cheeks warmed, but there was no denying he'd summed up Mama's position adequately. Almack's was the very exclusive pinnacle of the marriage mart, and Mama would be thrilled to gain vouchers so easily. As one of the club's seven patronesses, Mrs. Drummond-Burrell had the power to boost or blight a young woman's prospects. In Amelia's first Season, she hadn't received vouchers until well into the spring.

Quietly, Amelia said, "Speaking of Gifts, I wasn't able to ask my grandparents any questions last night. They didn't come to me. I'll ask as soon as they do."

"Very well. If—"

The French attaché, LeFebvre, brushed against Amelia's arm. As he begged her pardon, the ballroom vanished. Instead, she stood on a street corner. Men armed with everything from swords to hoes stormed a two-story stone building. Soldiers in blue fired on them. The crowd fell back but surged forward again, hurling stones ahead of them.

50

It's a vision, she told herself, though her heart hammered and her breathing felt shallow and fast. At least she stood apart from it this time, not in the midst of it.

"Amelia?"

Another power, faint but warm, vanquished the chill, though it didn't settle her breathing. Amelia blinked. She stood in the corridor with Julian, the concern in his eyes clashing with his bland expression. Robin and Sophie flanked him, both frowning.

People moved around them like a river flowing past a stone. "How long?" she asked Julian.

"A few moments, no more."

"Did you bring me out of it?"

"Yes. I apologize for presuming, but—"

"I'm grateful." She drew her shawl closer around her shoulders. "This is not the place to be so distracted. Did the Frenchman notice?"

"I don't believe so." Julian's gaze searched her face. "Perhaps we should discuss it. In private. Robin, will you find my aunt? I believe she's in the card room. We can use her insights. Meanwhile, we'll go to the library or some other empty room—please, God, let there be one in this crush!—and speak freely."

Robin veered toward the card room. Amelia, Sophie, and Julian continued to the library, which was, miraculously, empty.

The room was cool, the fire banked. Julian knelt, grabbed the poker, and stirred it to life. A scoop of coal from the scuttle soon smoldered, bright red flames licking the black fuel.

He cleaned his hands magically. "Robin and Aunt Augusta should arrive soon."

Most men she knew would've summoned a footman to stir the fire, but Julian had done it himself. For efficiency's sake? Whatever his reason, she liked that he had simply handled the matter.

Amelia and Sophie settled onto a gold satin, Egyptian-style divan with cats-head arms and no back. Julian took the chair beside it.

"I didn't have time yesterday to apologize for my delay in dealing with Adam's situation," he said.

"You've had other responsibilities. Ones that affect a great many more people. Living people."

He blinked. "Thank you for understanding that. I feared you might not."

"Grandmother Miranda and Grandfather Richard always made sure I understood priorities." She hesitated, but the warmth in his eyes encouraged her to confess, "Crispin's illness reinforced the importance of knowing what most mattered."

"I don't doubt that." His soft voice held an undercurrent of sympathy that also softened his eyes.

Their gazes locked in mutual understanding, and heat rose in her cheeks.

She looked at the fire in the hearth. If she'd cultivated her seer Gift before Crispin left for India, could she have prevented him from going and thus saved him? If she'd studied healing skills more intently before he fell ill, could she have truly healed him? Diseases that lurked in the body, seeming gone but later erupting again, were difficult to cure. But if she had learned more earlier, would it have made a difference?

"When Robin and Aunt Augusta arrive," Julian said, "we'll discuss your vision in detail. For now, though, can you give me an idea of what you Saw?"

Amelia took a deep, slow breath. "I think I saw a riot in France."

His gaze sharpened. "For or against Bonaparte?"

"I don't know."

~

As Amelia and her companions departed for the library, two men emerged from an adjacent parlor. French attaché Bernard LeFebvre frowned at his taller companion. "Why do you stare at that woman? This is no time for frivolity."

Silas raised an eyebrow. Really, the French had so little discretion. At present, he and LeFebvre had the corridor to themselves, but that could change in a moment.

He drew the short, swarthy diplomat back into the parlor. "Quietly, if you please. Did you not see how distracted she appeared, then shaken?"

She'd had a vision. Her mannerisms betrayed her. She was more powerful, and thus more dangerous, than he'd supposed.

"Bah. *Demoiselles* will forever swoon and flirt." LeFebvre shrugged. "Let us return to the card room."

"She's no ordinary widow on the catch for a protector or another title. That, my friend, is the Viscountess Buckton, a descendant of the Mainwaring line, which breeds powerful wizards and seers."

"*Oui, mais*—but what..." The gleam of understanding flared in the

Frenchman's dark eyes. "Seers, you say. With important events even now unfolding."

"Quite so. I'd heard she had little training, but perhaps that wasn't correct." The bitch of a great-great-grandmother who'd bred that talent into the line had had very little training but managed rather a lot of mischief.

In fact, she and her lord had watched his own great-great-grandsire as though they were hawks waiting to pounce. He'd never been able to implement his plan to bring the Gifted to power, as they deserved.

LeFebvre, who actually resembled a frog, as the English named their French rivals, scowled. "Shall we have to kill her then?"

Silas stared at him. God, what a typically Gallic over-reaction. "Never destroy what you can use. Her Gift is rare. Best to turn it to our advantage."

With a smile, Silas shot his cuffs. "I know that family's history inside and out, and I know precisely how to manage the viscountess. I'll offer her what she wants most in all the world."

"What is that?"

Let him enjoy his skepticism. He would see soon enough. In fact, given the interference of Aysgarth and Yeavering, with their tiresome support for the unGifted retaining political power, it would be wise to bring Amelia and her Gift under control as soon as possible.

Silas shrugged. "That's a closely guarded secret. I'll share it with her only, and not until the morning after our marriage, when she is irrevocably mine."

~

To think, Julian mused, he'd expected this evening to be a waste, another tedious occasion enlivened by the occasional need to dodge a snare. Instead, he was hearing a tale that fit disturbingly well with information trickling out of France. Amelia's composure and her orderly presentation as she created a scrying of her earlier vision were admirable.

If he asked, would she join the Merlin Club? Women could be members, though that was kept secret. To mask its true nature, the club needed to seem like the others in St. James's, which admitted only men. His aunt, who sat in an armchair by the divan, had declined to join.

"And then we came in here," Amelia concluded as the fiery image faded.

Julian glanced at Robin, who stood on the opposite side of the hearth from him. "Those soldiers wore the uniforms of the *gendarmie*, the military who provide security for the country. Do you think this is happening now?"

To her credit, she didn't answer at once but frowned, apparently examining her memories.

The firelight that cast a glow over the old leather books on the shelves also gilded her face and shadowed the hollow between her breasts. She made an enchanting picture. Perhaps too much so. No matter how much she had to offer, no matter how trustworthy he believed her to be, he would never lose his head over a woman again.

"I don't think so," Amelia replied at last. "It feels...uncertain."

"Could you tell this time whether they're rioting in Bonaparte's favor or against him?" If the mob was against him, that could be a boon to the allied nations.

"I still can't, no." The thoughtful look in her eyes sharpened into worry. "Do you think Bonaparte will start another war?"

"Almost certainly," Robin said. "Even if France cedes the government to him, he'll want to even scores against the Allies, to regain the reach he once had. It's heartening to hope some in France may not favor that."

Julian nodded. "Can you scry Bonaparte, Amelia, or summon a vision of him?"

"I'll try." Extending her hand, she poured argent power into the flames until even he could feel it where he stood by the mantel. The image of a small chateau formed.

"I'll try to see inside." Frowning, she fed in more magic, but the view didn't change.

She had so much power but less training than she should've, thanks to her idiot father's inability to stand up to her foolish mother. This was what came of marrying the unGifted. England's wizards were dying out or poorly trained while the more selective French and Germans, even the Italians, added daily to their numbers. Julian had the normal complement of Gifts, scrying, wielding witchlight and using it to ignite small flames, throwing it in larger volumes called witchfire, pushing or pulling objects or people, and projecting magic to light candles or create glamours, but he couldn't pretend he was as strong in any of them as his ancestors had been two generations back.

The flames turned blue at the edges. "I can't draw more," Amelia said.

"He's hidden," Julian responded. "Blocked from the scrying by French wards, no doubt. He could be anywhere."

He and Robin exchanged an angry glance. Julian added, "Only wizards raise wards. First the French Gifted helped him escape Elba, and now they shield him. They've broken accords going back to King Alfred's day."

Feeling his way, Julian said, "Amelia, you were scrying in the fire, not relying your seer Gift at all, were you not?" When she nodded, he continued, "Do you know the saying 'A seer need not scry to See—"

"—'what is, what was, and what will be,'" she finished with him. They smiled at each other, the same idea blooming in both their minds.

"Perhaps if I don't scry, if I simply open myself to it," she said, voicing that shared idea, "I could See something."

Scanning the shelves and tables, Julian frowned. "You know more than I about what spurs your Gift, but perhaps if we had something related to Bonaparte or to France?"

"That might help," Amelia said. "I've only used what my grandmother calls triggering objects that were related to my family or home."

Aunt Augusta walked to the table under the lone window. She picked up a porcelain shepherdess statuette and peered at the bottom. "Italian," she announced. The bust of Caesar was, oddly, German, as was the swan on the bookshelf. The dancing couple in Georgian attire on the mantel, though, were French.

"Better than nothing," she said, handing the figurine to Amelia.

Amelia turned it over, and the firelight picked out delicate gold detailing on the man's long coat and the woman's jewelry. Holding it loosely, opening her senses, she brushed Julian's magical awareness with her power.

"Don't watch me," she said. "I can feel your attention."

*F*rance, Amelia thought, *glory and Napoleon...eagles and sabers.* She called up the memory of the battle she'd envisioned. Moments ticked by, but patience was key here, essential to—

The room winked out of being. Purple-gray mists swirled around her with the stink of rotten eggs. The mists dispersed. Through the last wisps, stone and stucco buildings came into view, their roofs steep. A dozen men in the blue uniforms of the French army rode their horses at a walk down a narrow street. They stopped before an inn and walked inside.

Their leader, a narrow-faced man whose brown hair held traces of ginger, followed the stout landlord up the stairs.

The landlord knocked on a door and opened it, revealing a comfortable parlor. In the chair opposite the door sat Bonaparte.

Amelia's breath caught as the onetime Emperor of France rose. "Ney," he said, "so good to see you. *Bienvenue, mon frère*. With you at my side, who can prevail against us?"

Bonaparte and the man—Ney—embraced. Swirling fog obscured the vision.

"I lost it," she murmured. "Trying…"

But she couldn't recapture it. Rubbing her brow, she said, "It's gone."

Everyone looked to her, their faces hopeful. If only she had more to report.

She described the vision. When she mentioned Ney, her listeners' faces hardened.

"Who is Ney?" she asked.

Robin replied, "Possibly the bravest of Bonaparte's marshals. He commanded the rear guard in the retreat from Russia and is a brilliant cavalry officer. After Bonaparte abdicated, Ney made his peace with Louis XVIII and stayed in the army. If he has switched sides, that's a grave problem."

"I don't think he has," Amelia said slowly. "I think he will, but I don't know when. It feels…not definite."

Shaking his head, Robin said, "Ney commands six thousand men. He's doing well enough under the Bourbons. Why would he risk all that?"

An image flashed across her sight, a mounted figure in glistening armor and a cloth-of-gold surcoat waved a sword as though exhorting the men in front of him. Above, the fleur-de-lys of France flapped in the breeze.

"Amelia?" Sophie said.

The vision faded. She regained it but couldn't amplify it. Quickly, she told her companions about it.

"How odd," Julian said. "Nobles wore armor in the time of Richard III, so maybe it's to do with that. It wouldn't be anything to do with Bonaparte. Let us know if that happens again, but we've more pressing concerns than this mystery just now."

Robin shook his head. "If Ney turns his coat, if his command goes over to Bonaparte…"

"We must go," Julian said, "and alert the Merlin Club since the government will not listen. Amelia, we cannot afford to have word spread and panic people."

She gave him a wry smile. "Since most of my Gifted acquaintances are in this room and no one else would believe me, you needn't fear. Still, I give you my word I'll say nothing." Glancing at his aunt, she added, "Mama will wonder what became of me. I should return to her."

"Never fear." Augusta rose and shook out her skirts. "You've spent the time duly chaperoned and chatting with two well-regarded earls and a viscountess. Your mother, my dear, will have no complaints. Come, I'll walk back with you."

Sophie, too, stood and shook out her skirts. "I'll help distract her if need be."

"Speaking of Mama, Augusta, I must thank you for the Almack's vouchers," Amelia said. "They will ease any concerns she has over extended visits to your house."

"Indeed." Satisfaction rang in the older woman's voice. "When you're not helping the lads ferret out information about Bonaparte, you and I will see what we can find about your family curse."

"That would be marvelous." Amelia glanced from Augusta to Julian. "I cannot thank you enough."

"It's our pleasure," Julian said. He walked the women to the door. "Amelia, you've done your country, and perhaps all of Europe, a great service this night."

"Thank you." Smiling, she added, "I'm glad my Gift helped. I like to be useful."

"I'll send my carriage for you tomorrow," he told her. "You're coming to help my aunt, so we'll see to your transportation."

"I look forward to it." Partly because of the books and partly because he would be there.

She and Sophie left the room with Lady Augusta, and Amelia gave herself a swift mental poke. Best to focus on matters at hand and not become distracted by a man who likely had no interest in her beyond friendship.

⁓

I *look forward to it*, Amelia had said. For an instant, Julian looked forward to it as well. But there was no sense in letting himself become infatuated with her. He needed a sensible wife who would accept a sensible marriage. Amelia, who had been radiantly smitten with Buckton, likely would want a love match if she remarried. Julian could no longer offer any woman that depth of passion. In the end, he would only disappoint her and cause heartache for them both.

They should remain friends and nothing more.

Robin said, "You like her. More than you want to."

"She's Adam's sister." Julian shrugged. "I don't remember their father well, but I can't think why he agreed to cut his family off from the Gifted. Was he blind? Or merely stupid?" As Julian had been, letting Charlotte deceive him for so long. How many times had she cuckolded him before he'd realized he couldn't trust her?

Scowling, Robin ran a hand through his hair. "The man was a fool to have married a woman who didn't accept the Gifts in the first place and a weak fool to let her take the bit between her teeth."

"At least the Almack's vouchers should ease Amelia's visits. On top of that, Aunt Augusta will tell her mother Amelia's helping her find books for a charity sale Mrs. Drummond-Burrell supports."

Robin grinned. "That should outweigh any fears about Amelia seeming a bluestocking. One should never discount your aunt's wily mind."

"Indeed. She and my mother are much alike in that. With Bonaparte loose, we need a seer. Amelia has a great deal of talent."

"She's honest," Robin said abruptly. "No Charlotte to snare a man and then use him."

Unfortunately, Charlotte hadn't seemed like that sort either. At first. But Amelia was honest, and he already knew her better than he had ever truly known Charlotte. Had his wife deceived him because he lacked the intuition to sense her deceit? Or because he'd been too smitten to look for it?

"You know, Gifted, unattached women are rare," Robin said. "I was lucky to find Barbara, and you—"

"No. Enough of this. We've more pressing problems than my marital status or Amelia's. If the government won't act until they receive official word of his escape—and good God, what's delaying that?!—we must do what we can without them."

CHAPTER 7

Moonlight streamed through the tree limbs outside Amelia's window. As they shifted in the March wind, the dark lines of their shadows crossed and uncrossed and clashed, mirroring her emotions. *A great service*, Julian said she had performed. Perhaps she could help stop Bonaparte and, at the same time, find the information she needed to save her family.

That might mean spending more time with Julian. She would be wise not to anticipate that overmuch. For him, she was merely his friend's sister. Besides, she had no interest in looking for a husband with war looming and the family curse unresolved.

But surely there was no harm in anticipating his vaunted library.

A shimmer rippled through the air by the hearth. Miranda and Richard had arrived. Amelia sat up in bed and pulled her dressing gown around her shoulders.

"We need your help. England needs it." She explained about Bonaparte's arrival in France and the difficulty caused by his warded surroundings. "Can you learn where he is, where he goes?"

"Most likely." Richard frowned. "That should be simple enough, but his destination is obvious. To rule France, he must control Paris. Sooner or later, he'll go there."

"He seems headed there, but we can't be sure. No one in the government yet knows he has escaped. Can you learn how he did it? Can't you go back in time? Isn't that how you stay in touch with those who came before you?"

"It is," Miranda said.

"I need to know everything you can tell me about the afterworld. Julian thinks knowing more about it might help us find a way to help Adam."

Richard said, "I'll leave this to you, my love, while I see what I can learn in France." With a farewell nod, he faded from view.

Miranda shot him an annoyed look but turned to Amelia. "I saw how well you did tonight. You used an unfamiliar object to activate your Gift, and you obtained useful information about people you don't know and who weren't present. That's a sign of maturity in a seer."

"I was lucky to have you as a teacher. You had no one."

Miranda smiled. "When it comes to the seer Gift, one can teach only the basic skills required to direct it. All else, including range and scope of the Gift, is a matter of individual talent and power, as well as a bit of luck. You have great potential, Amelia."

"It isn't doing much good at the moment, though."

"All things come in their time." Miranda sat beside Amelia on the bed. "I truly believe the right Mainwaring at the right time will lift the curse. Until then, Richard and I have undertaken to ease the waiting for the others in any way we can."

"How are Papa and Adam?"

"They're slowly becoming accustomed to the afterworld."

Amelia climbed out of bed. Shoving her arms into her dressing gown's sleeves, she hurried to the desk and the writing materials she'd set out earlier. "I need to write down what you tell me, Grandmother. How did you first learn about that realm?"

A vision flashed over her sight, Grandmother, young and alive, in a big church. A man who resembled Lord Wyndon grabbed her, and they vanished in a flare of argent light. The vision shifted, to Grandmother and Grandfather—alive, Amelia knew through the vision—battling him in the shadow land. How was that possible?

If the living could go there...

Heart beating fast, she laid down her pen and turned to Miranda.

"I don't suppose— Is there any way I could come there?" As Miranda's face closed over, Amelia said, "Perhaps if I could be with Adam, it would help him."

"This is not a place for the living." Miranda's flat tone closed the subject. "Patience, my dear. Look for information on the curse every-where you can, and we will continue to do the same. For now, that must suffice."

"That means there is a way. I Saw it just now, Saw you—"

"I said no. Now write what I tell you so you have time to sleep tonight."

The curt tone stung. Worse, Miranda would not evade unless Amelia's questions touched on something important. One look at the ghost's stern face, though, and she knew better than to push. Amelia picked up her quill.

~

Five days later, Julian sat at the Merlin Club library table with the three men and one woman who had answered his hasty summons. "Word of Bonaparte's escape finally arrived at Whitehall earlier today. They are discussing what to do," he told them. "The French Army's Fifth and Seventh Regiments of the Line have gone over to him without firing a shot, and he entered Lyon today like a conquering hero. We must know how far this plot to place him in power again goes and who's involved in it besides our treacherous French counterparts."

Bess Lassiter, a short, sturdy brunette with strands of gray in her hair, smiled. "A laundress may go anywhere she wishes. I'll see that the French embassy needs me. Perhaps I can learn something of this M. LeFebvre."

Julian mustered a smile for her. "Bess, are you not weary of the laun-dress guise? You use it to great effect, but it must grow tiresome."

"Prying into the Frenchies' secrets never grows old. Besides, what else have I to do, save annoy my son by meddling in his business?" The widow of a tavern keeper, she lived with her son and his family above their tavern in Clerkenwell.

"Then I accept your offer with thanks."

"Bonaparte's making for Paris," wiry, young Pierre Charpentier said. "If he wants to seize power, he must hold Paris."

"But will the city accept him?" Julian rubbed his gritty eyes. He'd spent the last four days rallying the club's agents and questioning every source who might know something useful. "If the French mob turns on him, he must either capitulate or have his newly acquired forces fire upon them, a move that will hardly make him a more palatable choice."

Laurence Newberry, a retired Cambridge professor, spoke from his seat down the table. "France's financial woes are compounded by out-of-work soldiers who see the Bourbons as hostile and dismissive toward them. Bonaparte caused many of those woes, stifling industry by his Continental System that allowed trade only within his empire, taxing drinks and salt, requisitioning horses, fodder, grain and wine, and causing nearly an entire generation of young men to die or be severely injured. Some areas didn't have the farm animals to plow their fields last year. One reason the Allies were able to force Bonaparte to abdicate was that France was sick to death of war.

"Now, however, many of them are sick to death of Louis XVIII. If Bonaparte can evoke France's days of glory, can make the people believe he'll restore France's prominence, many will support him. Especially if he can convince them he doesn't truly want war."

With France in desperate straits, Julian couldn't find it in his heart to blame them, though anyone who believed Bonaparte didn't want his empire back was deluded. Yet he still wondered why so many were willing to overlook the devastation Laurence described. All of it belonged squarely at Bonaparte's feet. Dispatched to stop the former emperor's advance a few days ago, Ney had sworn to bring the Corsican back to Paris in a cage. But would he? Or would the events Amelia had Seen come to pass?

Owen Griffin, a stocky Welshman, leaned forward to take a pastry. "Not everyone will support him, but enough will."

"I cannot dispute what either of you says, but I'll see what I can learn from other sources." He could always ask Amelia to investigate the matter. After he'd had some sleep, which would—please, God!—be soon.

"I can beat him to Paris," Pierre said. "I can blend in there. I can be an émigré newly returned, an ostler looking for work, or whatever else we need."

Oh, to have the confidence of a seventeen-year-old. "You've done well thus far. I would hate to lose you now." Protest formed in Pierre's black eyes. Flinging up a hand to forestall him, Julian said, "The French Gifted appear to have engineered Bonaparte's escape. Their involvement makes all of this much more dangerous."

Pierre's expression turned mutinous. Hastily, Owen said, "I can go with him. Watch his back and all that."

Julian's gaze locked with Pierre's.

"It's my country," Pierre said. "I want to go home, but not under Bonaparte. Don't worry, Julian. I know what I'm doing."

He grinned, and that youthful confidence again wrenched Julian's heart. The boy had never lived in his homeland. His parents, a comte and comtesse, had fled France just before the Reign of Terror. Pierre had been born in London but nurtured on tales of a more civilized France. The work he had done in the war, decoding messages, hanging about stables in London, or lounging in taverns along the coast had, by design, kept him out of danger. Now he wanted to wade in full bore and would likely do so no matter what Julian said.

At last, Julian nodded. "We do need more eyes in the city. Don't make me come over there and rescue the pair of you."

He looked around at all of them. "I'm sorrier than I can say that I must ask you to do these things again, especially with France's wizards in violation of the Compact. We don't know how much farther over its lines they're willing to go. Whatever you do, be more careful than you think you need to be."

Everyone bade him farewell and left to begin their assignments.

Alas, his assignment was not going to bed. This meeting was only one of his list of tasks for the day.

Dare MacGregor was out again, postponing the conversation he'd requested, but Julian still had to alert the Gifted's ruling body, the Conclave Council. If he was lucky, they would supply the authorization he wanted and not chew over everything for a couple of hours. Or days.

Unfortunately, he'd never been that lucky. Even if they agreed to act, as he expected, they wouldn't do it quickly.

～

Despite hours of work, Amelia and Augusta had found nothing helpful about the Mainwaring curse. Now they were having tea before going back to the books Julian had left for them. Fighting frustration, Amelia savored the warm liquid going down her throat. At least she and Augusta had found several volumes of poetry and an old copy of Edward Gibbon's multi-volume *The History of the Decline and Fall of the Roman Empire* for the charity box.

She glanced to the side, at the secret room that held the oldest books and those about magic. Usually concealed by a bookshelf, it stood exposed today. A touch of Augusta's hand and a bit of magic had caused that shelf to slide behind the one on the left and revealed Julian's sanctuary.

Having such a collection of books about magic to read whenever one wished would be divine.

Augusta took a bite of caraway biscuit. "You know, Julian can introduce you to a number of Gifted antiquaries and historians who might be able to help you. In the meantime, you'll continue with your research here and sort a few books from time to time."

"That sounds lovely. Thank you."

"Are you ready to resume our hunt?"

Reading old-style type, with *f* for *s,* was fatiguing, but it was necessary. "Of course."

The two women settled back into their chairs by the hearth. If they could find a clue—even something to trigger a vision or a scrying—that could lead them to proof Richard III hadn't murdered his nephews, surely that would satisfy the curse.

Amelia had tried again to See or scry any link between the king and the armor she'd Seen a few nights ago. Images of a sturdy figure wearing it on the battlefield and others of it packed into a chest had offered no clue. The figure bulged oddly in the upper torso, but that could've been an ill-fitting surcoat. The French emblem in the vision posed another puzzle. King Richard had been an enemy of France. Did the flag mean someone he'd fought held the answer she needed?

For now, best to attend to her research and not worry about this mystery.

Amelia picked up the next book on her stack. She and her hostess read in silence.

The delicate chiming of six by the mantel clock drew Amelia out of her book. "This is interesting," she said. "Many more people than I realized defended King Richard's honor, no matter how subtly and carefully they had to do it. It's no wonder they waited until the Tudor dynasty ended."

Augusta's mouth turned up in a wry smile. "The more insecure a dynasty, the more likely they are to kill even a remote threat." She fished a book from her stack. "You should read this one, Horace Walpole's *Historic Doubts on the Life and Reign of King Richard the Third.* Take it home with you if you like."

"We're having a quiet evening for once, so I would like to have it." Amelia accepted the book. "I should go, though. Mama and Aunt Louisa will be wondering where I am."

"I'll have James send for the carriage and bring your maid from the kitchen."

They left the library without closing the secret room. With the Gifted footman away, calling for the carriage, was that wise? Before Amelia could think of a tactful way to ask, Augusta laid her fingertips on the doorknob. Faint silver flared around them, and she smiled. "Just a little ward until I return. Anyone who tries that door will find it stuck. Or so they'll think."

They strolled down the corridor to the stairs.

Descending, Augusta sighed. "One cannot help pitying Richard III when he learned his admired elder brother was perhaps not so admirable. Or feeling for poor Lady Eleanor Butler. Years before he met his future queen, King Edward secretly wed her, only to disavow the marriage when it suited him. She thought she'd won the heart of the most charismatic nobleman of the age, that she was Edward IV's wife and would be his queen."

"It must've seemed too good to be true."

"As it proved to be." In a voice as dry as earth in a drought, the older woman added, "She never married again, likely because she believed she would be committing bigamy. Julian says that in those days, a betrothal followed by a bedding made a marriage, with or without the ceremony. According to that book in your hand, a bishop married her to the king, albeit secretly. Of course she believed they were wed."

"If Edward IV did that to her and later secretly married Elizabeth Woodville, his queen, how many others did he treat the same way between them?"

"We'll never know. After King Edward died, the bishop told Richard of Gloucester, as King Richard was then, and showed his proofs to Parliament. Proofs that have gone missing. If Edward's marriage to Eleanor was valid, as Julian and I believe, then his later marriage to his queen was bigamous. That made their children, including the two boys who're still known as the Princes in the Tower, illegitimate and thus ineligible to inherit the crown."

Amelia's heart kicked. "If they had no right to the throne, King Richard had no reason to kill them. That would point to his innocence, perhaps even clear his name."

Why had Buckingham seen them as a threat? Did he fear the nobility would prefer the sons of Edward IV, illegitimate or not, to him? King Richard would not have shared that fear. He'd acceded to the throne after being asked to do so by the nobility, and he'd subsequently received oaths of allegiance from the higher clergy, the lords, and officials of the City of London. His nephews posed no threat to him.

"If we could find that proof," Augusta replied. "The Bishop of Bath and Wells is said to have revealed all to then-Duke Richard and Parliament. There may have been other witnesses as well. Odd, isn't it, that the Tudors, who had a strong interest in delegitimizing King Richard, came to power, and now the documents that supported his claim to the throne have vanished?"

"Indeed. Did Lady Eleanor at least live to see the truth come to light, to know she was vindicated?"

"Sadly, no. After King Edward repudiated her, she entered a nunnery. She died there in the late 1460s."

"How terrible for her." Amelia's heart ached in sympathy. If Crispin had treated her so wretchedly, she would never have recovered. Perhaps Lady Eleanor hadn't either.

There was something about Lady Eleanor. Something teasing the back of Amelia's mind as she and Augusta descended the last stairs to the foyer. What was it? If she could only grasp it…

The front door opened, and Julian walked in. His shoulders slumped with fatigue. The shadows under his eyes and the weary lines in his face turned her pleasure at seeing him into worry.

When his gaze met hers, though, he smiled. "Any luck today?"

She and his aunt reached the foyer floor. With a warning glance, Augusta said, "We found several books for the charity bin. We also discussed some Yorkist history."

"You left some books on the table," Amelia reminded him. Of course her hosts wouldn't want to risk unGifted servants overhearing a discussion of magic. "I hope you don't mind my borrowing one."

"My books are yours." His gaze sharpened, locking on her face, as James emerged from the back corridor with her pelisse, bonnet, and gloves.

Julian said, "I take it you found something of interest."

"I read something that made me want to know more. I'll see if I can find anything at my aunt's that will supplement it."

Comprehension flickered in his eyes. He knew she meant to scry or summon a vision.

He took her pelisse from James. Handling the coat with perfect courtesy, he merely brushed her shoulders with his fingertips as he helped her into it. His hands didn't linger even a moment more than was proper. The respect in his conduct underscored how presumptuous Lord Wyndon had been.

"Your maid is in the coach, my lady," James said. "It should arrive out front in a moment."

Amelia thanked him. He passed her gloves and bonnet to her, and she pulled them on.

"I'll walk you out." Julian's glance at his aunt conveyed something Amelia couldn't read.

Augusta said, "It's too cold out for my old bones. Amelia, thank you for your help. I'll see you in a few days."

Amelia thanked her and let Julian usher her outside. He closed the front door gently behind them. Augusta was right about the chill. The air seemed dank, too, and the lowering clouds promised rain.

"I've met with the Conclave Council," he said. "Do you know what that is?"

"My grandparents told me."

"They've taken the matter under advisement," he ground out. The words vibrated with anger. "I thought they had more sense, given that they put a watch on Bonaparte as soon as he became First Consul of France all those years ago. Now our French cousins are in this up to their bloody ears, and the Council wants to dither about it for a while."

"That's dreadful. No wonder you look so weary."

He blinked at her, and his brows rose.

Warmth washed into her cheeks. "I beg your pardon. I shouldn't have said—"

"It's all right." His lips curved in a slight smile, but his eyes searched hers. "Friendly concern is always appreciated. We are friends, are we not, Amelia?"

"Of course."

His expression softened. Their gazes held, and the warmth in his made her heart beat suddenly faster.

Before she could think of anything else to say, his carriage rounded the corner. It stopped neatly beside them. The footman at the rear jumped to the ground, let down the step, and opened the door. Amelia's maid, Mary, smiled at her from the rear-facing seat.

"Thank you, my lord, for the use of your library," Amelia said. Sometimes the social niceties offered a refuge. "Thank you as well for your concern about my brother."

"He was a brother to me," Julian replied simply.

Did that mean she was his sister? The thought, inexplicably, stung, but that was likely best. He needed an heir. He would marry a young woman, not one on the shelf.

He handed her into the carriage, his grip firm and steadying but, again, not encroaching. When he released her and shut the door, her palm tingled. She clenched her fist. What an odd reaction. It must've come from that unexpected moment of understanding.

A man's voice outside called, "My lord! Lord Aysgarth!"

Julian turned toward the sound. His shoulders tensed, and his expression went blank.

Amelia pressed her face to the coach window.

A young man in the worn clothes of a laborer hurried down the street. Julian stepped forward to meet him, and the coach pulled away from the curb.

None of your concern, she told herself. Still...why did this man's approach make Julian look so stony?

❧

As a rule, the Merlin Club was Julian's sanctuary. This evening, he was heartily sick of it. The young man who'd hailed him, a bricklayer and a club member, had borne a message asking him to return on urgent business, though, so here he was.

Divesting him of his coat, the footman, Harry, said, "I told Alasdair you'd had a long day, Julian, but he says his business is urgent. To be fair, he looked as though he'd ridden hard."

"If he says this is urgent, I won't delay. Where is he?"

"Room four. Should I send up food?"

"Straight away, enough for two if Dare hasn't eaten, and a bottle of claret. Thank you."

Mounting the stairs, Julian tried to put some speed into his steps. Plodding along only served to remind him how tired he actually was.

He knocked on the second door to his left. The guest rooms were nothing luxurious, but the canopied bed, writing table and chair, and two upholstered chairs by the hearth in each one offered cozy comfort, all within a layer of security provided by the building's wards.

Footsteps approached on the other side, and the door swung open. Alasdair "Dare" MacGregor, a member of Scotland's ancient royal line and one of her most talented Gifted, stepped aside to admit him. The tall, dark-haired Scotsman's usually serious expression now looked grim.

"Thank you for coming. I'm told I should beg yer pardon for draggin' ye back here, and so I do. I wouldna, but we canna keep missin' each other. This is important."

The emergence of Dare's brogue signaled worry or anger. A graduate of Harrow, he generally spoke in a more neutral accent. Whatever he wanted to discuss must matter a great deal to him.

Julian sat in one of the chairs by the hearth, leaving the other for Alasdair. "I requested food. Told them to send enough for two if you haven't eaten."

"That's kind."

The two men eyed each other as the silence stretched. Finally, Julian said, "If this is urgent, Dare, let's have it."

"Again, my apologies. This is…difficult."

"In what way?"

The other man grimaced. "I'm weighin' my oath to the Merlin Club with another, searchin' for a path between."

Someone knocked on the door. Dare opened it, admitting one of the kitchen lads with a tray. The delicious aromas of mutton stew, fresh bread, and honeyed parsnips filled the air. Setting up the writing table for the meal and unloading the food occupied the next few minutes.

When the lad had departed, the two men took their seats at the table. Julian didn't wait to start eating. The day had been excruciatingly long, and if Dare needed a few minutes to collect himself—though why he hadn't already done so was puzzling—there was no sense allowing the food to cool.

Dare stared down at his plate. Finally, he looked back at Julian. "The Romans slaughtered the Druids," he said. "Some survived. Enough survived, and they went into hiding."

"I know." Julian's godfather, his late father's best friend, had been a Druid. "But what do they have to do with the current problem?"

The other man opened his mouth, closed it, and took a long swallow of claret. "I'm sure ye know what happened after the '45. The Sassenachs destroyed the clans. Cleared the Highlands of those whose blood had lived there since before there was a Scotland."

"Yes. It was brutal." Unnecessary as well. The Jacobite rebellion, while a factor, wasn't nearly as important in the long term as the greed of absentee landlords who wanted to use the land for other, more profitable purposes than farming or raising cattle.

"It was..." Dare shook his head. "Again, enough escaped, evaded the redcoats, to mean something. I'm—some of my family were among them."

"Which makes you part of whatever bond they formed." Though Julian kept his tone bland, possibilities spun through his mind. Was there a cabal of Scottish Gifted in the Highlands? If so, were they dealing themselves into this current crisis? If they were, did they intend to help or...

"What our grandparents had is gone," Dare said. "The clans who built it are destroyed or scattered to the winds. To America. Or Australia. We'll never have enough of them back to regain what was." He took another drink of claret. "Oh, aye, we can wear our plaids now, and some of us clung to the Gaelic even when it was outlawed. It's not enough. Without the land, it never will be."

He stabbed his fork into his stew, took a bite, and ripped a chunk from the loaf of bread on the table. "Bloody Sassenachs," he muttered.

Julian understood that pain, but he couldn't let sympathy cloud his judgment. If Dare was bringing up these old grudges now, with Bonaparte running loose...

"Dare, are you telling me there are Scots Gifted who would aid Napoleon?"

The other man's shoulders stiffened. He laid down his fork and swallowed. "Not precisely."

"Then what, precisely? I've had a deuced long day, and I've no patience for games."

"It's no' a game," the Scotsman snapped. "It's bloody damned serious."

"Then open the budget, and let's deal with it."

Dare sighed and slumped in his chair. "The clans at Culloden lined up wi' their swords and dirks, facin' redcoats armed with muskets, and recited their lineage in a great, long roar. They didna know that was the obituary for the life they loved. Then they charged into a fusillade of musket balls."

"Blast it, Dare—"

"They're m'blood, and they've a right to their anger."

Julian studied the other man's stiff shoulders and defiant expression. Softly, he asked, "As you've a right to yours?"

"Aye."

Their gazes locked, Dare's blue eyes hard.

"Then why are we here?" Julian demanded.

"Because I took an oath. Because I think they're again chargin' to disaster. Because…it doesna matter what I think of Mad George and his fool of an heir. We canna reclaim the past and 'tis folly to try."

"Who's trying?" Julian clung to the shreds of his temper. Dare was a good man, obviously struggling, and alienating him would be a mistake. But if he didn't get the bloody hell on with it—

"I dinna ken. I mean, I don't know for certain. But I hear rumors. Of aiding Bonaparte's cause in exchange for French support to take back the Highlands."

"And do what there? As you said, those who left have built lives elsewhere. There aren't enough people to hold the area even if they win it. This sounds like a French scheme to occupy part of this island."

"Aye, it does." Grim-faced, the Scotsman added, "I willna stand by while my kinsmen shed more blood on a folly. Charles Edward Stuart wasna worth the muck his horse shat, and many of them still canna see it." He hesitated. "There's more, perhaps worse, though it may not be true. There are rumors—plans to eliminate the Royal Navy and open the way to Scotland, and they…well, as I said, it sounds like a fairy tale, but with magic, who can know?"

"Indeed. What are the rumors?"

"They've an ancient tome, one that tells of a way to travel from one place to another undetected. By going through the lands of the dead."

A chill rippled down Julian's back. "This is how they plan to eliminate the fleet?"

"Aye. Four men will board each vessel via this dead realm, kill the captain, and set the wood alight with witchfire."

Only magic could quench witchfire. The ships would burn to cinders, destroying the Royal Navy's defensive line along the Scottish coast and opening the way for invasion.

Bastards.

Dare continued, "Then they'll escape the way they came, moving from the dead realm onto another ship. If the French Navy can land Scottish and French troops and escape, they'll count that a successful diversion. That's how they plan to take King George and Prinny hostage as well. They'll smuggle them away through this dead realm and keep them until Parliament grants the Highlands separate and equal status."

"It could work," Julian said slowly. "But if you can do that, why do you need the French Navy? Why not simply move your troops through there?"

71

"I gather the place is infested with wraiths and perhaps other fell creatures, so moving through there requires inner steel. Most men don't have that when facing a supernatural foe. As for whether that plan can succeed, aye, it can for a while. England is distracted, her army is drawn away from the Continent, and Napoleon has a clearer road. But then what?"

The Scotsman glared at his plate. "What happens when the world's best navy and one of its strongest armies attack—again?" Bitterness laced the words. Dare took another swallow of claret. "My kinsmen die, that's what, and the plaid and our Gaelic again go under a ban. No. I won't have it."

"There's something else odd about this. If Bonapartists are supporting the Scots in this, why are they? This seems like a risky venture with an uncertain result. How can Napoleon support that when it'll cost him hundreds of thousands of francs to rebuild the army?"

"I don't know that he is supporting it, or even knows of it." Dare sighed. "I don't know where they get their money, only that I hear they don't lack for it. As for why anyone would underwrite this, think what an army could do with assassins or spies able to move from one place to another undetected and escape without fear of pursuit."

"Even if this venture fails," Julian said slowly, "if those behind it gain the ability to move with such stealth, they might count the money well spent."

"I would. Especially if I thought the great powers of Europe were about to descend on me."

"This book is the key, then?" There'd been something about a book in old letters between Jeremy and Cabot Winfield. Was this book connected? Or merely a coincidence? "Without the lore it holds, the plan falls apart?"

When MacGregor nodded, Julian asked, "Do you know where the book is?"

Alasdair shook his head. "I'm tryin' tae find out. That's why I've no' been here to talk to ye. There're rumors that book came from in or near London, but I've no' enough information to scry it. I canna hope to see one book out of many when I dinna ken its looks or title or origins."

"Very true." Amelia probably couldn't summon a vision of something that vague either.

"I've friendly ears to the ground, but they must take great care. These wizards willna hesitate to kill anyone who opposes them."

"Of course. You take great care as well, but see if you can steal that book." Perhaps Amelia's family ghosts would help locate it, but they weren't his secret to share.

When the Scotsman nodded, Julian asked, "Do you need any help from the club?"

"No' yet. I'll let ye know if I do."

"Very well. Thank you, Alasdair. I know this wasn't easy."

The other man shrugged. "I'm doin' it for Scotland. No thanks needed."

Perhaps not, but when a man put his life on the line, he ought to know others appreciated the risk.

CHAPTER 8

In her uncle and aunt's house a few streets away, Amelia closed the borrowed copy of Walpole's *Historic Doubts* for the night. Lady Eleanor Butler had occupied her thoughts for most of the evening, but this book mentioned nothing about her save in relation to her kinsmen. She'd been daughter to one earl, sister to another, and widow of a baron. She was no lightskirt, not someone even a king could trifle with. Yet Edward IV had.

That poor woman, bedazzled by the king, trusting his word, and utterly betrayed by him.

Shaking her head, Amelia doffed her dressing gown and laid it on the chair near the bed. Blowing out the candle on her night table left the room semi-dark, with clouds obscuring the moon. When she climbed into bed, the sheets were warm, thanks to Mary and a warming pan.

Once, Amelia hadn't needed a warming pan. She'd had Crispin. Snuggling into the sheets, she looked at the smooth pillow beside hers but didn't touch it. The time for that had passed with the grief that had burned in her chest and throat and stolen her breath. The soft, quiet feeling of loss that remained didn't demand such homage, nor would he have wanted it to.

She hadn't talked to him in a long time. Hadn't felt the need. But wherever he was, perhaps he could hear her. Turning toward the empty pillow, she told him about Lady Eleanor, the king who betrayed her, and the dignity with which she had borne his abandonment. What choice had she, really, against a king? But she had carried on with her life, honoring her vows even though he broke his.

"If you had done that to me," Amelia said, "I don't know how I would've kept breathing. Her story makes me appreciate what we had, what we gave each other, all the more."

And what she'd lost when he died, but she'd promised him she wouldn't dwell on that.

There'd been no vindication for Lady Eleanor. The Tudor chroniclers had needed to repudiate her marriage to Edward IV so that his daughter, Henry VII's queen, would be considered legitimate. Only thus could they secure the loyalty of Edward's followers. So Lady Eleanor had been shoved onto history's dust heap, just as her royal husband had consigned her to the dustbin of his forgotten mistakes.

Amelia turned over and punched her pillow. Someone should've punched King Edward, but no one had dared challenge him. Lady Eleanor's family had faced a situation remarkably like Edmund Mainwaring's had been after Richard III's death. They'd known the truth but hadn't dared to share it.

But had they preserved it?

Edmund had written a confession, now mysteriously lost. Had Eleanor Butler or someone on her behalf written down her account of her clandestine marriage?

Would proof of that marriage, of Richard III's unassailable right to succeed his brother, clear the king's name and lift the curse? It would demonstrate King Richard's right to the crown Parliament had offered him. If he had that right, not merely a paper claim, why murder his newly bastardized nephews?

There would be no marriage lines for a secret wedding, but if there were something else, an affidavit from Lady Eleanor, a letter from the king...

Best not to hope too much. Any proof Lady Eleanor possessed might've been presented to Parliament already, perhaps as part of the King Richard's claim. It might've disappeared when the Tudors came to power. The possibility was worth considering, though.

Would Grandmother and Grandfather know more about Lady Eleanor? If that place touched all times, they could find out. They hadn't come tonight, hadn't told her what, if anything, they'd learned about the French.

Were they avoiding her questions? That would be truly distressing. What could they be hiding? The secret to living beings coming to the afterworld, perhaps? Why would they care?

There was no sense worrying about that now, though. Amelia sighed and stared at the far wall. Gradually, her mind relaxed into sleep.

Purple-gray mists swirled around her, and the stench of rotten eggs pervaded the eerie twilight. The mists and the odor signaled a vision forming in her dream.

Could she direct it? See Lady Eleanor?

The fog rolled back, revealing a square chamber with dark-paneled walls, exposed beams overhead, a plank floor, and mullioned windows. The heavy, carved furniture belonged to an earlier time, as did the woman in the chamber. The green gown with a high waist and dangling sleeves and the headdress, like a flat-topped cone with silk veiling attached, spoke of distant eras.

The woman sat in an X-shaped chair by the window. She had a narrow, pleasant face with full lips and pale blue eyes. The hair tucked under her headdress was dark brown.

Was she Lady Eleanor?

Her head lifted, as though she'd heard something. She darted to the window, took one look, and dashed out of the chamber. The steep stairs to the ground delayed her not at all. She reached the courtyard as a horseman dismounted.

When he turned to her, grim-faced, her shoulders slumped. "Oh, John."

John Talbot, Lady Eleanor's brother? They resembled each other, his face shaped much like hers and his eyes the same blue.

"Not here, Nell," he murmured, embracing her.

Nell was a nickname for Eleanor. Amelia's heart beat faster.

The pair went indoors and back up to the room the woman had left in such a hurry. Her brother tossed his puffy velvet cap on a chest and ran his hand through his hair. "Nell, I—"

"There's no cushioning the news I believe you bring. Tell me straight away, and let's have done with it." She sat braced, her shoulders square, her chin up, and her clasped hands in her lap, white-knuckled.

Her brother dropped to one knee before her and took her hands in his. "I saw the king. He told me I must be mistaken, that there had never been troth plighted between you or any sort of marriage. That you had misunderstood."

As he spoke, his sister's eyes fired. "How dare he?"

"He is the king."

Amelia bit her lip. That said it all, didn't it? *Oh, Eleanor.*

"He assured me you should have no further difficulties over the manors he restored to you."

"Unless I cause His Lying Grace trouble." Eleanor set her lips in a tight line. "I wish I had let Thomas's father keep those manors, even though he'd no right to seize them. Then I would never have met—never—"

Eleanor shoved out of her chair and paced to the hearth and back. Despite the hurt in her eyes, her face set in hard lines of fury. "I did not spin this tale out of whole cloth, John. Bishop Stillington of Bath and Wells, himself, witnessed our vows and was there when we went to bed. He knows as well as I, as well as Edward, what transpired."

A long moment passed before her brother gently said, "Aye, but do you think he'll dare to contradict the king?"

Again, the look between them held. Eleanor finally said, "Apparently not." Lips trembling, she dropped onto the wooden settle by the hearth.

Her brother sat beside her and put his arm around her. She turned her face into his neck. Tremors ran through her body and her muffled voice. "I knew better than to hope, after all these months. Still I...oh, I was such a fool."

"With a bishop standing by, who would not have trusted him?"

They sat in silence for a few minutes before John added, "If he did this to you, Nell, he may have done it to others. We must have an account. Let me have our lawyers in, swear them to secrecy—"

"No." Eleanor raised her head. "This is too big a secret for anyone but a priest. Father Thomas shall witness my account, and you must keep it safe."

He frowned. At last, he said, "If that's what you want."

"It is." She walked to the window and stood with her arms crossed in front of her. "Someday, there may be room for the truth."

The fog swept across the scene. Its acrid stench stung Amelia's nose.

Amelia jolted awake. Blast! A few moments more might've made such a difference.

Eleanor Talbot Butler, rightful Queen of England. Where is her proof? What became of it?

An image floated across her sight, a coat of arms. Encircled by the famous blue, gold-lettered garter granted to members of the Order of the Garter, a shield held two panels of gold lions rampant on a red field with a jagged gold border. Those were quartered with panels of white with two red lions standing with a single paw raised in each. A coronet surmounted it all.

Amelia slid out of bed, tugged on her robe, and lit the candle on her desk. She should sketch this before she forgot it. She tugged out a sheet of foolscap. Her quill pen sputtered, but the memory might fade if she took time to sharpen the nib. She managed to quickly outline the arms she'd seen.

Alas, she'd no idea whose arms they were. They might well be the Shrewsbury arms, or perhaps the Butlers'. Or someone else's altogether.

If only one of the ghosts would happen by. If they'd looked in while she was sleeping, though, they would've gone on their way.

Well, there was always tomorrow. In the meantime, Julian might have some idea about these visions. She could send this to him, and perhaps he could meet her at the lecture on Egypt tomorrow.

Amelia blew out her candle and climbed back into bed. Pinning her hopes on this could be a mistake. If Eleanor's affidavit had come to light during King Edward's lifetime, his word would have prevailed over hers. When proof came to light after his death, however, Parliament had recognized the marriage. Whatever proof had supported its legitimacy had vanished under the Tudors. But if the affidavit still existed, it might clear King Richard's name and free her family's souls.

~

Hope did wonders for one's appetite.

Amelia served herself eggs, a rasher of bacon, and a slice of warm, yeasty-smelling bread from the sideboard dishes. Her note to Julian, with a better drawing of the coat of arms, was on its way. She would have time to read Walpole more carefully before Robin and Sophie fetched her for the lecture.

Sipping coffee, she thought again of Lady Eleanor. A woman with the steel in her to bear up under such callous treatment would've made a good queen. At least her life in the nunnery had provided companionship. She hadn't died alone.

Amelia sighed. Crispin hadn't wanted *her* to be alone. She'd promised him she would remarry if she could find the right man. And so she would try, when war was no longer a threat and she'd saved Adam and Papa.

Perhaps the delay caused by periods of mourning, first for Crispin and then for Adam and Papa, was as well. Her grief for Crispin had faded into the background. Sometimes days passed when she didn't think of him. That was probably good, but it also meant the precious memories had gone fuzzy.

"My lady?"

Simon, a thin, middle-aged footman, stood near the table. When he had her attention, he said, "You've a caller, my lady. In the front parlor."

"At this hour?" Ten was rather early for morning calls, which shouldn't start before eleven and preferably began after noon. Could it be Julian? If so, why did Simon look so excited? He tried to hide it, but his eyes danced.

Amelia opened to her Gift. The familiar purple-gray fog rolled across her sight. After it came a vision of Lord Wyndon in the front parlor. Her good mood plummeted. Of course he would do as he chose, and manners be hanged.

Firmly, she said, "I'm not at home to callers today, Simon. I'm going out."

His excitement faded into anxiety. "Yes, milady. You said. Your lady mother, though, she said you would see this gentleman."

Oh, of course she had! Blast it. There would be no sending him away until they spoke.

"Very well. Does the gentleman have a name?"

"Your lady mother, she said..."

"Never mind. Tell him I'll join him shortly." Sending him away would achieve nothing. Best to dispose of this problem today. Then she and Mama would have a very serious conversation.

Amelia deliberately finished her breakfast, though the food no longer tasted quite so good. If his lordship wanted to pay a call before proper visiting hours, he could bloody well wait on her convenience.

At last, she pushed back from the table and walked slowly to the parlor. A few feet from the closed door, she squared her shoulders and lifted her chin. There would be no room for him to misunderstand after this. No chance for him to take advantage. She walked in with a brisk stride and left the door open.

Wyndon rose, his eyes assessing. "Good morning, Amelia. I dislike waiting."

Despite the custom of using first names among the Gifted, his use of hers rankled.

"I dislike callers who use my given name without my permission and arrive outside the proper hours. Why are you here, my lord?"

"To speak privately with you, of course."

Magic prickled over her skin. From the corner of her eye, she could see the door. It slowly swung inward. She couldn't have closed it from here. His magic had more reach than hers. Did he also have more power?

"If you close that door," she informed him, her voice cool despite her pounding heart, "you will regret it." Screaming would draw an audience, which might allow him to claim he'd compromised her and they had to wed. Even a widow could be compromised by a great enough scandal. Setting him on fire, however, appealed strongly. She could certainly do that at this range.

"As you wish." The door stopped moving.

The smug look on his face, though—oh, how she longed to punch him. "Say what you came to say, my lord. I've a full day ahead."

"Should we not sit?" he asked gently.

"You won't be here that long."

Anger flared in his eyes. Her stomach clenched, but she stood her ground.

He shrugged. "Very well. My dear Lady Buckton, I've made no secret of my growing regard for you."

"If I have done anything to make you think I return that regard, I must beg your pardon."

He actually smiled at her. "You say that as though it matters."

"It matters to me." Where in all the world and time were Grandmother and Grandfather? A little support, even of the intangible sort, would be more than welcome.

"I suspect your father's and brother's souls matter to you as well. Perhaps more?"

Blood roared in her ears, and a chill swept down her spine. How did he know?

Amelia swallowed hard. "I don't know what you mean."

"Of course you do." He raised an eyebrow. "One of your ancestors was rather talkative when drunk. I know all about the Mainwaring curse. Princes in the Tower, Duke of Buckingham, and poor scapegoat Richard III. All of it."

He did. The truth in his words washed over her Gifted senses.

"Marriages among our kind, my dear, are made for strategic reasons more often than for affection. I have the means to prove King Richard innocent of his nephews' deaths and lift your family curse. To liberate all the souls who've suffered that fool Edmund's doom. If you will do me the great honor of becoming my wife, I will give you the proof you seek."

Marry him? Be…intimate with him?

Her friends' warnings roared into her mind, and her stomach churned. Again, she swallowed hard.

"What proof is this? How do I know you truly have such a thing?"

"You're a seer. Of course you know."

How could he have learned that? She was so cold. Her hands felt like ice.

Dear Heaven, would she actually have to go through with this?

"As for the proof," he continued, "it's a document that will do all you wish."

A vision flashed over her sight, the same document in the same dark chamber she'd Seen at his house. Amelia's heart kicked hard. "I need to see it in order to consider your offer."

"And so you shall, on the morning after our wedding. I'll place it in your hands when you are irrevocably my wife."

"I cannot—this is very sudden." If she could stomach him, she could free so many, including those who held her heart.

If.

"It's also something of a shock, apparently." He smiled, and his eyes glittered with triumph. With certainty.

Oh, dear Lord!

"I'll return tomorrow for your answer."

He walked toward the door. Amelia stepped aside, but he stopped in front of her. When he took her hand, revulsion swept through her.

"Never fear, my pet. So long as you comply with my wishes, you'll find me an indulgent lord." He lifted her hand and turned it to press his lips to the inside of her wrist.

A vision flashed across her sight. Of herself cowering beside a bed, naked, with welts marking her buttocks and thighs. Tear tracks stained her cheeks, and terror twisted her face. He stood over her, his eyes glittering and his hands glowing with power. "I warned you."

She jerked free of the vision. Lord Wyndon, mercifully, was gone.

Her stomach revolted. She raced out of the parlor, up the stairs, and through her chamber to the dressing room. Dropping to her knees beside the chamber pot, she lost all she'd eaten. For long minutes, she hung over the ceramic bin, her empty stomach heaving.

When the heaving stopped, she collapsed in a shivering heap on the floor. If she couldn't bear his touch without being sick, how would she ever bear having him bed her?

The mere idea had her rebellious stomach surging again. She gritted her teeth.

Obviously she couldn't bear it.

For the sakes of those she loved, though, if the document he held would do all he claimed, she might have no choice.

CHAPTER 9

Julian waited in the Liftons' front parlor for Amelia. He'd come to fetch her for the lecture while Robin and Sophie remained in the carriage outside.

When Amelia walked into the parlor, the smile of greeting died on his lips. Tiny tremors rippled through her. Her eyes seemed huge in her pale face, and worry creased her brow.

He clenched his fists to keep from reaching for her. "Amelia, what's wrong?"

"It—I—" She shook her head. "I can't talk about it now."

"Do you still want to go this afternoon? Everyone would understand—"

"No! I mean, yes. I particularly need to speak with you. Please, Julian, let's go."

As they left the room, her chin rose. She mustered a smile for the footman who returned his hat and gloves. As soon as they were outside, though, the smile withered like a rose in a desert.

What could have happened to make her so distraught?

The footman opened the carriage door, and Julian handed her in. She settled beside Sophie on the forward-facing seat, and Julian took his place by Robin, across from them. Robin tapped on the roof, signaling the coachman to drive away.

"What's happened?" Sophie demanded. "What has upset you so?"

Amelia shook her head, pressing her lips together. Her throat moved in a hard swallow.

At last, she took a deep, shuddering breath. When she turned to Sophie, fear welled in her eyes. "Lord Wyndon proposed to me," she said in a flat, almost toneless voice.

"And when you refused him?" Sophie asked.

"I haven't. I don't know—I may not be able to."

"Why ever not?" Sophie scowled at her friend.

Julian exchanged a resolute look with Robin. Wyndon would not have Amelia under his brutal thumb. On that, they were agreed. The mere idea made Julian cold with rage.

Amelia's throat moved in another hard swallow, and his heart twisted. He'd always thought of her as Adam's sister, but in the time he'd spent with her recently, he'd come to see her as more, as a friend and possibly an ally. Either way, he couldn't let Wyndon ruin her. Or take control of her abilities, though that, surprisingly, was a secondary consideration.

Amelia sighed. "He says he has a document that will prove Richard III innocent of his nephews' deaths. It will end the family curse. Free Adam's and Papa's souls. Everyone's."

"Did you ask to see it?" Julian demanded.

"He said he would give it to me when—on the morning after the, ah, wedding."

Bastard. Julian bit back a sharp curse.

"Do you believe him?" Robin asked.

"He's telling the truth. Thanks to my Gift, I know it."

Slowly, Julian said, "He's telling the truth if he believes what he says. That doesn't mean he's correct about what this document would do."

"Yes, but..." Amelia shrugged.

Sophie said, "This is far more important than a lecture about Egyptian pyramids. We need privacy to plan, which means someone's house. Julian, Ned is meeting with his business manager at Havelock house, and Mama is receiving this afternoon."

"I believe Aunt Augusta has guests, but we can go into the library without passing her parlor."

Robin raised the trap in the roof and directed the coachman.

"Aunt Augusta is very resourceful, Amelia, and sensible. I suggest we bring her into our conversation."

"Very well." If she had to marry Wyndon, everyone would know about it soon enough. But she would never agree to that without seeing his supposed proof and believing it would actually end the curse. "Julian, have you found anything about the coat of arms I sent you?"

"A little." In the circumstances, he wished it were more. "I stopped by the College of Arms this morning—"

"They know him well there," Robin interjected, his voice wry. "He's forever stopping in on a quest for some obscure information about heraldry."

Julian raised an eyebrow. "Some of us know how to read coats of arms. Those who don't merely poke fun to hide their jealousy."

"What did you learn?" Amelia asked.

Clearly, the banter had been mistimed.

Julian replied, "The coat of arms you saw belonged to John Talbot, First Earl of Shrewsbury in the second creation of the title. Second creation means—"

"I'm sorry," she said, "but does that matter here?"

"No," he answered gently. "Coats of arms often change from one generation to the next, but the one you describe likely belonged to Lady Eleanor's father."

"It will take time to find out," she said. Her lips trembled, and she pressed them together. "I must…he expects my answer tomorrow."

"That doesn't mean you must give it," Julian responded.

"I dare not delay unless I mean to refuse. He won't tolerate being crossed." The bleak look on her face must mean she was certain. As a seer, she likely was.

"Where are your ghosts?" Sophie asked. "Can they not learn what this document is?"

Amelia shook her head. "I don't know where they are, and even if I asked, they can't go through Wyndon's wards to enter his house. Or enter other warded places, unless the wards were set by a Mainwaring."

"There must be a way," Robin said. "Have you tried to See what this is?"

"Yes, but I can't find it. After our dinner at his house, I glimpsed a document, very old, with odd writing and a heavy wax seal. I Saw it again earlier today, but not its location."

"Of course you're distressed." Sophie squeezed Amelia's hand. "Perhaps tea and a biscuit will help."

Amelia looked doubtful but didn't say anything.

Julian hesitated. To persuade her, he must keep his own outrage on a tight rein.

With a deep breath, he plunged in. "You cannot marry Wyndon, Amelia, no matter what he offers. Marriage to him would destroy you."

She bit her lip. "I can set Adam and Papa free. Set all of them free. How can I not do that?"

"Because the price is too high, as I'm sure they also would say," Julian replied. "Oh, don't look so surprised. This isn't effrontery or imagination on my part. I knew your brother. I dare say Robin and I knew things about Adam you never did. I've read letters between Richard Mainwaring, Lord Hawkstowe, and my great-uncles Cabot and Jeremy Winfield. They were chivalrous men, all of them. Kind and strong as well. Hawkstowe would not want you to endure years of misery to free your kinsmen."

Amelia shook her head. Softly, she said, "You cannot know that."

"Anyone who would ask that of you doesn't deserve his freedom." Julian's gaze locked with hers. Again his heart twisted. The pain and fear and doubt in her eyes made him ill, and the urge to comfort her had him again clenching his fists to resist it.

I would wed her myself rather than see her tied to that evil piece of work.

The thought came out of nowhere, startling him. There was no cause for such drastic measures. He and Amelia's other friends would find a solution, one that included procuring this mysterious document. Besides, he and she might not suit. He'd chosen rashly with Charlotte, and look where that had gotten him.

Anyway, marriage wasn't the issue. Wyndon's lure was.

Julian glanced out the carriage window. "Robin, have Charles drive round to the mews. We'll go in through the kitchen." When Amelia shot him a startled look, he said, "I do it often when I'm in a hurry. No one will remark upon it."

He didn't do it with guests, but his servants were used to what he wasn't supposed to know they called his *odd starts*.

Robin complied, and they all walked through the back gate, across the yard to the house, and up the stairs to Julian's library.

When they were settled in front of the fire with a tea tray, Amelia said, "I feel as though it's selfish to balk at anything that could free them. When I die, I'll pass to whatever awaits. They can't. How can I risk losing the chance to end the curse and free them?"

Robin accepted a cup of tea from Sophie. "I'm telling you, Amelia, Adam would not want you to do this. If you ask him, I've no doubt he would confirm that."

"I cannot, not until he speaks to me. I don't know how to reach out to him. Even if I did, you're probably right about what he would say. I keep trying to think of another way. I'm certain Wyndon is involved with the French in some way more important than his friendship with M. LeFebvre, but I don't know how and can't prove anything. If I did, I could turn this around on him."

Sophie shot Julian a *say something!* look.

Thinking fast, Julian began, "There is a larger picture here, my dear. More at stake than several generations of your kinsmen, dreadful though their fate has been."

"What do you mean?" She cupped the tea in her hands as though desperate for its warmth.

"You have impressive Gifts. You're a seer. If Wyndon is in league with the French, if he has any involvement at all in Napoleon's escape, your power cannot fall under his control. Having a seer at his side could spell catastrophe for the allied forces."

He hadn't thought her face could grow any paler, but now it was ashen. "That's not fair," she choked. Her tea sloshed. She set it down hastily.

"It isn't." He kept his voice gentle. "Nor was it fair of Wyndon to put you in this position. Nor of your benighted ancestor Edmund to curse his blood. Fairness has little to do with what happens in life."

"I know that," she snapped.

Of course she did, having buried three good men, her husband, her twin, and her father. At least her irritation showed that her spirit wasn't entirely stifled.

He acknowledged her comment with a nod. "Regardless, if you marry this man, you endanger far more lives than the number of souls you could save."

Robin leaned forward. "Dear Amelia, Julian is right. Adam would not want his liberation at the cost of years of misery for you and thousands of soldiers' and sailors' lives."

Aunt Augusta entered the library and shut the door behind her. "Thomas said you wanted to speak to me—oh, my goodness! Child, whatever is wrong?" She hurried across the room to squeeze onto the settee by Amelia.

Amelia shot a beseeching look at Julian. With a nod to her, he briefed his aunt. As he talked, her face hardened.

"This is insupportable," Aunt Augusta declared. "Yet it's not something we could convince the Conclave to intervene in. What he has done is within all the rules of our society and that of the unGifted. I assume this news has convinced you to miss the lecture, so we've the afternoon for research. Things will go much faster with all of us working."

Or would they?

Staring at Amelia's wan face, Julian had an idea. Perhaps the solution was much simpler than researching old books.

He knelt in front of her and waited until she looked back at him. "I can put agents on Wyndon, perhaps obtain proof he's hand in glove with the French. Meanwhile, continue trying to scry or otherwise divine the location of this wondrous document. Once you know that—" He shrugged. "—we'll steal it."

Everyone but Robin turned shocked looks on him.

"You needn't stare at me that way," he grumbled. "It isn't as though I've never stolen anything for a good cause."

His aunt shook her head. Robin's lips twitched suspiciously, but Sophie and Amelia looked at him as though he'd sprouted an extra head. This probably wasn't the time to tell Amelia about her brother's ability to pick pockets.

"Julian's a very good thief, actually." Robin's voice vibrated with suppressed laughter, and his eyes glinted. "Many of the Merlin Club are. Did you know Adam was a rather accomplished pickpocket?"

Julian scowled at him, and Sophie's eyes widened.

"What?" Amelia asked.

"All for England's good," Julian interjected.

Amelia's eyes glinted with humor. "I look forward to hearing about it."

That brief, humorous light eased some of his distress for her. He squeezed her hands. "Give me time," he said. "I'll make a thief of you yet."

"Adam would love that, I'm sure." Her face sobered, and she looked down at their joined hands. "Even if we cannot steal the document, I cannot marry Wyndon. For all the reasons you list, I cannot put my Gifts in his control. If I were his wife, there would be no avoiding it."

The courage of her choice and the resolve in her voice stunned Julian. She'd looked at the larger problem and put strangers ahead of her family. Yes, her decision spared her a wretched marriage, but it also brought a vast burden of guilt. Making a sacrifice for beloved family members was difficult enough. Sacrificing that family for the sake of strangers could only be agonizing. Yet she had made that choice.

No one spoke. A log broke in the hearth. Robin rose to tend to it with the poker.

"Are you resolved to this?" Julian asked.

"Yes." Amelia squeezed his hands and released them. "So it seems our course is thievery, if we can find out where the document is hidden."

"Sit back, Amelia," his aunt ordered, "while I brew a tisane for you. The rest of you, go to work. The sooner we find a solution, the better."

~

The slanting sunlight coming through the window signaled the afternoon advancing. Amelia nibbled a ginger biscuit and sipped tea. Augusta's tisane had settled her stomach, and not feeling so queasy had helped settle her mind.

Behind her, the sounds of low voices started and stopped. Paper whispered as a page turned. Her friends were giving her quiet to scry or summon visions while they researched bloodline curses. Unfortunately, she hadn't managed more than the image of the mysterious document.

She shifted on the sofa to look at them, and her gaze fell on Julian, his head bent over his book as he sat at the worktable. Since his return, he'd proved she could depend on him. An image flashed into her mind of him sitting in a bedchamber. He wore loose trousers and a gold-embroidered, blue banyan. A little bubble of pleasure and longing welled in her throat. Then the image vanished.

You're friends, she told herself sternly. *He thinks of you as a sister. Clinging to him because he's kind and you're scared will ruin it.*

He looked up and smiled. "Feeling better?"

The warmth in his eyes was comforting, and she didn't feel quite so alone. If it also made her heart beat faster, that was her secret. Their gazes locked, and she caught another odd flash of Sight, of herself and Julian in each other's arms, her in a cherry-printed cambric frock and him in the same loose trousers and banyan.

The vision intrigued her, but of course it would never be. Her cheeks heated, and she looked down at her hands.

But if it would never be, why was she Seeing it? Did that mean it might happen?

Sophie asked, "Any luck, Amelia?"

Robin groaned. "Soph, you don't rush a seer."

"She isn't rushing me, as I've nothing to report." Another little bubble, this one of affection, brushed over Amelia's heart. When she'd decided to come to London, she'd cared only about finding information.

She should've realized how important it was to renew friendships as well.

Sophie settled on the sofa next to Amelia. "I hope you don't mind, but Augusta invited us to supper, and I accepted for you. You were absorbed in your scrying at the time."

"Thank you." If she dined here, she could delay seeing Mama, who must be bursting over Lord Wyndon's visit.

Julian said, "Amelia, can you either give us a more detailed description or show us this document Wyndon claims to have?"

"Twice when I was near him, I caught a glimpse of a document on a table. Under glass. The writing looked odd. I couldn't read it. A heavy wax seal hung from the bottom edge. That's what I've been Seeing, though not clearly. Look at the fire."

Amelia fed magic into the flames and opened her mind, thinking of the remembered glimpse but not holding to it. She wasn't scrying so much as feeding her earlier vision into the flames, so any wards around the document wouldn't block her.

The flames showed the windowless underground chamber she'd envisioned before. On a table in its center rested a selection of objects—a sheathed broadsword, two glass cases, an ornate vase. She pulled the vision closer to the case she recognized. The ornate script still defied her efforts to read it. This time, though, she could read the seal. Amelia froze. She'd seen that signature before, on documents in the muniments room at Hawkstowe.

Edmund Mainwaring, originator of the family curse, had signed this document. Could it be his confession? If so, it could mean—but best not to assume too much about a document she couldn't read. Still, finding that confession could solve everything.

She looked over the page, searching for words she could make out. But the dim light in the chamber and the unfamiliar script defeated her.

So where was it?

The image didn't change. She couldn't widen her view or shift to an exterior. Wherever this was, it was hidden well.

With a sigh, she released the vision and told her friends she hadn't been able to evoke a wider view.

"I know of no warding," Julian said slowly, "that would conceal it so thoroughly. As for the writing, though, I've an idea." He walked into the hidden room and returned with a large, leather-bound volume. Gold clasps on leather straps held it shut. Setting it on the table in front of her, he asked, "The script in your vision looked like this to me. What do you think?"

He undid the clasps and turned a page. The text on it...

"Yes," she said, "it looked much like that."

"This is fifteenth-century English," he said. "Old correspondence between a couple of my forebears in Edmund's era. By the Tudor period, letters were formed in ways we would more easily recognize." He turned several more pages, skimming, before holding the book out to her.

While still ornate, with tails and flourishes where no one would put them now, the writing was legible. Understandable.

She took a deep breath. "I think that document truly is important. If we can find it." Meanwhile, she could ask Edmund's ghost to verify it was his confession. If he said it wasn't, they needn't bother hunting it.

"It's likely at a Wyndon property, for all the good that does us," Robin commented. "We'll figure out which one. It will take time, I'm sorry to say, but we're good at solving puzzles."

She carefully closed the book. "I know that cannot be helped. Before we put this aside and I join you in your searches, we must plan how I'm to handle Wyndon on the morrow."

CHAPTER 10

"L ord Wyndon to see you, my lady." Simon offered a silver tray with his lordship's card on it. "I seated him in the parlor, as your ladyship directed."

Amelia's heartbeat kicked. Still, she managed to avoid looking at Sophie, who sat by her bedchamber hearth. "Thank you, Simon. Wait five minutes and then show him to the back garden."

"As you wish, milady." Simon looked baffled but knew better than to question. He gave her a slight bow and departed.

Amelia blew out a deep breath. "Thank you for coming out so early, Sophie. It bolsters my courage to know you'll be watching. I've managed to avoid Mama, but she'll be either furious or so dreadfully, sadly disappointed in me."

A housemaid could've been a witness but might hesitate to make trouble for an earl. Besides, Amelia might need someone able to counter magic.

"Which is intended to make you feel guilty and compliant, of course. Since we'll all be at breakfast, however, you'll have our support." Sophie stood and embraced her. Holding tightly, she added, "Robin and Julian are lurking in the mews under the pretext of talking to your stable lads. Now hurry, so you can take your position before your footman shows Wyndon the way."

Amelia picked up her rose-and-lavender paisley wool shawl, her

92

favorite, from the bed and squared her shoulders. Marching downstairs, she steeled herself. Wyndon was not a man accustomed to refusal, and he would certainly use every emotional lever he could devise.

Putting anonymous soldiers and sailors ahead of Adam and Papa and Grandfather and Grandmother and all the rest hurt bitterly. It was the right choice, but still…the guilt would haunt her until they were all freed.

When she walked outdoors, the morning air still carried a chill that made her glad for the shawl. Dew sparkled on the grass. She settled herself on the wrought-iron bench by the back path. The gate to the mews stood perhaps a dozen feet to her right, set in the six-foot brick wall across the property's rear. "Julian?" she called softly.

"We're here," came the quiet reply.

A glance up at her window earned her a smile from Sophie. They were as ready as they could be. That was fortunate because the back door opened ahead of Simon and Lord Wyndon. Simon bowed and departed.

Wyndon raised one eyebrow. As he descended the stairs at a graceful, unhurried pace, his gaze stayed locked on her. So might a cat watch a mouse's hole.

Her heart pounded in her throat, and her breath felt short. Her knees trembled. She held the shawl's edges tightly as she waited for him.

Before he could sit beside her, she stood. Propriety now forbade him to sit.

His face turned stony, as though he knew what she would say.

Amelia lifted her chin. "While I'm aware of the great honor you do me, Lord Wyndon, I must decline your very kind offer. We would not suit."

Anger flashed in his eyes, and his expression hardened further. Amelia needed all her courage to stand her ground and not take a backward step.

"You are turning down the only chance the Mainwarings may ever have," he commented in a voice silky with menace. "You do know that?"

The words stabbed her heart, but she had expected them. "Yes," she said, proud that her voice remained steady. "It's what they would want me to do."

His eyes narrowed. Fury rolled off him, rasping over her magical senses. His lips curved in the most ominous smile she'd ever seen.

"You had your chance," he said. "Good day, Lady Buckton."

He gave her a formally correct bow. Even as she curtsied, he wheeled and strode toward the house.

The door closed behind him, and she dropped back onto the bench. Thank Heaven that was over!

The gate hinge creaked. She looked up in time to see Julian and Robin hurrying toward her, concern etched on their faces. The contrast between that and Wyndon's bullying couldn't have been plainer. They halted before her.

"How are you?" Julian asked. His kindness warmed her more than it probably should. *Friends*, she reminded herself.

"You were brilliant," Robin added.

"Thank you both. Knowing you were there made standing up to him easier. I feel steady enough, and I'm relieved, although a trifle guilty."

"All understandable," Robin said.

"We will obtain that document somehow," Julian assured her. "I've some ideas for learning about those wards, but we must know where the document is before we can move."

"Of course," Amelia replied. "I'll keep trying to locate it."

That afternoon, Julian met with Alice Gresham, the head of the Conclave Council. Talking her into what he wanted might be a challenge and so warranted a careful approach. Though she was Gifted, she wasn't privy to the Merlin Club's secrets.

He started by explaining the situation, concluding, "I've feelers out but nothing concrete as yet."

"I have some strings I can tug." Past fifty, a fishmonger's wife, she had a sharp brain beneath her graying brown hair. Having a limited education didn't keep her from being canny, the trait that had elevated her to the Council's head.

"That's good," he said, "as my strings are spread rather thin."

Alice shrugged. "People went home to enjoy a world finally at peace. It will take time to gather them again."

"Time we may not have. If Ney hasn't joined Bonaparte already, he will soon enough. I'm certain Bonaparte is advancing on Paris, but we seldom actually see him. His coach deflects scrying, which means it's warded. We can only conclude French Gifted are involved."

"Or Scottish ones. They're always up to something," Alice said, her green eyes hard. "If they are now, they'd best take care. So should you. Any wizard who goes beyond intelligence-gathering, save in defense of self or others, breaks the Compact of Prague."

"I know, Alice." The Merlin Club construed *in defense of others* more broadly than the Conclave but stayed on the Conclave's side of the line as much as possible. "Have you heard from our French counterparts?"

"No, and that's ominous. I'll send a messenger."

"A clandestine one might be best. If we don't know how deeply they're involved, we don't want to risk a messenger's life."

"Indeed not."

Julian paused. If France welcomed the Corsican back, she was risking her future. Her Gifted might assume they had nothing to lose by going all out against their foes.

"Alice, if the French won't or can't control their rogue Gifted, there's no one to do it but us."

"No." She shook her head hard. "No, Julian. I forbid it. Their transgression does not excuse ours. It's one thing for us to dispatch Gifted in reconnaissance, as we did during the war. It's quite another to openly battle our counterparts."

"So we sit on our hands and do nothing." He leaned forward. "If they used magic to smuggle Bonaparte off Elba and across France, what makes you think they'll balk at using it against the allied armies?"

Her lips tightened, but she said nothing.

"If the Gifted of the allied nations don't defend our armies, we'll lose. Everyone who died before Bonaparte surrendered last year will have done so in vain. France will dictate terms to us all. Is that what the Council wants?"

"Of course not," she snapped. "But any response must be authorized by the governing Councils. We cannot have wizards running about causing more trouble than they prevent."

Slowly, carefully, he said, "None of us is stupid, and gaining this accord you want will take time. Time Bonaparte will use to consolidate his hold on power. We must act against him soon."

"No." The word sounded flat. Final. "Absolutely not. Most of the Councils will have delegates in Vienna. I've dispatched Jasper Clayton. You may join him if you wish."

That was better than nothing but still not enough. Julian shook his head. "Let's hope we can do this your way before it's too late."

T hat night, after everyone in the house was abed, Amelia stoked the fire in her bedchamber. Clad in her nightgown and robe, she sat in front of the hearth. "Grandmother, Grandfather, if you can hear me, I've important news. I may have found Edmund's confession, and I need him to verify it."

For long moments, there was silence. Her heart sank. She'd hoped they were near even though they avoided her questions.

She leaned forward to bank the fire, and Richard shimmered into view beside it. With him came a ghostly man clad in a green tunic and hose and low boots. His shoulder-length black hair bore streaks of gray, but his blue eyes and strong features were familiar from portraits at home.

"Amelia," Richard said, "this is your many-times-great grandsire, Edmund."

He bowed. "Your servant, my lady."

She inclined her head to him. "Greetings, Edmund." Anything more cordial eluded her.

"I expect there's more you would like to say," he responded quietly. "Believe me, I have heard it all before. Many times. I was stupid and rash and never dreamt setting matters right would take so long."

His frank admission of responsibility and the sadness in his eyes softened her anger. "I want you to see this," she said.

Explaining how she'd first Seen the document in Wyndon's presence, she called up its image and fed her vision into the flames. The document couldn't be scried, only Seen, but she could share it this way.

She hadn't thought a ghostly complexion could pale, but Edmund's did.

"It's...that's it. My confession. Where is it?"

"We still don't know," Amelia said.

Richard frowned. "When we knew it was lost, we tried to find it. Miranda couldn't See it."

"My Sight was spurred by Wyndon's proximity, I think. Once I'd Seen it, I could summon the image again."

"This is very good news," Richard said. "Amelia, my dear, well done." Shaking his head, he vanished.

He didn't usually depart so abruptly. Did he fear she would ask again about traveling the afterworld? Why couldn't he understand why the information was so important? Was he still nearby but not letting her see him?

Edmund's eyes looked suspiciously bright. "If there is aught I can do, any way I can help, you must call upon me."

"I will. Now that we know what we're looking for, surely finding it will be easier."

There was no certainty of that, but she had to offer him this shred of hope, the one she now clung to. In return, perhaps he would help her where Richard and Miranda had refused. "Meanwhile, I don't suppose you could explain travel in that realm to me, especially reaching there from here?"

"Alas, no." The pained look in his eyes seemed sincere. "I am sorry. Truly. I gave Richard my word that I would leave such matters to him and Miranda."

Despite the misery in his face, his tone was firm. There was no point in pressing him.

"I'll contrive to let you know if we discover anything of use," she told him.

"Thank you," he choked before he also vanished.

Amelia stared down at the flames. She would look for this document at every opportunity, but she wasn't so inexperienced or naïve as to think it would be easy to find.

CHAPTER 11

Julian generally avoided house parties. They were too often populated with scheming young misses on the catch for a title. With Bonaparte rolling toward Paris, such a gathering seemed doubly like a waste of time. French soldiers were deserting en masse to join the escaped Emperor's forces. Ney had declared for Bonaparte the previous day and would doubtless unite his forces with the Corsican's soon. Meanwhile, Merlin Club agents monitored Bonaparte in Paris and the allies in Vienna. The former Emperor had issued a public proclamation promising a constitution along with abolition of autocracy and the elimination of any feudal obligations reinstated by Louis XVIII. Unimpressed, the allies convened at the Congress of Vienna had declared him an outlaw.

None of that required action on Julian's part, nor was anything likely to until Bonaparte reached Paris. If he did. Much would depend upon the reception the city gave him. So Julian had agreed to join this gathering, primarily because Amelia and her mother were attending. He'd told himself he would come to keep an eye on her in case Wyndon tried something underhanded. The man wasn't one to accept refusal. The truth, though, might be a bit more unsettling.

Amelia was a friend. She was Adam's sister and so should be a sister to Julian. Having been part of a love match, she would likely want the same if she married again, and he couldn't give her that. Yet he found himself drawn to her against all common sense.

The day turned unseasonably warm, and Mrs. Dalrymple, the hostess, decreed that refreshments be set out on the terrace. Her guests could enjoy them between bouts of archery and walks around the small lake at the rear of the lawn. Standing on the terrace, Julian watched the archers but with only half his attention on them.

"Julian? Am I late?"

Smiling, he turned to greet Amelia. "On the contrary, we're so much earlier than everyone else that we may sit wherever we wish."

They chose a table with a view of the lawn. A footman brought them small cakes and sweet, almond-flavored orgeat, a truly disgusting drink but all that was offered.

"Thank you for all you've done," she said, removing her short gloves to eat. "I look forward to resuming my research. Your library contains so many intriguing volumes."

"It's at your disposal, but I've a selfish interest. England desperately needs a seer, as you know."

Amelia smiled. "I'm happy to do what I can."

The deep gold of her gown flattered her complexion, and the snug, high-waisted bodice with a bronze ribbon under her breasts emphasized the curve of her bust. Julian's blood stirred, and he wrenched his gaze back to the table.

"Grandfather came to see me this morning," she said. "He and Grandmother have been trying to learn how Bonaparte escaped. They confirmed he had help from the French Gifted." When she raised her eyes to him, worry shadowed them. "That will make him more difficult to stop, and he's now definitely bound for Paris."

That meant Julian could reassign all the agents except the one at the French Embassy and the three in Paris. That was the only good thing about her news.

"Their actions," he said, "break a compact among our kind dating back to King Alfred's day and codified four hundred years ago in Prague. They must have a powerful incentive to take such a risk."

"A risk? Could this lead to war among the Gifted?"

"It might." And damn the French for that. No matter what the Conclave Council said, some of Britain's wizards would respond to the French in kind.

Her frown deepened. "Will you play a role?"

"Almost certainly." As Director of the Merlin Club, he already did, but that information didn't belong on an open terrace. "Our kind hold grudges for a very long time. Any conflict between us wouldn't end with a treaty between nations, which is why we had the compact the French have now broken." Along with the Scots.

Again she frowned—concerned but without the panic so many women displayed at the mere mention of Bonaparte.

"I hope you'll be careful," she said with simple honesty. "I wouldn't like you to be hurt."

Her words brushed a cold, dark corner of his heart with an instant's warmth and light.

He smiled, resisting the urge to clasp her hand. "Thank you for that, Amelia. I'm not without experience."

"You've studied so much. Know so much." Sighing, she picked up her glass. "I look forward to my next visit to your library."

As he did to having her in his house. Her composure and natural warmth made him feel at ease. Less alone.

And therein lay a potential host of problems.

Trying for a lighter note, he said, "You already know enough to have provided timely warning of Bonaparte's escape."

"I like to be useful, as I said." Biting her lip, she turned her gaze to the couples wandering the lawn. "I've no wish to be decorative and pampered and—and idle. I'd be bored in a fortnight."

"I can understand that. What did you do at Leyburn Manor?"

"I visited the tenants and the merchants in the town. Crispin managed our lands, leaving any issues with the people for me unless I needed his backing." She paused, her expression wistful. "We worked well together. Now I must find a new path, and further developing my Gifts is a first step. Adam shared what he learned, of course, and Grandmother and Grandfather taught me much. Still, some lessons, such as complex healing, require a living teacher."

"Of course. We'll do what we can."

"Your aunt was very kind to help us secure Almack's vouchers. Their arrival made Mama ecstatic, though I'm not sure I see the point. I've met many gentlemen already and won't remarry simply for the sake of being wed. I've told Mama I'll be accepting fewer invitations."

"For some, the point of Almack's is that admission carries a certain social cachet. It also offers the richest hunting ground in Britain." He'd met his deceitful, manipulative, spendthrift wife there.

"You sound bitter." Her hand started toward his, but she checked the movement. "Julian, why—but that isn't my affair. I beg your pardon." She turned to watch the archers farther down the lawn, and the curls at her temples blocked his view of her eyes. "I suppose you titled gentlemen must feel like quarry on occasion," she said in a dry voice.

The fact the girl he'd once loved had seen only usefulness in him was also not her affair. He shrugged. "Fox hunting lacks the appeal it once held."

So did the idea of any woman who interested him walking into the courtship game at Almack's. No matter how much he wanted to deny it, Amelia did interest him. With her quiet, thoughtful temperament, she might be open to the sort of rational, affectionate arrangement he sought in a wife. Unless she was set on another love match.

And that was the second time this morning he'd thought of wedding her.

Despite his concerns, perhaps the notion wanted further considera- tion. Her worry over her brother and her willingness to put Britain's soldiers and sailors ahead of her own desire revealed her inner strength. Yes, he must consider this carefully.

Amelia sighed. "I remember the social pressures of my debut Season, and I've often observed young ladies on the hunt since my return."

"You'll see more of it at Almack's, you know." As she had with Wyndon, though not with such high stakes. Julian looked sidelong at her. "Prepare yourself, Lady Buckton."

She sighed. "To be honest, I found Almack's terribly tedious." Glancing over her shoulder, she wrinkled her nose. "I probably shouldn't say that too loudly."

"No." He grinned, and a rueful smile curved her lips.

For a long moment, they looked at each other in perfect accord. She abruptly turned away and took a sip of the dreadful orgeat.

Studying her, he cocked his head. "You truly don't want to go there, do you? Why not? Aside from the tedium, which I also recall too well."

Her glance flicked over the plates and cups on the table. "I had a good marriage, a fulfilling one. If I can't have that again, I would rather be alone."

"I understand that." She hadn't mentioned love. Would a partnership satisfy her?

"I've met more people here in London who resent their marriages than who cherish them."

She'd met one more than she knew. Loneliness rang in her words, and sympathy softened his heart. There could be loneliness inside marriage as well as outside it.

Smiling, she lifted her face to the sunshine. "At least we've a lovely day. I've ordered a mount to ride out to the old manor ruins. I like to look at ruins, as I can sometimes See people who lived there before. It will be nice to spend time on something simply for the pleasure of it."

"It would. I might go with you, if you don't mind."

"I welcome the company."

He liked her smile, but he should take care. His value to her might lie solely in his ability to help her, just as her Gifts were part of her appeal for him. Even without them, though, she had much to recommend her, not least that she wasn't on the hunt for someone to keep her in comfort.

Again, their gazes locked. He wrenched his downward.

"There's news from France," he said quietly. "Ney has declared for Napoleon. This despite having vowed to bring him back to Paris in a cage. Have you Seen anything that could explain such a drastic change of heart?"

"No, I—" Amelia froze. Her eyes lost focus, and Julian straightened in alarm. "Amelia?" he said softly.

She didn't reply, so he said nothing else. The vision might be important, but he would try again if she didn't come back to herself soon.

A long minute later, she looked back at him, her eyes wide and her expression dismayed. "I saw armor in a chest. Perhaps it isn't related to King Richard but to Bonaparte. Then the scene shifted. I saw London, Westminster Abbey, with crowds along Parliament Street as Bonaparte rode ahead of the French soldiers. Most of the people frowned, but some shouted his name. Surely the French cannot take London?"

He shook his head. "With Bonaparte, nothing is certain."

~

Watching from the lawn, Silas swore under his breath. Amelia's dazed expression, her initial failure to respond to Aysgarth, could only mean she'd had a vision. As for Aysgarth, he looked entirely too concerned. Leaned toward her far too protectively. Allowing him to gain any more influence over her would be a mistake.

Best to make sure of her today, then. With a little help, he could use her morning ride to isolate her. Once he did...some scandals, even a widow of good repute could not brush off.

Silas frowned. How unfortunate for her that she'd taken him in dislike. She would resist, but the independence that so troubled her mother would break quickly under proper discipline.

Meanwhile, he had an ally in LeFebvre and a tool in a man whose debts made him vulnerable.

He beckoned to a passing footman. "Bring me Monsieur LeFebvre and Mr. Pendergast."

~

Half an hour later, Amelia and Julian met on the terrace in riding garb. Her deep blue habit set off her eyes, which gleamed with anticipation, and her ruffled shirt framed the pale column of her neck. The jaunty angle of her black top hat proclaimed her intention to enjoy herself.

Julian smiled at her. The grin she gave him promised a lighthearted, enjoyable outing. With all the trouble on the horizon, he welcomed the chance for a pleasant distraction.

They descended to the lawn and followed the path to the stables. Halfway there, they met portly, cheerful Hugo Pendergast.

"There you are, Aysgarth!" The stout, gray-haired man waved. "I've been looking for you since I arrived a while ago. I want to buy that mare, the one you raced at Newmarket last year. Lucinda, ain't she?"

"This isn't the best time, Pendergast."

"You needn't rush," Amelia said. "I'll go ahead, and you can join me when you and Mr. Pendergast conclude your business."

"Very kind, Lady Buckton," the older man said. "Very kind."

"Amelia, you shouldn't ride alone this close to London."

"I'll take a groom." Smiling, she said, "You'll be mere minutes behind me, and then he can return to his duties."

"If you're certain."

"It'll be easy to arrange," she assured him.

She walked on toward the stables. Pendergast extolled Lucinda's virtues.

A few minutes later, mounted on a gray mare, Amelia set out across the meadow in the direction of the ruined Dalrymple manor. A groom rode behind her on a roan. She cut a fine figure on a horse, with a sure seat and steady hands.

"Tell me about the mare's lineage," Pendergast said.

They talked for several minutes, but half of Julian's mind was on catching up to Amelia. Groom or no, it was better to be too cautious than to relax with Wyndon in the vicinity.

Speaking of that rotter, there he went, toward the ruin, on a big bay.

That tore it.

"I'm sorry, Pendergast," Julian said, "but I can't keep the lady waiting any longer. We'll talk this evening."

Brushing off the other man's protests, he strode toward the stables. A group of guests milled about the stable yard while grooms matched horses and riders.

"Yes, yes," the French attaché said, "we'll depart for the ruins in a few minutes, as soon as we're all ready."

Amelia had ridden out with a groom, followed less than five minutes later by Wyndon, who had the authority to send that groom home if he chose. Now his bosom friend, LeFebvre, was preparing to ride out with a group.

Julian didn't need to be a seer to smell the stench in this arrangement.

"*Bonjour*, Lord Aysgarth." LeFebvre stepped into his path. "We are riding out shortly. Do you wish to join us?"

Despite his bland expression, a sly look tainted his eyes.

Julian brushed past him and marched into the stable. An elderly groom held the reins of a large, black gelding that was already saddled.

"Is he a hunter?" Julian demanded of the startled groom.

"Yes, but—begging your pardon, milord, but this here's Mr. Dalrymple's Beau. He can be difficult, he can."

"I'll manage." Julian grabbed the reins. "I'm sure Mr. Dalrymple won't mind if I borrow him." The path to the ruins meandered through the wood. If Julian cut across country, he might overtake Wyndon and would definitely beat LeFebvre's party. But that could mean jumping stone fences. Hence the need for a hunter.

Ignoring the groom's protests, Julian swung into the saddle. He wheeled the big gelding toward the stable door and tightened his legs on his mount's sides.

The horse surged forward.

The other guests gaped as Julian and Beau galloped out of the stable yard. Once they were clear, Julian leaned forward and gave Beau his head.

~

The manor had been abandoned in the early 1600s, and local villagers had helped themselves to stone from the site. Its original outlines and waist-high fragments of many walls, however, still remained. A ditch surrounded the main building, a remnant of the days when the manor had been fortified.

If Amelia closed her eyes, she could See it whole and envision the people who'd once lived here. Women in the rich, lush gowns of the Tudor period laughed and chatted in the entry.

She walked farther into the ruin, and now the clothes were simpler. Women wore long, straight dresses with dangling sleeves while the men wore tunics, hose, and boots.

Even though she summoned these visions with her Gift, they came to her without swirling fog. Miranda had said her early visions had sometimes included it and sometimes not, with no apparent reason, until she mastered her Gift. Amelia's training, however, meant she saw those mists only when she deliberately used her Gift. Spontaneous visions or those spurred by her location or her companions didn't involve that.

Footsteps sounded on the grass behind her. Would Julian think she was fanciful? Oddly, she trusted him to understand. She turned to greet him and froze.

Lord Wyndon stood in the opening that had once been a door. "I assume you don't mind if I join you."

"As a matter of fact, sir, I do." Raising her voice, she called, "Washam!"

"I sent him home, my dear, so you and I might talk privately." He strolled into the chamber.

"We've nothing to say to each other. My lord, I must ask that you leave." Amelia circled behind a pile of tumbled stone. If she set him on fire...

His magic swirled around her. Suddenly, she couldn't move.

Panic jolted her heart into her throat. The look on his face was one a cat wore as it stalked a mouse. Trembling, she strained against his power. He sauntered around the stone barrier and studied her for a long minute. With one finger, he stroked her neck.

"That's better. You'll learn, my poppet, when I want something, I have it."

He slid his hand into the neckline of her jacket and then under the shirt she wore with it.

Oh, no. Absolutely no.

Gathering herself, Amelia imagined fire and fed magic into the thought. When she tried to say the word, it emerged as a whimper that made him chuckle.

It must've been enough though, for his sleeve burst into flame. He quenched it and yanked the fabric he held, tearing the shirt and jacket to the waist.

Still, his hold on her loosened. Amelia wrenched free, tearing her clothes further, and darted through the opening.

He caught her, slung her against the low wall, and held her down with a hand at her back. A hard bulge pressed against her skirts. Then he was lifting them.

Fighting terror, Amelia slipped her hand under the rising hem of her skirt and seized Miranda's dagger. She jerked it from the sheath and stabbed Wyndon's leg.

"Aargh!"

His hold loosened. She twisted to the side, but not fast enough.

He caught her wrist and wrenched the dagger from her hold. Then he seized her by both shoulders. "You will pay for that, you little viper."

He shook her hard. She couldn't break free. Her teeth rattled, and her hair fell about her face.

Over his shoulder, a horseman approached. She couldn't see him clearly with Wyndon shaking her and her hair in the way, but he was a witness. To this scandal.

Perhaps he would help her, though. She kicked Wyndon. If she could break free, conceal her ripped clothes with a glamour—

The rider jumped the ditch. His mount had barely landed when he flung himself from the saddle. He seized Wyndon, breaking his hold on Amelia. She staggered backward.

The *smack* of bone on bone sounded. Fumbling with her torn clothing, she looked up in time to see Julian pull his fist back from Wyndon's face. He drove his other fist into Wyndon's gut and then slammed home another facer.

Wyndon collapsed.

"Are you hurt?" Julian asked, standing beside her with his eyes averted. He shrugged out of his jacket.

"No, but I—" Across the field, more riders approached, coming swiftly. One of them pointed. They gathered speed.

"We've been seen," she choked as Julian helped her into his jacket.

They looked at each other in shared dismay. If they hadn't been spotted, they might've used invisibility glamour to escape. But there were other Gifted in that group who would know what they'd done.

She pulled her hair back but couldn't put it to rights without the pins. Most of them were lost in the grass anyway. And where was her hat?

"Can you glamour your hair and clothes?" he asked.

Shivering, she tried, but she couldn't steady herself, and he couldn't do it for her without staying very close to her at all times.

The riders pulled up at the ditch. They stared from her to Julian and then at Lord Wyndon on the ground.

With her dress torn, her hair disheveled—Lord Wyndon would say she'd led him on, allowed him liberties, and then changed her mind. The story would spread, with many of the *ton* believing it.

There was no escape. Chilled and sick, Amelia clutched Julian's jacket around her.

His gaze met hers. The anger was back, but comprehension also shone there.

"Amelia," he said quietly, "follow my lead, and all will be well."

With no ideas of her own, she could only nod.

As the riders dismounted, Julian drew her against his side. "Steady," he murmured.

His tall, sturdy frame sheltered her, easing some of the panic. Amelia slid her arm around his waist and leaned into that security.

"Aysgarth?" one of the riders called.

"Lady Buckton?" a woman said.

The Frenchman, LeFebvre, scrambled to the edge of the ditch. "What—?"

Everyone stared at Lord Wyndon sprawled on the ground and Julian, in his shirt sleeves, embracing her.

His fingers tightened reassuringly on her shoulder. "Ladies and gentlemen," he said in a cool, relaxed voice, "you're just in time to wish us joy. Lady Buckton has consented to wed me."

CHAPTER 12

I simply cannot believe it." Seated on Amelia's bed at Dalrymple Court, Mama rubbed the bridge of her nose. "For Lord Wyndon to —to attack you in that way—"

Amelia wheeled from the wardrobe. "Do you doubt me, Mama?" If she did, Amelia would never forgive her.

"Of course not. Of course not, my dear." Tears welled in Mama's eyes. "How dreadful that must've been."

Amelia sat beside her mother and squeezed her hand. "It was. Until Julian arrived."

"And now you are betrothed to him." Mama shook her head and rose to pace. "I cannot like that. His family shares your dear papa's eccentric notions. He's a fine man by all accounts, but marriage to him…you'll be in danger."

"Why do you say that?" Amelia kept her voice cool with an effort. "He rescued me, after all." Yet his promise to *set things right* when he'd walked her to the door here implied a desire for the betrothal to be temporary. That was probably wise. They'd become friends, but only that.

Of course, she and Crispin had begun as friends. Perhaps it was best not to think of that now, though.

A cup of tea had helped her calm down. Now she wanted—needed— quiet. But Julian and Robin were waiting to escort her and Mama back to London.

"I don't want you to wed a man who toys with dangerous forces, as your dear papa did. I won't lose you, too. I want you to be safe. With a husband who'll take care of you. I cannot countenance this betrothal."

Mama seemed sincere, and she'd often voiced her worries about magic before Papa and Adam died. In the end, however, Amelia's choice of a husband, should matters come to that, was out of her mother's hands.

Quietly, she said, "I'm of age, Mama, and I control my lands and funds. My choices are no longer yours to countenance or not."

Her mother looked shocked, but Amelia continued. "It may be that Julian and I will not suit, but he saved me tonight. Even a widow could not weather the sort of scandal Lord Wyndon intended to cause. Julian and I, and only we two, will decide what happens between us now."

"I cannot stop you." Tears leaked from Mama's eyes, and Amelia steeled herself. "I want only the best for you," Mama said, "and I do wish you would listen to me. This is a mistake, Amelia. Please, please, I beg you, reconsider."

"I can't promise you that. I'm sorry." This business with Wyndon's proposal and Mama's reaction had all come about because Amelia had allowed her mother to have too much say in her affairs. No longer.

Mama sighed and dabbed at her eyes. Perhaps waiting for Amelia to give in?

"This has been a trying day," Amelia said. "I'd like to go back to Uncle Harry and Aunt Louisa's and go to bed."

"Of course, of course, my dear." Her mother leaned over and kissed Amelia's forehead. Despite her reproachful expression, she said nothing as she left the room.

Amelia sank onto the bed. It was just as well the ghosts weren't here tonight. She had thinking to do. Julian had saved her from disaster. Now they were destined for the parson's mousetrap unless they could find an honorable way to avoid it. The situation wasn't fair to either of them but especially not to him. He'd chosen the only strategy that would save her from either marrying Wyndon or losing her reputation.

They had agreed to ride in Hyde Park together early in the morning. Surely two clever people could find a solution to this problem. She couldn't let him pay for his chivalry and decency with his freedom.

Julian slowly rode his bay gelding, Percival, back and forth on Rotten Row near Hyde Park Corner. This early, mist still rose above the Serpentine. Dew sparkled on the grass in the weak morning sunlight. He hadn't had time to warn Amelia that he'd asked Robin and Ned to shadow her and her groom until she reached the park this morning. Wyndon's actions yesterday betrayed not only anger but desperation, which was always dangerous.

Despite the early hour, street noise rolled into the park from Knightsbridge Road to the south. It was too early, however, for the fashionable set to turn out. He had the Row to himself, with nothing to distract him from the wild idea he'd had last night. Perhaps it was truly mad, but it could solve both their problems. If he hadn't misjudged her. If she trusted him enough. If she was willing to forego the chance of a love match.

If, if, if.

He turned Percival toward the gate. Three stories high and built of red brick, Apsley House loomed out of the morning mist at the end of the park.

Amelia rode through the gate, her groom behind her. Julian trotted Percival over to meet her. She looked as uneasy as he felt, and that was somehow comforting. Her mulberry riding habit set off her dark hair but also underscored the pallor of her face.

"Good morning," he said. "Thank you for coming out so early."

That earned him a flicker of a smile. "Only the early hours are private. This was a wise suggestion."

He wheeled Percival to ride beside her. The groom hung back, allowing them to open a gap between him and them.

"How did you sleep?" Julian asked when they had a decent lead on the man.

"Not particularly well, but last night would've been much worse if not for you." She glanced at him. "Forgive me, but you don't look as though you slept much either."

"I was thinking about our situation."

She grimaced. "I'm determined you will not suffer for helping me, Julian. We'll handle this betrothal any way you wish. If you want to cry off—"

"You know I cannot. If one of us is to do so, it must be you."

"The rules again." She shook her head. "Tell me what you want. If we maintain this sham through the end of the Season, that will cost you any chance of finding a bride."

"I may have already found one," he said. Was that a flash of dismay in her eyes? Was he a scoundrel to hope it might be? "I've been betrothed to her since yesterday."

Amelia's head snapped around. She gave him a stunned look. "Are you serious?"

"Entirely. I've a question for you, one you needn't answer unless you're amenable to turning this sham betrothal into a real one. Are you still in love with Buckton? If you are, I can respect that, but I cannot marry you."

"You want—forgive me for being a slow-top this morning, but...you wish to marry me?"

"I think we might suit each other. I should say at the outset that I no longer have grand passion to offer. Whatever I possessed of that burned away during my marriage, which was not a happy one. I want a partner I can trust, as I couldn't trust my late wife. One whose company I enjoy and who has a sound head on her shoulders. I want to build a life, a family, with someone who wants the same from me."

They rode several feet in silence before Amelia raised an eyebrow. "Even though your marriage wasn't happy, I must be sure. Are you still in love with your late countess?"

"I would not have proposed if I were. Marrying one woman while in love with another is not only unfair but dishonest. I've no emotional attachments."

"But many friends," she said softly, "so you have attachments of other sorts. Crispin and I began as friends. Before we became betrothed, however, we had grown into so much more." She paused. "Do I gather it's the 'more,' not only grand passion, you cannot offer?"

"That's correct." At least she didn't look dismayed at that, only thoughtful.

They rode a little farther, the horses' hooves muffled on the dirt of the Row. "To be honest, I'm not sure I can offer that either," Amelia said. "I haven't thought much about it because I've been so preoccupied with worry for Adam and Papa. I would like to marry again someday, but as I said, I shall be fine if I don't."

"You would rather remain alone than settle for something hollow, I believe you said."

"Yes." She turned a thoughtful, considering look on him, and his pulse sped up. Silly, but a man didn't propose marriage to a friend every day.

"You mentioned building a life together. I believe we could do that. We are friends, are we not?" When he nodded, she asked, "But would that satisfy you? Is it enough?"

"For me, yes. You must decide whether it is for you." Treading carefully, he added, "I do need an heir. My marriage deteriorated rather quickly, so my wife and I ceased having relations before our first anniversary."

"So you need to know why Crispin and I had no children." Amelia shrugged. "We were married a little more than a year when he left for India to find his brother. He was gone the better part of the next twelve months and ill increasingly often and with increasing severity after he returned." She paused. "The lack of children was the one thing we both regretted at the end."

She hadn't flown up into the boughs. Had, in fact, been understanding and matter-of-fact. That she'd behaved as he'd assumed she would was extremely gratifying. "I apologize. I don't wish to pry, but—"

"You must think of the title, of course. When do you need an answer?"

"Take your time. Maintaining the betrothal to the end of the Season would protect you and give me a breathing space. I've no desire to bother with courtship when I have more pressing responsibilities."

"Very well." Her lips curved in a rueful smile, and humor brightened her eyes. "This is not the conversation I expected to have this morning."

"Nor is it the one I planned last night."

He grinned at her, and her face brightened. "Gallop?" she asked.

He glanced down the Row, for once clear of horses and carriages. "Down to the turn?"

Before he finished, she'd kicked her horse and dashed away. Leaning low over Percival's neck, he followed. Percival gained on her smaller mare, but slowly. Amelia was truly an excellent horsewoman. Perhaps that boded well.

⁓

How is Amelia?" Robin asked, joining Julian at his library table. "She looked composed when we followed her to the park this morning, but she must be shaken. Her mother did not seem best pleased last night."

"The betrothal lessens the scandal but doesn't prevent one altogether. As it happens, Amelia and I had an important conversation this morning."

He told his friend about his offer to her. Robin looked amazed, then thoughtful.

When Julian finished, Robin said, "It could be a good match. I must say, though, that she was truly smitten with Buckton. Remember their wedding? How happy they both looked?"

How much in love, Robin meant, and he wasn't wrong.

"I remember," Julian said, "and she knows I cannot give her that. Whether I can give her enough, only she can say. But I won't be the man a woman settles for as a last resort. Not again."

"You deserve better," Robin said.

"So I would hope." Julian pushed aside a stack of books and sat at the long table. "When does Barbara arrive?"

Robin's betrothed, Lady Barbara Gordon, would offer Amelia another possible friend. Barbara had a kind heart and a sharp mind. They should get on famously.

Not that Amelia's friendships were his concern as yet. Best not to rush his fences there.

"Mid-April." Robin leaned against the back of the sofa. "There's already an entry in the betting book at White's about you, Wyndon, and Amelia. Which of you she'll ultimately wed."

"Bloody gambling idiots," Julian grumbled. "We must devise a scheme to protect her. Having gone this far, Wyndon likely will not give up."

The memory of the panic in her eyes yesterday tore at him. He clenched his fist on the table. "At least our betrothal makes her research with my aunt and our work on the Bonaparte problem simpler to arrange."

Robin studied him for a long moment. "You're not as content with this as you would like me to believe."

"Not entirely, no. I don't see Charlotte in her, Robin. But neither did I see the treachery in Charlotte." Nor had he heard the gossip about her *tendre* for a married marquess until it was too late.

"So you doubt your own judgment," Robin said slowly, "and yet you proposed."

"I'm trying to set a logical course for a change. This is logical. I know Amelia better than I'm ever likely to know some flirtatious young lady. I need an heir, so I must remarry at some point. She is as good a choice as any and better than most."

"I hope you had the sense not to say that to her."

Julian threw him a withering look.

A tap on the door heralded a footman holding a silver salver with a visiting card on it. "Mr. Fitzhugh to see you, my lord."

"Do you know him?" Robin asked.

"Not well. Friend of Wyndon's, I think." Glancing at the footman, Julian said, "I'm not at home, George."

The man bowed and departed.

Julian hefted a large, leatherbound book and passed it to Robin. "If you'd like to help, look through these letters between Richard Mainwaring and Cabot Winfield. See if there's anything about traveling the land of the dead."

"If I must." Robin shed his coat and sat at the table.

A few minutes later, the footman returned. "Mr. Fitzhugh brought this for you, my lord. He begs your pardon but says he must await your reply."

"Bloody hell." Julian accepted the folded paper George proffered. "I'll ring for you when my reply is ready." To Robin, he added, "Wyndon's seal. What the devil can he want?"

He broke the wax seal and unfolded the parchment. As he scanned the sheet, a single word leaped out at him, *duel*.

"Julian? What is it?"

He read the note over before answering, but there was no mistake. "It seems I need you to stand for me, Robin. For the offense of striking him, Wyndon has challenged me to a duel."

CHAPTER 13

B loody hell, indeed," Robin said softly.

Julian passed the note to him. "I should've expected this. Wyndon is nothing if not proud. Because I was so busy pondering what to do about Amelia, I neglected to consider that."

Frowning, Robin scanned the note. "While I agree about his pride, there's a second consideration. Killing you ends the betrothal and frees Amelia."

"That cannot happen. Apart from anything else, she's too important to our defense." Her danger yesterday had made him realize she was important to him, too. He wanted her with him. If that made him a fool, so be it.

"I'll have to meet him." There was no help for it.

"You're important to our defense as well. Critical to it, even."

"If I don't meet him, he'll brand me a coward in the *ton*. While I could live with that, it would hinder my covert activities, both through the Home Office and via the Merlin Club. Much of what I do depends on the access that comes with social standing. I cannot lose that. Nor will I ask Amelia to marry a man so derided."

"Amelia," Robin said, scowling, "is no fool. She won't care about that."

"Perhaps not, but I do." With a wry smile, Julian added, "It seems I've more pride than I knew."

"Hellfire." Robin glared at him.

"Will you help me or not?"

"You insult me by asking." Robin leaned back in his chair. "Choice of weapons is yours, and I should convey your preference when I accept the challenge for you and set the day. Don't pick pistols. I've seen Wyndon shoot the pips out of a playing card at thirty paces at Manton's shooting gallery."

"With a pistol, traditionally, he has one shot. But he could demand we agree to two shots in case he misses."

"So could you," Robin said, "but I would be stunned if he missed. With swords, he needs only one opening to stab you through the heart or the throat."

A duelist who killed an opponent generally had to flee the country to avoid murder charges. Against an opponent as powerful and well-connected as Wyndon, however, Julian couldn't rely on that to save him.

"Have you seen him at Angelo's?" London's elite fenced at that salon.

"A time or two. He's good but no better than you if you were at top form."

"But better than I am when I haven't touched a blade in a couple of years."

Robin nodded.

Julian frowned at the table. Aside from his general desire not to die, he now had Amelia to protect. If he fell in a duel, Wyndon would move on her without delay. He'd been thwarted twice. He wouldn't risk failure a third time.

"You can take someone else along," Robin told him. "Any member of the Merlin Club would stand for you, but you would do well to choose Ned. His title gives him social standing that will matter in the gossip after."

"Whichever way it goes." There had to be a way to improve his chances. Wyndon simply could not be allowed to win. Julian pinched the bridge of his nose. "What about Jackson's? Does he spar?"

Robin blinked. "You can't choose fisticuffs. It's not done."

"Since dueling is illegal, I don't imagine there's a law limiting choice of weapons."

"There's the *Code Duello*."

"We've altogether too many social rules. I'm willing to flout those. So, tell me, how's Wyndon in the ring?"

"He has a punishing right," Robin said, his expression thoughtful, "but he rarely takes the ring at Jackson's."

"That could mean he doesn't like boxing. Neither do I, but I've been in my share of tavern brawls." Sometimes starting a brawl was a useful way to escape a situation. He'd hoped the days of needing escapes were behind him, but the experience might be useful now. "I can hold my own."

"You took him without difficulty yesterday."

"I surprised him." Scowling, Julian added, "He was too busy abusing Amelia to hear me coming behind him."

Robin shook his head. "Christ, I wish there were another way."

"No more than I do, believe me. So it's fisticuffs, preferably to first blood. Wyndon may want to kill me, but I doubt he would proclaim that openly by demanding a fight to the death."

"All right, then. I'll talk to Ned tonight."

"Without Sophie. Amelia mustn't know. It would worry her." Aside from the disapproval of dueling common among females and other sensible people, she already felt too beholden to him. Having his proposal accepted out of gratitude would be appalling. Nor did he want her fretting over something he couldn't avoid.

"She's a seer," Robin noted. "She doesn't need anyone to tell her."

"She isn't omniscient, though. I don't want her having any hint of this that could bring on a vision."

Julian moved behind his desk and drew out a sheet of foolscap. He quickly wrote his reply, sealed it, and extended it to Robin. "If you'll take this down to Fitzhugh, we'll set this sorry business in motion."

"Back in a moment." Robin accepted the note and left the room.

Julian stared at the fire. He could survive a punishing fight. He might even win it, but it would be a mistake to think Wyndon had only one arrow in his quiver.

What else might he do?

～

Amelia and Sophie sat on the rear terrace at Havelock House, Sophie's parents' London home, with a pot of tea and a plate of tiny sandwiches. Amelia told her friend about her ride with Julian that morning. "So I said I would think about it," she concluded.

"I admit I'm surprised," Sophie responded. "In truth, I can see the two of you as a match. I didn't have any idea he would, though, because he's so averse to remarrying."

"He needs an heir." It probably wasn't that simple, but she couldn't hunt for hidden motives. Julian was a good man who deserved to be taken at his word. If only she knew how she felt about his offer. On the one hand it was unexpectedly tempting. The short time they'd spent together in London had built on her earlier liking for him. Now she genuinely cared for him and trusted him. A marriage between them might well succeed.

On the other, marrying only for the logical reasons he'd cited could ultimately prove disappointing.

"I'm to attend a play at Covent Garden this evening with Mama and my aunt and uncle," Amelia said. "I can't possibly go and have everyone staring and gossiping."

"Oh, but you must. If you don't, everyone will assume you're too ashamed of your somewhat irregular betrothal to show your face."

"I am so very weary of worrying about what everyone assumes," Amelia snapped.

Sophie's eyes widened, and Amelia sighed. "I beg your pardon, Sophie. This situation has me peevish."

"It would anyone." Looking out at the lawn, which was just beginning to turn green, Sophie asked, "Any word from your ghostly grandparents?"

"No, and that worries me. In my entire life, they've never stayed away for more than a day or two at a time. When I do see them, they stay only long enough to give me whatever news they've gleaned. I don't know whether they're busy investigating the French situation or looking for clues to lifting the curse—or whether they're avoiding me because I might ask questions they don't want to answer."

"You've no way to summon them?"

"No." Amelia sighed. "For all I know, they could be standing directly behind you but simply not letting me see them. I don't know whether to be angry with them or distressed at their evasion or frustrated by my own helplessness here."

"Or a bit of each?" Sophie asked.

"Precisely. Aside from all that, I would like to talk to them about Julian."

Although...she did own the dagger that had once belonged to Miranda. Would it have enough of an affinity to its original owner to forge a connection? Perhaps Julian had a book that contained the answer.

While she and Sophie sipped tea and munched sandwiches, Amelia mulled over Julian's offer. Did she like him enough to marry him and share his bed? Or did she like him too much to be content with friendly affection instead of love such as she and Crispin had shared?

Did she even have that to offer anyone? She'd told Julian she wasn't certain she did. Before she could commit to a union such as he offered, she should be certain of her own feelings.

The terrace and lawn vanished, replaced by a group of men in a grassy clearing in a grove of elms. Two knelt beside a shirtless one on the ground.

She took a step closer, then another. Wyndon stood a short distance away, shirtless, red splotches on his face and body, as though from blows. Triumph glinted in his eyes. He must've fought someone, perhaps the man on the ground?

One of the men kneeling lifted his head. Robin. Did that mean—no, please no! She ran toward the tableau until she stood behind Robin. The man kneeling with his back to her was Ned, but she barely thought about that. The man on the ground, his face and body battered, was Julian.

~

As usual before an opera performance, the members of the *ton* peered from their boxes into others. Some were so rude as to point at Amelia and her family. Others merely trained the small telescopes known as opera glasses on them.

Seated beside lean, solemn Uncle Harry in the front row of the box, Aunt Louisa turned to offer Amelia a kind smile. "Never fear, my dear. Your engagement may be everyone's favorite topic now, but it will be a nine days' wonder. Something else always comes along." Oblivious to Mama stiffening at Amelia's side, Aunt Louisa added, "The Earl of Aysgarth is a marital prize. Twenty-five thousand a year and an ancient title. You've done very well, Amelia. Very well indeed."

Did no one but her care that he was also a kind, capable man? Did only his title and estates matter to them?

Her aunt faced front again, and Amelia scanned the boxes across the way. The Aysgarth box, third from the left in the second tier, was empty. But Sophie had said Julian was coming. Where in blazes was he? She had a very great deal to say to him if he had any notion whatever of fighting an idiotic duel. Although she'd never seen a duel, the scrying she'd done after that vision had shown her an encounter much like she assumed a duel must be.

Footsteps sounded behind the velvet curtains at the box's rear. Anticipation rippled down Amelia's neck, and she turned. Parting the curtains, Julian stepped into the box.

When his eyes met hers, he smiled. "Good evening, everyone."

Her breath caught, and she smiled at him.

The box's other occupants greeted him, Mama civilly and Aunt Louisa and Uncle Harry with genuine welcome.

To Amelia, Julian said, "Would you care to join us, my lady? My aunt very much wants to talk to you."

"Of course, my lord." Rising, Amelia flashed a smile around the box but held it only until they reached the corridor.

Julian blandly offered her his arm. "Why do I think you're displeased with me?"

"More worried than displeased." Bracing herself against unwanted visions, she slid her hand into the crook of his elbow. Nothing untoward happened, so she relaxed. With people strolling past, however, this wasn't the place to discuss her disturbing vision. "Did you not receive my note asking you to call?"

"I did, but too late to pay a call. Since Sophie said you would be here, I thought we might talk under cover of the play."

Talk about his fighting a duel, perhaps dying in it, in a box with hundreds of eyes on it? No. "That won't do. This is important, Julian."

His gaze searched hers for a long moment before he nodded. "Very well. Because of the gossips and our current situation, we must stay for a time, perhaps the first act. Then we'll leave on pretext of escorting my aunt home because she's feeling unwell."

"That isn't flattering to your aunt." Yet the fact he'd taken Amelia seriously meant a great deal. She couldn't bear to think of him dying on the grass somewhere in London.

"What is it?" he asked.

"We can't discuss it here."

He nodded, his gaze on her face. "Can it wait until after the first act?"

"Possibly." Watching him closely, she asked, "Have you any unusual plans for tomorrow?"

His face closed over, and her heart sank.

"No," he said.

Her instincts confirmed he was telling the truth. But he was also not elaborating, not explaining. Perhaps that was merely his way. Or perhaps he had plans, just not for tomorrow.

The scene of him on the ground flashed across her vision. She pressed her lips together. He definitely meant to fight Lord Wyndon.

Because of her? Regardless, she couldn't let him do that.

He ushered her into his box, and Augusta greeted her warmly. "Here, child, sit in front with Julian. Let's fling your betrothal in the tabbies' faces." She paused, studying them. "Smile, both of you."

Somehow they both managed it.

"Tell me about your horses," Amelia requested. She desperately needed a distraction from being the center of everyone's attention. Although she hadn't thought anything could draw more interest than she'd already endured tonight, she'd been wrong. The sight of her and Julian together apparently was like hay on a bonfire.

Below the level of the box rail, Julian's gloved hand closed over hers, a reminder she wasn't facing society alone. She had an ally.

He said, "We're only of interest until some new *on dit* makes the rounds. Ignore them, and they'll turn their attention elsewhere." Flashing a smile as artificial as hers, he added, "I've a string of four racing this year. Pendergast, the fellow who stopped me at the house party, wants to buy one of them, but I think he played a part in yesterday's trap. I scried afterward and saw him talking to Wyndon while we were preparing for our ride. I won't trust him with one of my horses. Besides, he's a cow-handed rider."

"Who do you consider good riders?"

"You, for one. You easily kept your seat at a flying gallop, in a sidesaddle, and never had to saw on the reins or abuse your mount."

She didn't need her Gift to know he was sincere. "Thank you, Julian."

"Riding with you was a pleasure."

The curtain rose, and the audience applauded. Still, Amelia knew better than to assume attention would shift to the stage. Seeing, being seen, and gossiping mattered far more to the *ton* than anything the actors did. But she had leisure to figure out how to dissuade Julian from this dangerous path.

At last, the interval arrived. Aunt Augusta feigned a headache, allowing Julian and Amelia to escort her out. He sent for the carriage and helped the two women in.

Despite staring fixedly at the stage, he'd noticed the sharp, sidelong looks Amelia cast him from time to time. She either knew about the upcoming duel or, judging by her question in the corridor earlier, suspected he had some sort of plan she wouldn't like. Given the short time until the duel and her seer Gift, odds favored her having Seen something about it. Especially after this afternoon's rather peremptory summons to her side.

Her concern touched him, perhaps more than it should. Only by staying within the bounds of friendship could they make this marriage succeed.

She had a set, determined look on her face he had to admire. She wasn't afraid to push for what she wanted, and he already knew, from Adam, she wouldn't do so with tears or tantrums.

The coach swayed on London's cobblestone streets. Aunt Augusta glanced from him to Amelia and back repeatedly. They were almost home when she said, "The pair of you look as though you'll be at daggers drawn shortly. Whatever is the matter?"

Daggers drawn. A more apt phrase than she knew, and the narrowing of Amelia's eyes meant she'd also read additional significance into it.

"I need to speak with Julian," she said. "I beg your pardon, Augusta, but the matter is private."

"I see." His aunt pursed her lips, clearly not seeing but respecting Amelia's refusal to elaborate.

They arrived at his Mayfair house, in Park Street near Grosvenor Square. He assisted the ladies to alight, and the three of them went inside. When they'd surrendered their outerwear to the footman, Aunt Augusta said, "I'll have tea sent to you in the library." She paused, a considering expression on her face. "Do try not to kill him, Amelia. He generally means well."

Amelia and Julian walked back to the library and sat together on the sofa.

Resigned, he asked, "What has you so unsettled, my lady?"

She stared at him, as though choosing her words, before she spoke. "I may as well be blunt. Julian, are you engaged to fight Wyndon?"

Bloody hell. "A gentleman doesn't discuss such matters with a lady."

"Because gentlemen have silly notions about protecting ladies from *matters* we're perfectly able to deal with knowing about." Frowning, she added, "Must I remind you I'm a seer?"

He sighed. "What did you See?"

"You, Robin, and Ned met Wyndon, Mr. Fitzhugh, and a couple of other men in a park. You and Wyndon fought, using your fists." Worry darkened her eyes. "You lost. You landed a fair number of blows, but the fight ended with you on the ground."

Apparently, choosing fisticuffs wasn't going to win the day for him. Heart beating fast, he braced himself. "Was I dead?"

"I don't think so, but I'm not sure."

Well, hellfire and bloody damnation.

She drew a shaky breath. "So tell me, are you planning to fight him? Or has this yet to be arranged?"

"He challenged me," Julian admitted. There was apparently no avoiding it. "I accepted, and we're to meet the day after tomorrow at dawn."

"He challenged you because you rescued me, didn't he?"

Julian shrugged.

"I forbid you to fight him. Do you hear me? I forbid it."

She looked so angry, so worried for him, that tender warmth stirred in his chest. "My dear, you know I must."

"I know no such thing. Are all men idiots?"

The arrival of the tea interrupted them. They sat in stiff silence while James, one of the Gifted footman, set out the sandwiches and the tea service.

"Will you pour?" Julian asked when they were alone.

"Will you promise not to do this stupid and—and possibly fatal—thing?" Anxiety darkened her eyes, and the warmth in his chest deepened.

He shouldn't trust that feeling. It didn't belong in the sort of marriage he'd offered her. "Why do you care?"

"What sort of fool question is that? Of course I don't want you to meet some dreadful fate."

"Why?"

Exasperated, she said, "Whatever else you are to me, you're my friend. You're a kind, decent man."

"Are those the only reasons?"

"Well, what other reasons could there be?"

A moment later, her eyes narrowed. "If you think I care more for the help you give me with the family curse and my other visions than I do for you, you insult me. And you had best not think I would marry you for your money."

"You wouldn't be the first." That slipped out unexpectedly, truth welling from deep inside him. That was enough of that, so he clamped his mouth shut.

Amelia's face softened. "Some women are fools," she said.

They regarded each other solemnly, the crackling fire the only sound in the room. Thank God, her eyes held no sign of pity, only indignation on his behalf.

Holding his gaze, she told him, "You were Adam's trusted friend. On his soul, I swear to you, I'm considering wedding you only because of the life you want us to build together. Only for that."

Looking into her clear eyes and earnest face, he believed her. Old humiliations had made him unduly suspicious, at least where she was concerned. Getting past that would take some time—assuming he had time and didn't die the day after tomorrow—but he owed it to her to try.

"I beg your pardon, Amelia. Can you forgive me?"

"We all have worries, and yours is understandable. Of course I forgive you."

The look between them held. Warmed.

"Amelia," he breathed. Without conscious intent, he lifted his hand to her warm, smooth cheek, caressing it gently.

Her eyes darkened. When he leaned toward her, she met him halfway. Her mouth under his was soft and welcoming. He kept the kiss restrained, out of courtesy, even though her hand rose to rest on his shoulder.

When the temptation to press grew too great, he raised his head. Amelia opened her eyes and smiled at him. Her face held no hint of regret or embarrassment, only tenderness.

Until that moment, he hadn't realized he'd feared kissing her would raise Buckton's ghost. He smiled and kissed her again swiftly.

They looked at each other. What to say after that?

Amelia flashed him a shy look and turned back to the tea, breaking the moment. "I implore you not to fight him. All else aside, he will certainly cheat. He's just that sort."

Julian accepted the cup she offered but kept his gaze on her. "Your concern touches me, my dear, truly. But I must fight him. If I don't, all the *ton* will take it as an admission I was wrong to hit him. I was not wrong. He deserved that, and more. In the circumstances, I would make exactly the same choices."

"I am so very sick of the bloody *ton*."

That made two of them.

"Is there nothing I can say to dissuade you?"

He shook his head. "But there may be something you can do to help me. Tomorrow, we'll have Robin and Ned over here. You'll scry the fight in the fire for us, and we'll see if there's aught I can do to change the outcome you saw. At the very least, we'll see how Wyndon cheats."

~

The next afternoon, Amelia fed her vision into the parlor fire for their friends to view. Repetition did not make it any better.

When it faded, it left the little group silent and shaken. Reliving it made her every bit as anxious as she'd felt the first time this vision had come to her. She and Julian sat together on the sofa facing the parlor fire. His aunt, Robin, Sophie, and Ned sat in chairs near the hearth. Halfway through, as though Julian knew she needed support—or perhaps because he did?—he'd taken her hand. She'd gripped his gratefully.

Robin's grim gaze turned to Julian.

"Don't say it," Julian told him, his voice flat. "You know I must go through with this."

Robin's eyes narrowed. After a moment, he shook his head.

Ned leaned forward. "His hands were glowing. At least, I think they were. It's difficult to be sure in daylight."

"We need to see it again," Julian said.

Amelia bit back a cry of protest. Watching him take such a pounding did not become easier with repetition. Yes, he landed quite a few blows, but he'd once again ended on the ground.

As though Julian sensed her distress, his fingers tightened on hers. "Someone else can do it. Looking only a day into the future should be simple for anyone who's adept at scrying. We need to determine how Wyndon will cheat, but you need not watch it again. You ladies should go down to the library and let us join you shortly."

"No." Amelia shook her head. "If you're watching it, I'll stay with you." He was in this dire scrape because he'd helped her. She wouldn't hide from any part of it he faced—other than the duel itself, because women were forbidden at those.

Of course, if no one knew she was there...

"I can manage the scrying," Robin said.

He directed a stream of silver magic at the hearth. The vision formed again, the Aysgarth carriage pulling up, then Julian disembarking with Robin and Ned.

Gritting her teeth and fighting tears, Amelia watched the seconds agree on the rules before Julian and Wyndon faced off. Julian dodged Wyndon's punch at his face and slammed his left into the other man's gut. Wyndon responded with a facer that knocked Julian backward, though he kept his feet.

"He's strong," Robin said. "But so are you. Those blows are hurting you more than they should."

"His hands definitely are glowing," Augusta said, her face granite.

"Only his knuckles." Julian scowled. "How is he using magic that way? Only glamours stay so close to one's body. Even when they cover a wide area, they're always close to whoever casts them."

Robin raised an eyebrow. "Are you more angry because he's cheating —or because he's using magic in a way you don't understand?"

"Both," Julian snapped. "We can't counter what we don't understand."

Appalled silence fell over the group. They watched the fight to its end, still unable to tell whether Julian lived when he fell to the ground.

Amelia frowned at the now-ordinary fire. "If what he's doing is like a glamour, could you not—is there a similar way you could perhaps summon magic to blunt his blows?"

The suggestion felt appallingly silly.

Julian, however, looked thoughtful. "There might be a way. If Robin and Ned will help me, we'll see what we can devise."

"You mean to have them hit you." Sophie glared at him.

"Well, of course," Julian responded. "The only way to test one's defenses against a blow is to take one."

"Happy to hit you anytime," Robin assured him.

Julian rolled his eyes.

How could they joke about such a thing? This entire situation grew steadily worse.

Julian looked to Robin. "What member of the Conclave Council has the highest social rank?"

"Allenstone, but he's out of the country. No one else on the Council has noble rank. If we go down to ordinary members, Ned and I both have old titles, but I'm your second, and he's your friend."

Amelia asked, "What are you looking for?"

"A witness," Julian responded. "One who won't tattle to the unGifted authorities but who can detect magic if Wyndon uses it."

"The best person is Alice Gresham," Robin said. "The Council head's word would carry weight, but a woman can't attend a duel. We could have her deputize someone."

"I've arranged for Tobias Waller to attend as your doctor," Ned said. "Since he's also Gifted, I'll have a word with him about watching for prohibited magic use."

Amelia's stomach lurched, and she swallowed hard.

Julian said, "Have someone who's on the Council come as his assistant. Perhaps that will deter Wyndon."

Robin scowled. "In a fair fight, you stand a good chance of taking him."

Julian shrugged. "I cannot very well bleat about that now. Anyway, we've something else to discuss."

"What is it?" Amelia asked.

He turned an intent, measuring look on her. "Wyndon seems to be biding his time until tomorrow's encounter. If he is, as we think, planning to cheat in a novel way, he's apt to feel rather confident. So he may plan to wait for tomorrow's outcome before moving against you again."

"You think he would assault her again?" his aunt demanded.

"We cannot discount the possibility. If, as seems likely, I don't return upright tomorrow, Wyndon may see my incapacity as leaving you unprotected."

His *incapacity*. Please let it be only that, not his death.

"Your aunt and uncle's house," Julian continued, "is not warded, as they're not Gifted. If we can devise a way for me to counter Wyndon's cheating, he may try to secure you while we're all flushed with victory."

"Secure me. You mean kidnap me, don't you?" Much as she wanted to, she couldn't dismiss the idea as implausible. Dread knotted her stomach.

"I put nothing past him," Julian said. "If there were a way to do so without ghastly social damage, I would move you into the Merlin Club today. It has the strongest magical wards in London, and every man there would defend you."

"I would go with her," Augusta announced. "I dare anyone to impugn my conduct."

"I don't care about social damage," Amelia said. "I've had more than enough of the *ton* and its rules. I do care about being immured there if—if you need me. To help you here, I mean."

Heat rose in her cheeks. Julian must've noticed, but he said nothing. She couldn't bring herself to say *if you're badly injured*. If he died, God forbid, Augusta would need her.

And Amelia would never forgive herself.

"If you think Wyndon would try to kidnap me, it would be easy enough for him to have someone lie in wait outside the club. I can't stay there forever, and if you're…injured, I want to be with you, Julian."

Surprise mingled with pleasure in his eyes. Whether he couldn't have trusted his late wife to do that or hadn't been sure Amelia cared to, she'd given him something he liked, and that was satisfying.

Robin said, "It would be harder than you think to lurk in that area, but you make a good point. If this thing goes as we've seen, all of us will want to be here with Julian."

"She could spend the night here," Augusta suggested. "Betrothed or not, that will lead to talk, but if Amelia doesn't care, so be it. We can reinforce the wards tonight, and I'm sure Robin or Ned can convince some of the Merlin Club to stand guard tomorrow. These wards aren't as strong as those at that club, but they aren't far behind."

Amelia responded, "I don't care what people say. I wouldn't sleep at all if I weren't here." Especially if he came home badly injured.

She glanced down at her and Julian's joined hands. At least she could be with him. She not only wanted to be but owed him that. Especially considering the reason he faced this duel.

"I'd best go to my uncle's house and pack," she said. "Mama simply must understand." Because Mama couldn't know the truth, she would be distressed and baffled and, yes, scandalized. Amelia couldn't allow that to matter.

Augusta offered, "I'll come with you and help manage your mama. I'll tell her I need your help, and that will be the simple truth."

"I'll walk you down." Rising with Amelia, Julian offered her his arm.

They descended to the entry hall together. The footman brought her spencer, bonnet, and gloves. He then retreated, and Julian assisted her with the short jacket.

As his aunt descended the stairs, he stroked Amelia's cheek. "All will be well," he told her, his gaze level and certain. "I mean to be back here tomorrow night to dine with you."

"I look forward to it." At least her voice was firm, not showing the terror for him that gnawed at her. "We haven't discussed the other problem."

Ney and the six thousand men under his command would likely join Bonaparte today. The deposed Emperor marched on Paris in force. But would the city accept him?

"One thing at a time," Julian said gently. "We can do nothing about that problem for the moment."

"I know, but you're needed to handle that, and instead you're doing… this…because of—"

His finger at her lips stopped her. "Do not say it's because of you. I won't have it, Amelia. None of this situation is of your making."

There was no use arguing with him, but she gave him her best stubborn look.

Sighing, he gathered her close. The warmth and strength in his body felt inexpressibly dear. He simply had to survive tomorrow.

She hadn't been this frightened since the doctors told her Crispin had dysentery.

CHAPTER 14

Even after Julian's practice with his friends, he couldn't reliably summon magic as a buffer against blows. The scrying of the duel had not changed. He would have to go through with it and hope to survive.

"You should've spoken to Amelia before we left," Robin said as the carriage rattled through the predawn fog.

"I didn't want to distress her further. Or have her try again to change my mind."

From the rear-facing seat, Ned said, "Women set great store by such little courtesies."

"She'll forgive me." If he survived. If he didn't, she would have other matters to concern her. His stomach churned, and he made himself take a slow, deep breath. "If this goes badly, she'll need you both to help her fend off Wyndon."

"It won't go so badly as that," Robin replied.

He couldn't be as sure as he sounded. Julian wasn't at all certain. If he could find an opening, knock Wyndon down, he would. But no scenario they'd scried showed him doing that.

Fortunately, the duel was not to the death. However much Wyndon might want Julian dead, he had not, as anticipated, wanted to proclaim that in the arranged terms. Neither had he settled for first blood. They would fight until one of them could no longer stand up.

Best not to think about how much punishment that would involve. Yes, Julian could throw the fight. Given what he already knew, that might be the wise thing, but he couldn't accept it. Anything less than his best effort would be an admission he'd wronged Wyndon. He would never concede that.

At least the women were safe this morning. Dare MacGregor and burly Wat Granger were on guard at the house, and Julian had reinforced the wards last night.

The coach turned into Hyde Park and veered right. They passed the Serpentine on the left and headed deeper into the park, so they ran less risk of someone observing them.

The coachman halted. Julian and his friends climbed out. The seconds had selected a copse of ancient elms well into the park as the dueling site. Wyndon stood under a tree a short distance away with Fitzhugh and a stout man who had the familiar feeling of a Gifted. Wyndon had stripped to his shirt.

Off to one side, clearly taking no one's part, stood Dr. Tobias Waller, a lanky, taciturn man. Short, wiry Ellert Chandler, a prosperous mercer who served on the Conclave Council, stood with him. Wyndon would know Chandler wasn't truly Waller's assistant, but arguing about the man's presence would insult the Council.

Fitzhugh and the other man came forward. Ned clapped Julian on the shoulder and went with Robin to meet them. Julian tossed his coat into the coach, and then his cravat. They'd agreed to fight shirtless, but there was no use dealing with the morning chill until he had to.

The seconds walked back. Looking grim, Robin said, "He offers you the chance to apologize and forego this."

"If anyone should apologize, it's he. No."

"I thought as much." Robin looked over at Fitzhugh and shook his head.

Wyndon pulled off his shirt.

Julian did the same. His gut felt taut with nerves. Somehow, he would survive this.

Escorted by their seconds, they walked to the little clearing appointed for their meeting. He and Wyndon stopped a couple of yards apart. The hatred in the other man's eyes came as no shock. No member of that family ever brooked opposition. The more effective the opposition, the more they despised it.

There was no way to know how much of a difference a small change could make. But in each scenario they'd scried, he'd let Wyndon throw the first punch. Perhaps he should seize the initiative instead.

Fitzhugh reminded them they would fight until one of them could no longer stand. "You will observe Broughton's rules, my lords, as agreed. No blows below the waist or striking your opponent when he's down. If either of you falls, you have until the count of thirty to stand. If you cannot do so, your opponent wins."

He looked to Robin, who said, "Begin."

Julian darted forward and slammed his fist into Wyndon's gut. The blow doubled him. His breath *whoofed* out. Julian followed with an uppercut to the jaw.

Wyndon seized his arm and wrenched it aside. Searing, magical pain speared upward. It rocked Julian. He couldn't block Wyndon's facer. Even though Wyndon was gasping for air, the blow connected with Julian's cheek like a hammer. Magic again, barely diluted by the magical defense Julian summoned at the last second. Black lightning flashed across his vision.

Fists raised, he danced backward. Had to summon his resources, prepare magic to block. That twist to his arm had surprised him. Put him off balance and lost the small advantage he'd gained.

He and Wyndon circled each other, breathing hard.

Wyndon swung a hook punch at Julian's head. Julian ducked. Came up behind the swing to drive his fist into Wyndon's ribs. Wyndon back-handed him. Despite Julian's magic buffer, the blow to his ear drove thunder into his head. Julian staggered.

Wyndon punched him in the jaw, then the gut. Blows like a horse's kick. Magic.

Something inside Julian gave. Agony seared his insides. Had to finish this. He gathered himself and slammed his fist directly into Wyndon's face. Broke the bastard's nose.

Julian punched his chin, then his ribs. Wyndon staggered backward, but Julian was failing, his vision going.

He blocked Wyndon's blow toward his head. Managed to twist aside away from one to his gut, turn it into a glancing strike.

The next one connected, hard, as though it had driven all the way through his skull.

The world scrambled like puzzle pieces, then went dark.

～

W hy were the men taking so long to return? Hyde Park was a short carriage ride away.

Amelia paced the upstairs corridor of Aysgarth House with fear scalding her throat and pounding through her veins. Julian was alive. She'd scried that, and she knew it, as only a seer could know.

That didn't mean he would recover fully. Scrying into the next several days produced only images of him in bed, sometimes sleeping but often looking bewildered. Her attempts to See with her Gift produced similar results, and she'd been afraid to See or scry farther ahead. Afraid to know.

She shouldn't have let Sophie and Augusta convince her not to sneak out to see the duel. If she'd gone to the park, she would know what was happening.

She reached the end of the corridor and peered out at the back lawn. A coach turned into the narrow alley behind the house. Its door bore the Aysgarth crest of a tower above two crossed swords on a blue field.

Had they let Julian out at the front? She hadn't heard anything from the entry hall.

The coach door opened. Grim-faced, Robin and Ned jumped out. Ned rushed to open the back gate, and Amelia's heart twisted. Paralyzed by fear, she could only stare at the scene below. A short, wiry man she didn't recognize braced Julian as he slumped in the coach's doorway. Bruises covered his face. Robin and Ned hurried back to the coach. They each tugged one of Julian's arms around their necks. Linking their free arms beneath him, they lifted him clear of the coach. The footman braced him from behind while the other man stepped down.

Tears stung Amelia's eyes. She whirled and dashed down the stairs.

When she rushed through the door separating the front of the house from the rear, she struggled to recall how to reach the back door. Judging by all the shelves of china and crystal, this was the butler's pantry. Voices came from ahead. She hurried toward them, pushing through a plain, wooden door. The pantry opened onto the kitchen, where a short, sturdy woman in a cook's plain gown and apron yanked open the back door.

"God save us," the woman gasped.

Amelia brushed past a couple of footmen and a maid in time to see the stranger bracing Julian as Ned and Robin carried their friend into the kitchen.

The damage looked even worse up close. He'd been beaten badly.

Because of her.

"Amelia, move," Robin snapped, and she stumbled backward, out of their path. Of course they needed to hurry. He should be in his bed as soon as possible. Besides, he was not a small man and must be heavy.

She fell in behind them. Her healing skills would help with the bruising, but there must be other damage. Why else would he be slumping that way, seeming unaware of his surroundings, his head lolling onto Robin's shoulder?

When they reached the front hall, Dare MacGregor and Wat Granger hurried from the parlor where they'd stationed themselves. Their dismayed expressions gave way to stony anger.

"Do ye need help?" Wat asked.

Robin said, "We have him, but I'll let you know if we need you."

With guilt choking her, Amelia followed them up the stairs and into Julian's bedchamber. Someone had turned back his bed. His friends laid him gently on it.

A slender, blond man with the familiar feeling of a Gifted rushed in from an adjoining room. His face paled. He must be Julian's valet.

Robin said, "Amelia, excuse us while we undress him. Go and tell Dare he should admit Tobias Waller and Ellen Drake. They're coming to attend Julian."

Glad for something to do, she rushed down the stairs. MacGregor paced the entry hall. When she rounded the turn at the top of the stairs, he wheeled to face her. The worry in his face stabbed at her heart.

Because of me. All because of me.

"How bad?" the tall Scotsman demanded.

"We don't know yet." She delivered Robin's message. "Do you know them?"

"Aye, from Conclave gatherings." His face grim, he added, "I'll no' admit them until I'm sure they're themselves and not others glamoured to resemble them."

Aghast, she stared at him. "I never thought of that."

"Why should ye?" His face softened, and he touched her arm. "We've matters in hand, Amelia. See to Julian. And bring me word when you have it."

"Of course. Of course."

Amelia climbed the stairs as fast as she could. Outside Julian's door, she met Ned and Augusta.

Ned said, "I'll go down and help watch the front."

"Some of the staff are Gifted," Augusta said, "including Julian's valet, Baker. But I doubt they're trained in defensive magic."

Ned scowled. "I'm feeling much more aggressive than defensive." He hurried down the stairs.

Amelia stared at Julian's closed door. There must be some way she could help.

"Amelia." Augusta waited until Amelia looked at her. The sympathy in her expression made Amelia's chest hurt.

"My dear, this is in no way your fault."

"If Wyndon hadn't wanted—it's because of me, and—"

"It isn't. It's because the de Veres of Wyndon breed greedy, selfish scoundrels. If you had sought his attention, that would be a different case, but you didn't. Julian will be extremely vexed if you insist on blaming yourself."

If he lived to be vexed.

Amelia shook her head. "There must be something I can do."

Robin opened the bedroom door. Both women turned to him. He shut the door behind him.

"We scried the fight," Augusta said. "We know what happened. How is he?"

"Not good. His eyes don't track, and he doesn't respond. Tobias found broken ribs, extensive bruising, and internal bleeding."

Fear wrapped ice around Amelia's heart, but Robin was continuing. "He fixed what he could at the park, enough for us to be able to move Julian. Now he's gone to fetch Ellen. Says she's better at healing internal injuries than he is."

"Who is that man who came with you?" Amelia asked. Apparently they trusted him enough to leave him alone with Julian.

"Ellert Chandler. He's a member of the Conclave Council. We needed an impartial witness so we could bring charges against Wyndon for using magic to cheat. So far he's been bloody disobliging."

"What do you mean?" Augusta demanded.

"Chandler admits he saw magic around Wyndon's hands," Robin said. "But he also saw it on Julian's body."

"Julian was defending himself," Amelia protested.

"He says that doesn't matter because that's cheating as well. He won't refer the accusation to the Council. If we do, he'll oppose it."

But Julian had not used magic against his foe, only to shield himself. Aghast, Amelia stared at Robin.

Augusta's face paled except for two bright, red spots on her cheekbones. She pressed her lips together. "We will see about that," she announced, the words slow and emphatic.

"A protest will gain us nothing, as Julian would be the first to tell us." Robin shook his head. "His only recourse is trial by combat, and he's in no condition for that anytime soon."

Trial by combat? Expose himself to a second pounding?

Not if I can prevent it.

But she had no right to prevent it or, truly, even to oppose it. She was only his friend, not his wife or even his genuine fiancée.

Perhaps that should change.

The thought brought a new rush of nerves, and she shoved it aside. Restoring Julian's health must come before all else.

James, one of Julian's Gifted footmen, led two people up the stairs. A lanky man with graying hair walked beside a short, sturdy woman who looked to be in her forties. Both wore clothes that were well made but not in the first stare of fashion.

"Dr. Waller and Mrs. Drake," James announced. He then walked down the corridor to his usual station.

Robin introduced everyone. In a gravelly voice, the man asked, "Do any of you have healing skills?"

"Mine are very limited," Augusta replied.

"I have some," Amelia said, "but no experience healing wounds I cannot see." Wounds such as Julian bore.

Ellen said, "I can teach you that. Come with us."

Robin and Augusta also followed them into the room. Ellert Chandler rose from a chair by the bed. "Now that you've healers on hand, I'll be going."

"Thank you for helping us bring him home," Robin responded, his tone grudging.

Chandler shrugged. "Sorry I can't do as you wish. I hope he'll recover quickly." He nodded to the newcomers and departed.

Amelia slipped past Robin so she could see around the bed curtains. Julian lay on his back with his eyes closed. His pale, battered face looked even worse than it had a short time ago.

Tobias looked at Ellen. "I'll stay in case you need me."

"Very well." To Amelia, she added, "Come with me." She moved to the bed and pushed the hangings back farther. When Amelia stood beside her,

Ellen drew the coverlet down to Julian's waist and pushed up his night-shirt to bare his torso. Bruises covered his ribcage and his belly.

Amelia swallowed a gasp. It was all very well for Augusta to say this wasn't because of her, but she couldn't help feeling responsible.

Ellen's hands glowed argent. She moved them over Julian's body, her palms about an inch away, then did the same with his head. Barely touching him, she laid one hand lightly against his side.

"Cracked ribs," she said. "Amelia, place your palm against my side. Probe with your magic and tell me what you feel."

Amelia complied. "I can sense the smoothness and the pallor of the bones and the warm, living tissue behind them."

"Good. Now, very, very gently, place your palm against his side."

Terrified of hurting him further, Amelia did so.

"Now probe again." When Amelia hesitated, Ellen added, "It won't hurt him. You'll see."

Carefully, Amelia sent a trickle of magic through his skin. "I can feel... cracks in the smoothness. And a...wrongness beyond it."

"Very good. Now, just as you envision a cut closing when you apply magic, trace the crack with one finger and imagine it smoothing."

"I can feel...it's working, but it isn't altogether closing the crack."

"Nor will it. This must be done several times, a little power at a time, as bone is difficult to heal. Now move your hand to the bruising on his waist and probe behind it."

"There's more of that wrongness."

"That's internal bruising. You fix it the same way, but instead of imag-ining it closing, you imagine seeing him healthy. We'll leave the bruises on his skin for last, as they're the least serious problem."

Under Ellen's guidance, Amelia also touched Julian's brow, and the confusion and pain behind his forehead stunned her.

"Steady," Ellen murmured. "Envision him speaking to you, concen-trating on something. His brain will remember the feeling. Health is its natural state. With a boost of power—very slight at any one time, mind you—it will correct the injuries... Yes, like that. Just that bit is enough for now. Too much will overwhelm his body's natural healing."

"Will you stay here and tend him?" Augusta asked.

Ellen nodded. "For a few days, until he recovers enough for Amelia to manage."

Amelia lifted her hand from Julian's brow and clenched her fist in her skirts. He looked so helpless. And his brilliant mind was such a jumble. What if he never—

His eyes opened. Amelia smiled. Everyone moved closer.

But his gaze held no recognition, only confusion, and her chest went tight.

"Speak to him," Ellen urged. "Use his name."

"Hello, Julian," Amelia said.

His brow furrowed, but the confusion in his eyes didn't clear. Disappointment and guilt welled into her throat.

Robin stepped up beside her. Despite his strained expression, his voice was light. "Told you this was a bad idea. Perhaps in future you'll listen to me."

Still no recognition. No change. Robin gripped Amelia's hand, and she squeezed his fingers.

"Don't be alarmed," Ellen advised as Julian's eyes closed again. "Now that magic has begun the healing, sleep will continue it. I'll treat him again this afternoon and this evening. Each time, he'll be a little better."

"I'll sit with him," Amelia said, and propriety be damned.

"We'll take it in turns," Robin stated. "He won't be alone."

Ellen nodded. "That will benefit you more than him, but it's good to keep an eye on him. Now, if you'll excuse me, I'll find my chamber."

"I'll come with you," Augusta said.

She and Ellen left the room, and Ned and Sophie entered. The fear in Sophie's face and the anger in Ned's echoed Amelia's feelings.

"He'll recover," Robin declared. "He must. He's far too bloody brilliant to—" Blinking fast, he set his jaw.

"Of course he will," Amelia said, and hoped with all her heart it was true.

CHAPTER 15

The King of France bolted from Paris on March nineteenth. Royalists were already fleeing the country. By the next morning, according to Merlin Club reports, Bonaparte was once again ensconced in the Tuileries Palace. One of his ministers had announced that the emperor was open to any proposal for peace, but no one believed that. Europe braced for war.

In Julian's house, that was no one's first concern. Robin dealt with the Merlin Club by messenger because someone had to, but he spent every minute he could with Julian.

By the twenty-second, the third day after the duel, there had been only slight changes. Julian's eyes were open more, sometimes appearing to follow people moving about the room. He hadn't yet spoken. His valet, Baker, managed to feed him some gruel and barley water, but not much.

No one else had a strong appetite either.

At least his ribs were entirely healed. That would make little difference, though, if his brain didn't recover.

After picking at her luncheon, Amelia went up to Julian's chamber. She met Baker coming out with a tray. "Any better?" she asked.

The young man tried valiantly to smile. "He scowled at the gruel. That's—I mean to say, he loathes it, so that must—must be a good sign, my lady. Mustn't it?"

Because one of the unGifted staff could come down the corridor at any moment, they couldn't use first names. Amelia also had to be a bit more formal than she would've preferred in the face of his obvious worry.

"Of course." She patted his arm and hoped he was right. He'd spent the last three nights on a pallet in Julian's chamber while Robin or Ned slept on the sofa by the windows.

When she entered the room, Ned rose to his feet. "If you'll be all right alone for a bit, I'll take Sophie for a walk round the square. It would do her good, do us all good, to be out in the sunshine. Even though you can't leave the property, you could sit in the back garden with Robin or Dare on guard."

What a tiresome prospect. "You cannot all guard me forever, Ned."

His expression hardened. "Once we've seen to Wyndon, you won't need protection. We will see to him, Amelia. It may take us a while, but he will get his deserts. I promise you."

He was probably crowing about his triumph—and thus his vindication—all over London. Well, let him. Sooner or later, as Ned had said, they would see to Wyndon.

She thanked Ned, and he left the room.

Amelia leaned over the bed. Julian's head on the pillow turned. His gaze met hers. He looked less confused but still didn't seem to recognize her. His fine muslin nightshirt hid the healing bruises on his body, but the ones on his face still showed as faint green splotches. With the coverlet up to his chest, his arms lay on the bed. Should she take his hand?

If he were well, she would hesitate because of their unsettled status. She shouldn't do it now, when he couldn't protest.

"Hello, Julian," she said. "You didn't eat much gruel."

He scowled, so he must have understood her. That little reaction cheered her immensely.

She settled into the chair Ned had vacated. Sunshine pouring over the leather-upholstered sofa called to her, but it was too far from the bed.

The volume of Wordsworth's poems she'd left on the bedside table still lay there. Amelia picked it up and opened it.

When she glanced at Julian, he was watching her, frowning.

She smiled at him. "Do you need something?"

His frown deepened. He shook his head, not seeming to mean no but as though in frustration.

Desperate to comfort him somehow, Amelia caught his hand. His fingers closed on hers in a tight grip. He stared at her as though trying to summon her name.

"Crumple," he said. Anger flashed through his eyes. His lips tightened. This time his headshake definitely conveyed *No*.

Was his mind so badly scrambled still? Trying to guess what he meant might frustrate him more. Heart pounding, she waited.

"Hammer," he said, and fury boiled in his eyes. He closed them and took three slow, deep breaths. When he opened them, he looked determined. With his free hand, he pointed to the book.

"You want the book?" Amelia asked, holding it out to him.

Another head shake. He released her hand and mimed opening a book and turning pages. Then he pointed to her.

"You want me to read to you?"

He nodded. That small bit of communication had to be a good sign.

"I must let Ellen know you're talking. Then I'll happily read to you."

She stuck her head out in the corridor. When James, the footman stationed there, turned to her, she said, "Please inform Mrs. Drake his lordship is talking."

The man's face split in a wide grin. "At once, Lady Buckton."

Amelia shut the door and found Julian watching her, a slight crease in his forehead.

"There," she said. "I'm sure Ellen will be down directly."

She returned to her chair and opened the book. There were no poems about horses, but perhaps he would like "Composed Upon Westminster Bridge," with its images of London in the stillness of early morning.

She found the sonnet and started reading. Julian continued to watch her but didn't say anything else.

Someone knocked on the door. Amelia glanced at Julian. He nodded, and she called, "Come in."

Ellen turned a keen gaze on the bed. Julian stared back at her with that same expression, as though he should know her name but didn't. She smiled at him. "Welcome back, Julian. May I lay my hand on your brow and use magic to see how your head is healing?"

He looked to Amelia, who gave him a slight nod. After studying Ellen a moment more, he also nodded.

"I hear you've been talking." Ellen laid her hand gently on his forehead. A silver glow appeared around it. "That's an excellent sign, so I'm not surprised there's much less swelling now."

"Crumpets," Julian replied, and he scowled again.

"Are you having difficulty saying the words you want?" she asked. When he nodded, she patted his hand. "That's not unusual with a head injury. It should pass as your brain heals. In the meantime, would you like a slate and some chalk? I imagine they're somewhere in this house."

His eyes lit at that.

"I'll see to it." Amelia hurried into the corridor and gave James his errand. Again looking delighted, he hurried away.

Amelia returned to Julian's chamber as Ellen said, "Since I'm here, shall we proceed with your next healing treatments?"

He nodded eagerly.

Amelia sat on the sofa, out of the way, to watch. Her throat tightened, forcing her to realize how grateful she was for these small signs of progress and how much she'd feared he would not recover.

When Ellen departed, Amelia asked, "Shall I resume reading?"

He nodded. She was halfway through "Lines Composed a Few Miles Above Tintern Abbey" when someone knocked on the door. She looked to Julian, but the footman entered before he could respond.

James closed the door behind him. With a slight bow, he presented Amelia with a slate, a stick of chalk, and a rag. When he turned to the bed, he had tears in his eyes.

"If I may, Julian, I must say it's a great pleasure to us all to see you improving. We're praying for you below stairs, all of us."

Julian smiled and gave him a nod of thanks.

The man's throat worked. He swallowed hard and hurried from the room.

Amelia knew exactly how he felt, but she tried to seem calm when she handed the slate, chalk, and rag to Julian. He balanced the slate on his raised thigh and wrote something. When he turned it to her, it read, in blockish letters, *Thank you.*

"You're very welcome," she managed around the lump in her throat.

She quickly sat and opened the book. As she read, however, one part of her mind examined her reactions. Her intense relief didn't merely signal a lessening of guilt but also the deepening of her feelings for Julian. Not to a degree that would create an imbalance between them, but perhaps enough to build on?

She needed time to know.

～

Two days later, Julian clearly recognized people. He'd printed each of their names on his slate, and he could summon some of the words he wanted to say. Yet he seemed restless.

He couldn't read for very long, but he could write names. Was the reading difficulty due to trouble making out words? Or was it an issue of sustaining his attention?

Amelia had an idea and consulted Ellen. With Ellen's approval and over Robin's objections, Amelia asked James to bring Julian's chess set from his library.

Robin hovered outside Julian's door. "If he can play, that's excellent, but trying is risky. If he doesn't know what to do with the pieces, I can't see how that's good for him."

"It will tell Ellen things she needs to know." Amelia patted Robin's arm. "Don't worry. I'm taking in only one pawn and leaving the set and the box of pieces here with you and James. If Julian doesn't seem to recognize the pawn, I won't take this any further."

"I guess that will do," Robin conceded. "But I'm coming in with you."

When they walked into Julian's room, Sophie was sitting by the bed, reading from *The Sporting Magazine*. "There's an article on the Derby," she said. "I thought it might interest Julian."

Or it might remind him he wasn't strong enough to work with his horses, but he didn't seem distressed. It was so hard to know what to do for him.

"Will you excuse us, Soph?" Robin requested.

Her eyebrows rose. She looked at Julian, who shrugged.

When the door closed behind Sophie, Amelia opened her hand and showed the white pawn to Julian. His eyes gleamed, and he smiled.

"Shall we play?" she asked.

He nodded emphatically.

"I'll watch," Robin said. He likely wanted to be there if trying to play distressed Julian.

Amelia sat by the bed with Julian propped up on his pillows and the board between them. He'd handed the white pawn to her, so she would play white. That meant making the first move.

She nudged a pawn forward. Julian did the same.

Gradually, they spread out their pieces, but his made steady inroads on her side of the board. After perhaps a dozen moves, she knew she was outmatched. That was all right, though. Winning wasn't the purpose of this game.

He took his time when it was his turn, but he never moved a piece incorrectly. His knights leaped in an L, his bishops stayed on their colors, and the queen had the freedom of the board while his king didn't move at all until Julian castled, moving the king two spaces to its right and placing the rook on its left.

In the end, he had her king pinned. Amelia tipped the piece on its side in token of surrender. Julian grinned, first at her and then at Robin, who had moved a chair to the bed so he could watch.

Perhaps it was her imagination, but Julian seemed as pleased as she was that he could develop a strategy and follow it.

He wrote on the slate and turned it to her. *Tomorrow?*

"Yes, if you like." She flicked a glance at Robin. "Perhaps you need a better opponent, though."

Julian erased the slate and wrote again. *He wishes he were.*

Robin mock-frowned at him. "Now I must uphold my honor and trounce you."

Smirking, Julian shook his head.

After a moment, his smile faded. He looked out the window.

"Julian?" Amelia asked. "What is it?"

His lips tightened. He wrote on the slate again. *Boney. Report.*

She and Robin shared a look of dismay. Ellen had said Julian mustn't be allowed to worry over things he couldn't change.

Robin shrugged. "Bonaparte is in France, as he was days ago. Let's set the board up so I can remind you how well I—"

"Knitting," Julian said, and his eyes flashed. He waggled the slate at Robin.

"If he wants to know that badly," Amelia pointed out, "not telling him won't help."

Robin sighed. "Very well, then. Bonaparte has been busy. He recently issued a proclamation to the effect that all he wants is to rule France in peace."

When Julian's lip curled, Robin added, "Indeed. No one believes that. The army is delighted to have him back. Everyone else seems to be waiting to see what happens. Save in the royalist-leaning areas of the west, where there's a clear lack of enthusiasm that will likely swell into opposition."

Our men in Paris? Julian wrote. *Safe?*

"Thus far. Pierre reports that Bonaparte isn't the man who rode away a year ago. His breathing is harsh and sometimes labored. He looks older and tired, is often pale, and keeps a handkerchief on hand to blot saliva that trickles from his mouth. That last probably is because of his suicide attempt last year." Robin scowled. "God forgive me, but I wish he'd succeeded."

"A great many people may wish that before this is over," Amelia said quietly.

The chess game made Julian feel as though his mind was working for the first time in days.

He helped Amelia gather the pieces of the set. Their fingers brushed, and the contact brought awareness of her that rippled into his gut. Their gazes locked. Smiling, he brushed his fingers over the back of her hand.

She could take that as a gesture of thanks if she chose. Judging by the pink in her cheeks and the little smile on her lips, though, she wasn't taking it that way. Good. He'd touched her because he longed for the connection. Perhaps she'd liked it as much as he had.

She placed the box of pieces on the board and lifted it like a tray. "I'll bring this back tomorrow. Augusta will be in shortly."

He nodded and watched Amelia walk out of the room. She moved with easy grace, which shouldn't have been a surprise. She'd been light on her feet when he danced with her. How had he forgotten that small detail?

If she didn't marry him—an increasingly unwelcome prospect, but one he must face—he would still look after her as a friend. That meant he needed to recover his strength so he could get out of this blasted bed and deal with Wyndon as well as that Corsican scoundrel.

The day Julian recovered his ability to speak, Ellen had insisted he sing, explaining that something about the music would strengthen his ability to summon the words he wanted. Though he refused to *warble* in front of his friends, five days of singing and magical therapy, together, had produced marked improvement.

Now that he was noticeably on the mend, his friends turned more of their attention to the Bonaparte problem. Robin convened a meeting in the Aysgarth House library with Ned, Sophie, Amelia, and Dare MacGregor. Wat Granger remained on guard while Augusta read to Julian. He was restless and easily bored but couldn't yet read for himself. They all hoped that would change soon.

They sat around the long table while Robin reported the findings of the Merlin Club's various agents. In Julian's absence, they'd dealt with him, as was their custom.

"Most of the news is bad," he said. "The army is solidly behind Bonaparte. Still no explanation as to why, though the dismissive treatment the Bourbons gave them probably has much to do with it. Our agent in Paris reports projects designed to put men to work. They're to build a new market at Sainte Germaine, work on the fountain at the Bastille's old site, repair the Louvre, rebuild fortifications around the city, and repair rifles, ironwork and other military equipment. In all, he'll give nine thousand Parisian families an income. The city is behind him, but the countryside, especially in the west, is not rejoicing at Bonaparte's return."

"It's odd that anyone does," Amelia said. "So many Frenchmen followed him to their deaths, especially in Russia. Yet they flock to his banner now. Are matters in France truly that bad?" At least the Scottish plot Robin had explained earlier was easier to understand.

"For enough people, they apparently are," Robin said. "Or perhaps they're just unwilling to die for King Louis. On top of everything else, Bonaparte has announced the formation of eight units he's calling corps of observation."

Ned frowned. "I'd wager those corps can easily be converted to armies should he decide to do so."

"Convenient," Robin said, "since they'll be stationed along the borders."

The group exchanged grim looks.

Ned asked, "What else has happened while we were distracted?"

Robin shrugged. "The Allies formed a new coalition, the seventh. Meanwhile, Bonaparte has ordered all royalists out of Paris, requiring them to stay ninety miles away, and arrested some." He shook his head. "Despite growing dissatisfaction in France, he holds Paris securely. He has the bit between his teeth, and we'll soon have the devil to pay."

That anyone would welcome him still seemed inconceivable.

Turning to Dare, Robin asked, "Any word on the book you were seeking?"

"We've narrowed our possibilities, but we don't yet know where it is."

Robin shook his head "Of course. Keep looking."

"Aye, o' course." Dare pushed back his chair. "If that's all—?"

Robin thanked him, and he left the room.

"I may be able to help with that," Amelia said, "but I need to go outside." She hadn't seen her grandparents in more than a week. It was time to face whatever made them so uneasy. She couldn't confront them from within the house's wards, though, and she hadn't wanted to reveal their existence in front of Dare, whom she scarcely knew.

Ned and Robin exchanged frowns. "You and Julian aren't wed yet," Ned said. "Wyndon won't give up, especially since he won that duel. The agents Julian set to watch him say he has watchers on the house."

"We can have our Gifted grooms observe from the room above the stables, though they can't see anyone glamoured to be invisible. Then if we ward the gardens," Robin began.

"No wards," Amelia told them. "I need to speak to my grandparents' ghosts, and they can't penetrate warding that isn't Mainwaring-raised."

"You're a Mainwaring," Augusta noted. "You could ward the area below the rear terrace, just outside the cellar, while some of these gentlemen stand guard."

Of course she could. "I'm a bit out of practice." Admitting it was embarrassing, but she should be candid with her friends. "I never thought to ward my uncle's house because there didn't seem to be any danger then."

"I'll help you," Sophie offered. "Ned and Robin can stand guard."

Thus inconveniencing them more. But there was no help for it. They were right. Wyndon seemed determined to control her and her rare Gift. She shouldn't take unnecessary risks.

"There's no time like the present," Amelia said.

"I'll ask Augusta for the supplies," Sophie offered.

The rest of the group trooped down the stairs to the cellar and out its rear door. The area was visible from the mews and the rear gate, but not from above because of the terrace.

Robin asked, "How do you want to do this?"

"Cast a circle, I suppose." That would at least protect them from magical attack and from scrying, though not from ordinary eyesight. Amelia frowned at the flagstoned surface. "I wouldn't trust myself with anything more complicated."

The simplest ward to create was a structural one, infusing an existing wall with magic and feeding it into the floor and ceiling that way. Casting a ward from nothing required a little more work. Unlike with a structure, which could be warded against intruders yet allow the use of windows and doors, a ward circle couldn't be broken.

Sophie bustled out of the cellar with two small bags in her hands, one gray and one white. "I brought salt and charcoal, as I wasn't sure which you would want." She hesitated. "Julian overheard me asking for these things. He's putting up rather a fuss about coming down."

"He isn't supposed to be out of bed." Robin scowled. "Yesterday, Ellen said at least three or four days more of rest."

He also couldn't talk normally yet, which meant his brain had more healing to do. No one wanted to say that, though. Merely thinking about it was unnerving enough.

"Augusta will manage him," Ned stated. "Let's get on with this and have it done. Julian can be damn—dashed persistent."

"I'll use salt." Amelia reached for the white bag.

Robin asked, "Do you want us in the circle or outside it?"

"You're safer inside it, are you not? If we're taking precautions to protect me, we should also protect the rest of you." An odd feeling skittered over her back, and she frowned at the mews behind the house. "Do any of you feel as though we're being watched?"

"I do." Ned also stared at the mews.

That probably meant there were invisible watchers. Regardless, this was necessary.

Amelia opened to her Gift, but it showed her nothing. Yet the unease remained. "Yes," she said, pouring salt, "let us have this done and go inside."

She had to ration the salt to make a large enough circle for them all. "All right," she said. "Everyone step inside."

When they complied, she bent and held one hand parallel to the ground above the salt circle. Faint argent streamed down from her palm and made the circle glow. "Salt of life, pure as snow, take my power for walls that glow. Build them high, build them hard, protect us all within this ward."

To her friends, she said, "Please don't watch me. It makes me nervous."

They pointedly turned their backs. That would do.

Amelia drew Miranda's dagger from under her skirts and fed a tiny trickle of magic into it. Facing the lawn, she softly called, "Grandmother. Grandfather. Please come talk to me. I need your help."

She called three times before Miranda shimmered into view outside the ward.

"What do you need, my dear?"

"I need to know why you've been avoiding me."

"You've set us rather a list of tasks. We're dealing with those."

"I'm grateful. But you're also avoiding me."

Her grandmother hesitated. Finally, she said, "Not that so much as we're evading your questions. There are some we simply cannot answer."

"I suspect you mean 'will not,' but that's neither here nor there. Scots rebels and their French allies have a grimoire that talks about moving from one place to another by traveling through the land of the dead."

That slight tightening around her grandmother's blue eyes and the tension in her face she quickly masked confirmed Amelia's suspicions. "So it is possible to come there."

"Even if that were true, it doesn't mean you should do so."

"Well, someone's planning to. We need to know where that book is so we can steal it. Our friends are looking, but we could use help." Julian apparently had decreed Dare was to have first chance to crush this plot. If he failed, though, the Merlin Club would act. That meant they needed information.

Miranda frowned. "Did you not hear me? That's dangerous knowledge. I won't help you gain it."

"Would you rather let England's enemies control it?"

Miranda's lips tightened.

Amelia said, "Grandmother, someone has that book and will master the methods in it. None of us here plans to go prancing through that realm as though it were Almack's. But if the French and the rebel Scots learn how to do that, they can wreak much worse harm, across greater distances and faster, to help Napoleon's armies. I assume you've seen what two decades of war did to us in our island—and to the people on the Continent."

Robin said, "Bonaparte's brother-in-law Joachim Murat is King of Naples. On March fifteenth, he declared war on Austria. That conflict continues."

Amelia shot a startled glance over her shoulder. He still faced away. "Can you hear her?"

"No," he replied. "But I hear you and have pertinent information to add. Bonaparte is rebuilding his army. This is not a time for being overly nice."

Annoyance flickered over Miranda's face. "Your friend is rather a pushy young man."

"He has the virtue of being correct."

"Based on what he knows. One should never think one sees the entire canvas. Still, Richard and I will discuss this."

Before Amelia could reply, Miranda vanished. Amelia turned to Robin. "You didn't say anything about Murat earlier."

"It didn't affect our situation," he replied.

Amelia bent and extended her hand over the salt circle. She drew the power back into herself, and the salt once again became salt. Her friends helped her gather it into the bag.

"We can go in now." Though being outside was a pleasant change, she wanted to see how Julian fared.

As they walked into the gloomy cellar, she asked Robin, "What could possibly make so many French soldiers turn to Napoleon? They must've lost much of a generation in all those years of war."

"The men of the army were treated as heroes under Bonaparte. They idolized him, even after the Russian fiasco. The Bourbons gutted the officer corps, refused to pay pensions, and denied medals. They've wiped their boots on the army. On top of that, Bonaparte has always possessed the knack of touching people's hearts. Inspiring them. If I didn't know such a thing to be impossible, I would say he has bewitched them all."

Could he have? "If walking the land of the dead is possible, why isn't bewitching an army?"

"Anything is supposedly possible," he returned, "though Julian would know better than—that is, I'm sure there's information in the library on such things."

They all knew what he hadn't said, though. Until Julian's brain healed, they wouldn't learn how much of his vast store of knowledge he retained.

Robin continued, "As far as I'm aware, however, such widespread bewitchment has never been achieved. Joan of Arc, who inspired men to follow her, was burned as a witch and a heretic. Now, however, even the most patriotic Englishman knows those charges were fabricated to justify her death."

Yet men had followed her, a woman, in an age when women were even more restricted than now. A vision flashed over Amelia's sight. A sturdy figure in armor and a cloth-of-gold surcoat stood on the battlements of a castle and addressed an attentive army. The French fleur-de-lys banner flapped above the ramparts. This was the figure Amelia had Seen before, but she'd assumed it was a man. Now she Saw it after Robin mentioned Joan of Arc.

Was this a woman, perhaps Joan? If so, that could explain the odd bulge of the figure's upper chest.

Inside the parlor door, Amelia paused, trying to make the vision clearer. Instead of knights and foot soldiers, however, the familiar, wispy fog swirled, then parted to show a wooden chest, perhaps three feet wide and four long, with a high, rounded top. It sat on a plank floor under a mullioned window.

Odd. Why this, and why now? She concentrated on the wooden chest, on where it had been. Time rolled into the past, to an unfamiliar room—plaster over stone walls, suits of armor and pieces of it lying about in the candlelit darkness. Two men packed one particular set into the chest. The breastplate was smaller than the rest of the ones on the wall racks, with an odd curve to the chest. As though for a woman?

Someone carried the chest away, and the vision ended.

She came back to herself to find her friends staring at her.

"Are you well?" Sophie asked. "Was it a vision?"

Amelia nodded. Perhaps they would think she was mad, but she had to know. In her bones, this felt important. She would see if she could extend the vision shortly.

"Do any of you know what became of Joan of Arc's armor?"

CHAPTER 16

The group returned to the library, and Amelia told them what she'd Seen. Robin frowned across the wide table at her. "So you believe the armor in your vision was Joan's."

"I'm fairly certain. As we talked about Napoleon bewitching his army, I had a vision of a young woman in armor. I've seen that same figure but didn't think it might be a woman. Then I saw someone taking that armor. Because they were moving stealthily and at night, I think they may have stolen it. Joan drew men to her in defiance of all the customs of the age. What if that's a form of magic? And the armor absorbed it?"

They all exchanged doubtful looks.

"I realize that sounds far-fetched," she admitted. "But that doesn't mean it's wrong. We should at least explore the possibilities."

"Agreed." Ned nodded. "So that means researching unusual forms of magic and the history of Joan herself? If we could learn who had the armor before you saw it removed, that might confirm it as hers—depending on who came away from France with it."

"There can't be many sets made to accommodate a woman's breasts," Sophie noted. "I'd say that raises the odds."

"We should ask Julian what he knows," Amelia said. "Or where we should look. It's his library, after all."

"Yes," Robin replied, "and if he doesn't remember, it will distress him. We should find what we can, and we should also check with those he has watching Wyndon. If we don't turn up anything about the armor, we can speak to him about it in a few days, when he's better. He's recovering fairly quickly."

But would he recover enough? That was the question worrying them all.

Amelia rose. "I need something to focus my Gift so I can try to summon a vision. I can control them better when they don't leap at me from nowhere. Is there a book about Joan here anywhere?" A book had given her awareness of Lady Eleanor. Why couldn't it work with Joan?

Someone knocked at the door. James stepped into the room. "Lady Buckton, my lord wishes to see you."

"I'll come at once." Amelia hurried toward the door.

"We'll see what we can find that might help," Sophie called after her.

Amelia walked down the corridor with James. He stopped at his accustomed post several feet from Julian's door. She tapped on the oak panel.

"Come in," Augusta called.

When Amelia entered, Julian's aunt rose from the sofa by the window. No chair sat by the bed today, and a battered copy of *The Canterbury Tales* lay on the coverlet near Julian's hand. Beside it sat the slate, chalk, and rag.

Because the sofa seemed so far away, Amelia stood by the bed. "You wanted to see me, Julian?"

He nodded. Frowning, he hesitated, and finally managed, "James."

"I'll call him." Amelia stuck her head out and beckoned to the footman.

When the man followed her back inside, he greeted Julian with a smile. This and James's emotional expression of support were reminders the staff cared deeply about Julian, and not only because their livelihoods depended on him. They cared for the man.

"James." Julian nodded, and the footman's chest puffed.

Julian pointed at the chair by the hearth and then to its former spot by the bed. James moved it as directed. "Will that be all, Julian?"

"Th—think—*thank*—you."

The man hurried from the room, his eyes glistening suspiciously.

Julian looked at her. "Amer—Amanda—America." His lips tightened.

Heart pounding, she waited.

"Amelia," he ground out, delighting her. "Please." He nodded at the chair.

Amelia seated herself. "I realize you may be weary of people asking you, but how do you feel?"

He shrugged. "Bet—butter—bench." He paused, scowling, and added, "Better."

"I'm so glad. Why did you wish to see me?"

"Wat—Watchers. Wyndon."

"I know. Your agents told us. We set guards, and I cast a warded circle."

Nodding, he grabbed the slate. Amelia waited while he wrote.

When he turned it to her, she frowned. "I mustn't go outside? Whyever not?"

He mimed firing a gun with his right hand. "Wards...not...bullets."

"A ward won't stop a bullet?" she tried. At his hard nod, she added, "You think he would have me shot?"

"If he can't—if you—"

"If he can't use me, no one will?"

"Yes."

The fierce expression on his face was some comfort. Julian would help her in any way he could.

"Stay...indoors," he said.

"I can use my Gift, or try to, to learn whether anyone's watching us, but I can't talk to the ghosts indoors." She told him of her discussion with Miranda. "I don't know what they'll do, Julian. I did my best to persuade her."

"Dare's...do...tending it."

"Yes, I know." Robin's warning about frustrating Julian had been logical. With Napoleon making gains every day, however, they had no time to waste.

Cautiously, she said, "I had an odd vision. Do you want to hear about it?"

⁓

Of course he did. He was going out of his bloody mind, what there was of it, lying here. At night, despite Ellen's assurances, he worried that he would never regain the mental sharpness and memory he'd had before. This would be a good test, even though it might produce dismaying results.

Every time Amelia sat with him, he basked in her concern and savored her presence, but what if he never recovered his full abilities? He wanted to protect her. How could he do that if he couldn't analyze situations?

"I had another vision of that armored figure near a French flag today. Immediately before that, Robin mentioned Joan of Arc. If the figure is Joan, or any woman, that would explain the bulge over the chest in my first vision. But if it is a woman, who could it be other than Joan?"

When he nodded, Amelia continued. "Then I Saw what I think may have been her armor. I'm almost certain it was stolen from someone, from a stately house. I need to See it again."

"Why?"

"Because it occurs to me that the power to sway men's minds, to draw their allegiance, as Joan did, might be a magical Gift. If it is, Napoleon must have some measure of it, wouldn't you think?"

Clever. Very clever. And logical. He grabbed the slate. *Armor could absorb power.* When she frowned, he erased that. *Old grimoire said.*

Amelia's brows rose. "So if Joan had that ability, if she used it constantly while wearing her armor, the armor could become infused with it?"

He squeezed cramped letters into the slate. *As staff absorbs magic if used long time by one wizard.* When Amelia nodded that she'd read it, he said, "Rare but...possible."

That would explain Bonaparte's astounding success in winning over soldiers sent to capture him.

He grinned at Amelia, who smiled back at him.

"You don't think I've run mad, then?" she asked.

"No."

"We don't know where else to look or whether it even matters who had it before the theft. We haven't been able to track that down."

"John...Bedford. Lanky." Scowling, he grabbed the slate and wrote, *John of Bedford, D. Lancaster, her gaoler. May have taken armor.* Simply knowing that obscure fact must be a good sign.

He showed the slate to Amelia. When she'd read it, he wiped it with the rag and added, *Relative may've inherited. Debrett's?*

"You have a copy?"

He nodded, and she added, "I didn't see a coat of arms or anything else identifying the owner, and continuing to look felt intrusive. Besides, it's possible whoever had the armor is so many generations from John of Lancaster as to not be a peer anymore."

That was possible. The grandson of a duke's younger son might or might not have a title. His younger children might not have a lesser title to inherit.

"I like...way...way you...think," he said.

They smiled at each other, and in that moment, he wanted her more than he ever had. Each day, she proved how different she was from Charlotte. His first wife would not have sat and read to him or thought to see if he could play chess or simply sat with him while he slept. Amelia was the sort who stuck. She'd tended Buckton unceasingly in his last illness.

But she'd loved Buckton. She didn't love Julian.

The knowledge stung, but he pushed it away. He didn't want her to love him. To want something he couldn't give in return. She was loyal. That counted for a great deal.

A knock on the door heralded James, who stood aside for Baker. The young valet carried a tray with a plate of chicken, potatoes, and stewed apples along with a chunk of buttered bread. It smelled divine.

As James closed the door, Julian pushed himself up in the bed. "That's...food, Wyatt."

"Yes, Julian." The young man smiled at him. "Mrs. Drake says you must eat only what you want, not force yourself. I've also brought small beer instead of barley water. And you should sit up for a time, perhaps whilst you eat?"

Overwhelmed by this good news, Julian nodded.

"Right, then. I'll just set things up for you."

"No...more..." Unable to summon the word, he made a circular motion with his hand.

"No more gruel," Baker confirmed, setting the tray on the desk. He looked almost as happy about that as Julian felt.

"You're in good hands," Amelia said. "I'll share your suggestions with everyone."

"Later?" he asked.

"Yes, I'll tell you what we learn afterward." With a smile that touched his heart, she said, "Enjoy your meal."

Baker bustled around the room, placing a small table in front of the sofa and setting out the food. Julian watched him but paid scant attention. He wanted Amelia for his own, yes, but he didn't want her to marry him out of pity or gratitude.

Of course, she might decide not to marry him at all.

Baker fetched his favorite blue banyan, or embroidered robe, from the dressing room. With the valet hovering, Julian walked carefully to the sofa and sat.

So far, so good. As long as Amelia stayed here, she was safe. He could worry about her choice later. There were more pressing problems on the horizon, ones far more important than his recovery.

It was time he picked up the reins at the Merlin Club again.

I n his house near Hampstead, Silas considered his agent's report. "Did you see what happened inside this circle after she cast it?"

Stout, rough-hewn Gil Shockley was observant and Gifted. Aysgarth, though, was wily.

"Yes, m'lord. She talked, but I didn't see no one talk to her. The others was inside it, as I said, but she weren't facing them. She'd talk a bit, wait a bit, and talk some more."

As though talking to a ghost. That art was supposedly lost. How many other unusual skills did the bitch possess?

"So you saw Lady Buckton and several others, but not Lord Aysgarth."

Shockley nodded. "I chatted up one o' the kitchen maids. His lordship was eating gruel, not talking right, yesterday. Today, he's some better."

Amelia had not posed a problem thus far, but one never knew what a seer might See. Once properly trained, she would've made a useful countess. Out of his control, however, she was a liability they could not risk.

He looked up at Shockley. "Take Wilson with you and watch that house. I want to know anything you can learn about Aysgarth. If you've an opportunity to snatch Lady Buckton, take it. If you cannot capture her, kill her. By whatever means you find convenient."

"Aye, milord." Shockley didn't flinch. Hardened from an early age, he would do whatever served his employer's needs with no hesitation.

Shockley departed. Staring into the fire, Silas shook his head. Executing a woman with such prodigious Gifts was a sad waste. Better that, however, than having her expose his plans. For the welfare of all Britain's Gifted, one woman's life was a negligible price.

Julian had gone to the club over Ellen's objections. He'd said he wouldn't stay long. Day had turned to evening, though, and he and Dare, who'd accompanied him, still had not returned home. He had said not to hold dinner for them, a sure sign he meant to be gone longer than he'd told Ellen he would be. She had pronounced him able to finish recovering without her, so she'd returned home.

Amelia walked into the corridor to listen again. Still no sound from the front door. She could only hope he had the sense to rest for a while at the club.

She paced back to the chair by the hearth. Grandfather had found the Scots and French conspirators and their mysterious book, and Robin had dispatched a messenger to Julian at the club. Perhaps he was already planning what to do about that book. Or was he leaving that to Dare? He hadn't told the Scotsman about her ghostly grandparents feeding them information.

Grandfather had not been pleased at the prospect of Julian having the book, but he had agreed to look for Joan's mysterious armor. At least that didn't seem to nettle him.

If he and Miranda didn't trust her not to do foolish things by now, when would they?

Perhaps it was as well Julian wasn't here. His absence saved her from hovering about his chamber, trying to see enough signs of recovery to ease her guilt.

With all that had happened of late, she'd avoided thinking about his proposal. He'd asked her whether she was still in love with Crispin. She didn't think she was, but there was one way to be certain.

Amelia turned the chair to face the hearth and settled herself in it. This would be painful. It was necessary, though.

Casting her power at the fire, she summoned the day she and Crispin met. He turned to face her in a tent at a spring breakfast, and their hostess, Lady Marlowe, introduced him. At the sight of his smiling, healthy face, her heart kicked hard. He'd been a handsome man but not breathtaking, tall but not overly so, and bookish. He'd also had a wry sense of humor and a kind heart. All perfect for her.

They'd liked each other at once. Soon enough, with speed that startled them both, liking became much more.

Amelia watched the parade of images in the fire. The happiness in her face and his brought tears to her eyes. They'd had no idea their time together would end so soon and so horribly.

By his last day, his face was gaunt and weary. He was ready to pass on. They both knew it. Had made such peace as they could with it.

With tears rolling slowly down her face, she saw herself climb into the bed beside him and nestle against him. His shoulder had been so bony, not the muscular pillow she'd rested her head against so often.

She didn't want to watch this part. Yet looking away from it seemed cowardly. Disrespectful.

The image of Crispin took its last breath, and she let it fade. She fetched a handkerchief of fine cotton from the dressing room and wiped her face. Yet the tears kept rolling, the first she'd shed in nearly a year.

Staring into the fire, she knew her heart beyond doubt. It was time to give Julian his answer.

CHAPTER 17

Julian lounged on the sofa in his bedchamber with one leg up on the seat. He'd had a much-needed bath and a shave before he left home. Wearing loose trousers and his favorite banyan, heavy blue satin embroidered in gold, he was more comfortable, felt more himself, than he had since the duel.

Yet he couldn't keep his attention on his book. Not even his favorite Chaucer, "The Reeve's Tale."

With a sigh, he shut the book and set it on the end table. He might as well pay attention to the problem. How could he keep Amelia safe?

If Wyndon was true to his family history, he would destroy her rather than let her Gift serve anyone else. Julian had watchers on the watchers, with Dare, Wat, and Robin ready to confront them if need be, but the Merlin Club agents were no more impervious to knives and bullets than Amelia was.

Someone tapped on his door. He sat up and called, "Come in."

Amelia stuck her head into the room. His pulse kicked before he noticed her hesitant expression.

"Is something wrong?" he asked, rising to his feet.

"No. Oh, no, it's only that I thought you might have tired yourself out today. I didn't want to disturb you."

"Ellen would be pleased to know I rested for a bit in one of the bedchambers at the club."

Yet Amelia still looked uneasy. Had she come to refuse him?

Even though he'd begun to see his feelings for her as a potential powder keg, he wanted to marry her. Not only as a matter of logic and convenience but because doing so felt right.

"Please sit," he invited.

With a nod, she perched on the sofa near him.

"I don't bite, you know," he said gently.

That earned him a brief smile. "I know you don't."

Turning to him, she stared into his face. Unfortunately, he couldn't read hers.

"When you proposed to me, you asked me whether I was still in love with Crispin. You probably remember you said I need not answer you unless I were inclined to make our sham betrothal a true one."

"I do recall that."

The firelight picked out lines of strain in her face, and her eyes were slightly puffy, as though she'd been weeping. What did that portend?

"Before you answer me, however," he added, "I must tell you I've no wish to be married out of gratitude." Or out of guilt. Thank God, pity no longer came into the matter.

"I wouldn't marry for that. Without more, gratitude is a poor basis for any sort of relationship. I have examined my feelings today, Julian."

He braced himself as she said, "I haven't thought much about such things in recent months. With Papa and Adam dying, then my efforts to help my cousin settle into being the new lord at Hawkstowe, and then coming here, I've had other things claiming my attention. So I gave this evening to Crispin."

"Forgive me, but you don't look as though the doing gave you much joy."

"It gave me peace. As he would've wanted." She took a deep breath. "I've been watching us in the fire—our courtship, our marriage—and remembering."

She glanced at the carpet and then at Julian. "We loved each other very much."

The words stabbed him in the heart. So be it then. He schooled his face to impassivity lest he make this harder for her in any way.

Amelia looked directly into his eyes. "I will always love him, but what I felt tonight, watching those memories pass through the fire, was not what I felt when I lived those moments. I can honestly tell you I am no longer in love with him. Being in love means sharing and hoping and planning, and those days ended for Crispin and me nearly three years ago."

Hope hummed in his veins. "Are you accepting my proposal?"

"If you still want me, yes."

His happiness burst into a wide grin, and Amelia smiled at him.

"I do want you," he assured her. "Very much." He lifted her hand to his lips and kissed it.

Her fingers tightened on his. "So there we are." She sounded slightly breathless, and her amazement filtered into her eyes. "It seems we're betrothed."

"We definitely are." Leaning forward, he kissed her.

Amelia put her arms around his neck. He drew her close and deepened the kiss. She welcomed him, stroking his tongue with her own and sliding her fingers into his hair.

～

Amelia leaned into Julian's kiss. Her hands roamed his broad shoulders, and his stroked her back. With a muffled, wordless sound, he tugged her into his lap. Leaning into his solid chest, she gave herself over to kissing him.

Julian tugged his mouth free and pressed kisses along the line of her jaw and down her neck. He cupped her breast through her cambric frock. A rush of hot pleasure blinded her. Amelia arched into his hand and moaned.

Then his mouth captured hers again. Her hand slipped into the open neck of his shirt, feeling warm, smooth skin and soft, curling hair.

Julian groaned. He broke the kiss and drew her against him, tucking her head into the hollow between his neck and shoulder. Amelia bit back a moan of protest.

"I'm being chivalrous," he announced.

He had a lovely neck, solid but not bullish. When she trailed her fingertips over it, the skin was warm over corded muscles.

"Amelia, sweetheart—"

Wondering at her own daring, she looked up at him. "Do you want to be chivalrous?"

He smiled. "No, but are you certain? Most of the household is abed, but we still could meet someone in the corridor when you return to your chamber."

"It doesn't matter. We're to be married. We'll be discreet, and your staff adore you."

Julian's expression softened. "Then here's to the future." He shifted her off his lap and rose. Although she didn't need his offered hand, she accepted it just to touch him. She'd forgotten how lovely it was to touch and be touched.

Their kiss this time was gentle, tender, and possessive. Kissing and caressing each other, they made their way to the bed. He shrugged out of his banyan and let it fall. Amelia tugged his shirt out of his trousers and over his head. As he drew her close, she pressed kisses over the muscular planes of his chest. Julian groaned, his hand in her hair holding her but not controlling.

His muscles tensed and relaxed under her hands and mouth. When she licked his flat nipple, he made a choked sound. Tugging her head up, he kissed her again.

"Let me see to your clothes," he said with his mouth against hers.

Heart beating fast, eager to go on with this, Amelia presented her back to him. Julian made short work of the buttons on her frock and the lacing of her short stays. Both garments landed on the floor beside his banyan, and she didn't care.

He slid his arms around her waist from behind and nibbled the side of her neck. Pleasure shot through her, and she moaned. One of his hands slipped up to her breast, rubbing the nipple through her thin chemise. Amelia whimpered, again arching in his hold, desperate for more.

His mouth covered her ear. "You smell exquisite," he murmured, and his breath teased the sensitive channel. His other hand slid down between her legs, rubbing her through the slit in her drawers. The hard bulge at his groin pressed against her buttocks. Driven by craving, she wriggled.

"I love that you're so wet for me," he groaned.

"I want you," she gasped.

Julian turned her in his hold and took her mouth, this time with driving, demanding passion. Then he tugged her chemise off. Amelia untied her drawers and pushed them down.

He dropped to one knee and yanked them the rest of the way. Then his hands cupped her buttocks, pulling her to him, and he licked her belly. The sight of him kneeling, the feel of his hands and his tongue, made her breathing erratic. Her hands in his thick, soft hair caressed him as he pressed kisses and small nips over her belly. He bent lower and kissed her mound.

A wave of heat and need rolled through her. Amelia let out a choked cry. He kissed and licked through the hair, his hands kneading her buttocks, until she was nearly weeping with desire.

As though he sensed her craving, he stood to kiss her mouth again. Amelia worked the buttons on the fall of his trousers while his hands caressed her breasts and their tongues slid together.

The trousers dropped, and she knelt to push them down. When she wrapped her fingers around his hot, hard erection, he choked, "Wait."

He picked her up and laid her on the high bed. Joining her, he tugged her over him. They kissed and touched and explored each other before he rolled so he was on top. When his soft, wet mouth closed over her aching nipple, Amelia cried out. Her thighs parted, and Julian settled between them. He kissed and sucked and stroked until she was mindless with wanting.

When he rose above her, she lifted her hips to receive him. He slid into her, filling her, and hot pleasure surged through her.

"All well?" he ground out.

"Yes. Yes." Tugging on his hard buttocks, she bucked under him.

With a groan, he turned his face into her neck. He withdrew, thrust again, and withdrew. With each thrust, the pleasure inside her tightened, pushing her higher, deepening her craving.

Amelia wrapped her legs around his hips and rocked with him, holding onto his solid shoulders.

The pleasure grew so strong that it blinded her. Whimpering, she met his pounding thrusts. Almost—

Julian thrust hard, and the tension burst, flooding her. Amelia cried his name. Vaguely, consumed by the crashing wave of pleasure, she felt him shudder. He groaned her name into her ear.

They lay together, warm and sweaty, as their heart rates settled. Eventually, Julian raised his head. His gaze searched her face. What he saw there must've reassured him, for he smiled. "Am I heavy?"

"In a nice way."

He propped his torso up on his elbows, taking some of the weight, and kissed her again. With a sigh, he pressed his face against her neck. They stayed together that way until his body slid out of hers. Then he rolled onto his back. Amelia cuddled against his side.

Only now did she realize how much she had missed this intimacy, this pleasure of lying naked and sated with a lover she trusted. Now she had years of it to look forward to. *Please, years. Don't take him from me too.*

She took a deep breath. If she let fear creep in, it could paralyze them. Better to think of the future they would build together. To trust that it would come. But that was so much more difficult than it once had been.

Julian pressed a kiss against her hairline, and she slid her arm farther across his chest.

They dozed a little. When Amelia opened her eyes, the hearth fire had burned low.

"I should return to my chamber," she murmured.

"Not yet." His hold tightened. "I like holding you."

"I like it too." She brushed a tender kiss over his shoulder.

Julian groaned. "More of that, and I won't want you to stop. I had best walk you back. Baker is the soul of discretion, but I don't think you would like for him to come in and see us."

"Baker! Oh, my word! Does he come in to help you prepare for bed?"

"If you're asking whether he already saw us, the answer's no. He doesn't come in unless he's summoned, as a rule, and if he heard voices he would back away and pretend he heard nothing."

Voices. That was one word for it.

Oh, well, what was done was done. Amelia pushed up on her elbow to look down at Julian. "You needn't walk me back. It's only a few doors down the corridor."

"Beside the point." He rolled off the bed. "Wait here."

At least she had a superb view of his sculpted backside as he walked into his dressing room. He emerged a few minutes later shrugging into a dark blue dressing gown.

Amelia sat up as he came around the bed. Julian scooped up his discarded banyan and held it ready for her. "This will be faster than dressing you again."

"That's certainly true." She slid her arms into the sleeves. He wrapped the heavy garment around her and tied the belt from behind. Pressing his face to her hair, he inhaled deeply.

"One more thing," he said.

"You've changed your mind about stopping now?" she teased.

When she faced him, though, his expression was serious in the dim light.

"Amelia, sweetheart, how do you feel about marrying by license?"

~

The next morning, Amelia adopted a casual air while she dressed. Yet she could scarcely believe Mary didn't notice her excitement. She and Julian would announce their betrothal at breakfast. Avoiding the entertainment that kept most of the *ton* up until nearly dawn allowed everyone here to start the day early, and he had resolved to go down for the meal.

Afterward, matters would move swiftly. A license would allow them to marry without delay instead of waiting for the banns to be called. They meant to wed as soon as possible, and they had much to do before then.

Someone tapped on her door, and she hurried to open it. Julian smiled at her.

"Good morning," he said, and he kissed her quickly. Despite his cheerful expression, his eyes searched hers. "Are you ready for this?"

"Entirely. Before we go down, though, there's something I want you to know." Looking into his eyes, she said, "I recall what you said about not trusting your late wife. Whatever she did or didn't do, my dear one, I keep my word. That includes marriage vows."

His expression softened. He kissed her gently and held her close. "Thank you, Amelia."

"I wanted to be sure you knew."

They walked down the corridor toward the stairs. "I've been thinking," she said, "about our other problem, the possibility Wyndon wants to kidnap me or—or worse."

"He can't reach you here."

"I can't stay in this house forever." She flicked him a sidelong glance. "Not long after Crispin and I were married, there was a problem with highwaymen outside Leyburn. He devised a scheme to lay a trap for them. Perhaps we should do that now."

"With you as bait? Out of the question."

They started down the stairs. "We must do something," she said. "Why allow him to retain all the initiative?"

"'We' will not include you. Hear me on this, my lady—"

"If you're about to put your foot down, Lord Aysgarth, you had best reconsider."

He narrowed his eyes at her, and she sighed. "I won't take any foolish risks, but I will be part of planning anything to do with this because it concerns me so directly. That's only fair."

"I suppose so," he conceded.

They walked into the breakfast room, a bright, sunny space with large windows, to find hot food on the buffet, their friends milling about, and a footman waiting by the buffet in case anyone needed anything.

The next few minutes passed in a flurry of exchanging morning greetings, choosing food, and finding seats. Julian maneuvered everyone so Amelia had the seat to the left of his usual one on the end. When everyone was served, Julian dismissed the footman, who was not Gifted.

He flicked her a glance so full of mischief that she had to press her lips around her fork to keep from laughing. A few minutes later, he said, "We've a busy day ahead, so we had best plan it. I need the assistance of the Merlin Club." All heads turned to him. "The club members are sworn to Britain. I need ones who're also personally loyal to me."

Robin said, "You're planning to do something about Wyndon. I'll see to gathering our allies. Where do you want to meet, and when?"

"At the club, two o'clock this afternoon. Thank you, Robin."

"My pleasure." Glancing at Ned and Sophie, Robin added, "I think there'll be quite a few ready to help with that project."

"Good. We cannot allow Wyndon's threat to shadow Amelia indefinitely, and we must do something about his French ties."

"I should hope so," Augusta said. "The man is a villain and a traitor. If the Conclave Council won't see it, they cannot blame us for acting on our own."

"They will, though," Robin put in. "We all know it. So we must lay our groundwork with care. What are we doing this morning, Julian? Library research?"

Julian laid down his fork. "I hoped one of you would accompany me on an errand. I must go to Doctors' Commons to see about a marriage license."

Their friends needed a moment to absorb what he'd said. He grinned at Amelia, whose smile was so wide that the corners of her mouth ached.

Sophie squealed, leaped out of her chair, and rushed to hug Amelia and Julian. "I knew you were both too clever not to appreciate each other!"

Ned and Robin rose to shake Julian's hand, clap him on the back, and kiss Amelia's cheek.

Augusta, though, stared down the table at them. Despite her smile, tears glazed her eyes. "Nothing you could have done," she announced, "would have pleased me more. When do you plan to marry? Do tell me you'll have it done at St. George's and not in some mean little way."

"We must settle the problem of Wyndon's watchers first. We cannot discount the possibility they've orders to kidnap Amelia if they can, and perhaps to do other mischief."

He didn't mention that they might try to kill her. He was protecting his aunt, but he didn't try to downplay matters with his future wife. That boded well.

Augusta said, "She must have a lovely gown for the ceremony, and surely a small wedding breakfast is in order. I suppose there's no time for a trousseau. I know it's the second time for you both, but that doesn't signify." Smiling at Amelia, she added, "My dear, Julian's mother will be delighted but sorry to miss the occasion. I'm sure your mother will be pleased. Have you told her?"

Amelia shook her head. "We only decided last night. She believes us officially betrothed already, but of course, since that was a sham, we hadn't set a date." Glancing around the table, she said, "I want her to hear it from me, directly and not by letter. How shall I do that?"

Julian raised an eyebrow at her. "How are you with glamours?"

"Fairly adept, as it happens. Grandmother Miranda began teaching me how to use them when I was very small. I haven't had much occasion to practice, however."

"You do now. I think it's best your mother not come here. Wyndon wouldn't be above using her to get to you, but I suspect she's safe enough as long as she's with her family. While moving against her would get your attention, it would also draw the Council's. It's a low-probability risk, but we cannot discount it entirely."

"Then I need to go to her as soon as we can manage it."

Julian reached over to squeeze her hand. "The outriders can go with you and glamour themselves to be invisible. You can glamour yourself as your maid."

Keeping outriders on one's staff had fallen out of vogue, but Julian sometimes wanted the eight Gifted men as reinforcements on long and dangerous journeys.

His aunt frowned down the table. "If I were trying to learn what went on in a house, I would befriend someone young and trusting on the staff. People feel safe in their homes. I doubt any of our people would discuss anything they thought could be used against you—the layout of the house and the locations of valuables, for example—but few London servants can resist gossiping about the household's doings to some degree."

"You'll see to that?" he asked.

"I'll talk to Mrs. Beadon and to Harris. The staff are more likely to confide in the housekeeper and the butler, less likely to be intimidated by them than by any of us. I'll begin that this morning."

"Right, then. You see to that, Ned and I will tend to matters at Doctors' Commons, and Robin will organize this afternoon's Merlin Club gathering."

After obtaining the license, he had another errand to run. There was no need to share that with everyone, but Amelia had written a letter inviting her in-laws, the Earl and Countess of Bainbridge, to the wedding and asking the earl to negotiate the marriage settlements.

"We'll need someone to replace Dare," Robin pointed out, "as he's leaving to go after that book. I'll find someone."

"What shall Sophie and I do?" Amelia asked. "Everyone else is having all the fun."

Julian replied, "If it suits you, perhaps the two of you might devise some ways we can decoy and perhaps trap Wyndon's henchmen."

What a superb idea. Sophie gave her an approving nod, and Amelia smiled at Julian.

"I cannot wait to begin." That he would assign her a strategic task said good things about his trust in her ability.

"I thought so." His voice was wry, but his eyes were warm with affection. He squeezed her hand again before returning to his breakfast.

Amelia savored her meal. After all these days of worry and research and outright fear, the prospect of taking action held tremendous appeal. First, however, she had to inform her mother of an impending wedding.

Later that morning, escorted by half of Julian's eight Gifted outriders, Amelia returned to her aunt and uncle's house. The escort cloaked themselves in invisibility glamour before leaving home. On arrival at her aunt and uncle's house, they positioned themselves in front of it. She held the glamour that made her appear to be Mary, her maid, until she was safely indoors.

Mama sat in her parlor, reading. Amelia's stomach fluttered with nerves. Despite her Gift, she had no hint of what her mother would say.

She tapped on the door. Her mother looked up. Her eyes widened with surprise, and time hung suspended.

Then Mama smiled and rushed to the door, her arms held wide. "My dear girl, you've come back!"

Amelia's eyes stung with tears of relief as she embraced her mother. If only the rest of this would go as well.

Mama rang for tea, gave orders she was out to callers, and sat down with Amelia by the fire. She studied her daughter's face and slowly said, "You haven't returned, have you? Is Aysgarth—has something happened to him?"

Augusta had told Mama about the duel and Julian's injuries. Knowing that, Lady Hawkstowe had raised no objection to her daughter tending her supposed betrothed. She would surely not like this next bit, however.

"No, Mama, thank you. Julian is much recovered. But we wish to be married soon."

"Well, neither of you is getting any younger." Her mother hesitated. "You should know, however, that the duel has filtered into London gossip."

"With Wyndon's aid, no doubt."

"I cannot speak to that, but I wonder whether, considering all the gossip, you might delay your wedding."

"I take your point, Mama, but Julian may need to travel." Or not, but the possibility would be a sop to Mama's concerns. "I want to accompany him, and the best way for me to do that is as his wife."

"Oh, of course. How soon do you intend to marry?"

"The day after tomorrow, at St. George's. Julian's procuring a license." Mama's face fell, so Amelia quickly added, "I know that will feed the gossips as well, but it cannot be helped. We thought to wed quietly and wait until summer to have a larger celebration."

"The delay will allow the talk to die down. That's probably wise." Mama sighed. "I'm not blind to Lord Aysgarth's qualities, my dear, but his Gifts concern me. If you are set on this course, however, I will support you."

"Thank you, Mama." Amelia hugged her mother.

The conversation had turned out much better than she expected. If only the plan she and Sophie hatched would do the same.

～

While Amelia visited with her mother, Julian took a hackney to Bainbridge House, the home of her late husband's parents. The earl didn't keep him waiting. When the footman ushered Julian into the study, however, Bainbridge's expression was more assessing than welcoming. His lands and Julian's adjoined, and they'd always had an amiable relationship. The reserved welcome wasn't a good sign.

"I'm glad to see you looking well," the older man said. "Word is that you took quite a pounding."

"I've recovered, as you can see." Julian reached into his coat and extracted Amelia's letter. Offering the square of folded paper to his host, he said, "I imagine you've heard I'm betrothed to Lady Buckton."

"Betrothed in a damned havey-cavey way." Bainbridge frowned but accepted the letter. "I must say, the story making the rounds—we traced it back to the Earl of Wyndon—doesn't cast a favorable light on you or my daughter-in-law."

His frown deepened to a scowl. "Makes her sound no better than she should be but skates the edge of provocation that could give me or my sons cause to call him out."

Of course, because Wyndon was not only a vengeful bastard but clever. "Amelia's note will explain. As for calling him out, I don't recommend it. It would distress Amelia. Besides, he cheats."

Bainbridge raised an eyebrow at that but said nothing. He broke the seal and unfolded the single sheet of paper.

As the earl read, his expression relaxed. He pursed his lips for a long moment before he looked again at Julian. "You're aware she wants me to negotiate the settlements?"

"I am, but I doubt that will take long. She and I agree that she should retain her present control of her funds and property. I'll supply quarterly pin money and establish a fund for her use and that of any children after my death."

Bainbridge's gray eyes lit with humor. "Not going to give me a chance to play the hero, eh? Well, so be it. I'd rather she marry a reasonable man than a martinet. I assume you also know this letter invites our family to the wedding and asks me to give her away."

"Your family's presence and your escort would please us both very much."

"Then we'll call it done. I'll order some coffee while we do whatever hashing out we need. Then you'll join my lady and me for luncheon and tell us how all this came about."

~

Daffyd, Julian's Gifted coachman, slowed to a stop in front of the Merlin Club just before two o'clock. The four outriders, glamoured to be invisible, dismounted and took positions around the steps, their movements betrayed by sound. Julian felt like a right fool having so much security around him in London, but Wyndon's enmity was nothing to take lightly.

Waiting for the footman to lower the step, Julian looked to Dare on the opposite seat. "Do you need any of us to help you find the conspirators and obtain this book?"

The Scot gave him a crooked smile. "You'd do as well to say 'purloin,' as that's what we'll do. I thank you, but no. I know where they are, thanks to your information, and those of us who've a stake in the Highlands will see to it."

Thanks to Amelia's ghostly kin, actually, but their existence was a secret.

"As you wish," Julian replied. "I appreciate all you've done, Dare. Never doubt that, and you may call upon me at any time."

"I know. Helping your brave lassie was my pleasure. Wyndon's a vile snake, and she's a lady with few peers. You're a lucky man."

"If you conclude these conspirators are dangerous or if you need help, call on me. Should you run into trouble, remember, Aysgarth Hall is always open to you."

"I will, and I thank you for it." Dare's expression hardened. "If they're idealistic fools, that's one thing. If they're dangerous, I'll see to them."

Their gazes held. At last, Julian nodded. This was Scotland's business, so Dare should have first say in managing it. Having the Mainwaring ghosts on the lookout couldn't hurt, though.

The coach door opened. Julian and Dare climbed down. Before Julian touched the merlin plate, Josiah opened the door, smiling broadly. The porter said, "It's good to see you again so soon, Julian."

The footman, Harry, hurried to the door. Julian and Dare passed their outerwear to him.

Dare said, "I'm leaving in the morning, Josiah. Won't return for a while."

"We'll be sorry to see you go."

At that, Julian hid a smile. Josiah was always sorry to see anyone go, and he was always sincere about it.

Julian and Dare climbed the stairs to the library. At the door, Dare laid a hand on his arm. "Amelia charged me to be sure y'don't overdo."

"Not yet wed, and already she meddles." Julian sighed to hide his pleasure at her concern.

"We should all have such good fortune," Dare replied.

Julian only smiled. He opened the library door and walked in.

The men and women of the Merlin Club either rose from their chairs or straightened from their slouching positions along the bookshelves. They applauded, and Julian's throat went tight. He'd been here a couple of days ago, of course, but this was the first time he'd seen members other than staff.

Although he held up a hand, the applause continued. Only when Robin stepped forward with his hand raised did it die away.

Robin's eyes looked suspiciously bright. "Julian, on behalf of your friends among the membership, allow me to tell you we rejoice in your recovery and are delighted by your return."

They applauded again, with Robin joining in. Julian scanned the group. There must be upwards of thirty members here. They included all classes, from laborers to gentry to a few of his fellow peers. Even some servants who'd been excused from their duties to accompany their employers.

"We saved you a chair." A middle-aged woman, a modiste, at the far end of the table pointed to the empty seat at its head.

Feeling bloody conspicuous as they all watched, Julian made his way through the throng. It was slow going as his comrades clapped him on the back or patted his shoulder.

At last, he took his seat. Looking down the table, preparing to direct this meeting, felt like settling into a familiar, comfortable coat. Yet an odd pain pulsed near his heart. Until this moment, he hadn't realized how much he'd feared he would never again lead a meeting here.

Buying time, he cleared his throat. "Well. Let us begin." He laid out the situation. "I must spike Wyndon's guns," he concluded. "I cannot allow him to menace Amelia or to continue, as we believe he's doing, to aid the Bonapartists. We must dispose of his accomplices as soon as may be. Others are devising a plan for capturing them. Once we have them, however, what shall we do with them?"

"It'd be no loss to kill the scurvy knaves," someone standing far down on his right offered.

"It wouldn't be," Julian said, "but I cannot countenance killing prisoners in cold blood. Other solutions?"

"Lock them up somewhere, maybe Kent," a man suggested.

"Ship them to Jamaica," someone else offered.

Similar suggestions rolled through the meeting, all receiving some degree of approval. Julian met Robin's gaze. Robin shrugged. Relocating the men would merely transfer a menace elsewhere. Absent killing them, though, there was no other solution.

They would, however, be less of a menace without their Gifts. "There's one aspect of this we've overlooked," Julian announced. "These men rely on their Gifts for their effectiveness. Without them, they're the same as any other petty criminal."

Danby Moore, an aged butcher, stepped away from the shelves. "How do we remove their Gifts? Is that possible?"

"It is," Julian confirmed. One of Cabot Winfield's letters referred to that, and Julian had found a method in an obscure text. "At least, I believe it is. Once we have them in custody, we can bring them before the Council. Slow as they usually are to move, they would at least scry the men's activities and find proof of their misdeeds."

"The Council might kill them!" A bloodthirsty soul at the room's far end spoke with relish.

"If they do," Robin put in, "it's an execution under our laws. If we do it out of hand, it's murder."

That would not be too high a price to keep Amelia safe, if there were no other way.

The thought jolted him. He cared for her deeply, but he needed to remain rational about their relationship. A certain distance was best. But he could worry about that later.

"What the Council learns could also justify moving against Wyndon," Julian noted. "Regardless, I don't see the Council ordering these men executed for general brutishness, even if they use their Gifts for it. Other suggestions?"

"If I may." Seated a few chairs down on Julian's left, Donald Marsden looked thoughtful. His narrow, dour face under thinning brown hair gave him an inconsequential appearance despite his well-made coat. Behind that unremarkable face, however, lurked a sharp mind that had fueled his rise through the ranks of his chosen business.

"As some of you know," Donald began, "I am a director of the East India Company. We are always in need of laborers on our docks and in our warehouses—in India."

"You're saying we ship them to India?" Julian asked. "Englishmen there don't have a reputation for treating the local people well, and I would hate to add to that."

A thin woman down the table said, "My brother's in the navy. The press gangs know how to handle troublemakers. We could give these men to them."

"I like that," Robin said.

Press gangs forcibly conscripted men to serve in the navy. They were unpopular for many reasons, but it was hard to feel much sympathy for men who would commit murder so readily.

Julian looked around the gathering. "Does anyone object to the press gang solution?"

No one spoke up.

"Then that's it," Julian said. "I also need help to guard my house and capture these men. If you can assist us, let Robin know when you're available."

Almost everyone volunteered. Watching them, Julian saw years of working together rebound to his credit. By the time this gathering ended, they would have plans in place for disposing of Wyndon's tools. Then he would see whether Amelia and Sophie justified the faith he'd placed in them.

CHAPTER 18

Darkness fell. Amelia joined Julian in an upstairs bedchamber of his house. With the lights here and in the corridor out, they had a good view of Park Street. Now they would see whether the plan she and Sophie had devised would work. Julian had found more people to help than she'd dare hope for.

If their plan failed, she was trapped in this house.

Sturdy Bess Lassiter, the tavernkeeper's mother, climbed out of a hackney cab across the street from Aysgarth House. Holding a basket of folded laundry on her hip, she limped down the walk to the kitchen entrance as though her feet hurt.

At the same time, Merlin Club members who had trickled into the mews and the Aysgarth stables, some glamoured to be invisible, trickled out again, heading into the streets around the house. The staff who were not Gifted had been given an overnight holiday at Julian's expense so they would be safe and the Merlin Club could operate freely.

Julian and Amelia watched those of their friends who were visible fan out through the neighborhood. Each would have magical senses open, receptive to magic but not using any. Despite the cool evening, the window was up so she could call a warning if she Saw an imminent attack. With Julian's outriders stationed at the ends of the block, surely the plan would net at least one attacker.

"If only there were a simpler way," Amelia said.

"It's an excellent plan."

"Yes, but it depends on finding people who're glamoured to be invisible. If they're even there at all."

"We have alternatives. Don't worry." He paused, a thoughtful expression on his face. "Warding defeats scrying, but glamours don't. Or shouldn't. Neither should deflect your seer Gift."

"You said that earlier, and then we were interrupted. I don't know how to use my Gift that way. For the most part, the visions come upon me unpredictably."

"Yet you can summon them at times."

Amelia sighed. "Yes. Sometimes, though, knowing the future doesn't bring any comfort. When I see awful things there's no way to avoid, I wish I had seen nothing instead. Do you understand?"

"Of course." Yet he didn't take her hand, as she'd hoped he might. In fact, he seemed a little distant. "Julian, is all well with you?"

"Yes, certainly." He flashed her a surprised look. "Why do you ask?"

"You seem…subdued."

"My apologies, my dear." He smiled but still didn't touch her. With a glance at the mantel clock, he said, "The next group should move in shortly."

Footsteps came up the stairs. Bess tapped on the door and entered the room.

Julian rose. "Please sit," Amelia said.

"Don't mind if I do." Bess sank onto the bench at the foot of the bed. "We've two possible spies. One a couple of doors down on t'other side of Park Street, and one across from the entrance to the mews. They're glamoured, so we can't see them. Felt their magic, though, as our folk went by. James Lindsay glamoured hisself invisible and is keeping watch, his brother says. Though how he can keep watch on what he can't see, I don't know. Still, I credit him for trying."

Julian looked at Amelia. Did he expect her to say something? Do something?

"Bess, can you show me the spot across Park Street?" he asked.

She nodded. Taking care to keep a distance from the window, so the darkness could conceal her, she frowned down at the street. "Look at the door across from you," she advised, "and then count three down to the right. There's at least one of the rogues there."

"Thank you, Bess. Will you go back to the kitchen and take the reports of those who come in?"

Robin was down there, coordinating everyone.

Bess left the room. Julian turned to Amelia. "Sweetheart, we need you to See who's over there." Before she could protest, he added, "I know you've never done that. But other seers have. Will you try?"

"Of course, but do you know what those others did?"

"They stared." At her incredulous look, he shrugged. "That's what the old grimoire said. The seer stared at a spot until he pierced the glamours around it and Saw what truly was."

That was not much help.

Amelia shifted in her chair to stare at the spot Bess had indicated. Summoning power, she stared harder.

Nothing.

"Perhaps not every seer can do this," she said.

"You're very powerful, though. Can you summon a vision of what's over there while you stare at that spot?"

That sounded truly strange, but if it pierced their enemies' glamour… "I can try."

She looked again at the sidewalk across the street, narrowing her vision so the wrought-iron fencing between the front walk and the kitchen lane filled her sight. Trying to feel what was there. To open to it. Tightening her lips, she pulled more magic into the effort.

An image winked across her sight, then vanished. "Two men," she said, breathing hard, "one stocky with a crumpled face, one thinner and sour-looking. Between the front walk and the kitchen path."

"Good job." Julian squeezed her shoulder. "Keep watching. I'll send a runner to alert the riflemen." He walked to the door and spoke to someone in the corridor.

On the roof of his house, watching the street and the mews from behind the chimneys, perched two Merlin Club members. Expert marksmen in their thirties, Roger Southwell and Peter Randall had served in the 95th (Rifle) Regiment of Foot in the Peninsular War. They carried the latest type of rifle, a Baker, according to Julian. All reports were being passed up to them by the lead outrider's eight-year-old, towheaded son, Jamie.

"But if I can't see the spies all the time," Amelia asked as Julian resumed his seat, "how will we know where they are?"

"We may not have a better chance. Keep trying, sweetheart."

Amelia kept her attention on that one spot. Every once in a while, she caught a flash of Sight, piercing the glamour around the two spies. They looked bored and irritated.

She could only hope they would be aghast at their own defeat soon.

The Aysgarth coach, sent to Ned's family's London home earlier today, clattered up the street. In the back sat Ned. Glamoured to resemble Amelia, he carried a dagger and a brace of loaded pistols.

This was the dangerous part. Anticipation chilled Amelia and churned her stomach.

"I'm going down, darling." Julian kissed her swiftly. "Keep your distance from the window."

"Be careful," she called after him. If anything happened to him—No. Dwelling on that fear would only make it worse. Amelia took a slow, steadying breath.

Moments later, Jamie ran into the room. "Beggin' your pardon, milady, but them villains as was at the mews is moving up the street."

She thanked him, and the lad dashed out. Amelia took a breath that did little to settle her nerves and stared at the corner. Two more men winked into view, then out.

Really, this was rather a handy trick if she could only learn to do it consistently.

∼

Standing behind the front door, Julian held his pistols, two of Manton's finest, ready. The riflemen would shoot to kill. The rest of them would strive to capture at least one of Wyndon's accomplices.

The coach pulled up in front of the door, at the extreme range for anyone in the house to start a magical fire near it. Disguised as a footman, Bess's son Edwin let down the steps and opened the door.

In his glamoured guise as Amelia, Ned stepped out of the coach. If Julian hadn't known she was safely upstairs, he would've believed—

"Down!" came her shriek from above.

Ned and Edwin dropped flat as the *crack* of a shot sounded. The ball stuck the side of the carriage door, where Ned's head had been.

A heartbeat later, "Flame," roared a voice in the parlor and one across the entry hall in the morning room.

Harris, Julian's sturdy, sixtyish butler, yanked open the front door. Julian stepped out and dropped to one knee on the stoop as argent power flashed out of the open windows of the two front rooms. The magic flickered out at the corner and across the street, but nearer, by the coach's boot and the lead horse's head, flames erupted. Aiming was purely a guess based on where those generating the fire thought the attackers would close in. In each spot, two men became visible as the fire pierced their personal wards.

Rifles barked from above. One man in each pair of attackers dropped, twitched, and lay still. Julian sighted on the survivor by the boot, his shabby coat aflame, as Edwin lunged for the one still standing at the corner. Ned scrambled up, pistol in hand, and rushed to help. The besieged man managed to fire a shot. It *spanged* off the brick near the parlor window.

Julian fired at his fleeing, blazing target, who fell like a dropped stone. With grim satisfaction, he checked the other man. Ned and Edwin had him in hand, the fire in his clothing extinguished, and were hustling him toward the rear of the house and the mews. Julian cast a glamour over the street to hide the corpses.

Just in time, too, as lights came on in nearby houses and doors opened. Julian handed his pistols to Harris and walked into the street.

Turning in place, Julian called, "I beg pardon, everyone. Had a raucous guest, but we've settled him now. Very sorry!"

In the morning, his aunt would write notes to that effect. Practicing magic in the heart of Mayfair carried certain risks. Given everyone's desire not to believe they'd seen something they knew to be impossible, though, he and Aunt Augusta should be able to smooth this over.

He walked back in. Harris beamed at him. "Superb showing, Julian. I wouldn't have believed it if I hadn't seen it."

"It went rather well, didn't it?" With pride swelling in his chest he added, "When you have the chance, you might say so to Lady Buckton and Lady Whitestone. It was their scheme."

"Indeed, sir?" Harris, never completely able to adopt the informality of the Gifted, smiled anew. "How splendid!"

Footsteps sounded on the stairs, rushing down. Amelia rounded the turn from above and dashed into the entry. "You're all right," she said, her lips trembling. "That man shot at the house, and I—I feared."

"All is well." Walking toward her, he opened his arms. Amelia darted into them, her own closing around his waist.

"Oh, thank God," she breathed, pressing her face against his neck.

She felt good in his hold, nestling against him, worried about him. Her soft hair brushed his cheek, and the scent of her rose soap wafted into his nose. He pressed his face to her dark hair. If he wasn't careful, she would soon own his heart.

"Your scheme worked brilliantly, my dear. We've a man in custody."

"Sophie's scheme too. We feared you would think it was silly. So much depended on breaking their glamours."

"Yes, and that worked as well."

"The fire was her suggestion."

"I must go," he said. "We're transporting Wyndon's man to one of the East India Company warehouses, over by their docks. I must be there to question him."

"I wish you wouldn't go." Amelia looked up at him. "Wyndon likely hates all of you, but on top of everything else he holds against you, he'll resent you for surviving his vicious tactics."

The easy reassurance died on his lips. She looked up at him with such concern in the depths of her clear, blue eyes. It was seductive.

That made it dangerous.

Smiling like a proud father, Harris walked past them and through the door to the rear of the house.

Julian pressed a quick kiss to her hairline and released her. "I must do my part, sweeting. But a small army of the Merlin Club will remain here to secure the house in case Wyndon comes hunting for his assassins."

"Wait." Her fingers tightened in his shirt before she released him. "Will you—that is, shall I—I'll wait up, shall I?"

A wise man would tell her not to, would gain some distance. Apparently born stupid, Julian smiled. "I would like that."

The Merlin Club's unmarked, warded coach breached the wards around an East India Company warehouse off Seething Lane, near the Tower, and drove through the wagon entrance. The hackney and team used to transport the prisoner sat a short distance away in the cavernous space stacked with various crates and boxes. Standing beside it, Ned lifted a hand in greeting. That coach, the property of a club member, also was warded. Any chance to secure Wyndon depended on his not knowing they had one of his men in custody. Warding Park Street would've been wise, had it been possible to do without alerting Wyndon's spies that they'd been spotted.

The Merlin Club would simply have to depend upon Wyndon's arrogant belief that no one would touch him.

Alice Gresham, Ellert Chandler, and Ralph Dibny, a tall man with a thin face and a long nose, shared the forward-facing seat. Alice glanced out the coach window and raised an eyebrow. "You take your secrecy seriously."

"When dealing with murder and treason," Julian responded, "one must. I'm fortunate to have helpful friends." Since the Councilors not only were unaware of the Merlin Club's true nature but would disapprove if they knew, he couldn't speak frankly to them.

They climbed out of the coach. Ned nodded a greeting and led the way to the office in the far corner. A desk stood below a high window in the rear wall, and shelves along the walls held stacks of paper. Behind the desk stood another Merlin Club member, young, sturdy John Wade. He left the room as they filed in.

Their prisoner, a heavyset, scowling man, sat alone by the hearth. He wore shackles bespelled to prevent him from opening them magically.

The Council members took the seats arranged for them by the hearth, facing the prisoner.

"I assume Julian has told you of our evening," Ned said. "Perhaps you would care to see it for yourselves."

He directed energy at the flames and scried the battle at Julian's house earlier. As the images rolled through the flames, the Council members' demeanor went from doubtful to outraged to stony. But at whom were they displeased?

Watching events unfold reignited Julian's anger. This man and his friends had tried to kill Amelia. Impressment into the navy was too good for him.

The fight came to an end. Ned flicked a glance at Julian. "Now we come to the very interesting part," he said. Again, his magic slid into the flames and evoked images. This time, they were of the prisoner and his dead comrades coming and going from Wyndon House.

"The house is warded," Ned stated, "so we cannot know what occurred inside it."

"I work for Lord Wyndon," the man protested. "That don't prove nuffink!"

Alice Gresham turned cold eyes on him. "Would you have us believe you undertook to murder a Gifted woman on your own initiative?"

"I—my—what did you say?"

Ellert frowned at him. "Was it your own idea to attack Lady Buckton?"

The man looked started. Now he saw the trap. Blame Wyndon, and he gained an implacable enemy. Assume the blame for attempted murder himself, and the Council might kill him for it. They likely wouldn't since the intended murder weapon was an ordinary firearm, but he had undeniably used magic in the attempt.

"I—that is to say—I mean, we—"

Julian watched him flounder.

"We was having a bit of a joke," he finished feebly. "On Lord Aysgarth, as m'lord don't much care for him."

Dibny raised an eyebrow. "So Lord Wyndon put you up to this?"

"No!" The man licked his lips. "I mean to say, that is—we thought we'd amuse him."

"So this was your idea," Alice stated, "and you will bear the penalty for it."

"No! No, I—see here, it were a joke, naught more."

"Rather a deadly joke," Ellert commented.

The Councilors studied the prisoner in stern disapproval while he squirmed.

Dibny mused, "The use of magic in an attempt to kill another Gifted can carry the death penalty. Should the Council see fit to impose it."

"No! Please, your worships, no. We didn't mean nuffink by it."

Alice tapped one finger against her chin. "If you will tell us who put you up to this," she said slowly, "we can offer you a chance to start anew far from here. If you are merely the tool of the true villain, why should you suffer for that?"

"That's right, it is. That's right." Desperately, the man grasped at the offered straw.

"If we are to take his testimony," Alice decided, "we should bind him to truth-telling and record it. Ralph, can you serve as our scribe?"

Ned put in, "We've paper and ink at hand."

Of course they did. The Merlin Club was always prepared.

Dibny moved behind the desk and seated himself.

Alice told the prisoner, "You will look at me at all times." The air crackled as she wove magic around them both. "If you lie, we have no bargain."

Was she bluffing? Julian had studied what he could find on magical interrogations and never heard of shared magic revealing a lie.

Alice leaned forward. "Did you fire a gun at a lady in Mayfair this evening?"

"It weren't her, though. 'Twas him." The man jerked his head toward Ned.

"You believed him to be Lady Buckton, did you not?" Alice demanded.

Hanging his head, the man mumbled that he had.

"Who put you up to this?" she pressed.

He'd been recruited by his friend, now dead, on Lord Wyndon's orders.

As he talked, Julian looked at Ned. Did they not have a direct witness to Wyndon's involvement?

Apparently not, for Alice was looking grim.

"Very well," she said at last. "Mr. Dibny, Mr. Chandler, I hold this man's bargain to be fulfilled. What say you?"

They both agreed.

"So you'll let me go?" he asked, his gaze hopeful.

"Indeed," Alice told him. "Into the Royal Navy."

"The navy? I ain't going to no—"

Ned thrust a gag into his mouth and tied it in place. Over the outraged noises it muffled, he said, "He'll soon be in the navy's hands."

Before delivering him to the press gang, Julian and Ned would stifle the man's Gifts. The Merlin Club would not send a menace into the navy.

"If he has family," Alice said, "we must see they're taken care of."

"He has none," Ned reported. "There's a girl in Covent Garden he sometimes sees, but no family."

Alice walked out of the office. Julian and the other two Councilors followed her.

"You've no direct link to Wyndon," she said. "Close but not direct."

"But surely enough to question him, Alice," Julian said. "If you can read a lie in the magic, as you said in there, you'll know if he's telling the truth."

Alice smiled. "I bluff rather well, don't I?"

"The circumstances imply his guilt," Ellert said. "We should question him. With a bit of advance notice, we can have some water from Morgan's pool on hand. If he drinks that, he cannot lie."

Morgan le Fay's pool lay in a cave at Pendragon, the Gifted steading in Cumberland. Its attendants, known as Morgan's handmaidens, kept a small supply of its water on hand in London. Occasionally, if they deemed the proposed use fitting, they gave a tiny amount to the Council.

Alice glanced at Julian. "He'll argue that you accuse him out of spite because he thrashed you."

That stung, but Julian kept his face impassive.

She continued, "Some on the Council may give him the benefit of the doubt. If he challenges his accuser to drink the water from Morgan's pool, will you?"

"I will. I've nothing to hide."

"Be careful before you say that." Tilting her head, she studied him. "Are you certain you wish to divulge everything that transpired tonight?"

Had she guessed Amelia's role? Or did she refer to Merlin Club secrets? Regardless, he would do what he must to bring Wyndon to account.

Julian shrugged. "I've studied Morgan's pool. One who drinks its water cannot answer untruthfully, but one can refuse to answer."

"Secrets don't encourage people to trust what you say."

"I'll testify if I must, but unless the rules have changed, scrying is also proof." A seer's testimony surely would be, but the fewer people who knew of Amelia's rare Gift, the better.

"Very well." Alice turned to her fellow councilors. "Send word to have Lord Wyndon brought before the Council on the morrow."

If the Council's agents let him escape... One look at Alice's face, though, and Julian knew she would never agree to have anyone connected to him arrest the rogue wizard.

"Be at the Green Bull by noon," Alice said. "We'll need to pay Peter to shut down for the day, but it won't be the first time." Studying Julian, she paused. "If you've witnesses to bring, have them there at the same time."

"I understand."

Alice and her comrades climbed into the unmarked coach. Hugh, Julian's Gifted groom, drove them out of the warehouse. Ned and Julian, with John Wade's help, would block the prisoner's power and then turn him over to a press gang. Only then would Julian return home.

Ned walked up to him. "So Wyndon faces his reckoning tomorrow."

"If there's any justice, yes."

"It's past time he did. The man's a blight on the *ton*." Clapping Julian on the back, he added, "Once that's settled, you can plan your wedding."

"Indeed. Ned, I don't want Amelia to know about tomorrow's hearing. She would want to attend and make her own accusations. I would have the devil's own time dissuading her. It's far better if she simply doesn't know."

185

"She won't hear of it from me." With a grin, Ned added, "You do recall she's a seer, do you not?"

~

When Julian returned home, light showed under Amelia's door. Of course. Idiot that he was, he'd asked her to wait up.

Steeling himself, he tapped softly on the door.

She opened it. Wearing a loose, burgundy satin dressing gown over her night rail, with the firelight gilding the curve of her cheek and glinting on her unbound hair, she awakened a longing he'd thought he'd expunged from his heart years before.

That way lies danger.

"You're unhurt?" She kept her voice down, but it was probably best to talk in her chamber.

He stepped inside and shut the door. "Yes. The man we captured confessed to the Council, and they're seeing to him. As we discussed, he'll be enjoying a new vocation in the Royal Navy."

"And Wyndon? Are they arresting him?"

No fear in her face, only outrage and resolve. Her boldness threatened his peace of mind. "They're looking into it."

"Julian, are you telling me everything?"

That narrow-eyed look didn't bode well. How did one deceive a seer?

"Sweetheart, this has been a long day, and it's past time we were abed. You've a wedding to plan, after all."

"It's your wedding as well. Aren't you going to plan it?"

"I thought to leave that to you and Aunt Augusta, as I've other matters to attend to."

"Other matters." Amelia pursed her lips.

"Yes. Good night, my dear. I'll see you at breakfast."

"You're leaving?"

The disappointment in her face smacked him with guilt. And with treacherous longing.

"I thought to let you have a good night's rest after this rather trying day."

"The day was unsettling," she told him quietly. "I wanted to relax with you for a while, but I don't wish to keep you up. Good night." She turned away, and he felt as though he'd kicked a kitten.

"I could stay for a while," his foolish mouth offered, apparently without consulting his brain.

Amelia's smile, though, warmed him. Perhaps staying wasn't so foolish. She would be his wife. He had no right to protect himself by creating emotional distance if that hurt her.

He settled into the chair by the hearth and tugged her onto his lap. "Was all quiet here after we left?"

"Very." Nestling in his arms, she rested her cheek against his hair. "While your aunt and I plan a wedding, what will you be doing?"

"Talking to the Council about Wyndon." Telling her a little of the truth might be the best way to avoid alerting her Gift.

"I should talk to them too. Tell them what I've Seen."

Bloody hell, no.

"He assaulted me magically at the house party. Can I bring charges against him for that?"

"Yes, if you wish. It's probably better to let that go, not stir up the talk again, though."

Amelia sighed. "Papa Bainbridge did tell you there'd been rather a lot of that. Wyndon is such a nasty man."

"He is that."

They sat in silence and watched the flames, their warmth welcome on a cool spring night. Julian's tension slowly eased. Thank Heaven, she was not a chatterbox. The idea of quiet evenings like this stretching ahead held a great deal of appeal.

"Julian?"

"Hmm?"

Amelia sat up and stared into his face. "Why do I think you're keeping something important from me?"

CHAPTER 19

Bloody hell. His peaceful mood evaporated.

He couldn't outright lie to her. Charlotte's deceit and dishonor had been the undoing of their marriage. Whatever course he and Amelia charted together must be an honest one.

He raised his eyebrows. "Is that what your Gift tells you?"

"No, it's only a feeling. Even seers have ordinary intuition. So are you? Keeping something from me?"

She didn't seem angry, only worried and perhaps a little hurt.

"I am," he admitted.

The hurt grew more pronounced, and he stroked her hair. "Amelia, sweetheart, there will be times in the years ahead when I want to shield you from something. Can you trust me to do so? Will you allow me that privilege?"

He had been honest—sort of—with her. Flying up into the boughs wouldn't encourage him to do so again.

Amelia bit her lip. "That doesn't seem fair," she said at last.

"It's a husband's privilege to shield his wife."

"And to rescue his friend's sister and fight—"

"Rescue his friend," Julian corrected, his voice firm. "You are my friend as well, Amelia."

"I appreciate that, but it changes nothing. You took a beating for me, Julian."

"No, for my own honor." Now he looked mulish.

Best to begin as they meant to go on, though. "Because of me, and I'm not speaking of blame here, so let's not argue that. My point is that you've already shielded and sheltered me. I'm to be your life's companion. Is it not only fair that I stand on my own sometimes?"

"Sometimes you may," he agreed.

"But you'll decide when?" She frowned at him.

He sighed. "Sometimes, merely telling you of an event would distress you. I won't apologize for wishing to spare you that."

No matter how frustrating she found the sentiment, apparently. "I think you forget I'm not some delicate young flower of the *ton*. I managed our lands while my husband searched for his brother in India. I nursed him through dysentery, which I can tell you is not a task for the faint of heart, and I held him as he died. The evils of the world do not frighten me."

"You are a prime English rose, my dear, for you've steel at your core." Julian stroked her cheek with his knuckles. "I've no doubt of your courage. But there are evils in this world beyond your conception."

The shadows in his eyes triggered her awareness—whether from Gift or mere intuition, she couldn't say. "You've waded through those evils," she said softly.

"Bonaparte's return and all that comes with it bring back memories I thought to pack away forever."

Yet he had plunged into his duties at the Merlin Club, with all they entailed, and had let Wyndon pound him to protect her good name. No matter what he said, that protectiveness was part of what drove him. Part of who he was.

"I understand what you're saying, Julian. I do. But can you not understand that as your friend, as your wife to be, I would also like to spare you?"

His expression shuttered. "So we're at an impasse."

"Not at all. At least, not today. If you wish to stand for me tomorrow, so be it." As surprise washed over his face, she frowned. "Be warned, however. If you return home injured, I'll demand a full accounting."

"That's fair." He kissed her quickly, and then longer. Kissing him back, Amelia relaxed against him.

He tipped up her chin so he could nibble a path down her neck. Shivers of pleasure rocked her, and she let her hands roam his broad shoulders and chest. He stroked her thighs and buttocks. When he cupped her breast, Amelia gasped at the blinding pleasure.

She tugged his head around to kiss him again, senses reeling. Julian groaned and turned her more securely against his chest.

"Stay," she murmured in his ear. "Stay the night with me."

He raised his head, his eyes hot.

Someone knocked on the door.

They sprang apart like guilty children. Heat rose in Amelia's face. Really, this was silly. She and Julian were betrothed. If they anticipated their vows, it was no one's business.

Finger-combing her hair, Amelia hurried to the door. She opened it to find Baker, Julian's valet, standing in the corridor.

Red-faced, he avoided looking at her. "I beg your pardon, Lady Buckton. If you should happen to see his lordship, would you tell him Lord Yeavering wishes to speak to him? On a matter of, ah, some urgency?"

"Of course. Thank you, Baker."

The young man bobbed his head and scurried away.

Grinning, Amelia shut the door and leaned back against it.

"You did that nicely." Julian cupped her face in his hands and kissed her. "'Of course. Thank you, Baker,'" he parroted.

"Well, what did you want me to say? 'Hang on while he puts his clothes to rights?'"

"Taking them off is more what I had in mind, you impertinent baggage."

He kissed her again. Resting his brow on hers, he sighed. "If Robin sent for me at this hour, it cannot be good news. I'd best go see what he wants."

"I wish I could come too." Unfortunately, not even in this casual household would she appear outside her chamber in her nightclothes.

"If whatever he wants is involved and requires time, I'll send you word. If not, I'll return shortly."

～

Julian walked along the corridor to the library. Robin paced before the hearth, his face set in grim lines.

Julian shut the door. "What is it?" he demanded. "What's happened?"

"Wyndon's run for it."

"What? How can that be?"

"He must've scried the fight in the street. Or else we slipped up somewhere in warding what came before and after."

"If only we could've warded the street without their knowing we did it."

"We took a calculated gamble." Robin ran a hand through his hair. "Whatever the reason, Wyndon's gone. Lit out with his valet and his coach about an hour before the Council's agents came to arrest him."

"He could be anywhere now." Julian scowled into the fire. "In his place, I would dash for one of the ports."

"Wouldn't he expect us to think that?"

"Perhaps. Or he might hope we would think it too obvious." Mulling possibilities, Julian said, "He owns a yacht. Keeps it moored at Chatham, I think. If he can beat us to it, he might sail to the Continent. Or he might avoid the yacht as too obvious and go anywhere."

He bit back an oath. He'd counted on Wyndon being in custody before Amelia stepped out of a coach at St. George's for their wedding.

"He can ward his coach so we can't see inside, but we'll still know it's his." Robin shook his head. "He might abandon that somewhere, take a mail coach. What better way to throw us off his scent than to take the mail coach with people he would ordinarily consider far beneath him?"

"That's a good point, though warding a mail coach, with all the stops and comings and goings, wouldn't be effective. Damn it, by the time we figure out where he's headed, Wyndon could be in Calais."

Robin frowned. "You haven't asked my advice, but I have some for you. Don't delay the wedding for this. We can guard the church, put agents in place well before the ceremony. Marriage to you protects Amelia from a forced one to Wyndon."

"As far as that goes, it also transfers Wyndon's target from her to me." Where he preferred it. A husband shielded his wife. Of course, marriage to Julian wouldn't stop Wyndon from forcing her to use her Gift for him if he could capture her. Nor did it guarantee he wouldn't try to kill her, but it did put Wyndon and the world on notice that anyone seeking to harm her would have to face Julian first. The duel had revealed a new danger, but Julian would eventually master the defensive techniques he'd devised. When not constrained by rules, he had other methods to hand.

"Here's something else we haven't considered," Julian said. "We know Wyndon is in league with the French, and he likely suspects that. So why does he still fear Amelia's Gift? What else is he up to?"

Could he be involved in the Scottish-French plot to invade Britain? Or was he planning something else? If he could've moved between places via the dead realm, he would've already kidnapped Amelia. So what was he doing?

"Perhaps we should ask her that," Robin suggested.

~

What was keeping Julian? Something dreadful must've happened. Amelia paced in front of the fire. That accomplished nothing, so she sat in the chair she and Julian had shared.

Too restless to sit, she resumed pacing. Being in his arms felt right. It also served to remind her how much she had missed that simple pleasure of marriage, cuddling. Naked cuddling was even sweeter.

Was it selfish to worry that whatever had drawn him away would preclude naked cuddling—and its prelude, shared pleasure—tonight?

Someone tapped on the door. As she hurried toward it, Julian opened it and stuck his head in. Judging from his grim face, cuddling was indeed to be postponed.

"I need to consult you," he said. "Do you mind receiving Robin in your dressing gown?"

"Of course not." She checked the belt to be certain it was secure and the front fully wrapped.

Amelia sank into the chair by the hearth. Julian sat opposite her, and Robin retrieved the straight chair from the desk before joining them.

"What's happened?" she demanded.

"Wyndon has escaped," Julian stated.

"What? How?" Feeling faintly ill, Amelia listened to Julian's explanation.

"So that's as much as we know." His expression turned wary. "It occurs to us that your Gift might help us locate him. Or, if we're fortunate, learn what he plans."

"I'll do whatever I can, of course." So much depended on capturing him.

"There's something else," Julian said, and he knelt to take her hands. "What about the wedding? We'd hoped he would be in custody, that we could proceed without any threat to you. If you step out of a coach at St. George's, you'll be exposed during the time it takes you to cross the church portico. It's not deep, but sometimes several feet can feel like several miles."

She tightened her grip. "I don't want to wait. We don't know how long it will take to find Wyndon. From what everyone has said, he's the sort to take revenge on anyone who thwarts him, so until he's apprehended and dealt with, he'll remain a lurking threat. If we delay until we're certain it's safe, we may never be married. And truly, Julian, lovely as your house is, I'll go mad if I'm confined here much longer."

He smiled. "I've an idea that could help. But first, can you See anything to help us find Wyndon?"

"I tried scrying before I sent for Julian," Robin said.

"So you need a seer's talents. Very well." Amelia squeezed Julian's hands and released them.

As though he realized she needed separation, he returned to his chair.

Amelia closed her eyes and summoned the memory of Lord Wyndon's face. Holding it in her mind, she opened to her Gift.

Purple-gray fog rolled over her mind's eye. She caught a flicker of Wyndon's face, but it winked out like a snuffed candle.

"I had him," she murmured, "but I lost him." With her perceptions open, the two men's disappointment brushed over her mind. "I'll try again."

Yet her efforts yielded more of the same flickers. At last, she said, "I'm sorry. I'm afraid nothing is coming to me."

"You tried," Julian replied. "Perhaps tomorrow matters will come clearer."

"You know," she told him, feeling her way, "for days I tried not to think of him. Not to let dread of what he might do next intrude into my thoughts. That may have been a mistake."

"Understandable, though," Robin said.

There must be a way. Warding defeated scrying, as glamours defeated ordinary sight. Nothing was supposed to defeat a seer's Gift, though Wyndon had managed it with that confession the Mainwarings needed. Objects could cue that Gift, though.

"What is it, Amelia?" Julian asked.

"You remember when I had that vision of Marshal Ney joining Bonaparte. I used a porcelain figure made in France to bring up that vision. I wonder what might happen if I held something that belonged to Wyndon. I suspect his house is full of things that would do."

Robin grinned. Comprehension glinted in Julian's eyes but faded into worry.

"We'll take care," Amelia told him. "But haste is important, is it not?"

"Not as important as your safety," Julian stated.

His concern touched her heart but posed an obstacle just now. Before Amelia could reply, Robin spoke.

"Wyndon gains distance every hour," he said. "Merlin Club agents are at the house and can secure a perimeter. Julian, if Amelia is willing to take the risk, we should allow it."

Allow it? If either of them thought he could *allow* her to do something, she needed to correct him. That argument, however, could wait.

"Very well," Julian said. "But when we reach Wyndon House, Amelia, you wait in the coach until I say it's safe."

"Of course." She offered him her sweetest smile. "Whatever you wish, my lord."

He had the sense to look suspicious, but she ignored that. Thanks to Robin, she'd won the chance she wanted. But that didn't mean Julian was wrong. Wyndon was unpredictable. Anything might await them at his house.

～

My lord is not at home," Wyndon's fiftyish butler, answering the door in a dressing gown, informed them.

He pushed the door toward them. Robin pushed back. Over his shoulder, he said, "Julian, I told you we should go straight in."

A shoving match would waste precious time. Julian laid his palm flat on the door, envisioned it moving away, and slammed magic into the vision. The door flew inward, knocking the butler off his feet.

"This is outrageous," the man shouted, scrambling into their path. The sense of familiarity about him meant he was Gifted, which would simplify matters.

"Your employer," Julian said, "is a fugitive from the Conclave Council. If you interfere with us, you'll answer to them." Probably. Julian had sent a runner to Alice Gresham with a note explaining their plans, but he hadn't waited for a response. Instead, he'd gathered reinforcements in the form of the two riflemen, Roger Southwell and Peter Randall, and climbed into the coach.

Southwell was tall, burly, and dark, in contrast to Randall's shorter, thinner frame and fair coloring, but they wore matching expressions of grim intent. Now armed with pistols, they waited beside the coach to guard Amelia.

Julian directed a stern look at the butler. "If you'll stand aside, we'll conclude our business as swiftly as possible and depart."

"I can't stop you." Scowling, the stout man moved out of their path. "But my lord'll make you sorry, that he will."

He was welcome to try. When Julian went to the coach for Amelia, the two riflemen escorted them inside. Together, they all mounted the stairs.

Julian asked, "What would be best for you, give you the strongest clue?"

"Honestly, I've no idea. Using objects to key visions is new to me. But the places that have the strongest links to him might be best. Objects he handles often, perhaps clothing, that sort of thing."

"Then let's try his bedroom or his study." To the riflemen, Julian added, "Start looking. Let us know when you find either of those."

Senses open to the possibility of a magical ward, he opened the first door he reached. Amelia checked the chamber across the hall.

After finding several more unused bedchambers, he began to wonder how many bloody rooms this house had.

"Julian," Southwell called. "Looks like a library." As Julian and Amelia hurried toward him, he added, "Desk with papers on it. Fire burning low."

He stood aside so Julian and Amelia could enter.

"Watch the corridor," Julian requested.

The two men took positions on either side of the door, pistols at the ready.

Amelia walked a little way into the chamber, surveying it. Bookshelves lined the walls. There was no table such as the one in Julian's library. At the far end of the room, a desk sat at a right angle to the window. Armchairs upholstered in maroon damask flanked the hearth and sat near a couple of the shelves. Beside each chair stood a small table.

"What is it?" Julian asked, joining her.

"I'm trying to decide. This is all so new to me, but I think...he will have used the desk more than anything else."

She marched toward it and around behind the chair. With her hands above the chair back, she hesitated. Dread darkened her eyes. "I have no control over what I See, Julian. The more we learn of him, the more I understand what a truly horrid person he is. I don't want—I would rather not—"

"You can change your mind," he assured her. Though how they would learn Wyndon's plans if she did, he didn't know.

"It's not that." Her throat moved in a hard swallow. "It's only…I may discover more than we seek to know. Things I would rather not know. Things such as you warned me about."

He put an arm around her shoulders. She leaned into him and sighed.

"I'm sorry to be such a coward," she said into his shoulder.

"None of that, now. We each have limits to our tolerance. I don't like the idea of your wading in the cesspool of Wyndon's character. Say the word, my dear, and we'll return home at once."

Amelia locked her arms around Julian's firm waist. He could have no idea how beguiling she found his suggestion.

He held her close, waiting. No hint of impatience came from him.

He'd taken a beating because he believed that was the only honorable course. Now he'd deployed the Merlin Club, calling on his personal credit with its members, to protect her.

How could she not do her part in turn?

Nestling against him, she inhaled the bay fragrance of his soap. "Stand beside me while I do this. If I seem—if what I See is too dreadful, call me out of it."

He pressed a kiss into her hair. "I'll do whatever you wish. Including taking you home straight away."

She looked up at him. The respect and concern in his eyes steeled her spine. "I know you would," she told him. "That's what makes this possible."

Squaring her shoulders, she stepped away from him. "The sooner we're done with this, the better."

She laid her hands on the back of the chair, took a deep breath, and opened to her Gift. The room wavered out of focus in purple-gray fog, then returned. Now Lord Wyndon sat in the chair, rummaging through the drawers. His butler sat opposite him. A leather portfolio lay open on the desk. "I'll take my coach to Chatham. They'll assume I'm the passenger, but I'll have a good start on them."

He rummaged through the desk drawers, pulling out documents and laying them in the portfolio. "I must go," he said, "before they can convince the Council to send agents here."

The servant rose. "Good luck, my lord."

"I can use it. Watch out for yourself. They'll come here sooner or later."

He grabbed a caped greatcoat from one of the chairs and hurried out. But to go where from Chatham? Had he told his butler before the vision began?

Amelia reached backward. In a swirl of stinking mist, the scene changed. A girl in a maid's uniform of gray dress and white apron hesitantly approached the desk. Fear darkened her eyes. "You sent for me, sir?"

"Bend over the back of the chair."

The girl's throat worked in a hard swallow. She obeyed.

"Raise your skirts." Undoing his falls, Wyndon walked toward her.

Amelia's stomach heaved.

"Amelia?"

Julian's voice. A lifeline. He gripped her shoulder. Laying her hand over his, she swallowed against nausea. Reached again for Wyndon.

The mists rolled across the revolting scene and parted, revealing Wyndon and his butler seated as in the earlier vision.

"Where are you going?" the butler asked.

"It's better if you don't know." Wyndon hurried to the shelves and tugged on a book.

His hand hid the title, but it was the third volume from the left.

That single shelf slid back, dropping behind the one below it. He laid his hand against the metal square set into the wall behind the shelves. The square slid aside, disappearing into the wall. Wyndon reached in and withdrew a fat purse and a slim packet of papers. He applied magic to the wall, and the metal square slid back into place. A moment later, the shelf of books rose to its earlier position.

He stalked back to the desk and seated himself. Rummaging through drawers, he said, "I'll take the coach."

This was what she'd originally Seen. Steeling herself, Amelia reached farther back, past his assault on the girl.

LeFebvre...

She summoned the Frenchman's image, and the scene changed again. Wyndon and the French attaché sat in front of the fire. Its light glinted off crystal brandy snifters and the amber liquid inside them.

LeFebvre shook his head. "Talleyrand and those like him are fools. They try to—how do you say?—butter their bread on both sides. I've wasted this day preparing a draft of a trade agreement that will become meaningless within the year."

He took a long swallow of his drink. "You are certain the Scots suspect nothing?"

Wyndon's lip curled. "The fools are too enamored of their Highland nation delusion to question the particulars. Once MacKenzie masters the spell for entering the dead realm, he'll train his wizards and ours, never realizing the scheme can serve other ends as well as it serves theirs."

"Will he have sufficient numbers? The Royal Navy—"

"Are only as good as their ships. Mere water will not douse witchfire, my friend. All will be well."

An image flashed across Amelia's vision, of sailors and Royal Marines thrashing in the water. Desperately, she pushed it aside. What had Wyndon meant by *all*?

"By the time they know they've been gulled, they will have done what we needed. If they fail..." He shrugged. "Better to lose barbaric High-landers than trained soldiers."

She summoned other visions of the two men, other conversations, but all of them occurred in this chamber.

"Amelia? Amelia, come back to me."

She ignored Julian's voice. The answer must be here. They must've discussed it.

"Amelia." Julian pried her hand off the back of Wyndon's chair.

"I can't find it," she said, shaking her head. "I need to try longer."

"You can try when your lips aren't white. Sit down." He pulled the chair around, but she shook her head again.

"I won't sit there. I can't. He's—I won't."

"All right, then. We'll go into another room."

They crossed the corridor to a parlor, and Amelia sank onto the sofa.

"I'll fetch you some brandy," Julian offered.

"No. No, I want nothing of his. Just sit with me." When he gripped her hand, she clutched his, grateful for its warmth. Amelia took a deep breath and described her visions. "I couldn't find out what Wyndon meant by *all*. It feels important, Julian, like the missing piece of the puzzle. But I do know he has a secret cache in his study, and I know how to open it."

"We'll search it before we go." Rubbing his jaw, he stared at the banked coals in the hearth. "I've never studied your particular Gift. Seers are so rare that other subjects seemed more likely to be useful."

"Grandmother might know why I've had difficulty tonight."

"She might. We'll return home and see if you can summon her."

With Wyndon's whereabouts unknown, Julian insisted Amelia work within a warded circle. She cast her ward in the familiar area outside the cellar, with riflemen on the roof and Robin and Ned keeping watch on the mews. Julian stood between her and the rear lawn.

She appreciated his concern for her, but putting everyone to so much trouble had grown wearisome already. If she had tired of it, surely her guardians must have.

Besides, what was Julian's concern? For his promised bride? Or for Britain's only seer?

Perhaps she was better off not knowing.

Miranda shimmered into view. "You've had a busy evening, Amelia."

"I need your advice, Grandmother. First, though, I've news. Julian and I are to be married." The nervous tremor in her stomach shouldn't have surprised her. Miranda and Richard had been her guides and teachers and friends all her life. She needed their approval.

Miranda smiled. "That's wonderful news. Richard will be so pleased. Cabot Winfield was his closest friend. Tell Julian we welcome him to the family."

Amelia let out a relieved breath and passed the message.

Julian flashed a smile in the general direction of the circle. "Thank you."

"Tell Adam and Papa, will you? I want them to know."

"Gladly, but perhaps we should address your questions. What are they?"

Amelia told Miranda about the visit to Wyndon's home and her difficulty summoning the vision she wanted.

The ghost listened, first with a thoughtful expression and then with a frown. "Sometimes, summoning a vision in a place where its subjects have spent a great deal of time limits one's scope to that place."

"So if I tried the same thing elsewhere, perhaps here, I might have better luck?"

"Perhaps, but, as I said, it's a contrary Gift. You cannot always summon whatever vision you wish, whenever you wish. Of course it's worth an attempt. If that fails…" Miranda cocked her head. "Aysgarth is a scholar of magic, is he not?"

"That's probably a fair description."

"Does he know of Morgan's pool?"

"He has never mentioned it. What is it?"

"In the steading at Pendragon, there is a cave. Deep within it lies a pool Morgan le Fay used to summon her visions. When Richard and I faced a difficult test, the handmaidens of Morgan, the order who tend the pool, granted us a vial of its water. We used it to…expand…my power, to give me more control over what I Saw."

"You think I should do that."

"I do, but only if you've a secret place with flowing water. I later learned that was necessary. At the old Hawkstowe house in Bishopsgate Street, there was a hidden cellar. The new one, however, doesn't have such a thing. You should ask Aysgarth if he does. If not, you'll need to go to Pendragon."

"I've never been there. Mother was against Adam and me studying there."

"Of course she was." Miranda sighed. "Be careful, my dear. The pool itself carries far more power than a mere vial of its water. The visionary magic in it may show you things you would rather not see. Things that distress you. You must bear in mind that any vision of the future can change as preceding events take one path or another."

Lovely. This entire experience was a lesson in the risks of magic use.

Amelia said only, "I'll remember."

"I had Richard with me in the vision. At the time, we chose to do that because he had so much more magical training and knowledge than I did. When I looked back on it, however, I realized his presence anchored me. The pull of visions is seductive. With part of my attention always on him, I couldn't become lost in them. You should have Julian accompany you."

"That makes sense."

Miranda smiled. "You're a clever young woman. Needle-witted, as I believe the current saying is. You can do this. At Pendragon, Richard and I can come to you when you're out of doors but cannot penetrate the manor wards. One of us will always be near the steading."

Amelia thanked her grandmother. When she turned to Julian, questions lurked in his eyes, but he said only, "Let's go indoors and discuss this."

~

They sat together on the library sofa. As Amelia talked, Julian's disquiet grew ever greater. He'd been trying to avoid this risk, but he should've anticipated Miranda Hawkstowe, a powerful seer, telling Amelia about the pool.

When Amelia finished, he stared into the flames. He couldn't justify hiding the truth from her. They needed to know what Wyndon and his allies planned.

"I know of the pool," he admitted. "It's dangerous. All blood magic is."

"Do you have a secret cellar with flowing water in it?"

"No. The wizard who built this house thought such things an outmoded tradition. We've discarded many of the old ways. That wasn't always wise."

"If the pool is more dangerous than using a vial of water, can we not procure a vial and take it to some safe location to use it?"

"If we had such a place. No public location is truly safe. We would need to be both protected and unobserved. We might manage that in some obscure spot on the river, but the Thames would dilute the water from the pool too much. Even if it didn't, additional danger in using that water calls for a protected location. As I said, it's blood magic, which can rebound in unexpected ways."

"Hmm." She frowned but didn't seem frightened by the prospect of blood magic. Had she ever used it?

"Perhaps," she murmured, "we're anticipating too much. I should try to summon a vision here, now, in a place neither Wyndon nor LeFebvre has ever been."

"I stole Wyndon's pen. Perhaps that will help."

Amelia grinned at him, and his heart turned over. "Practicing your thieving skills?" she asked.

"No skill involved. I merely pocketed it, though that did break the end off the feather." He fetched it from the desk and handed it to her. Instead of sitting beside her, he chose a footstool in front of her, so he could better see her face.

She held the broken quill lightly in both hands and closed her eyes.

When she experienced a vision, her eyes usually opened, staring into some unseen distance. Now they remained closed.

Her brow furrowed.

The mantel clock ticked off seconds. Amelia set the pen on the cushion beside her, but her expression didn't change.

At last, still frowning, she opened her eyes. "What the pen showed me was mostly things he had written, generally instructions to his estate managers, and various conversations in his library. Once I set it aside, I did see him and LeFebvre in several locations, but they discussed nothing important."

"So it's the pool then."

"I fear it must be. Grandmother suggested having you with me to anchor me."

"I'll do whatever you need. Much as I hate to say this, the longer Bonaparte is at large, the greater the havoc he can wreak. The stakes here are very high, especially with this Highland plot. Even if we had a safe place to use a vial of water, it might not give us what we need."

"I just remembered something," Amelia said. "I told you about it, the vision I had of Bonaparte in London. Could that be Wyndon's goal?"

"Only if he has a very great deal to gain by it."

They stared at each other. He didn't want to be the one to say what had to come next.

"I must risk the pool," Amelia said, her face grim. "We cannot afford to delay while I try lesser measures, only to have them fail. We must take the path with the greatest chance of yielding the answers we need."

"I fear you're right." He took her hands in his and peered into her face. "I'll be with you, Amelia, every step of the way. Anything you require, I'll do, and gladly."

Sadness tinged the smile she gave him. "For England," she said.

No, for you. But he wasn't ready to hand her that power. Instead, he said, "For us all."

～

On the last day of the month, they set other concerns aside for their wedding. Amelia stood before the altar in St. George's with her hands in Julian's as they said their vows. Sunlight streaming through the stained glass cast rainbows over the burnished woodwork and brightened her yellow gown, a new one with green leaves and white flowers embroidered around the hem and the cuffs of the long sleeves. In lieu of a bonnet, she wore similar white flowers tucked around the bun at her crown.

She had stood here with Crispin. Julian had stood here with Charlotte. For different reasons, both marriages had been doomed.

Looking into Julian's eyes, though, the gray soft and warm and tender, she put the memories to the side. She and Julian were marrying to build a future. They mustn't let the past overshadow their hopes.

He slid a simple gold band onto her finger above the square-cut emerald ring that was his engagement gift to her.

Smiling, the rector pronounced them married and gave the benediction.

Julian grinned and offered his arm. The delight in his face lifted her heart as she slid her hand into the crook of his elbow.

Standing at Julian's side, Robin gave them an approving nod. Sophie returned Amelia's bouquet of white flowers and hothouse daffodils tied in white ribbon.

The small group of guests smiled at them. Mama and Papa Bainbridge sat with Crispin's brothers Oliver and Gabriel. The eldest surviving son, Lucian, now the viscount, hadn't been able to come on short notice. Mama, Aunt Louisa, and Uncle Harry sat in the front pew on Amelia's side of the church. On the opposite side sat Julian's Aunt Augusta, Ned, and Robin and Sophie's parents, the Earl and Countess of Havelock. All would join them for a wedding breakfast.

She'd arranged a surprise for Julian during the celebration. Augusta had told her about a Yorkshire custom of crumbling a piece of wedding cake over the bride and groom's heads. Julian had wanted to do that at his first wedding, but Charlotte had thought it silly and refused to have cake in her hair.

How foolish.

If serious, dedicated Julian wanted to do something frivolous, if it would make him smile, what was a little cake in one's hair? The bits of cake and fruit would brush out, after all. So Amelia and Julian would do that today. She could give him that.

Amelia's heart overflowed with hope and happiness. In that moment, she didn't care that the threat of war hung over their heads.

CHAPTER 20

F ive days later, Amelia followed Julian through the woods at
Pendragon, the secret retreat of the Gifted. The path led upward,
a ribbon of packed earth winding along the rocky, wooded slope.
Although late-season frost glazed shady patches of ground to either side,
the path remained clear. More remarkable was the magic that permeated
the ground and the air. If she opened to her Gift, the sense of it
surrounded her like a lush blanket.

She took a deep breath of the clear air. The breeze coming through the
newly green-leaved branches carried hints of frost-dampened earth and
of hearth smoke from the manor behind them but no wintry bite.

"You're managing the steep path well," Julian commented.

"In Leyburn, I loved to take long walks." Unsure how he would react,
she added, "After Crispin died, walking the land he loved consoled me."

"It's good you had something that did." He reached out, and she laid
her hand in his. "I hope you know you needn't ever fear to mention him
to me. He was important to you, and I don't expect our marriage to blot
out your memories."

"Thank you for that." She leaned into him briefly. "I cannot believe
how strong the magic here is. It's as though the very ground were
engaged in a working."

"Ah, you've noticed the power of Pendragon." When she raised her eyebrows, he explained. "So many people have worked magic here for so long that it suffuses the very ground. The drawback is that it makes working magic here nearly impossible. Only a group can do so. A single wizard can't counter the power in the air."

"It sounds like something out of a legend," she said, thinking of Avalon.

"As well it should. Legends like Morgan, Merlin, and Arthur once walked these lands. Now, though, let us hurry. I don't know how long this will take, and we should return to the manor before dark. Even with witchlight, the trail is hard to follow after the sun goes down."

Amelia quickened her pace, grateful for the flat-heeled half boots Julian had told her to bring. In place of a pelisse, a cloak of rich, blue wool over her paler blue cambric round dress countered the morning chill. She fingered the cloak's soft fabric, admiring the color.

Julian moved through the woods with the sure stride of one who belonged there. Watching him, she said, "You look much at home here."

Affection and pride softened his face. "I love this place."

"Will you tell me more about it? Coming here makes me realize how little I know about this, and it's my heritage. Our heritage."

"What do you want to know?"

"I know the women of our line are daughters of Merlin and the men are sons of Morgan, as a salute to the peace forged between the Gifted after Merlin's death. I know Morgan wasn't the evil sorceress of legend, but I don't understand what led to their quarrel."

"My people, those of the new Gifts—"

"I'm sorry, but what are new Gifts?"

"Those are the skills, such as using glamours and performing certain types of scryings, that came with those who arrived about the time the Romans left Britain. The older blood and related talents, including the seer Gift, are native to Britain. Merlin and Morgan, with others of our kind, served the man legend calls King Arthur. They came from these lands, from ancient Cumberland. As the Saxon push gained strength, the Britons withdrew into Wales, and the twins found themselves increasingly at odds."

"Why?"

"The law of the Gifted, set down when we arrived here, forbids the use of magic for personal or tribal—national, if you will—gain. When matters grew desperate, Morgan advocated breaking that law. Merlin swore to oppose her, and Arthur agreed with him. Rather than battle those she loved, she withdrew into the south of England, to Avalon."

"Where is Avalon? I've often wondered."

"At Glastonbury, yet not." He smiled briefly. "That's a lengthy tale for another day. In due time, Morgan's fears came to pass. Arthur suffered a mortal wound, and the Britons lost all chance of retaking their lost realm."

"Just as the stories say, then."

"In that regard, yes. Both Merlin and Morgan had served their principles, so our people decided to honor them by styling ourselves as you noted. We do it in respect and gratitude and to remind ourselves of our kinship to one another."

"I never knew that. I fear my magical education has been more deficient than I knew." At least in part because of Mama. If not for Richard and Miranda's lessons and for Adam sharing what he learned, her skills would be far less developed.

"You know a great deal more than many do, and your seer Gift is strong."

"That's thanks to Grandmother Miranda. But where did this steading come from? Was it Morgan's?"

"The house, named in Arthur's honor, as you likely guessed, was built by the Romans. You may have noticed the warm floors. A pump—now worked by magic instead of muscle—keeps hot water circulating in pipes beneath the flooring. Say what you will of the Romans, but they knew how to build. The Gifted took possession after the Romans withdrew. A few hundred years later, when the manor needed more space, they added the tower."

"No wonder the place feels like something out of myth. I wish Adam could have seen it. He loved those chivalrous tales."

"I know." Their eyes met in shared grief.

Cresting a rise, he stopped and pointed. "Look there."

They stood in a clearing. The ground fell away before them, sloping to the valley floor. In the distance, wispy gray spirals wafted up from the Pendragon Manor chimneys. Amelia caught the scents of wood smoke and cooking rabbit.

A faint mist off the river beyond blurred the lines of the long, low stone house with its thatched roof and the high, square tower at one end. Through the mist, the river gleamed faint silver in the spring sunlight. The valley road led from the manor through the trees along the riverbank, then wound into the forest, narrowing until it vanished behind a stand of holly and yew. This place felt like home, even though she'd never been here before.

Julian put his arm around her waist. "Our kind have admired this view since before William the Bastard left Normandy. Since before Alfred fought the Danes in Wessex. Let's conclude our business so we can explore."

Around the next bend, the path ended in a clearing backed by a steep rock face.

Julian raised his free hand to shoulder level. Silvery light glowed around his fingertips. He pointed at a rowan tree to one side of the clearing, and the light drifted over to twine among the branches. They gave off a faint chime like a score of tiny bells all struck at once.

He lowered his hand, and the glow faded. The sound died away.

The rocky face of the hill shimmered.

Amelia gasped. She took an instinctive step backward. Julian had told her what to expect, but hearing about it was very different from seeing it happen.

The shimmer dimmed and died to reveal a candle-lit opening. In it stood a woman garbed in a simple gown of silver velvet. It had no waistline, but a girdle of leaf green embroidered in gold encircled her hips. From the left side of the belt dangled a sheathed dagger.

The woman stepped from the cave mouth and smiled at Julian. "Welcome, son of Morgan."

He bowed slightly to her. "Greetings, daughter of Merlin and handmaiden of Morgan. I bring with me my wife, Amelia Winfield, a woman of the Old Blood and a seer. We seek counsel through shared visions in the waters of Morgan's pool."

The woman nodded at Amelia. Her thin face showed no great age, but silver threads glinted in her long, black braids. "Well met, Amelia, Lady Aysgarth. I am Elspeth, daughter of Merlin and handmaiden of Morgan. Come inside, both of you."

They followed her into the cave and took the seats she offered. Amelia found herself settling onto an x-shaped wooden chair that had a comfortable, flat seat and arms just the right height. Worn a bit by years of use, an intricate knot pattern gleamed in the dark wood of the armrests.

A small fire crackled in a brazier, surely giving off scant warmth, but the air carried no chill. Instead, the cave radiated coziness. Bright tapestries of forest scenes graced its walls. Beeswax candles on the scattered tables gave off soft light and a subtle, mellow aroma. From the rushes covering the packed-earth floor rose scents of lavender and verbena.

"You've not used the pool before," Elspeth said to them, "so I must tell you what it does. It cannot show you the future, though it can spur a seer's Gift to show possibilities. It can show you the past. It can show you a dream or a vision and any trails that lead to or from it. Within these limits, you can direct it."

"We want to share the visions in the pool," Amelia said.

"Then you must each cut your left hand, clasp them so that the blood mingles, and plunge them into the water."

Such a cut would be simple to heal, but the idea of doing it was still unnerving.

Too much was at risk to quail over a little cut, though. "We understand," she told Elspeth.

"Very well, then. But I warn you both, as we have warned every user of the pool or its waters since Morgan created it, that the pool shows true, not only the vision within it but the hearts of those who use it."

She paused as though to give her next words greater weight. "No one pays a fee for its use, but many have paid a price. We who guard it have seen betrothals and marriages, business dealings, and long friendships wither in its mist. As a seer, you may find it affects your Gift in unpredictable ways. Use it only if you dare."

Amelia and Julian looked at each other. The resolve in his eyes echoed hers.

"Let's go," Julian said.

Elspeth looked from one to the other of them and nodded. "Follow me."

She led them behind one of the tapestries and down a flight of stairs. The stairs ended in the mouth of a narrow passage that sloped gradually down into the heart of the rock. Julian had to stoop to make his way through it.

As they walked, the air around them grew cooler and faintly damp. It smelled of wet stone and moist earth, like a garden in the spring rain.

Elspeth lit their way with green witchlight glowing around her hand. Darkness enveloped the path before and behind them.

At last, their guide rounded a corner and stopped. "Close your eyes," she warned.

Amelia obeyed. Light flashed, so bright that it came through her eyelids like day.

"You may look now," Elspeth said.

Amelia opened her eyes. She and Julian and their guide stood in a chamber as large as the great hall of a castle. Its white crystal walls glowed with soft, eerie light that cast bluish shadows around the three who stood within.

"The pool is there," its guardian said, nodding past them.

Amelia and Julian turned. A few feet to their right lay a body of silvery gray water several yards across, a perfect circle that hinted at unnatural origins. Its opaque surface reflected the gleam of the crystals but showed not a ripple of movement. Whatever spring fed it must come into it far below the surface.

Not large enough for a boat but not too small for drowning, she thought. Cold danced up her spine.

Though colder than it had been before, the air had lost its rainy, earthy aroma. Instead, the scent of roses pervaded the chamber. Amelia could see no source for it other than the pool.

Eerie, ancient power whispered across her senses, and her stomach twisted. She forced her chin up.

Elspeth took the silver dagger from her belt sheath and offered it, hilt-first, to Julian and Amelia. Standing closer, Julian accepted it.

"The left hand, remember," she said. "When you plunge your hands into the water, the mists will rise. You can then summon the vision you seek. The mists respond to the slightest thought. You must remain intent on what you want, or they will lead you through your lives or those of your friends and family. I'll await you by the entry to the passage."

He nodded, studying the water. "Our thanks, Cousin."

"Luck to you." She turned away.

Amelia gathered herself. "You called her cousin because she's Gifted, did you not?"

"Yes. Were you not aware of the custom?"

Despite the nerves dancing in her stomach, Amelia smiled. "I knew of it. But most of the Gifted around me were actual kin, or else friends. So there was no need for another form of address."

"I see. Are you ready?"

She nodded.

Holding the dagger, he said, "Blood magic usually heals the wound that gave the blood. This pool should do the same. If it doesn't, I know you can heal mine, and I should be able to tend to yours. If we cannot manage it for some reason, Elspeth will see to it."

"Very well, then." Despite her quavering insides, she managed to sound calm. "We've nothing to gain from delay."

Approval shone in his eyes. "I'll go first." The blade flashed, raising a thin line of blood just below the base of his fingers. To her amazement, he smiled. "Ready?"

Steeling herself, she extended her hand. Again he moved quickly. Not until she saw the blood welling did she feel the stinging pain it brought.

Julian set the dagger down. He held out his bloody palm, and she laid hers across it. Warm and sticky, their mingled blood oozed through her fingers. She took a deep breath, preparing herself. He did the same. Together they knelt and plunged their joined hands into icy water.

It lapped against their knees. Ripples spread outward from their hands. In the center of the pool rose a silvery mist, shimmering like dew at sunrise. It thickened, and the shimmer became a billowing cloud that rushed toward them.

"Steady," Julian murmured. His grip tightened.

The mist surrounded them. It blotted out the sight of him, the feel of his hand on hers, the icy chill of the pool.

Alone in a ghost fog, Amelia fought panic. She couldn't see Julian and no longer touched him, but awareness of him floated over her senses. There he was, not far away.

Pain vibrated in the magic, old hurt he didn't want anyone to mention. Would he hate that she had sensed it?

Instinctively, she called, "Julian, I need you."

~

Amelia?" Surrounded by purple-gray fog, he turned slowly in place. If this was what she Saw in her visions, she deserved a medal. The rotten-egg stench of the mists bade fair to turn his stomach.

"I'm here," she answered.

He walked toward the sound of her voice. The fog thinned, and he saw her. They embraced.

Relieved to have found her, he caught her hand and raised it to his lips. Her fingers tightened on his, and she smiled.

The fog rolled back, revealing the dining room of Aysgarth Hall. He and Amelia sat at opposite ends of a long table set with snowy linen. In the center of the far side sat Aunt Augusta, next to a brown-haired tot who likely perched on a stack of books. The other chairs held children. The oldest couldn't have been more than twelve, a dark-haired girl with his gray eyes. Two other girls and three boys filled the other seats.

Eyes wide with wonder, Amelia turned to him. "Julian, is that—are they ours? I mean, will they be?"

"You would know better than I, my sweet. We've still much to do before we reach that point, with the outcome far from certain." Yet he wanted that scene of domestic peace, wanted it so badly that it burned in his throat.

The clouds thickened. With them came the stink of gun smoke and the weight of unpleasant memories. On the whole, he preferred the rotten egg stench.

The boom of artillery filled the air. The mists rolled back over shadowy ground to show them rows of tents around a low, white farmhouse. Men in blue uniforms darted to and fro, shouting.

"A French camp," Julian breathed. "But when?"

"Let's see if the armor is there, perhaps in the chest I Saw." The vision changed, as though they rushed past the tents, and toward the white, wooden house at the center of the encampment.

They passed through the outer wall, then inner ones, as though they weren't there. The vision showed them a narrow bed with a canopy draped over it. Baggage of various sorts lay around the room.

"That's the chest," Amelia said. "The one I saw them put the armor in."

She knelt beside it. The lid rose easily. Inside lay a small suit of armor such as she'd described to him.

Brow knitting, Amelia said, "Let's see if it's as important as we thought." She held out a hand to Julian. When he clasped it, she laid her other hand on the breastplate.

The fog rolled in, swirling its nauseating odor around them. It rolled back to show a castle under siege. The French fleur-de-lys flew from the ramparts. French heraldic banners flapped in the wind. So did red and blue ones that might've been Burgundian if Amelia remembered her history correctly. The din of cannons and men's cries was deafening.

Mounted on a white horse, a slender, armored figure slashed its sword at men wearing Burgundian blue and red. The sun glinted off the figure's cloth-of-gold surcoat. A man reached up, grabbed the garment, and yanked the rider off the horse.

Julian winced in sympathy. Amelia shifted closer to him.

The Burgundian soldiers ripped the surcoat away and revealed the same armor as in Amelia's vision. Someone snatched the rider's helm off, exposing sweaty brown hair cropped in a bowl cut above the delicate features of a woman.

This was the armor of Joan of Arc.

"We were right. That's how he's winning them over," Amelia said.

"Probably not all of them, but I expect this is a powerful influence on those who might waver. He may have someone wear it, but merely having it with him might suffice." Slowly, feeling his way, Julian added, "Along with the jobs he's providing, this could explain why those in Paris support him enthusiastically while the country's more remote regions don't."

He paused, and Amelia prodded, "What is it?"

"Perhaps nothing, but I wonder…is there a way we could use that armor, if we had it, to turn people away from Bonaparte?"

The Burgundian soldiers yanked Joan to her feet.

"I don't want to see this," Amelia said, and the fog closed over the vision again. "Joan was so brave, and so…betrayed. Shut out of the city, sold to the English, murdered on a flimsy pretext."

"She deserved better," Julian agreed.

"Speaking of deserving better," Amelia said, "let us see what Wyndon was holding over me."

"I know that's important, sweetheart, but more urgent is learning what Wyndon has in mind," Julian reminded her. "Remember the records we found in his secret cache, the purchases of so many muskets and bayonets, so much canister shot. Where did they go?"

She stiffened, as though to protest, and he braced himself. She controlled what they Saw. If she chose to put her brother first, he couldn't stop her. Or even blame her.

"Very well." Amelia straightened, and the mists slowly thinned. She and Julian stood in the green square outside St. Margaret's and faced the long, uneven façade of Westminster Palace. The members of Parliament stood assembled in New Palace Yard under French guard. Silent crowds jammed the street and spilled into the churchyard and the square beside it. To Julian's right, the great hulk of Westminster Abbey dwarfed the smaller church beside it.

Down Parliament Street marched the French army, Napoleon in the lead. Julian set his jaw. He would do anything he must to prevent this from happening.

"Can you see how we came to this point?" he asked.

"I'll try."

The scene shifted again, to Dover, where French longboats put soldiers ashore at the base of the fabled white cliffs. Boat after boat.

"Why did they land here instead of the Highlands?" he asked. "Were the Scots duped by the French? Or did they land in both areas? Those don't look like French naval vessels."

"I don't think they are." She changed the angle to see them more closely.

"They're merchant ships. Damn it." Julian ran a hand through his hair. "Who the bloody hell is—wait. Do you remember the documents we found at Wyndon's, receipts for shipping companies?"

They'd been in his secret compartment. Amelia cocked her head. "Where would you land if you meant to put soldiers ashore in Scotland?"

"To invade the Highlands, Glasgow or Dundee to cut the area off from British troops. Possibly Inverness to sweep south." Julian narrowed his eyes. "That cannot come to pass unless their scheme to remove the Royal Navy succeeds. Let's see what happens in Scotland if Bonaparte takes London."

Nothing. Nothing at all happened.

"The Scots are betrayed again, it seems," Julian murmured. "Or else they lost before this happened. But he cannot take London without a larger army than we think he can raise."

"Unless he defeats the Allies and brings his entire army down on us." Amelia swayed on her feet. "If he wins on the Continent, that may be his plan. Or his hope."

Sliding an arm around her shoulders, Julian said, "Perhaps you should stop now."

"Not without knowing where Wyndon has Edmund's confession."

The fog churned. No image appeared.

Amelia and Julian looked at each other in shared bewilderment. "I was so certain the answer would be here, Julian. How can he block a seer, especially when I'm using this pool?"

"I don't know, but we'll figure it out. Can we See what he's doing now?"

Amelia shifted the vision to find Wyndon. He appeared in the fog, sitting by a fireplace in a small room with a glass of wine. When she pulled the vision back, a waterfront with many ships moored came into view.

"He's in Calais," Julian said. "What the devil is he doing there?"

"Perhaps going to meet his French allies?" Leaning against Julian, Amelia sighed. "Whatever he's doing, Bonaparte must come first. We must steal the armor. If we undercut his support, perhaps that will force him to surrender."

~

That night, the fog invaded Amelia's dreams. For once, she resisted it. She was so tired. So very tired. Yet the fog persisted. A man's hand, spotted with age, held a small, square book with a battered leather cover. Amelia stared at it, and Lady Eleanor's face flashed into her mind.

Could this be her book?

The man's other hand lifted the lid of a glass case, and he laid the book gently inside. The blue, red, and gilt decorations on the leather binding had faded over the centuries, but the book itself remained intact.

The man's shirt sleeves were of the modern style, a ruffle showing at the edge of his black coat's straight sleeve. Who was he? Why the prayer book? Could Edward IV's abandoned queen, Lady Eleanor, have hidden her testament inside it?

The room faded, and Amelia awoke. She lay beside her sleeping husband in a soft bed in a dark room. The narrow window high in the wall to her right showed stars twinkling beyond the treetops. The glow of the hearth fire, now dying to embers some ten feet beyond the end of the bed, cast enough light to let her see her surroundings.

This was her and Julian's chamber at Pendragon.

Had the images of the prayer book been a dream? Or a vision?

Regardless, she should see if she could expand it. Perhaps learn more about the book and the man who owned it. The table by the bed held a candlestick with a beeswax taper, a ghostly blade in the dim light. She lit it by pushing out a flicker of her power, avoiding the glow of witchlight or witchfire. If she moved carefully, perhaps she could avoid disturbing Julian.

When she swung her bare feet off the low bed, the floor tiles warmed them. She flattened her feet to savor the odd feeling, so different from the chill of a plank floor. Although she wore only a muslin night rail, she didn't feel cold.

Magic again.

She set the lighted candle on the polished oak mantel so she could stoke the fire. Prodding the logs with the poker, she sat back on her heels and summoned the vision again.

Behind her, Julian's sleepy voice said, "You need your rest, sweetheart."

"In a bit. I had a dream vision, so I thought I would see if I could expand it."

The bedclothes rustled. He joined her on the rug.

"The magic all around us may block your scrying unless your seer Gift can slide through it. You must be careful not to wear yourself out. That would delay action on any of the things you've discovered. You need to sleep."

"I need to save my family. Or do you consider that unimportant in the face of all else that's happening?"

"That isn't what I meant. I don't want you to fall ill."

"Nor do I, but I will not leave here without learning all I can about Lady Eleanor and Edmund's confession. I delayed at the pool for other things. I've had a dream that could help, so I must pursue it. Or don't you think that's important?"

She'd thought he would understand. If he valued and trusted her as a friend, wouldn't he share her concerns? He'd downplayed them earlier.

"Of course it's important." Impatience crackled in the words. "But surely it can wait until morning. I'm trying to take care of you."

"Then let me do what I need to do now. Or do you want this always to come last?"

"Amelia, what—?"

"Never mind. I'm tired, that's all. I'll finish this and go back to bed. It's nothing."

He gently tipped up her chin with two fingers. His face solemn, he studied her. "On the contrary," he said. "I think it's rather more than 'nothing.'"

～

The hurt in Amelia's eyes made Julian's stomach churn. Did she truly think him indifferent to Adam's fate? Perhaps so, given his delay in doing anything about it.

"Amelia, sweetheart, surely you know how important Adam was to me. I understand how much this matters to you."

Her smile flickered, weak in the firelight. "I hope so. Regardless, I need to do this."

"Amelia, I…"

What could he say? Had he pushed her concerns to the side in his worry over the larger problem? Seeing the wider view, allocating resources for the most urgent needs, was his job. No matter how much he cared for her, he couldn't let her distract him from that.

Yet he had a nagging sense he should've paid more attention. He'd promised to do what he could to help with her family curse, after all.

"Go back to bed, Julian. I don't need help with this."

Lie in bed while she sat before the fire and worked? No.

"I would rather go see what I can find in the library. Do you mind?"

Amelia shrugged. "Do as you like, of course."

He pulled on pantaloons and his banyan and walked down to the big room at the end of the long house. In the library, he summoned blue witchlight at his fingertips and sent it zipping around the room to light the beeswax candles in the sconces. The chamber was a jumbled mess. Wizards tended not to put books, scrolls, and the occasional tablet back where they belonged, but he didn't mind. He enjoyed putting them in order.

While he put the room's contents to rights, he would see what he could find about how someone could block a seer's Gift. Solving that problem might help them locate Edmund Mainwaring's confession.

He set to work slowly, methodically, examining the titles of the books he held. As he sorted the books, unbidden memories of the women he had known intimately ran through his mind. He had always chosen them with care.

Ever since he'd learned of Charlotte's betrayal, capped by the knowledge she'd never loved him, he'd been careful in his liaisons. He'd kept them rare and casual.

That was easy to do with women he didn't truly know. Or admire.

With Amelia, holding himself apart was harder than he had thought it would be. She had such courage, such determination and loyalty.

Such a kind and generous heart.

A kind woman would never cuckold or embarrass her husband. That was probably why he already cared so dangerously much for her.

The thought went through him like a blow to the head. It froze him in place.

"Not *care*," he admitted to the empty room. "I don't only care for her. I love her."

He'd told her he couldn't, had made it plain he didn't expect love from her. He'd been wrong.

If he were a stronger man, he would banish that feeling, lock it away where it could never pose a danger. But it was too late for that. Amelia was already inside his guard.

She obviously cared for him, but did she love him? Could she? If he wooed her carefully, could he win her heart?

CHAPTER 21

Amelia sat on the floor in front of the fire, arms crossed over her raised knees, and watched the flames. Julian had been gone rather a long time. Had she driven him out?

Perhaps she was being unreasonable.

With a sigh, she rested her head on her arms. Marriage to Crispin had shaped her expectations, and Crispin never—No. Comparing Julian to Crispin was not fair. They were different men.

Different marriages, begun in different ways and for different reasons.

Measuring Julian and her marriage to him against Crispin would poison any hope of the future. She simply must not do it.

The door opened. Julian slipped in. He hesitated before coming toward her.

Folding his tall frame onto the floor at her side, he asked, "Did you find what you needed?"

"I confirmed that the book in my dream was Lady Eleanor's prayer book, but I couldn't tell who has it. Since then, I've been having odd visions."

"Scrying?"

"No. The pool did something to my Gift, Julian. I've Seen the oddest things, just sitting here while they drifted across my Sight. There was a ballroom full of people, with many of the men in various uniforms instead of evening dress. A uniformed man I didn't recognize arrived, and another man in a different uniform came out to see him. Then they sent for the Duke of Wellington, and then for another man. They talked and then separated."

"Did you try to See where they went?"

"No. I was curious about what would happen if I simply let the images come. I saw Wellington and one of the men beside a bed with a map on it. Wellington looked vexed. He said Bonaparte had 'humbugged' him, gained twenty-four hours' advantage. Then the scene changed to a battle at a crossroads, a place called Quatre Bras—French and Allied infantry and cavalry. After that came an image I've Seen before, of soldiers sleeping, their hats over their faces while rain poured down on them."

"I brought along a book of maps compiled by the Merlin Club over the years. We can try to locate Quatre Bras in the morning. Are you still Seeing these things?"

"Not anymore, but it's nice here by the fire."

They sat in silence for a few minutes, watching the flames.

"About earlier," he began.

"It doesn't matter. Of course the struggle against Bonaparte must come first. I realize my Gift is an asset for us in that. I was upset over nothing." She couldn't expect him to care about Adam and Papa and Grandfather Richard and all the others as much as she did, no matter how close he and Adam had been.

He shook his head. "I don't think you were." Turning to face her, he held out his hand. She laid hers in it, heartened by the warm grip of his fingers closing around hers.

"I must ask you to bear with me," he said. "When I have a goal, I often let it...absorb me, for lack of a better phrase. I lose sight of all else, filtering everything through progress toward that goal. So my first concern was learning what we could about Bonaparte."

"I understand."

"You shouldn't need to." He rubbed his thumb over the back of her hand. "I didn't marry you for your Gifts, or even for Adam, dear as he was to me. Or even because you're clever and determined. I married you because I don't feel alone when I'm with you."

He felt alone without her? She never would've suspected it.

"You have scores of friends," she reminded him.

"Yes, and I'm grateful for each of them. It isn't the same, though. You know it isn't." As she nodded acknowledgement, he added, "I don't want you to feel alone, either, and I fear I made you do so earlier."

She squeezed his hand. "Not alone. Frustrated, perhaps."

He raised her hand to his lips to kiss it, and heat shot up her arm. Holding her hand in both of his, he said, "If I become too absorbed—or perhaps it's better to say when I do—never hesitate to tell me. The habit of years is difficult to break, but you're my wife, Amelia. My life's companion, as you once said. You've a right to demand I pay attention to our personal concerns."

His life's companion. That's what she had promised to be when she agreed to marry him. Looking at his earnest face, at the anxiety lurking in the gray depths of his eyes, she put aside her disappointment at not having more.

"Do you forgive me?" he asked.

"There's nothing to forgive." She glanced at the fire, but no images rolled across it now. "Let's go to bed. Using the pool is exhausting, but perhaps we should try it again tomorrow. I still don't know what we should do next. We can scarcely sit at home and wait for Bonaparte to make his move. And I still don't know who has Lady Eleanor's prayer book."

"I can write to the Talbot family and inquire. As to Bonaparte, let's see what the Merlin Club has discovered in the morning. Perhaps that can spare us the need to use the pool again."

He rose and tugged her to her feet. Holding her hand against his heart, he said, "Never doubt I cherish you."

His mouth brushed hers in a soft, tentative kiss, as though he were unsure of his welcome. Amelia rose on tiptoe to kiss him back, locking her arms around his lean waist. With a groan, Julian slid one hand down to her buttocks and pressed her against the hard bulge at his groin. Pleasure rolled through her, and she clung to him.

They undressed each other by the fire, kissing and touching. By the time they went to bed, they were both impatient to join.

Julian tugged her over him, his mouth and hands at her breasts driving her ever higher as she rode him. The pleasure surged with each rocking motion of her hips, each nip of his lips or stroke of his fingers or swipe of his tongue. When he pressed his thumb to the sensitive nub of flesh at her groin, the tension burst. Amelia shuddered with release. Julian caught her thighs, pulling her down as he thrust upward. He made a choked sound, back bowing, as he found his release.

Amelia collapsed on top of him. He pulled the covers over them and locked his arms around her. Warmth and security combined with satiation in drowsy contentment.

"Am I heavy?" she murmured.

"Uh-uh." Pressing a kiss against her hair, he tightened his hold.

She snuggled closer and let herself drift.

The purple-gray, stinking mists rolled behind her eyelids. Slowly they parted.

In a forest clearing, Dare MacGregor knelt beside a young, dark-haired man lying on the ground. Beyond them, two horses stood in the shadows.

Grief and anger twisted Dare's face, but the other looked tired and pained. And far too pale. Blood spilled from his belly, staining Dare's hands and the white fabric—a shirt?—he pressed to the wound.

"They're comin'," the other man choked. "Take the book, Dare, and get ye gone."

"I willna leave you."

The other's rasping cough might've been a laugh. Blood burbled on his lips. Dare gently wiped it away with his sleeve. "Aye," the man said, coughing again, "but I'm leaving you."

"Geordie, no, I can—" Tears glazed MacGregor's blue eyes.

Geordie shook his head. He lifted his right hand.

Dare clasped it in his right hand, his expression threatening to crumble. "I've healed the wound. I'll boost you onto Fergus, and we'll run for it."

"I've...bled too...too much."

"No. I canna—"

"Until—" Geordie coughed again.

Dare's throat worked. He leaned closer until his face was inches above the other man's.

"Until...the break..."

Dare's lips trembled. He set his jaw.

"...break of day." A paroxysm of coughing racked Geordie.

Dare waited for it to pass. Carefully wiping the blood from his comrade's waxen face, he ground out, "Until the break of day." He leaned down and kissed the other man's brow. "Just so ye know, the bastard who shot you's a dead man."

"Amen—to that."

Geordie's hand went limp. Grief contorted Dare's face. Holding his comrade's hand to his chest, he gently closed the now-unseeing eyes.

He sat unmoving for several heartbeats. His grief tore at Amelia's heart, and she bit back a sob.

Scrubbing his sleeve across his eyes, he squared his shoulders. His face set in stony lines. He removed his coat and gently laid it over the other man's face. "Ye'll be seen to right and proper."

He rose and hurried to the two horses. From the saddle bag of one, a big gray, he removed a large, fabric-wrapped rectangle. With his head cocked, as though he were listening, he hastily tucked the rectangle in the saddle bag of the other horse, a tall chestnut.

He turned to the gray and laid his forehead briefly against its neck. When he straightened, moisture glazed his eyes again.

"Yer a good lad, Fergus. Lead them a merry chase." He slapped the horse's rump, and it galloped out of the clearing.

Dare mounted the chestnut. With a last look at Geordie's still figure, he wheeled the big horse and trotted off through the trees.

But where was he? Where was he going? When was this?

"Amelia."

She ignored the voice. Dare was in trouble. He'd helped her and Julian, and now he needed help. Now, tonight.

But where?

"Amelia. Come back to me, sweetheart."

Straining to know, she kept Dare's mounted figure in sight. He cleared the trees, leaned low over his mount's neck, and kicked it to a gallop on a narrow path.

"Amelia!" A warm hand gripped her shoulder.

The vision shattered. She opened her eyes.

She lay on her back in the bed at Pendragon with Julian leaning over her on one elbow.

"Are you with me?" he asked.

"Yes," she choked. He slid his arm around her, as though to draw her in, but she stopped him with a hand on his chest. "Dare's in trouble, Julian. He has a book, and there are people chasing him to recover it. I think it's the book the Scots rebels were using."

In the flickering firelight, his face tensed. "What did you See?"

She told him, concluding with, "Who is Geordie to him?"

"His younger brother." Julian pushed back the covers. "Thanks to Richard, I think I know where he's coming from. I need you to show me what you saw in the fire, and then we may need to scry."

Scrambling out of bed, she asked, "Do you think that's the book you told me about?"

"I can't think what other book he would care about enough to steal." Julian scooped up her dressing gown and held it for her.

Belting it, she hurried to the fireplace, where the logs had burned to embers. "We need to stoke the fire."

"I'll see to it." Now wearing his blue banyan, he took logs out of the basket by the hearth and used the poker to roll them into the embers.

The wood crackled, then caught. Julian slid his arm around her, and Amelia nestled against his side while they waited for the flames to rise.

"We could sit on the settle, you know." He nodded to the high-backed wooden bench beside the hearth.

"I like to be closer when I'm scrying." Frowning, she said, "I've a strong feeling this is urgent."

The log finally caught. Tongues of gold and orange flame rose in the hearth.

Amelia summoned the vision. As it played out in the flames, Julian grew ever grimmer.

When it ended, he said, "Can you scry where he is now? If I could see the countryside, I might have some idea where he is. Or not. It's night, after all, but—"

Amelia summoned the image. Dare walked his horse, leaning forward to pat its neck as its sides heaved. The lines of grief etched in his face made her throat hurt.

"Bloody hell," Julian muttered. His hold on her tightened. She reached out to grip his free hand. He ached for his friend, and she could do so little to help.

"Sweetheart, can you pull back, give me more of a view of the landscape?"

"I'll try." She'd done this a time or two, growing up, to find Adam when he was late for a meal.

Slowly, the image of Dare and his horse dwindled, the countryside expanding.

Julian's fingers tightened on hers. "Can you show me the road ahead of him?"

When she obliged, he grinned. "I know where he is. That's an old trading track, and he's about half a dozen miles outside of Kirkoswald. See that tower on the hill? It's the tower for Kirkoswald church."

"That's fairly far away."

"From here, yes, but not from St. Oswald's Manor. It's the ruin of a small hermitage, once attached to the collegiate church, outside Kirkoswald. It's a Merlin Club bolt hole, heavily warded and well off the main roads. If he can make it there without being scried, he'll be safe. At least for a while."

Frowning, he added, "Of course, if they scry him and see him disappear behind the wards, they'll know where to look. There's no help for that, though. At least they can't scry from a moving horse any better than anyone else can. Or so we must hope."

"Are we going after him?"

Julian's smile faded. "I won't take you into a possible fight, and I won't leave you here, even with our outriders."

"But is it not essential to keep that book out of enemy hands? Besides, he's our friend. If they catch him, they'll surely kill him."

"What they'll do if they catch you doesn't bear thinking about."

The warmth in his eyes made her breath hitch. Amelia raised her hand to his face, and he leaned down to kiss her. The kiss deepened. They pressed closer until he eased them to the floor in front of the hearth.

When the kiss broke, he gathered her in. Staring at the fire, he said, "Dare knows to head for Aysgarth if he's in trouble. We'll go there in the morning. I'll send half our guard to meet and escort him. He knows them from the ambush at our house."

"Don't all members of the Merlin Club know each other?"

"A few do. Most know only those who live near them. The Londoners, for example, each know the others on sight, and many are friends." He pressed a kiss into her hair. "The bed would be far more comfortable. If we're leaving for Aysgarth in the morning, we should sleep. We'll be on the road most of the day."

Amelia let him help her up. By unspoken consent, they climbed into bed naked and snuggled together.

Julian's breathing deepened, but Amelia stared up at the exposed ceiling beams. This place was doing something to her power. Increasing it in some way. The man beside her probably knew more that could help her understand than anyone else—except possibly the guardians of Morgan's pool.

There wouldn't be time to speak to Elspeth or one of the pool's other guardians tomorrow. Besides, she might not know anything helpful, the seer Gift being so rare, and the effect might be unique to Pendragon. If it persisted, though, Amelia would need to return here and see where the manor's magic could take her.

~

They rose early the next morning. Julian scried a Merlin Club report full of dismal news he then shared with Amelia. On April 3, Bonaparte had sent out a series of messages intended to reassure the governments of Europe. Around the same time, he'd secretly ordered the creation of a new cavalry force. With forty-six thousand men, it would outnumber Britain's and Prussia's combined.

Bonaparte clearly wanted a war, and Amelia felt as though all she had were more questions. She and Julian hadn't yet located Quatre Bras, but the maps in his book, compiled by club members on missions, had only minimal indexing.

While Julian supervised the brief loading of their baggage, she waited in the spring sunshine by the drive. In addition to their eight outriders, Southwell and Randall had accompanied them on this journey. Southwell had taken four of the outriders to meet Dare, but Randall and the remaining four moved with quick efficiency, their horses saddled and waiting in the drive.

"Your friend recovered the book," Richard's ghost said at her shoulder.

Amelia turned away from the coach so no one would see her lips move and assume she was talking to herself. "Yes, and we must learn how to do what it says." She paused, eyeing him. Although his grim expression didn't look promising, she added, "We don't know whether those who had it mastered that skill. If they did, the only way we can stop them is by going through there."

"This realm is full of perils, and it's an avenue to endangering the living world."

"Then teach me about it. We're going to learn this anyway, assuming this mysterious book truly contains the key. You might as well make certain we travel it wisely."

Stone-faced, he shook his head.

"Dear Heaven, Grandfather! Do you think any of us has any interest in wandering that realm if we can avoid it?" Though she would give a great deal to see Adam and Papa face-to-face again, not merely envision Adam when he spoke to her. "We need to stop the French plot. Beyond that, none of us has any desire to roam there. Do you want us bumbling about in ignorance? If this place is as treacherous as you say, could we not do a great deal of harm with an innocent mistake?"

"Yes." His lips tightened. "We'll consider it. If you're going to Aysgarth, you need a place where we can come to you."

"I'll see to it."

His gaze softened. "You're a true Mainwaring, Amelia, ready to do what must be done. However, that doesn't mean I can countenance this plan. I'll talk to your grandmother. Beyond that, I promise you nothing."

Still, that was something. "Thank you, Grandfather."

"I saw your friend's escape. He's safe, at least for now, heading southeast from Kirkoswald. Pursuit has split, four men headed for the coast at Whitehaven and four following your friend. They've actually overtaken him and are now south of his position, watching the back roads. He should be safe if he keeps to the main roads."

"Wait." Narrowing her eyes, she said, "How did you know about Dare's problem? Were you in our bedchamber—"

"Heaven forfend!" The pained look on his face would've been comical had the idea of ghostly spectators not been so embarrassing.

"Your grandmother and I take great pains to avoid such, er, intrusions. When we think of you, if our initial image—always fuzzy, as though looking through gauze, and we take care to approach from great distance —is not fully clothed and, ah, decent, we back away."

Well, that was something.

"I overheard Julian's discussion with his outriders early this morning. Regardless of our concerns about your using that book to come here, we agree it's safer in your hands than in the conspirators'."

He brushed his spectral hand lightly over her hair. "Safe travels, my dear."

Before she could reply, he vanished.

Safe travels, indeed. She could only hope Dare had the same.

CHAPTER 22

They reached Aysgarth Hall in the early evening. The coach clattered along a gravel avenue lined with trees. Amelia took a slow breath to settle her nerves. Most of Julian's household staff had known him from the cradle, and many of their families had served his for generations.

What would they think of his hastily acquired wife?

Julian gestured toward the coach window. "Horse chestnuts. Planted by my grandfather, who ripped out over a hundred lime trees to do it."

"What was wrong with the lime trees?"

"His countess didn't like them."

"That was rather extravagant."

He grinned. "I found a letter to him from Cabot, his great uncle, that scolded him vigorously for the costly indulgence."

"His great uncle felt he could do that?"

With a shrug, Julian replied, "I gather his father was not what we might consider a forceful man. Cabot, however, certainly was."

The coach rolled through a stone gateway and swung into a turn, bringing the gray stone front of the house with its banks of glowing windows into view.

"I should've asked you about the staff. I don't want to put my foot wrong." Instead, they'd talked about what to do next most of the way here.

"They'll like you," he said as the coach slowed to a stop. "Never fear.

You'll meet most of the staff a few at a time, but the primary three will greet us tonight. Mrs. Kirby, the housekeeper, is always eager to please, but if you ask her to show you round the house and take Mrs. Pettijohn's suggestions for meals every now and again, you'll quickly become a prime favorite."

Judging from the shadows in his eyes, his previous countess had not done those things. All the more reason, then, for Amelia to make allies of the women who managed Julian's—no, her and Julian's—home.

A stout man in black and two women clad in dark gray filed through the central archway and into the drive. The footman let down the step and opened the door.

Julian climbed out first and offered Amelia his hand. The evening light softened the stone façade. Framed by empty niches in the walls, a deep archway led to a lantern-lit courtyard. Above the arch, pairs of windows rose to a clock set in an ornate pediment.

Her feet touched the ground, and Julian offered her his arm. Smiling, he said, "Lady Aysgarth, welcome home."

Home had meant Leyburn Manor, but she must stop thinking of it as such. Her place was with Julian, who was saying, "This is Newbold, our butler. Newbold, will you do the honors?"

The plump man, whose black jacket and gray waistcoat looked a bit snug around the waist, stepped forward. The feeling of familiarity that came with him signaled that he was Gifted.

With a bow, the man said, "Thank you, my lord. Welcome, my lady. We are all delighted that you've come, and we wish you both many happy years." Turning to the woman beside him, he added, "This is Mrs. Kirby, the housekeeper."

The petite, gray-haired woman he indicated wore a plain gray gown and did not carry the feel of a Gifted. She dipped a curtsy. "Welcome, my lady. I've prepared an inventory for your ladyship's approval."

Although her words and her manner were perfectly correct, wariness filled her eyes.

Amelia smiled at her. "Thank you, Mrs. Kirby. I depend upon you to help me learn my way round my lovely new home."

"I await your ladyship's convenience." Smiling, the woman bobbed another curtsy.

Newbold indicated the next woman, who appeared to be Gifted. "This is our cook—"

Distant hoofbeats drummed on the avenue. Julian wheeled toward the sound.

In the dusk, Amelia's Gifted eyesight could barely make out a group of six horsemen cantering up the approach. If they were cantering, they weren't under threat. Did they pose one?

No, for Julian was smiling. He gave her a slight nod.

Amelia turned back to the butler. "It appears we're about to have guests. Newbold, his lordship told me earlier that you know how to settle these gentlemen, so I leave that to you and Mrs. Kirby. And our cook...?"

"Mrs. Pettijohn, my lady," Newbold said.

"Mrs. Pettijohn," Amelia repeated, smiling. "I understand you've experience feeding a small mob of hungry men, so I leave that to your discretion."

The stout woman puffed up her chest. "I won't fail you, my lady."

Julian said, "I know you'll all help my wife settle in. Newbold, please alert the stables to our visitors' arrival."

My wife. The phrase felt less strange now.

Julian continued, "Darling, if you want to see your things settled in our chambers, I'll take our guests to the blue room. You're welcome to join us if you wish."

"Of course." He likely intended to learn how Dare had obtained the mysterious book and what had happened. She also wanted to know, so she would hurry.

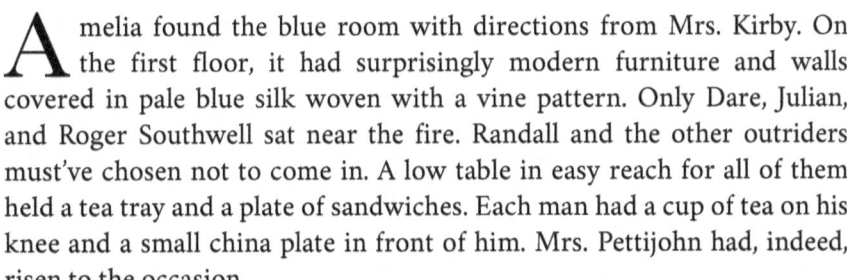

A melia found the blue room with directions from Mrs. Kirby. On the first floor, it had surprisingly modern furniture and walls covered in pale blue silk woven with a vine pattern. Only Dare, Julian, and Roger Southwell sat near the fire. Randall and the other outriders must've chosen not to come in. A low table in easy reach for all of them held a tea tray and a plate of sandwiches. Each man had a cup of tea on his knee and a small china plate in front of him. Mrs. Pettijohn had, indeed, risen to the occasion.

The men stood, holding their tea, as she entered.

Julian smiled at her. "There you are, my dear. We saved you the seat by the tea tray in the hope you would pour."

"Gladly, though you seem to have managed well enough without me."

Amelia seated herself on the sofa by Julian, and the others quickly sat. Pouring herself a cup, she said, "Don't let me interrupt you."

"We'd barely begun," Julian replied. "Dare just told us his brother Geordie infiltrated the conspirators and helped him gain access to the book."

Amelia turned to the young Scotsman. "I'm so very sorry for your loss." The words felt woefully inadequate, especially given that he'd watched his brother bleed to death.

"Thank you, Amelia." Dare ran a hand over his face. "There're nine Scotsmen and three French involved. Geordie helped me sneak into the manor where they're based. It's an old reivers' stronghold on what used to be Armstrong lands. I used glamours to ease in. The book was in a chest, but I picked the lock. Everything went smoothly until then."

He sounded bitter, and the lines of strain in his face deepened. "On m'way out, one o' them stumbled. Fell into me. A glamour won't protect ye from touch. Then it was a race. They must've stopped from time to time to scry us, to follow us so closely without taking any of the side trails. I was glad for Roger and the lads ye sent."

Southwell shrugged. "We had a bit of excitement outside Brough. No one was hurt, but they decided not to follow us farther."

"But they could have scried you," Julian said slowly. "Or scried the book. They would know where it is, at least until we brought it within the house's wards."

"Perhaps we should destroy it," Amelia said. Everyone turned to her with shocked expressions, but she continued. "If their aim is to use the knowledge in this book, the surest way to prevent that is to destroy it."

Her gaze and Julian's locked. He would be particularly against any destruction of knowledge.

Without looking away from her, Julian asked, "Dare, do you know whether they've mastered the secret of traveling the dead land?"

"I dinna—do not know for certain. Geordie said they'd practiced it a good deal, that they knew the ritual but hadn't managed to cross over. At least, so far as he knew."

Julian said, "If even one of them has figured out how to do it, we must master it in order to counter them."

They had allies among the dead as well, but neither she nor Julian would share that information outside a tight circle of family and close friends. Besides, they didn't know whether the Mainwarings trapped in the afterworld would be able to help.

Talking to Grandfather or Grandmother was now imperative.

melia walked into the walled garden with Julian. He'd agreed to an immediate attempt to contact her grandparents, but she knew he didn't fully trust them, perhaps because they were withholding information. He didn't know what wonderful allies they could be. Even with the tension between her and them about the afterworld, her trust in them would never waver. They had supported her during all the most difficult times of her life.

Julian shut the garden's wrought-iron gate with a click. "I don't like this," he said. "I won't feel sure of your safety until this is over."

"Our Gifted friends are all around us and heavily armed. The garden walls are another barrier. In truth, I'm glad I needn't cast a circle."

This far north, the night air carried a chill, even in April. Amelia hunched into her cloak.

"Grandmother? Miranda?" she called.

Light from the library windows and the terrace lanterns washed over the garden walls. From the sundial in the center, the garden paths radiated toward the compass points, the beds in between tidy and just beginning to show green for spring.

Amelia seated herself on the bench at the north compass point. Julian stood at her side.

When she cast him a questioning look, he shrugged. "If trouble finds us, I prefer to meet it on my feet."

If trouble blew past their friends on guard, he would have time to stand and meet it. If being on his feet made him more comfortable, however, she wouldn't argue.

"Grandfather?" she called. "If you can hear me, we desperately need to speak with you."

The spring breeze rustled the new leaves on the trees and on the garden shrubbery. No answer to her summons came.

"You did say they don't always respond."

"If they're near, they do. Or so I've always assumed."

They sat in silence a few more minutes. Neither ghost appeared.

"Amelia—"

Miranda shimmered into view on the path. A moment later, Richard appeared at her side.

Amelia smiled at them, but Julian tensed.

"They're here?" he asked.

She nodded.

"Good evening, my dear," Richard said. "You can tell Aysgarth to sit. No threat hovers anywhere near."

Amelia relayed the message, but Julian merely shrugged again.

Richard and Miranda exchanged a glance. Her lips curved in a slight smile. "He reminds me of you," she told him.

"Or of Cabot," Richard replied. "Well, let us not waste time. I hope you've warded that wretched book securely. If you haven't, they can scry it."

"Julian has it in a warded chamber," Amelia said, glancing at him.

He rolled his eyes, as though to say he wasn't so stupid as to fail in that precaution.

Neither ghost seemed to notice.

"That book," Richard grumbled, "is full of pretentious nonsense. It says you need all sorts of rubbish for the ritual of crossing over. A winding sheet from a year-old grave, the fragment of a dead priest's fingernail, a hair from an unshriven witch's corpse, dirt from a crossroads. It's useless, all of it. Unfortunately, the core of the ritual it details is accurate."

"How do you know that?" Amelia asked.

"I listened to them, of course. They've warded their tower but not their stables or their grounds. They also have copies of the ritual."

Amelia relayed the information to Julian, who frowned and asked, "Does he know whether they've mastered the rite?"

Amelia turned back to Richard, who raised a hand to stop her. "We can hear him."

"Of course. I forgot."

Miranda said, "If they haven't mastered it, they soon will. Richard thinks their obsession with using all the nonsensical props that book demands is actually slowing their progress. One or two of them have managed to form portals, the first step for the crossing. None has yet passed through."

"If they do pass through," Amelia asked, "can one bring through others?"

"Yes, if they're touching," Richard replied, "though we don't know how many they can bring through at one time that way. So far as we know, only we and the Wyndon of our day have ever made the crossing. He came through alone, and we brought only each other."

Amelia relayed that to Julian, who scowled. "That's a deuced disturbing possibility," he noted.

"It's an important one," Richard said. "One we had best hope doesn't become crucial. Each of our family's souls is trapped within the years he lived. Only Edmund, Miranda, and I can exist in the present. The three of us likely cannot stop them alone." Looking grim, he added, "We'll teach you and Julian how to pass over. If they manage it, we'll need living wizards here to battle them. But for the love of Heaven, destroy that book."

〜

J ulian looked up when Amelia entered the library. Perhaps he would one day grow accustomed to seeing her in his home. At present, though, each such glimpse gave him a jolt of happy surprise.

The book that had cost so much, an ancient grimoire bound in battered, brown leather, lay open on his desk. He couldn't argue with Hawkstowe's point about destroying the book, but he wasn't entirely certain he trusted the spectral Mainwarings. Amelia did, but they'd been extremely defensive about allowing access to the dead realm. Could their promise to teach Amelia and Julian be a mere ruse?

Thus far, however, the book had provided little useful information.

Dare lounged on the sofa, a book beside him unopened and his face set in weary lines.

"Our other guests are settled," Amelia told Julian. "Roger preferred to stay over the stable with the outriders, but Dare and Peter are in guest rooms off the gallery."

"Sorry to put you to the trouble," Dare said. "A pallet above the stable would do well enough."

Amelia made a dismissive gesture. Her smile, kind and yet devoid of pity, struck the perfect note. "You've had a wearing two days. You should sleep in a bed and rest. Besides, Mrs. Kirby seems to like having a house full of men to cosset."

Julian smiled. "She always loved it when my school friends came."

Amelia's expression softened. Quietly, she told him, "Adam loved coming here. Open study of magic and beautiful horses delighted him."

"His enthusiasm was always such a pleasure." Julian paused. "Don't tell Mrs. Pettijohn it wasn't the food."

"I won't." Amelia seated herself in the chair by his desk. "I thought I would stay with you while you work. If you find something interesting, perhaps I can help you untangle it."

Julian thanked her and went back to the book. Frowning at the page, he said, "It's a wonder no one using this has died. This recipe for a disguise potion uses nightshade and monksbane. A disguise as a corpse isn't very useful."

"It is for someone who only needs to seem a corpse," Amelia commented.

"Yes, but…hmm." Pretending to be dead, if one could revive in a short time with no ill effects, actually could be useful. Unlike, for example, this spell for ensuring one's unborn child was a boy. Or a girl, depending on one's wishes.

"Are you skimming at random?" Amelia asked.

"Unfortunately." He shrugged. "This is a collection of magical odds and ends with no appreciable organization."

Dare looked over at them. "Geordie said the spell for entering the dead realm was about two thirds of the way through."

Though Julian pretended to read, he watched Dare. The other man's shoulders slumped, and he rubbed his hands over his face.

"I'll seek my chamber," he finally said. "Unless you need me, Julian."

"No, go and rest. Any questions can wait until morning." Besides, he had a seer within arm's reach. Amelia could help him find answers.

Julian and Amelia wished Dare a good night. He walked out of the room and gently closed the door behind him.

Amelia turned to Julian. "He doesn't look well, which of course is not surprising. I have a good sleeping potion, one far more reliable and certainly safer than anything you'll find in that book."

"He won't take it, but you're kind to think of it."

Amelia looked uncertain, and Julian would have wagered he knew what troubled her. "I'll destroy the book when it's no longer useful."

"You don't trust my grandparents."

"I don't know them."

"But I do. Julian, Grandfather would never have told us the core of the ritual for crossing over was accurately described if he intended to trick us."

"Except possibly to seem sincere."

Annoyance flashed in her eyes. "You'll see. You do realize they're right about the book being dangerous? Aside from the lore it contains, it can lead the conspirators here."

"I know. We'll destroy it as soon as I'm sure there's nothing else in it that need concern us."

His habit of suspicion prodded him to make a copy of the rite without her knowledge and hide it away. But she trusted the ghosts, who'd been honest with her if not always cooperative. Julian's great-great-uncle Cabot had also believed in Richard Mainwaring's integrity.

In deference to Amelia and Cabot, Julian decided against making a secret copy.

Amelia curled up in the corner of the sofa and watched the fire. Julian returned to the godawful book. The more he read of it, the less likely it seemed to contain anything useful.

Looking for the crossing ritual, he flipped the pages casually. Not reading in order seemed reckless—who knew what he might miss?—but he wanted to see that rite tonight.

The handwriting was dreadful, some of it old English, some in Norman French or Latin and some few bits more modern, all of it cramped and hard to read. Some of the pages even had the lines crossed. It would be a miracle if he could make it through this book without his eyes crossing permanently.

"Here it is," he murmured. The supplies were listed at the beginning. "A winding sheet from a year-old grave, as Richard said. Lovely."

Amelia wrinkled her nose. "This would have to be important to be worth pilfering that."

"To the conspirators, it's everything." Rubbing his eyes, Julian leaned back in his chair. "I despise what the Scots're doing, but I understand it. Some might say they deserve to be hoaxed and used. Perhaps they do. But I can't help feeling some sympathy for men who so love their homeland."

"Nor can I." Amelia shifted to face him. "Yet you're a realist, Julian. You must be, to do what you do for the Merlin Club and the Conclave."

"I try. Dreamers are easy to lure astray, yet I sometimes think it's their aspirations that drive progress."

"Perhaps so." His wife smiled at him. "But without realists to anchor them, dreamers sometimes drive progress directly off a cliff."

He grinned. "It's good to be useful. I doubt there's anything useful here, though. I'll take a quick look through and then burn it. You needn't wait up while I do that."

"This was rather a long day," she admitted, "and there's more to come tomorrow."

Their lessons in crossing through to the dead realm would start tomorrow, as both Richard and Miranda insisted attempting it without enough rest was dangerous. They'd also insisted on somewhere more private than the garden for the lessons.

Since Julian refused to risk taking Amelia anywhere remote from the warded house, that posed a problem. Especially since only she could talk to the ghosts.

By morning, he would figure it out.

~

Amelia rubbed her eyes as she closed the library door. Going to bed sounded ever more appealing. She turned toward the nearest stairs, but light spilling from the blue room across the entry hall drew her. The fire should be banked if everyone was going to bed.

She hurried toward the room, only to stop on the threshold. Dare MacGregor sat on the sofa, his shoulders slumped and a glass of something amber in his hand.

Eyes widening at the sight of her, he rose. "I beg pardon, Amelia. I was on my way to bed, and the fire drew me."

"You're welcome to use any chamber in the house, of course." The torment on his face was painful to see. "Can't sleep?" she asked quietly.

He shook his head. "I should be abed, but...I can't."

Oh, how well she knew that feeling! "Would you like me to stay, or would you rather be alone?"

"It doesn't matter." He shrugged.

Amelia sat on the sofa near him. Once she was seated, he also sat.

"I lost my brother," she told him. "About eighteen months ago."

"I'm sorry for it," he said, staring into the fire.

"As am I. It was a magical accident. Papa was trying to store magic in crystals. When he tried to draw it out, the crystals exploded. The backlash killed him and my brother, Adam."

He nodded but said nothing else. Leaning forward with his elbows on his knees, his face haggard, he was the very image of dejection. Perhaps she should leave him alone.

Or perhaps he needed an outlet for his grief.

"Would you like to talk about him?" she asked.

Dare took a long swallow of his drink—brandy, by the smell of it. "He was just another Highland cattleman. Not anyone important."

"Everyone is important, at least to family and friends."

"Aye, so they are." Another long swallow.

Minutes ticked by. Perhaps he wanted her gone but was too polite to say so, especially in what was now her home.

Amelia shifted, preparing to rise.

"He loved chess," Dare said abruptly. "We had an ivory set, one some old MacGregor brought back from the Indies."

"Adam, my brother, played chess too. Was Geordie good at it?"

"Oh, aye. Good against anyone and a far sight better than me. He had the patience for it." With a sidelong look, he added, "He and Julian were cut from the same cloth. Patient, always analyzing, always thinking half a dozen or more moves ahead."

"Was your brother bookish, too?"

"When he had the time." Dare sighed. "He left a wife and three bairns. I must tell them, and soon."

"Where do they live?"

"Outside Dunblane." His face quivered. He closed his eyes and clenched his jaw.

Perhaps she should leave, but instinct had her reaching out, grasping his hand. When he gripped hers, she knew she'd done right.

"We'll sit here a while," she said.

Nothing else in that bloody book had seemed useful. Julian watched the pages burn. The leather smoldered and reeked. It was just as well Amelia had gone to bed. He would have to leave the windows open to clear the smell. That would have to wait until tomorrow, though. He wouldn't go to bed and leave such an easy opening into the house in these circumstances.

Burning only the pages might've sufficed, but it was best to take no chances with Gifted foes. Julian gathered witchfire around his hand and streamed it to the hearth. The leather crackled, caught, and disintegrated.

That should do it. Tomorrow, they would scatter the ashes to make absolutely certain no one could use the book's remnants to anchor a scrying.

He banked the fire and magically extinguished the candles around the room. As Amelia had said, this had been a long day. A good night's sleep would benefit everyone.

Shutting the library door, Julian magically locked it, as he'd done earlier with the terrace doors and windows. No one else would be able to enter until he'd disposed of those ashes.

The soft gleam of candlelight and a hearth fire spilled from the blue room. Had someone left the fire burning? He strolled over to check it.

In the doorway, he froze. Amelia and Dare sat on the sofa, close together and with her hand in his. The sight slammed into Julian's heart like a horse's kick. He couldn't breathe.

Not again.

But this was Amelia. She wouldn't…

He'd thought Charlotte wouldn't. He'd been wrong.

CHAPTER 23

As he fought to master himself, Amelia looked up at him. "Julian. There you are." She withdrew her hand from Dare's and walked toward the doorway. "Dare was telling me about Geordie," she said.

A few feet away, she stopped, her brow furrowing. "Is something amiss?"

"Of course not."

The furrow deepened, but he looked beyond her. "Dare, be sure to bank the fire when you go to bed."

"I'll see to it." Dare stared into the flames, apparently oblivious to the undercurrent flowing between Julian and his wife.

Looking down into Amelia's puzzled, concerned face, Julian bit back an oath. "I'm going to bed." He turned on his heel, heading for the nearest staircase.

Amelia hurried after him. "What is it?"

"Nothing. It's nothing." God, he hoped that was true.

On the landing, she caught his arm. "It isn't nothing. You were relaxed in the library. Then you came in the parlor, where Dare and I were sitting, and your face closed over."

Comprehension dawned in her eyes, followed by hurt. "How can you think that?" She swung away from him and hurried up the stairs.

Either his expression or her bloody Gift had betrayed him.

As she reached the second floor, he overtook her. "I don't think it."

"Perhaps you don't want to, but you do. Or you did." The wounded look she shot him made him feel about the size of a barn rat. "I thought we had trust, if nothing else."

Did that mean there was nothing else between them?

He could worry about that later. "I do trust you. I hope you trust me."

"For a moment, at least, you didn't. Perhaps you're now wondering whether you can. As I'm wondering whether I can rely on you to have faith in me."

Struggling to explain, to not seem as idiotic as he felt, he said nothing.

"I was comforting our bereaved friend," she said, "a friend who is rather more yours than mine, actually, and yet you..." She compressed her lips. "I won't justify myself when I've done nothing wrong. Good night, Julian."

She stalked through the corridor to her chamber and quietly entered. He stared after her. That hurt and outrage had felt true. At the end, Charlotte's protestations had seemed hollow. He'd finally learned to see through her pretense, and he'd almost regretted that.

Amelia, however, showed none of the calculation that had always lurked in the depths of Charlotte's eyes, had he not been too besotted to see it.

Now he'd seen Charlotte in Amelia, who hadn't deserved it. Amelia wouldn't soon forget this, so he'd put a blemish on the closeness they'd been building. It was entirely his fault.

～

I *thought we had trust, if nothing else.* Her own words echoed in Amelia's mind as she stared into the flames. Dare wasn't the only one who couldn't sleep tonight.

Wrapped in her favorite shawl, she huddled in front of the fire. Lying alone in the bed she'd assumed she and Julian would share would be unbearable.

Julian had never suffered more in comparison to Crispin.

Crispin had never been deceived and used, as Julian had been in his prior marriage.

Could she forgive him?

Perhaps, if he admitted his mistake and didn't repeat it. His absence now, though, said much about his true feelings.

A soft knock on the door that connected to his chamber made her pulse kick. Shifting to see the door, Amelia raised her chin. "Yes?"

Julian came into her chamber and shut the door behind him. The grave look on his face could mean anything. He'd changed into his nightshirt and banyan.

She turned back to the hearth. Had he come for physical intimacy, with this between them? If so, she couldn't bear it after the tenderness they'd shared. She raised her knees and rested her crossed arms on them.

He sat beside her on the thick rug. "I'm sorry. I was wrong."

Staring into the flames, she said, "I won't spend the rest of my life paying for Charlotte's sins. I can't."

"You won't have to." He took a deep, audible breath. "Of course I want you to be kind to our friends. To comfort them when they need it. When I saw you, it took me back for a moment."

"For longer than that," she said, remembering that conversation on the stairs. She laid her cheek on her crossed arms and studied him. "When I agreed to marry you, I told you I keep my word. Yet at the first test, you doubted me."

The pain in his eyes tugged at her heart, but she had to stand firm. If she yielded too quickly, she would always have to second-guess every gesture toward every man in her life.

"I don't ask you to forgive me," he said, staring at her. "Forgiveness means a clean slate, no repetition of errors, and I'm not certain I can promise that. At least, not yet."

"Then we have a problem," she replied, her heart aching.

"It's my problem. I'm determined it won't be ours." He scrubbed both hands over his face. "Until now, I didn't realize how much suspicion had become a habit."

That didn't bode well at all.

"Habits can be broken," he added. "I'm resolved to break this one. When I do, perhaps I will have earned your forgiveness. Can you give me the chance to do that?"

The regret and the uncertainty in his face convinced her. Amelia held out her hand. "I want that life we're to build together." That meant she could not hold tonight against him and must behave as though it didn't matter.

Even though it did, very much.

Julian caught her hand and kissed it. "Thank you."

He pushed to his feet. "We have much to do tomorrow. We should try to sleep."

She let him help her up, but he still looked uncertain, even contrite. His expression twisted her heart. "I'm sleeping here," she told him. "What about you?"

"All things considered, I was waiting to be asked."

Amelia smiled at him. "Come to bed."

∾

The orchestra played a waltz, the notes drifting through the familiar purple-gray fog. It rolled aside, revealing a ball in progress. Tent-like draperies of crimson, black, and gold created an exotic feeling in the long, low room with its rose-trellis wallpaper. Girls in pastel gowns and women in deeper colors danced with men in formal black or in the various blues, greens, and reds of military uniforms. Garlands of ribbons, leaves, and flowers adorned the room's pillars, and the light glittered off crystal chandeliers, jewelry, and gold and silver uniform braid.

Halfway down the room, she and Julian smiled and chatted with another couple. If this were only a dream, she would see it through her own eyes, not observe as though she were someone else.

Outside the ballroom, a footman stood with a man in a blue uniform jacket with crimson facings on the lapels and cuffs and gold braid trim. The footman went into the ballroom and returned with an officer in a scarlet jacket with more gold braid. The first man passed the second a folded paper. Over the music, Amelia caught the words *Charleroi* and *Prussians*.

The Duke of Wellington arrived, his narrow face and the hawkish nose that had spawned his nickname of "Old Nosey" familiar from newspaper sketches. The young officer in scarlet read the paper. His lips tightened, and he passed it to Wellington. The duke tucked it into his jacket without looking at it and stepped out of view.

The last of the couples leaving the supper tables entered the ballroom. With the hallway clear, Wellington returned. To the man in the scarlet uniform jacket, he said, "Your Highness, I need you to return to headquarters. We mustn't alarm the duchess's guests. I'll pass the word to the officers and follow you shortly."

The other man nodded and strode away with the soldier who'd brought the message. A middle-aged man in evening dress walked out of the ballroom. "What is it, Arthur? Boney?"

Wellington nodded. "I'll stay a bit longer to avoid letting the French sympathizers here think we're worried, but my men must return to their units. Meanwhile, Richmond, find me a map."

Amelia jolted awake, her heart pounding. Days ago, she'd Seen Wellington with a map. He'd mentioned a place called Quatre Bras. Where was Charleroi?

Julian spooned against her back. "All right?" he mumbled, apparently half asleep.

"I may know where Bonaparte is going." She told him about her dream, ending, "Do you know where Charleroi is?"

"No, but I know where the Duke of Richmond is. My mother often sees him and his duchess. They're in Brussels."

Julian shifted onto his back and drew her close. "Bonaparte isn't ready to move yet. He's still building his forces. If we're lucky, he won't have sufficient strength to attack before the Allied army is fully gathered, likely in July."

"If we aren't lucky?"

"Then Wellington will need all his skill. This must be a future vision. Can you scry the invitation to this ball? That would give us the date."

"I can try."

They slipped out of bed. Julian stoked the fire while Amelia settled herself in front of the hearth. She fed the vision of the ball into the flames and then summoned the invitation. It formed slowly, flickering, but with the date, fifteenth June, evident.

Julian frowned. "Can you tell whether there's a battle before this one? Or when Bonaparte will march from Paris?"

Amelia tried. A fuzzy, wavering image of Bonaparte riding out of Paris in a coach, his elite Old Guard surrounding it, flickered in the hearth.

"I can't find more." Slowly, she said, "Yet the ball is clear, and I feel certain it will lead to battle. To my dream of armies sleeping in the field. The ball must be important."

"Agreed. So we have until fifteenth June to steal that armor."

"Sooner would be better." If only they knew how to accomplish that.

Before breakfast, Julian asked Amelia to join him in the library. Having her participate in this difficult conversation with Dare would demonstrate his trust in her, or so he hoped, as well as bolster his own spirits.

When he explained what he meant to do, she looked at him for a long moment before she simply nodded. She sat beside him on the sofa.

A few moments later, Dare tapped on the open door and walked in. "You wanted to talk to me?"

"Yes," Julian said. "Amelia and I have news to share. Please sit down. First, I've a party of men ready to accompany you north. They'll provide security while you recover Geordie's body and take him home."

Dare's eyebrows rose. "That's kind, but it isna necessary."

"I think it is. By now, the conspirators must surely know who you are and who Geordie was to you. They'll expect you to return for him." Dare frowned, and Julian added, "The Merlin Club looks after its own, Dare. Would you not do the same for any of us?"

"Very well. Thank you for the escort."

"It's our privilege to help," Julian said. "If you want to lead a raid, I can put together—"

"No." Dare's eyes glinted with cold anger. "I'll see to them. This is Scotland's problem. We Scots will put an end to it."

"If you're sure," Julian said slowly. "If you don't see to it, however, I must."

"Fair enough."

Dare studied him for a long moment. "You've done the Scots a good turn," he said at last, "even if they don't know it. I'll do one for you as repayment. There are magics you don't know. Magics my kin have kept close for centuries. From what Robin told me of your duel, this Wyndon knows some of them. When I've seen to Geordie and the rebel fools, I'll teach you how to counter them."

When Julian thanked him, Dare shrugged. "As you say, the Merlin Club looks after its own. If that's all, I'll see you at breakfast."

He left the room, closing the door behind him.

Amelia said, "That went better than I thought it might."

"It did, and now we've more pressing concerns. We must be in Brussels before the events you dreamed last night occur, but I need to make certain those Scottish and French plotters have been dealt with before we go. Can you See or scry where Bonaparte is hiding that armor?"

She glanced at the mantel clock. "Everyone will be gathering for breakfast, but I think I should attempt it now. I feel as though our time is running short."

Julian walked toward the door. "I'll have James tell our guests to eat without us. Someone can bring the two of us a tray here. The more information we have, and the sooner, the better equipped we'll be to act."

Amelia needed only a moment to begin the scrying. The image of a large, gray stone building with a dome in the center formed in the flames. "Julian, do you know where this is?"

"Paris. It's the Tuileries Palace." He sat beside her on the sofa. "Can you see inside?"

"I'm trying." No matter how much power she pushed at the flames, however, she couldn't penetrate the wards.

"I'll try to See it," she told him, "but if the building is warded, Grand-mother and Grandfather cannot go into it to search."

She closed her eyes, concentrated on the image of the chest, and saw it through wispy purple-gray fog. It seemed to be in a small, Spartan chamber beside an elaborately decorated bedchamber. With a sigh, she released the vision and told Julian what she'd Seen.

He shook his head. "Sneaking into the Tuileries and then out with that chest would require a miracle. Perhaps they'll have something to suggest when we see them today."

~

Two hours later, Amelia and Julian stood together in his bedchamber. No one would disturb them here for anything not urgent. If they could rebuild the wards around this chamber, combining her magic and his, that might enable her family ghosts to enter.

Amelia took a deep breath to still her nerves. "I sometimes renewed the wards at Hawkstowe and Leyburn but never worked with any others."

Julian smiled at her. "It's easy," he said.

They walked to the exterior wall, where the windows looked out over the estate's rolling parkland. He placed his right hand flat on the wall. She placed her left beside it.

"When you heal," he said, "you feed magical power into your patient. One creates a ward the same way, as you may recall, but it's protective magic, not restorative." He caught her free hand. "Feed magic into me. Then I'll feed it into you. Then we both feed it into the wall."

"So what we use on the wall combines us both." Amelia nodded. "Right, then. I'm ready."

"You first."

She gathered power and channeled it down her arm, into their joined hands so that argent magic crackled around them. Julian's gaze darkened.

"Now me," he said, his voice rasping. The heat in his eyes created bubbling restlessness deep inside her. Magic flowed around their hands again, his rolling up her arm and down into her body, and the restlessness grew more insistent.

Amelia licked her lips, and desire flashed in Julian's gray eyes.

"Now," he gritted out.

Still holding hands, they each fed magic into the wall. The tides of argent from his hand and hers mingled, flowing up the wall, down to the floor, up to the ceiling.

"Keep it contained," he reminded her.

Of course. They needed the blended ward only for this wall.

The silver tide spread, but she saw it only peripherally. Her gaze was locked on Julian's hard face. On his eyes, warm and brilliant with desire.

His grip tightened. "That's done it," he said. "We can stop."

Amelia forced herself to look directly at the wall. The silvery glow faded into the structure, but she could feel the magic around them. Within them.

When she looked back at Julian, he dropped her hand and pulled her close. His head came down for a hot, deep kiss. Amelia welcomed him, pressing close, reveling in the hardness of his body where it pressed into hers. His tongue speared into her mouth. When she sucked it, he groaned.

"Shall we go away for a while?" Richard's dry voice behind her asked.

With a gasp, Amelia jerked free. Julian gave her a dazed, bewildered look.

"Richard's here," she choked out. "So's Miranda."

Comprehension dawned in his eyes, then annoyance. "Their timing's dreadful."

"They offered to go away." She half hoped they would.

"My mood is broken," Julian said. "But if you—"

"No. No, let's proceed." She absolutely could not talk to her husband about marital relations in front of her grandparents.

Turning to face them, she laced her fingers through Julian's. "We're ready to begin."

"Uh—one thing," Julian said, staring toward them. "Are you standing by the wall sconce, or am I imagining you?"

CHAPTER 24

Stunned, Amelia gaped at Julian. "You can see them?"

"Your grandfather's grinning at me as though his horse won the Derby."

He was, and Miranda was smiling. But how could Julian know?

Julian squeezed her hand. "You channeled your magic through me, and now we're touching. I suspect it's to do with that. Let's find out."

He released her and raised one eyebrow. "Now I can't see them."

She caught his hand again, watching his face.

"Yet there they are. So I can see them as long as you and I are connected. Or until the shared magic wears off."

"Then we've no time to waste," Miranda stated. "Julian, I gather you know who we are. We know who you are. So let us not waste time on introductions. Did you each fetch a twig or pebble, one not shaped by anyone, to anchor you?" When they both nodded, she said, "Excellent. Richard was ever better at this than I, so he'll instruct you while I go keep watch on those pesky Scots."

"How is Adam?" Julian asked.

"If we succeed at this," Richard replied, "you can ask him yourselves."

Face to face, he meant. Amelia's heart kicked hard. Being with her twin again would be wonderful.

"If the Scots conspirators master this before we do," Julian asked, "how will you stop them? From what MacGregor says, you'd need an army."

247

Richard's smile held a lethal edge. "Not if we simply eliminate the first few who succeed. The others will assume they failed, perhaps even be deterred by that."

Eliminate them. Kill them, he meant, as soon as they entered the afterworld. Amelia's heart pounded.

Richard raised an eyebrow. "This is war, my dear, and they are the enemy. They're prepared to kill hundreds of Royal Navy sailors and Royal Marines. I won't balk at shedding their blood."

"Of course," she replied, and Julian's hand tightened on hers. Richard was right, a fact Julian's failure to argue underscored.

"Amelia scried for something we need to steal." Julian explained about Joan's armor. "Her scrying showed her the Tuileries Palace, but we can't see past its wards. Have you any suggestions?"

"From here," Richard said, "you may be able to find the armor and other items you seek. The living can go where those of us who abide here cannot. If either of us were to try to pass into any other part of this house, for example, the Winfield wards would stop us. We could not penetrate them, even in ghostly form. Someone alive, however, someone not trapped here, can pass through those wards."

"That could be extremely useful," Julian breathed. Amelia could almost see plans and strategies churning behind his eyes.

"There are two parts to this," Richard began. "The first is forming a portal and stepping through it. The second is remaining alive when you emerge here. This realm is infested with wraiths, damned souls who were the worst of the worst in life and must remain here for a very long time, if not forever, as penance for their evil deeds. They're vicious and devour souls. Miranda or I can protect you from them and teach you to protect yourselves. You mustn't run from them, however, or otherwise move far away from me until you master that skill. Have you questions?"

They shook their heads.

Richard continued, "You should do this one at a time, and I suspect Amelia will learn faster because she has an indirect familiarity with this place."

Julian said, "That's probably what the winding sheet and other tools the book mentioned are designed to do, to help one feel the land of the dead."

"Perhaps." Richard shrugged. "Not that they will. This realm is unique. Now let's try. If either of you succeeds in forming a true portal, you should walk through it holding the other's hand. After you've crossed over once, attuning your magic to this realm and coming through will be easier. Be certain you have whatever you chose as an anchor."

When they nodded, he said, "Good. Now keep part of your attention on me. Just as you feed magic into a fire to scry or into a wall to form a ward, cast magic around the edge of a doorway. That one will do." He nodded to the open door between her chamber and Julian's. "There's no ward between that room and this, so I can move through there. You want to use a true doorway to avoid walking into a wall if you're unsuccessful. There also seems to be something about a doorway that magically helps form one."

"If magic is intention coupled with power," Julian mused, "a door image could help form the intention."

"Perhaps so." Richard gestured to Amelia. "Whenever you're ready, my dear. Until you have the doorway formed, do not hold onto Julian, as he could anchor you here."

Julian released her hand. Amelia took a deep breath and squared her shoulders. Extending her right hand, she envisioned power flowing from it to the doorway. Argent wreathed the opening, including the threshold.

"I can see that," Julian breathed.

"Anyone Gifted can," Richard said. He crossed the room, walked through the wall—which gave Amelia a jolt—and reappeared beyond the glowing doorway.

"It has the feel of a portal. Very good. Now take Julian's hand and walk through it to me."

Lacing her fingers through her husband's, she asked, "Could you see Richard before I took your hand? Or only the portal?"

"Only the portal. I couldn't see beyond it."

"Also as it should be," Richard said.

Together, Amelia and Julian walked toward the portal. As they neared it, the magic in it resonated within her. "Do you feel it?" she asked, looking at Julian.

"I do, a faint, barely noticeable tingling over my skin."

They paused on the threshold. Richard smiled and took two steps backward. "Come through," he urged.

They walked forward, into biting cold and thick air and...past it to Amelia's chamber.

"Never mind," Richard advised. "That was a good first effort. Julian, you try it."

The same thing happened with him, and then again when she tried.

They each attempted passage half a dozen times before Richard called a halt.

"It's neither easy nor pleasant," he told them, "and the matter isn't yet urgent."

"We still shouldn't delay," Amelia said. "We need to take that armor as soon as we can. Losing it could stem the rush of people to Bonaparte's standard. Perhaps even undercut their loyalty on the battlefield, should matters come to that."

"Possibly," Richard conceded. "Or possibly not. Your theory about the armor is only that. You've no proof of any of it. The French wizards could've stolen it merely to rescue it from English hands. Or believing it was needed, whether or not it truly was. We've no way to know."

"Until we touch it," Julian said. "If it possesses magical allure, we'll know when we have it in hand."

"That may be so," Richard acknowledged, "but if it does, you must take care not to be swept up in its net."

Judging by Julian's expression, he hadn't thought of that either, but Richard was correct.

Richard suggested, "You should rest and recoup your power. We can try again tomorrow morning."

Another delay. Yet he had a point. This was, indeed, a difficult rite, best attempted at full magical strength.

"How long did you need to master this?" Amelia asked.

"Quite a while." He shrugged. "Edmund taught me, although he did it reluctantly. In the end, I mastered it because Miranda was in danger. I needed to reach her quickly, and that was the only way."

Amelia asked, "Does that mean we need an urgent situation to goad us?"

"I've no idea. I only know the course my efforts followed. That's why I know you should rest."

"There is something you could do, if you will," Julian said. "We need to know where Bonaparte is. Once he starts marching, we must move." He glanced at Amelia. "There's a battle coming, somewhere near Brussels. It's better for us all if Bonaparte goes into it without that armor. If we cannot steal it by passing through that realm, we must sneak into his encampment. Either way, we cannot risk his having such an asset going into the battle."

〜

On the evening of the eighth day after Dare's departure for Scotland, Amelia found thoughts of him sliding into her mind often. Perhaps she should scry him or try to summon a vision. If she did, though, how would Julian respond?

Tonight, she sat on the sofa, reading another book about Richard III's claim to the throne while Julian worked on pieces of an ancient document at his worktable. She glanced over her shoulder at him, and the sight of him intent on his task stirred a wave of tenderness within her.

He'd said he would work on eliminating his suspicions. She'd said she would give him a chance. So perhaps she should risk being honest.

"Julian, I've been thinking about Dare."

He straightened, and his carefully blank expression didn't bode well. Still, she needed to act on this nagging unease.

"I feel that I should scry him or try to summon a vision and see how he fares."

"I would never argue with a seer's hunch. Do you need any help from me?"

"Not yet. I'll try a scrying first. If that doesn't succeed, if you have a bit of MacGregor tartan, that might help me summon a vision."

Julian hesitated. "Thank you for looking out for him," he said in a voice that was relaxed and easy, not stilted at all, before bending over his work again.

Perhaps his earlier stiffness had been uneasiness about her reaction rather than his own.

Amelia turned back to the fire and directed her magic at it. The image that arose seemed unreal. "Julian, come look at this."

Dare led a group of men and women on horseback down a narrow lane. Globes of blue witchlight bobbing above the horses lit their way.

Settling beside her on the sofa, Julian said, "He's not worried about secrecy, obviously. Twenty-three riders. If they're attacking a group of twelve, the odds favor them."

The riders pulled up just inside the tree line and dismounted. In the large clearing ahead of them, about forty yards away, stood a round pele tower four stories high and about thirty feet across. Lights glowed in its narrow windows.

Each rider, including the women, wore a tunic and loose breeches of dark green or blue with knee-high boots. Their only visible weapons were dirks on their belts at their right hips. Over the tunics, they each wore a different plaid looped diagonally across their torsos and pinned at their left shoulders by large, elaborately worked silver brooches set with smooth pebbles of smoky brown.

"Those are cairngorm stones," Julian said. "Smoky quartz. Interesting that all the brooches match. So do their garments, even the women's, except for the color."

She hadn't noticed that. "As though they were part of a particular group?"

"They well may be."

The image of Dare in the flames gestured. His comrades split, half going left and half right, all trailing a faint shimmer that implied magic.

One by one, the lights in the tower went out. The paths Dare's comrades had taken glowed faintly, as though they'd warded the area, an impressive feat with a space so large. The group reunited, fanning out in a semicircle with Dare at the center. He stepped to the fore and raised both hands to chest height, pointing them directly at the tower. Argent crackled around his hands, building until its glow lit his entire body.

Men poured from the tower's door with silver, blue, or green magic streaming from their fists.

The other wizards also built power around their hands. When Dare loosed his, the blast sheared off twenty feet up the left side of the tower. His companions shot bolts at the tower's defenders. Some fell. Others flung up shields of ice or fire.

Such use of magic wasn't possible.

Amelia looked at Julian and found him looking at her, his expression as stunned as she felt.

"I was right," he stated. "There are many magical Gifts or skills we've lost over time, not only the ones Wyndon used. The Scots didn't entirely lose this one, but we English seem to have."

"Perhaps it isn't entirely lost. If you could do that and knew few others could, wouldn't you keep it a secret, as they have?"

Their gazes met in shared awareness of the threat to her because she possessed a rare Gift. Would a rare skill be any less dangerous?

Julian shook his head. "I've heard tell of English Gifted who could do such things a hundred or more years ago but have never seen a written record." Rubbing his jaw, he continued, "The 1600s were a turbulent era. We had the Civil War, the Protectorate, the upheaval between that and the Restoration, and, of course, the witchcraft trials."

"We needed such skills to survive then."

"But the 1700s were less perilous, at least for danger to our kind. The witchcraft trials died out, and we fought our wars outside our own soil. A good bit of that conflict was in Scotland. Perhaps that explains why they kept that skill and we've lost it. A skill that isn't needed falls out of use and, if not recorded, becomes lost."

Amelia nodded at the battle scene in the fire. "Do you think Wyndon's ability to use magic in his fists might be some form of this?"

"It well could be." Julian frowned. "I wish I knew how they do that."

Of course he did. Such power would be invaluable against a magical foe, as Dare and his allies were proving. The glare of so much power in the air made seeing what happened difficult. The glow faded, though, as the defenders died.

At last, the battle ceased. Bodies littered the ground, but Dare and his companions still stood.

"We've seen what we need to, I think." As Amelia let the scrying fade, he continued, "It's good to know Dare is safe and doing well."

"I wonder if those are the magics he means to teach you."

Julian grinned, the expression fierce in the firelight. "I do hope so."

~

Another week passed. Each evening, Amelia and Julian conferred with Richard or Miranda about Bonaparte's status and that of the three French conspirators who had escaped Dare's net. They also asked about the magic they'd seen the Scots use.

"Some in our time could do it," Richard had told them. "Not many, though. It was a difficult skill to master."

"Can you teach me?" Julian asked.

"Us," Amelia corrected, frowning at him. "Teach us."

"I don't want you going into battle," Julian told her.

Amelia raised an eyebrow. "Sometimes battle comes to us, whether or not we seek it."

The reminder of the threat to her stopped him, but his lips tightened.

"Alas, that I cannot teach you," Richard had said. "I don't know how to do that, nor does Miranda. Your Scots friends are your best hope there."

They could do nothing about that until Dare returned, so they turned their attention to other matters. Each morning, they practiced making portals. Access to the afterworld seemed their best chance of stealing Joan's armor.

"I wish I could think of a way we might use it," Julian said as they lay in bed one night. "Bonaparte likely had it with him when he addressed army regiments on his way to Paris. Did it sway them to join him, or would they have done so anyway?"

"We may never know. Now those units are part of his very large army." Amelia sighed and snuggled closer. This problem kept Julian awake at night, and there was so little she could do to help. "They cannot all be in range of whatever magic the armor holds, yet they still follow him. Joan exhorted entire armies wearing it. If we tried to do that, perhaps by standing on the chest holding the armor, would that win their loyalty? Or would someone beyond the reach of its effect shoot us before we said three words?"

Julian's arm around her tightened. "There is no *we*. I will run any necessary risks in using that armor, not you."

He was welcome to think so for now if it eased his mind.

"That's an excellent question, though," he continued. "It might be more effective with a smaller group."

"But how big a group would that include? And what good does drawing off a small group do? Unless they were engaged in something vital?"

"Not much. Even if I could entice a hundred or so away, the effect would doubtless fade by the time I faced the next hundred."

"We would be chasing our tails," she agreed.

He seemed not to notice her use of *we*. So much the better.

"Once we obtain it," he said, "perhaps inspiration will strike. Or a situation may arise that seems to present an opportunity. Joan could exhort an army, but that was Joan herself, with her own power to inspire. The armor naturally has a weaker influence, but we cannot know how much weaker without testing it. We likely won't have a chance to do that outside a battle."

"So the key is remaining alert and open to possibilities?"

Julian chuckled in the darkness. "You just described ninety percent of what the Merlin Club does."

His breathing slowly deepened, and he relaxed against her. Sleep eluded Amelia, though.

Bonaparte had issued letters to the allied coalition claiming he accepted the terms of the prior year's Treaty of Paris, an offer made too late because he had already been declared an outlaw. A couple of weeks later, he'd ordered one hundred thousand muskets to be ready within fifty days. That would mean the end of May. Did he intend to attack then?

Wyndon remained in Calais. Why?

Julian said little, but the worry in his eyes troubled her. She scried and tried to summon visions but couldn't evoke anything other than her earlier images of battle. Each passing day brought them closer to the fifteenth of June and gave Bonaparte time to strengthen his hand.

~

The next morning, Amelia looked at Julian across the library table. "I begin to despair of mastering the afterworld entry rite, but we simply must. A glamour can hide us from sight as we go through a camp, but if anyone bumps into us, or if any wizard passes near enough to feel the magic in the glamour, that could ruin everything."

"So could a stray bullet."

"As could our current concern, an aimed shot. I know you've concerns about our security out of doors, but I'll wager a ride would do us good. The weather's warming, too."

"Yes, but we're safer in the house."

He'd given up his regular rides because of her. "This is supposed to be your time to work with your horses. You could go riding without me. No one's hunting you."

"So far as we know." He gave her a wry grin. "Wyndon may have won our duel, but he must see me as an obstacle. He needn't be present to do us mischief."

A tap on the door heralded Newbury. He carried a silver salver with a stack of paper packets on it. "The post, my lord."

Julian accepted the papers and thanked him. Amelia went back to her book, a history of warding written in cramped, tiny script she could barely read.

"The invention of the printing press did us all a great favor," she commented, frowning at the page.

"Indeed." He broke the seal on a folded packet and opened a note. "Letter from Mama, forwarded from London. I should write to her and tell her we'll be descending on her. Accommodations in Brussels are scarce, Bonaparte or not."

"Well, most people don't know he'll eventually head that way."

Julian glanced over his mother's letter. "She's sorry to have missed the wedding. Wants us to come to Brussels so she can host a dinner for us."

"That could be an excuse for us to go there."

"Yes, it could—bloody hell!" He sat up straight in his chair and stared at her. "Wyndon's expected in Brussels."

"With Napoleon headed there, his presence seems ominous. Though perhaps we're reading more into it than we should."

"It's better to be too cautious than not cautious enough."

"Can you send someone to capture him?" *Someone who isn't you*, she added silently.

"Possibly. Whoever did it would need to apprehend him secretly, and for a wizard with his Gifts, that means more than one agent. He isn't wanted by the British government, only the Conclave. Transporting a Gifted prisoner to London from Brussels would be a challenge, which is probably why they won't do it. The journey takes at least two days via Ostend or Antwerp, and that's with favorable winds."

He hesitated.

"What is it?"

"The simplest solution is assassination, but that requires sanction by the Conclave Council, which they're unlikely to give."

Amelia looked down at her book. Although she couldn't argue with his reasoning, the idea of simply dispatching someone, even Wyndon, still bothered her.

"I can send agents to watch him," Julian added. "We're stretched thin, but some people can be shifted. Perhaps Richard and Miranda can help, though we've asked much of them already. Now that we know where Bonaparte is and what he's doing, information our agents glean in London will be outdated, if it's reliable at all. I'll also ask Robin to turn managing the Merlin Club over to Ned and make ready to meet us in Brussels. With all we're facing, I want our best agent at our backs."

≈

Another several days dragged past. Amelia and Julian took to sitting in the walled garden, which supplied a protective barrier around them, each afternoon. They wrote letters or read in the sunshine. Julian had sent inquiries about Lady Eleanor's prayer book to her family, but no answers had yet arrived.

Though this was usually a pleasant interlude, sometimes even romantic, Julian stared at nothing today.

"What's wrong?" Amelia asked.

He shrugged. "Sorry, sweet. I scried one of our men in Paris this morning. Bonaparte claims to have approved additions to the French constitution that would require trials of members of the press to be heard by juries, not judges alone, and ban military tribunals hearing civilian trials. He promises complete freedom of religion, with the nation having no religious affiliation, and says their governing chambers must approve all conscription. Not for a moment do I think he means that. If these measures pass in this plebiscite he's announced, I believe he'll abide by them only so long as he must."

"That's dreadful." The idea of war again still made her sick to her stomach. "But how do you know that? One cannot talk through a scrying."

"No, but one can read what someone has written." He grinned. "At a designated time of day, an agent writes a report and sits before it in a private place. Robin or I scry that agent, either in the present or later, by looking into that day's past, and read the report. I can scry well enough for that. The agent sits with the report for five minutes before burning it with witchfire."

"Because that utterly destroys it."

"Precisely. The good news for us, such as it is, is that he has effectively beached the French navy. Initially, he excepted five ships of the line, but then he rescinded that. Their artillery and personnel are to be used for the defense of the interior. Smaller ships will defend the ports."

"So you know he plans a land battle."

"It seems that way, but we must watch to see whether he suddenly revives his navy. The vote on this new constitution will be on the first of June, so perhaps he won't move before then."

"That isn't as far away as I would like."

Julian shook his head. "Nor I."

Someone's footsteps rustled in the ankle-high grass of the lawn. Julian braced, but Dare stepped up to the wrought-iron gate and entered.

"Am I intruding?" he asked.

"Not at all," Amelia answered, hoping Julian wouldn't take that amiss. "Welcome back."

"How is your sister-in-law?" Julian asked.

"As well as I could hope. M'brother Jamie lives nearby, and he'll help her. She says having me lollin' about the place just reminds her Geordie's gone. I expect that's true, so I took m'self off."

Despite his matter-of-fact tone, pain shadowed the depths of his eyes. Amelia would've reached out to him, but she didn't want to aggravate Julian. How unfair that she must watch herself so. He'd best resolve his jealousy problems soon.

"It's good to have you here," Julian said, and his tone was as welcoming as she could wish. "There's news from France that may interest you."

He told Dare about the sidelining of the navy. "The conspirators had planned to use merchant ships to land at Dover, but they've allotted none for the Highlands." When Dare's brows rose, Julian added, "They lied to their Scots allies."

"They wouldna be the first." Dare shook his head.

"Could it be a ruse?" Amelia asked. "To make everyone think he plans to attack by land when he actually intends to attack by sea? If he could take Britain off the board, would that not be an advantage for him?"

"It would," Julian said. "As yet, though, there's nothing we can do."

"In that case," Dare said, "let's talk about your situation. I'll help if you need me to guard your backs against any threat, but I also have things to teach you."

Julian raised an eyebrow. "I don't suppose you would like to explain the group we saw attack the conspirators?"

"I cannot, for my word binds me there." Dare paused, studying them both.

"This is the conflicting loyalty you mentioned in London," Julian said. "Isn't it?"

Dare nodded. "I'll say no more about that. I'll instruct you, Julian, and Amelia if she wishes to learn. I'll not teach the Merlin Club. As I told you, I carry secrets that are not my own. I've some leeway in deciding who can share in them, but exceptions must be rare. Is that acceptable to you?"

"It is," Julian said. "I'll swear to it if you like, on the sword of Aysgarth, by the blood of Morgan, and into the dawn tomorrow morning."

"Amelia?" Dare asked.

"I accept your conditions," she answered. "If you need an oath, I also will give it, though I don't actually have the sword of Hawkstowe. It's at the manor in Cumberland."

"I'll take the both of you at your word, but I do thank you. We should do this privately. Is there a place we could use?"

"Any of the vacant bedchambers should do," Julian said.

"With these magics, there's the possibility of, ah, damage."

"We noticed that," Julian admitted, "when we scried your battle with the rebels. That was an impressive performance."

Dare grimaced. "Not impressive enough. We eliminated the Scots, but their French allies escaped. At our last scrying, they'd taken ship for France."

"That's too bad," Julian said. He already knew from Miranda and Richard, but their existence shouldn't be shared widely.

"Particularly as one of the Scotsmen's widows admitted the French were behind all of this. They'll likely recruit new allies in France, and we can do nothing about it."

"Still, what you did was astounding."

"Work hard at your lessons, laddie, and you can do the same."

Julian grinned. Amelia could almost feel his delight and anticipation. On the one hand, she shared them. On the other, if this involved combat...he'd been hurt enough already.

Dare added, "Somewhere out of doors would be best. Barring that, a chamber with as few breakables as possible."

"There's the ballroom," Julian said. "I had my fencing lessons there. To keep up the pretext, you and I should change our clothes while the staff open the ballroom. Not that doing so requires much. The furniture's at one end under covers, and the chandeliers are covered as well. But they can open the draperies for us."

"Chandeliers. Breakables," Dare noted. "Amelia, let me go first in case anyone who's a threat has sneaked onto the grounds."

He walked out of the garden and eyed their surroundings while Amelia followed him. Julian came behind her.

They hurried into the house. Mrs. Pettijohn stopped Amelia to confer about menus. By the time Amelia reached the ballroom, which over-looked the rear lawn, the terrace doors were flung wide. Sunlight streamed in. She carefully shut the corridor door behind her for privacy.

"...if you mean to challenge him," Dare said, "this'll help you." Near the right-hand end of the long room, out of view from the terrace, he and Julian stood facing each other.

"I must challenge him," Julian replied. "Otherwise, he escapes unscathed for his attacks on Amelia."

He could not be serious. The last time he'd fought Wyndon, he'd nearly died. Now he wanted to do it again? Oh, no. Absolutely not.

Amelia hurried into the room. The two men fell silent, as sure a sign of guilt as any she'd ever seen. She turned her sternest look on Julian. "I am the one Wyndon insulted. You are the one who allowed himself to be brutally beaten for the sake of my honor, and now that's done. As the injured party, I'm putting my foot down. You must not fight that scoundrel again. I forbid it."

Julian glanced at Dare. "Would you excuse us?"

The Scotsman shrugged and walked out to the ballroom terrace.

Judging by Julian's obstinate expression, he intended to ignore her wishes.

"I'm entirely serious, Julian."

"As am I, sweetheart." Before she could reply, he added, "You were the original injured party, but when he cheated in our fight, I became the one insulted."

"Injured, you mean. Seriously, dreadfully injured." The memory of him lying in bed, looking so confused and helpless, made her stomach churn. "You cannot do this, Julian. You must not. He knew one use of magic you didn't. What's to say he doesn't know others?"

"I'm considered something of a scholar of magic. The odds that he knows more than one use of it that I don't are extremely low."

"So were the odds he would know one."

Julian's lips tightened, and his eyes flashed. She'd made him angry. Unfortunate, but she would not waver on this. She couldn't.

"The Council," he said slowly, "wishes to question him. But that's primarily about his attack on us. We know he's up to his neck in treason, though proving that is another matter altogether. The material in his secret cache was inconclusive. Trial by combat avoids the need for proof. It solves the problem neatly."

"Only if you win." Her voice shook. Amelia swallowed hard. "Julian, you promised me we would build a life together. It isn't fair of you to risk it with another unnecessary duel."

His expression softened. He stepped close and cupped her cheek in one hand. "My dear," he said, "where you and I differ is on what we deem necessary."

Aghast, she stared up at him. "Please. Please do not."

"I'll offer you this compromise. If we can prove his treason, I won't challenge him."

"You want to, though. I can see it in your eyes. You want to pay him back for cheating."

"Of course I do, for that and for crowing about trouncing me all over London. Even more, I long to ensure he's never again a danger to you. If the opportunity presents itself, I won't walk away from it. But I won't seek it unless it's necessary for a greater purpose."

"But—"

"That's the best I can offer you, my lady." He drew her close and kissed her temple. "I've started this, and I must see it through. As a member of the Merlin Club countering an unscrupulous wizard, but also as your husband. The world must see that I stand for you, and they must see I can do it effectively. One way or another."

There was no budging him. She leaned against him but couldn't relax.

"Julian…"

The scene changed abruptly. Clutching his solid warmth, Amelia stiffened.

"Amelia?" His voice seemed to come from far away.

She stood in a crowd in a long, low-ceilinged room with plaster walls and exposed ceiling beams. Robin stood beside her with his arm around her. Sophie, Ned, and various Merlin Club members formed a protective wall at her back. Within a circular ward, Julian faced Wyndon. Magic crackled around the two men.

It wasn't supposed to do that. It never did that. How—?

A bolt of argent power shot from Wyndon's hand. It struck Julian in the chest, and Amelia cried out in fear.

The vision vanished. "No," she choked, tightening her grip on Julian's shirt. "No, please."

"Amelia, you're with me. You're safe." He stroked her cheek. "Sweetheart, come back to me."

She looked up into his worried face.

"What did you See?" he asked.

As she told him, his expression turned grim. Would this dissuade him?

"Well," he said at last, "it appears I need Dare's lessons more than we expected. Wait here, and I'll go fetch him."

Watching him walk out of the room, Amelia swallowed a shriek of frustration and fear. She couldn't even argue with him about the need for lessons, not after that.

Was it her destiny always to stand by while men she loved suffered?

Loved?

Her breath caught. Did she love Julian?

Yes. Yes, she did.

Amelia swallowed against pain in her heart. He'd been clear as a pane of polished glass that he couldn't offer her passionate love. She'd known better than to expect it.

Yet now she'd fallen in love with her husband.

CHAPTER 25

H it me again," Julian said.

Standing on the ballroom terrace, Amelia winced. In the ten days they'd worked with Dare, Julian had learned to blunt magical attacks, though he couldn't yet deliver effective ones of his own. Still, she couldn't bear to watch Dare—or, she suspected, anyone—hitting him.

Instead, she practiced magical summoning. The time might come when they needed help or a distraction, and Miranda believed Amelia had the power to create an avatar without resorting to the ritual she had used to summon Julian to London. She envisioned a dragon and poured magic into a spot about three feet away. The swirl of power created tingles along her nape and arms.

Cautiously, she opened her eyes. A dragon's form glimmered in the morning sunlight. But she could see through it.

A moment later, it dissipated.

She tightened her lips. Still more work to do.

Dare's lessons had led them to conclude someone versed in this magic must've taught Wyndon. These abilities were too difficult to master for him to have developed them spontaneously. Knowing that enabled her to call up a vision of Wyndon learning from an elderly Scots wizard. Unfortunately for his teacher, Wyndon murdered him as soon as he'd mastered the lessons.

The man had been foolish to trust him, but he hadn't deserved to die for that. Besides, no one descended from Edmund could criticize anyone else for misplaced trust.

"Again," Julian's grim voice said in the ballroom.

Amelia braced herself.

"Better," Dare replied. "How did that feel?"

"Like an ordinary blow."

"Excellent. You've countered the magical push in it. If you can learn to counter a strike with no magic behind it, that'll be a handy trick. But that's enough for now. It's Amelia's turn."

"Must it be?" Julian demanded, his voice low.

She marched back inside. "I heard that."

Sweat from their sparring dampened the two men's shirts and darkened Julian's hair. They'd worked hard this afternoon.

Julian frowned at her. "I won't apologize for wanting to spare you."

"Nor am I ungrateful." She laid a hand on his arm. "But do you think Wyndon or any of his treacherous allies would hesitate to strike me?"

His frown deepened to a scowl. He didn't answer.

Amelia squeezed his forearm. "You cannot always be beside me, and we cannot spend the rest of our lives in the house."

She turned away from him. "Dare, shall we?"

As they faced each other, her heart beat fast—not so much from nerves now as from excitement. She'd never imagined how empowering the ability to absorb a blow could be.

Dare twisted, his left hand rising in a backhand. Amelia jerked her head back, and his right fist drove for her side. She created a magical pad there just in time. The pad absorbed the magic but not most of the ordinary force of his blow. He'd pulled it, of course, so it bumped her back only slightly.

"Very good," he said. "You're also learning to anticipate."

"Not entirely. I didn't expect that punch."

"Yet you sensed it coming." He cocked his head. "Part of being a seer, perhaps?"

Amelia had no answer for him. "Let's go again," she said.

In the next ten minutes, she successfully blocked most of his blows. Sweat dampened her hair and trickled down her neck into the valley between her breasts.

Dare raised his fist and drove for her shoulder. Amelia summoned a magical cushion.

His blow, with no magic behind it, connected. It forced her back a step.

He shook his head. "If you can use that technique to block magic, why can't you block a blow that lacks it?"

"A better question," Julian put in from the side of the room, "is why it isn't difficult for you."

"I learned it as a child." Dare held up a hand. "Let's rest for a few minutes."

Amelia picked up a cloth from a stool and blotted the perspiration on her face and neck. Julian frowned at the clinging front of her yellow cambric frock but said only, "I'm next. Let's practice hurling magic bolts."

Looking at his set face, she didn't argue. Instead, she seated herself on the stool to watch. The two men didn't hit each other in this exercise.

They took positions facing a wooden archery target at one end of the long room, standing about six feet from it. Once she and Julian succeeded at that range, they would move farther back.

Dare said, "Pull the magic and gird your fist with it. Yes. Good. Now aim it at the practice target as you do when you scry or push magic into a ward. Then shove it at the target."

Argent power crackled around Julian's hand. A burst of it shot forward but died a few feet away. "Bloody hell. I thought I had it."

"I thought you did as well." Dare rubbed his jaw. "Perhaps you're having difficulty because you weren't trained to feel the magic around you, seeing as you've always believed magic came from within."

"Centuries of lore say so. Grasping a different idea is challenging."

Dare shook his head. "Huh. That explains a great deal."

Julian glanced at her. "Amelia should practice at the same time. We need to know this if we're going into enemy territory."

Dare nodded to her, and she joined the two men.

Unfortunately, her results echoed Julian's. She could send a burst of power away but not far enough to reach the target.

Dare frowned. "You can ignite fire at a distance, can you not? Or create ice? Repel an object or a person?"

They both agreed they could.

"Other than requiring more power, this is no different," he told them.

Perhaps it wasn't. Grandfather had said a wizard could bring down a wall. While that required touching the wall, it also involved a great deal of power.

Basil, one of the Gifted footmen, tapped on the ballroom door and opened it. "Sergeant Randall, my lord." His formality felt strange, but there might be unGifted staff nearby. They couldn't overhear a footman calling his employer or a guest by their first names.

The young rifleman walked in, and Basil shut the corridor door behind him.

"We've news that may be nothing," Randall informed them. "Or it may be important. Your man Derek was over to Bainbridge this morning to see his sister. He stopped in for a tankard of beer or two at the White Rose before he returned. He overheard some fellows in a side chamber talkin' about the prize they planned to snatch."

Julian edged closer to Amelia. "What sort of prize?"

"They didn't say, but they did say Wyndon would have their hides if they failed. And they had a coach ready to make for the coast."

"Hellfire," Julian muttered.

Amelia tensed. There might be someone or something else Wyndon wanted in Yorkshire, but that seemed unlikely.

"They'll make their move soon, mebbe tonight."

Julian turned to Amelia. "Shall we see what you can learn about these charming fellows?"

~

That evening, Julian led his men into the bushes along the narrow lane leading to his house. "You didn't need to come," Rafe Henshaw, his muscular, fiftyish lead outrider, told him. "We could've handled it."

"I have questions for these lads," Julian replied, "and I refuse to bring them anywhere near my wife."

Despite jealous qualms he knew to be foolish, he'd left Dare and the Gifted staff to protect Amelia. The best way to defang fear was to confront it. He'd put two Gifted grooms with Roger Southwell and his Baker rifle on the manor roof. Four of Julian's outriders, armed with muskets and pistols, stood guard at the house's outer doors.

"We're as certain as we can be that there are four of them," Julian continued. "This is the most likely route from Thornton Road to the manor. The other fields are surrounded by walls or hedgerows, and they're bringing a coach."

"Difficult thing to hide," Rafe said. "They'll likely leave it in the lane somewhere with the idea of rushing back to it with Amelia."

"Most likely." Julian scowled into the twilight. He'd had more than enough of people wanting to injure or capture Amelia.

Farther along the lane, near its end just past the avenue to the manor, three of his Gifted outriders waited in the bushes with Peter Randall. They would block the way forward while Julian and Rafe fell in behind, with Peter's Baker rifle trained on them all. Each of the outriders had a brace of pistols.

Minutes ticked by. The horses grazed or shifted restlessly.

A faint, rhythmic drumming and rattling wafted on the evening air. Julian strained to hear. Gifted ears had farther range than others, but they did have limits.

The sounds grew louder. A coach and a trio of horsemen came into view down the lane.

Julian and Rafe glamoured their mounts to be invisible but merged the glamours so they could see each other.

Three riders cantered past them—on mounts far better than the average hired villain should be able to afford. After them came the coach, a nondescript, black affair with no crest or other marking. One man sat on the box. None of the men wore livery.

Again, the four horses that pulled it looked like they would fetch prime prices at Tattersall's in London. These men had money behind them, someone who hadn't stinted on equipping them. They also carried the sense of familiarity that signaled they were Gifted.

A few yards short of the drive, the group halted. The horsemen dismounted and tied their horses to shrubs or trees by the road. The coachman set his brake, looped the reins around it, and jumped down.

Julian nodded to Rafe. Dropping the invisibility glamour, they drew pistols from their saddle holsters and urged their horses onto the lane. That cued the men at the end of the lane to magically ignite the brush piled on either side of the drive. A fiery barrier sprang up. The kidnappers' horses shied but couldn't flee, and the three men who'd hidden with Randall rode into view with pistols leveled.

The invaders sprang for the horses, but a shot from Randall's rifle drove them back.

"Do not move," Julian ordered, "unless you want to die here. Very slowly, put your hands on your heads and drop to your knees." They hesitated, glancing at one another, and a pistol shot kicked up a small fountain of dirt near one of them.

One man lunged for his mount. Julian shot him in the throat. He dropped, thrashing and coughing.

"You're under the aim of a rifle and five pistols," Julian announced, drawing his other pistol. "Lie face-down in the dirt with your hands behind your heads."

This time, they complied without hesitation.

Julian and Peter kept them covered while the others bound their hands behind their backs and hobbled their ankles with manacles ensorcelled to block their magic and prevent escape.

When Rafe nodded to him, Julian dismounted and stalked forward. "Which of you is in charge?"

The men looked at one another as best they could in their prone positions. No one spoke.

"Which of you brought the others into this?" Thanks to Amelia's Gift, he already knew, but would these brigands turn on their mate?

Now the survivors looked toward the man on the left end of the clump. Loyalty obviously counted for little among them.

"Bring him." Julian turned on his heel and walked down the lane. As planned, Rafe and Jarrett, one of the other outriders, hauled the man up and shepherded him down the lane.

While the fellow seemed docile enough, that might not last. Rafe and Jarrett kept their pistols trained on him.

Julian halted. Rafe pushed the fellow to his knees.

The prisoner directed a surly stare at Julian. Keeping his own gaze, like his pistol, leveled on the brigand's face, Julian told him, "I am Aysgarth. You are on my lands with the intent to kidnap my wife and to harm me and perhaps others. This area is not warded, so the Conclave Council will scry a very good look at your faces."

The man spat in the dirt. "So kill us if that's what you've a mind for. Don't talk us to death."

Whether his bravado was genuine or covered nerves, he sounded as though he faced death with nonchalance. His grit would've been admirable had he not come here to kidnap Amelia.

"Who ordered you to kidnap my wife?"

Judging by his guilty expression, he knew or had a pretty solid guess. Julian already knew but wanted to see whether the fellow would crack.

"What do I get if I talk?"

"A trip to Newgate."

"I'd druther die here than hang at Newgate."

"Suppose I allow you to explain yourself to the Conclave Council instead. If you tell me the truth—and I will verify what you say—you have that choice. The Council likely won't be as severe with you as the courts would be." Perhaps.

"No Newgate. D'ye swear it?"

"You have my word that I will not send you to Newgate, but your fate will be in the Council's hands."

The man's shoulders slumped. "The Earl of Wyndon, he hired us."

"And your plan?"

"We was to snatch your lordship's countess—not hurtin' her, y'understand—and take her to France."

"Then what?"

"Lord Wyndon, he was to meet us at Calais."

"You have passage booked?"

"On the *Lively Lady*, out of Hull."

Julian studied the man. "What other instructions did you have?"

The man shifted uneasily. "We was to...that is, we was to, ah, rough yer lordship up a bit, and make certain ye knew we took yer lady. That y'couldn't defend her."

That would, indeed, have burned. Especially after the trouncing Wyndon had given him. But Julian would even the score for that. And for this.

"Rafe," he said, "let's escort these gentlemen to their temporary quarters."

The tiny town of Aysgarth had no gaol. Rafe would have the outriders stash them in a disused tenant cottage and set a guard for the night. In the morning, they would escort their prisoners to London and a meeting with the Council.

Meanwhile, Julian and Amelia had plans to lay. With Wyndon plotting, they would do better not to be where they were expected to be.

∽

Two of the outriders took the corpse for burial in a remote spot several miles away. With Henshaw and Randall on guard at the cottage and their prisoners rendered unconscious by a sleeping potion, Julian rode back to the house. The night was growing cool, and the idea of sitting by the fire with his wife held tremendous appeal.

The ground floor was dark, but light shone in the windows of the upper floors. Dare and the house's other defenders were reliable, but Julian needed to see Amelia for himself, see her and know she was safe.

After surrendering his mount to a waiting groom, he walked through the courtyard and into the house. Grange, another of his Gifted footmen, paced the entry hall with a brace of pistols in his belt and a dagger in hand.

"All quiet?" Julian asked.

The lanky man nodded. Julian crossed the entry hall and mounted the main stairs.

When he reached the upper corridor, he breathed a sigh of relief. Dare stood outside Amelia's door, arms crossed and feet planted.

The Scotsman raised his eyebrows. "All went as planned?"

"They confirmed what we'd already learned. Now they're trussed like Christmas geese and awaiting transport to London. The Council should hear their account."

"The Council, even though they didna use magic in their attack?"

"They planned to kidnap a Gifted woman and are, themselves, Gifted. So yes, the Council will take an interest."

They bade each other good night, and Dare walked down the corridor toward his chamber.

Julian tapped on Amelia's door. She didn't answer. Frowning, he walked into the room.

Amelia sat in front of the fire. She didn't turn to greet him or move at all.

Julian closed the door behind him. "Amelia?"

She didn't respond.

He hurried to kneel beside her. In the firelight, tear tracks glistened on her cheeks. Moisture spotted the lap of her frock, as though she'd simply let the tears roll. Fresh ones welled in her eyes and spilled over.

Bloody hell.

"Amelia? Sweetheart? Come back to me."

A shudder rippled through her frame, but she didn't respond. Her eerie stillness chilled Julian's heart and clawed at his throat.

Everything he'd read said jolting a seer out of such a deep vision could harm her, but he had nothing subtle to distract her. Only himself.

He hooked an arm around her shoulders and took her near hand in his. "You can come back, Amelia. Step out of it and come back to me."

"So much death," she choked. "Everywhere."

"Where is everywhere?"

No answer.

"What do you See?"

Amelia shuddered again, harder. Julian gritted his teeth in frustration. His gaze fell on the dressing room door. The washstand should have water.

He hurried into the dressing room and splashed water into the basin from the ewer. Carrying the basin and the cloth from the washstand, he returned to his wife's side. He set the basin on the hearth in front of her to let the water warm. Cold would shock her more.

He held the cloth between his hands so it wouldn't be chilly. When it seemed merely cool, he put his arm around her again and gently blotted her tears. Wiped the tear tracks away.

All the while, Amelia stared into the fire, unmoving.

"Amelia, sweet," he said, fighting to keep his voice bland, "you're beginning to frighten me."

He dipped the cloth into the tepid water and wrung it out. Gently, he bathed her face.

Amelia blinked.

"There she is," he said. "Come back, sweetheart." He dipped and wrung the cloth again. Wiped it over her brow, then her throat.

She blinked again. Her brow furrowed. "I... What..." But she didn't look away from the flames.

Julian lifted her hand to his mouth and pressed a kiss onto her knuckles. A tremor rippled through her.

She swallowed hard again, but this time, she turned to him. "Julian?"

Her confused expression made his throat burn.

"Yes, my dear." He cupped her cheek and peered into her eyes. "You're with me at Aysgarth. We're safe."

Amelia closed her eyes and shuddered. "Julian." She leaned into him.

Thank God. He locked his arms around her. "Are you with me, Amelia?"

"I—Yes. It—I keep Seeing it."

"Seeing what, sweetheart?"

"A battle. A vast, bloody battle." Her hold on him tightened. "Men and horses falling, some of them blown to bits."

"I'm sorry." That was a ghastly sight for anyone, and he would wager she'd never seen the like. "Are you still Seeing it?"

"No, but it's as though there's a ghost of it in my head. I don't think I'll ever be able to forget it."

271

"Did anything cause this vision? Or did it happen spontaneously?"

"I was thinking about the ball I Saw, trying to figure out what Seeing us within it meant. And then I Saw this battle. It went on and on. I was amid British infantry, standing in squares—"

"Were you actually in the square with them or only observing?" Please, let it be only—

"I wasn't there, or at least, I don't think so. Then I saw the Duke of Wellington talking to some other men in uniform. He said, 'We're holding, but barely. Where is Blücher?' Do you know who that is?"

"There's a Prussian field marshal named Blücher. Could be him. Or not. It's a common enough name." He pressed a kiss to her brow. "How long were you caught up in this?"

"I don't know. Since not long after you left. I summoned the vision of that ball twice, trying to figure out what it meant. What we were supposed to do—whether we're supposed to do anything at all about it."

"Do you want something to drink? Water or a posset?"

Amelia shook her head and burrowed closer.

"Do you know whether this is happening now or whether it's a future event?"

"I think it hasn't yet happened because that ball hasn't. The vision moved directly from the ball to the battlefield."

"We can see where Bonaparte is. If he's still in Paris, this hasn't yet happened." Resting his cheek on her hair, he said, "Perhaps you shouldn't summon visions when you're alone. I couldn't break you free of this one for some minutes. Did you hear me calling you?"

"Not at first." Frowning, she added, "Possibly I did, though, faintly. There was so much noise. So much chaos. It was...when you wiped my face, that didn't fit with the battle. Then I did hear you, but the vision was so strong that I had to struggle to break out of it."

They sat in silence for some minutes.

Amelia looked up at him, her eyes dark with grief. "A great many men are going to die, Julian."

"Can we prevent that?"

"I don't know, but I've a feeling we cannot. That, for good or ill, this battle will happen."

"Do you know where?"

"I'm not certain. Someone mentioned a ridge at Mont Saint Jean, near Waterloo, but I don't know where those places are."

"Nor do I. They must be near Brussels if the battle follows so soon after the ball. We'll check the map book."

She took a deep breath, and her expression turned grim. "I scried the ball as well as having a vision of it. Sometimes being in a vision only means one is observing it deeply, whereas scrying shows the physical scene. I learned the ball was given by the Duke and Duchess of Richmond, as we suspected. We were in the scrying. Julian, I think we're supposed to go to Brussels before that ball."

"Then we will. We should go soon anyway. I'll let Robin know. Wyndon failed tonight, but he may have other plans to act against us here."

"There's something else." She hesitated. "When I Saw it—not in the scrying, only in the Seeing—it was as though a voice said to me, 'This battle will decide all.' Whether for good or ill, I couldn't tell."

"We'll do our best to sway the decision against Bonaparte. We must resume our lessons so we can breach the Elysée Palace, where Pierre says Bonaparte is now residing, and deprive him of that armor. I can't imagine he doesn't keep it with him."

She nodded against his shoulder. "I haven't asked you whether you intercepted Wyndon's minions."

"We did. All of us are unscathed, though I can't say the same for them." He told her about the encounter in the road.

"I'm sorry you had to kill one," Amelia said. "But I suppose he decided death there was better than on the gallows."

"Or perhaps he panicked. Either way, he was warned. I'm sending them to London under guard in the morning. I'll also send a letter for the Council. Then you and I can make our arrangements for going to Brussels. Before we do, though, you should consult Miranda about this vision and your difficulty breaking free of it. Perhaps she'll have insights for us."

In the morning, Miranda arrived to help them attempt afterworld entry. Amelia held Julian's hand so he could see the ghost too. When Miranda manifested, Amelia had a brief pang of regret. Matters were no longer as simple, as easy to resolve with familial advice, as they once had been.

Mourning that, however, would change nothing.

Amelia asked, "Were you here last night?"

"No. Since your marriage, we don't visit you in the evenings, as we've no wish to intrude. One of us is always near, but we won't come into your bedroom at night."

They once might've *intruded* at any time of the day, but not since Amelia and Julian had started the magic lessons that filled so much of their time.

Julian asked, "Did you see what happened in the lane?"

"Richard did, and he told me. Wyndon left Calais early this morning. We assume he scried the failure of his effort. Even at a distance, though, he's dangerous."

"So we've seen," Amelia replied. "Before we begin our lessons, I should tell you of a problem I had last night." She explained about the engrossing vision and concluded, "It was only one vision, repeated as I tried to determine what it meant. What we should do."

The corner of Miranda's mouth curved upward in a wry smile. "That's always the problem with visions, interpreting them correctly."

"You once told me you had a vision you couldn't shut out, couldn't make stop. What should I do if I have another that absorbs my attention so completely?"

"I wish I knew." The ghost sighed. "While scrying, I saw danger to Richard, but it didn't prevent me from being aware of my surroundings. An infusion of his magic blocked the scrying and freed me from it, but it was only a scrying—much shallower, for lack of a better word, than a vision. Your Gift is so much more developed than mine ever was that you've passed beyond my knowledge. Obviously, common sense dictates that you avoid summoning visions when you're alone. If you practice having visions and choose a particular word Julian can say to bring you out of them, perhaps you can teach yourself to respond to that."

Amelia glanced at Julian and read agreement in his face. "We can try that," she said.

"Richard is watching Bonaparte while Edmund keeps an eye on the French plotters. There is a danger, should they manage to reach this realm. The living have power over the dead here. Unless Richard and Edmund can catch them unawares, they may not be able to vanquish them."

"Then the Royal Navy is at risk," Julian noted, frowning. "A few days ago, to no one's surprise, Bonaparte converted four of his supposed observation corps to armies. Our agent learned he plans to have three-hundred thousand men under arms by June. We still think he plans a ground assault, not a naval one, but he's devious."

"He is," Miranda agreed. "He has forty thousand cavalry staging at Versailles and other areas, thirteen thousand pieces of artillery on the coasts and with the army, in the cities, and in some parks. There's a ceremony set for June first to announce the results of the staged plebiscite on the new constitution. The results are sure to be favorable and will ratify his power. Richard thinks he won't move before then."

"I hope he's right," Julian said. He glanced at Miranda. June first was a little more than three weeks away.

"We'll learn whatever we can," Miranda continued, "but I urge you to remain vigilant. As for Amelia's visions, based on my own rather limited experience, the more urgent the events you see, the more often you'll see them, and the clearer and more persistent the visions will be. Something that doesn't seem urgent at first can, as time rolls forward and some events foreclose the possibilities of others, rise in importance and in urgency. The stronger your vision, the more you should pay attention to it."

Amelia nodded. "So the ball is urgent, as is the battle. I don't See Bonaparte marching out of Paris unless I look for that. I haven't been able to determine the date."

"Then he may have different choices under consideration. I'm certain you would prefer to steal that armor before he moves. Should we practice crossing over now?"

"Yes, let's," Amelia said.

Miranda asked, "Do you each have your anchor?"

They picked up the pebbles they'd chosen. Miranda nodded. "Tempting though it might be to have them made into pendants or fobs or something easier to carry or wear, you mustn't do so. An anchor must not be shaped by human hands in any way. If it is, it will no longer bring you back to the living world."

"It's odd," Julian said, "to depend on something unliving to bring us back."

"I didn't set the terms." Miranda smiled. "I do, however, know well the importance of complying with them. When you manage to steal that armor, you may need a quick escape. Let's begin."

Amelia formed a portal. At least that was easy. Miranda appeared on the other side of it.

When Amelia and Julian started toward it, Miranda frowned. "Come quickly," she urged, extending her hand. "Take my hand. Hurry."

Amelia reached for her. She and Julian picked up their pace.

Cold enveloped them, the air thickened, and then...the bedroom vanished. The stench of rotten eggs filled the air, and purple-gray mists surrounded them.

Out of the mists came ghastly, skeletal shapes, all shrieking and extending claw-like hands.

CHAPTER 26

Julian froze. Amelia backed into him.

Miranda's hands rose. Pale purple magic crackling out of them streamed toward the frightening creatures and repelled them.

"Wraiths," Miranda said. "New souls and living bodies draw them. Stand still so I can shield you before they return."

Amelia's skin tingled as power swirled around her. In moments, faint, silver-purple auras enveloped both her and Julian.

The mists swirled around their knees and Miranda's.

No longer translucent, Miranda smiled. "Welcome." She held out her arms.

Amelia stepped into them. The embrace felt solid and real. She tightened her grip.

Holding her close, her grandmother's spirit smiled. "All your life, I've wanted to truly hold you. I only wish it were a happier occasion."

"As do I," Amelia said.

"I can see you," Julian announced.

"That's because we're in the same realm now." Releasing Amelia, Miranda smiled at him. "It's a pleasure to meet you in person, Julian. And, as I may have mentioned indirectly, to be truly related to your great-uncles Cabot and Jeremy at last."

"Ah, thank you."

Amelia said, "What was different? Why did you urge us to hurry?

When you reached out for me, and I reached back, that allowed us to pass over."

"I thought perhaps urgency would aid you. Dire need helped Richard cross through the first time."

"The reaching probably extended your power in a new way, even though you weren't aware of it," Julian suggested. "I cannot do that because I can see your grandmother only when I'm touching you."

"Now that you've been here," Miranda responded, "crossing over should be easier."

"That would be useful in a number of ways." His eyes glinted.

Amelia cocked her head. "You're planning something."

"Indeed." The idea had only just come to him. "Miranda, am I correct that traveling through this realm allows one to cross vast distances in very little time?"

"It does. You can also see anyone or anything you like."

"And we could emerge at whatever destination we chose. And return here from there?"

"Yes." The ghost nodded. She and Amelia both were smiling.

Amelia said, "You're planning to avoid any chance of confrontations with more of Wyndon's hired brutes by traveling to Brussels from here."

"Yes, but we'll send our baggage on with our outriders. If we can make any pursuers think we took ship, that could buy us a breathing space. If no one scries for us, of course." He grimaced. "I'll also ask Robin to set out for Brussels."

"That's all very well," Amelia said. "But there's something I want to do first. If we cannot manage to come back here, I'll miss my chance."

"You want to see Adam and your father." Julian slid his arm around her.

"I do. I must."

Miranda said, "I can take you to them. As for making the crossing again, you should have no difficulty. Now that you've done it once, you know how it feels."

"Julian, will you come with me?" Amelia asked.

"I want to, but I also think you and your brother should have privacy for your reunion. Miranda, perhaps I could join Richard in keeping an eye on the French plotters."

"Of course. Let's escort Amelia to Adam in 1813, the year he died and the most recent one he can reach, and then I'll take you to Richard. Until you can learn to shield, you cannot safely travel this realm alone."

"How do you know where to go?" Julian asked.

"I envision Adam and start walking. Stay close to me, both of you."

"After that," Julian said as they set out, "we should move ahead with our plans. If we can easily travel back and forth through this realm, there's no reason not to go to Brussels as soon as possible."

Miranda raised an eyebrow. "You must learn to shield first. Fortunately, that's easier than the portals. You've exerted yourselves enough for one day, so we'll do that when you're next here."

"Wait," a man's voice called. They turned as Richard emerged, grim-faced, from the stinking fog.

"A French wizard came through," he announced. "When I attacked him, he beat me back."

"As Wyndon beat back Edmund, all those years ago," Miranda said. "The power of the living over the dead in this realm."

"I fear so," Richard replied.

"Wait," Julian said. "What does that mean?"

Miranda and Richard looked at each other. She shrugged, and he replied, "In 1674, we fought the Lord Wyndon of that era here. Edmund attacked him, and Wyndon knocked him back with a bolt of magic. Edmund wasn't injured, but the bolt flung him far away."

"Could Wyndon do that in the living world?" Julian asked, frowning.

Richard answered, "I never saw him do so, but that doesn't mean he didn't. However, Miranda and I could do that here, where we couldn't in the outside world." He paused, studying them. "You can draw on the magic here, as we do. It's all around you, created by the life force souls shed as they pass through here to final judgment."

Draw on the magic. That was what Dare had told them to do. If they learned to do it here, could they apply that skill in the living world?

"Can you teach us to do that?" Julian asked.

Miranda replied, "That's how I'm shielding you and how you'll shield yourselves, by drawing on the magic of this place."

"Then I could fight them with you," Julian said. "I could recruit members of the Merlin Club to do the same. Live wizards would have a better chance against the intruders." Especially since some of them—Dare, at least—already knew how to draw magic from their surroundings.

If Dare would agree to have others learn. But this was Richard and Miranda's secret, not Dare's. Surely learning the skill here wouldn't break Julian's promise to the Scotsman.

Richard shook his head. "In the first place, the secret of coming here is too dangerous to share widely, no matter the circumstance. The more people who know a secret, the more likely someone will acquire the knowledge who cannot be trusted with it. Napoleon is a blight upon Europe, but some things that could be done through here would be far worse."

"How could anything be worse?" Julian asked. He glanced at Amelia, whose face reflected his own bewilderment.

Richard replied, "Some secrets are best kept forever. We ghosts will do what we can."

With every Mainwaring restricted in time to the years his life spanned, they didn't have the numbers to face numerous living foes. Yet Richard's adamant expression left no room for argument. They would simply have to hope the Mainwaring ghosts could prevail.

CHAPTER 27

A short time later, Amelia walked through the roiling fog with Miranda. "We're going back in time?" she asked. "It feels the same as when we walked to the house."

"It's the nature of this place, part of its magic. As I told Julian, if you wish to see a place—or a person or an object—you can. That's how Richard found those Scots and French plotters. Walking merely makes it happen faster."

Richard had grimly returned to watching the French cabal with Julian's help. That one of them had made the crossing was not a good sign. Since Richard had managed it only in the face of urgent need, however, and Amelia had done so with Miranda urging haste, the other rebels might never succeed.

The mists thinned, revealing a round, blue tent with a peaked top.

"Where did that come from?" Amelia asked.

"It's a manifestation of our magic, just as our clothing is," Miranda replied.

Edmund, the cause of the family's trouble, sat outside the tent. Knowing he regretted what he'd done, though, she couldn't resent him as she once had.

A resigned expression crossed his face. Rising, he bowed to her. "Greetings, Amelia."

She managed a civil nod. "Thank you again for helping Adam and Papa."

"Amelia!" Adam dashed from the tent and enveloped her in a tight embrace. Tears stung her eyes, and she pressed her face against his shoulder. He felt solid and real. Smelled of the same sandalwood soap he'd always preferred.

"I miss you," she choked.

"I miss you too." He drew back, keeping his arms around her, and gave her a narrow-eyed look. "Please tell me you're not dead. Miranda, if she were dead, she would've passed directly through, would she not?"

"I'm not dead." Smiling through tears, she cupped his cheek. "How I came to be here is rather a tale."

"You must tell me everything." He looked around them. "Where's Julian? Richard said the two of you had wed, and I'm so glad to hear it. He deserves someone like you, and he'll make you happy."

He was trying to, anyway. "That's part of the tale," Amelia said. For the first time, she noticed her father standing in the opening of the tent. "Papa!"

She rushed to him, and he caught her close.

"I'm sorry, my dear," he said. "I should've taken more precautions. This is all my fault."

"Not all." Amelia shot Edmund a stern glance. To his credit, he met her gaze.

"I am sorry," the older spirit said.

"Come into the tent," Papa requested, "and tell us about your marriage. And your dear mama." With a wry smile, he added, "Alas that I cannot offer you tea."

"I don't care about tea if I can actually be with the two of you."

"We'll wait out here," Miranda said.

Amelia followed Papa and Adam into the tent, which held only two low beds as furnishings. She and Adam sank onto one bed, facing their father on the other. Describing everything that had happened since she and Adam last spoke took less time than she'd expected.

"That is grave indeed," her father said, "but I've a different matter to raise with you. Are you happy in your marriage, Amelia?"

"Yes. Yes, I am." Mostly. Once she was sure Julian had mastered his suspicions, all would be well.

Her father's gaze remained level. "Are you certain? You don't seem as lighthearted as you did when you wed Buckton."

"War is coming, Papa. Because of my Gift, I must help determine how we can win it. I didn't have that burden before." Nor had she carried the burden of losing a husband, her twin, and their father, but she couldn't say that to him.

"I suppose not," he said.

Richard poked his head into the tent. "Staying here for a long time isn't good for the living. You and Julian should return to the living world, Amelia."

Staying here wasn't good for the dead either, but they had no choice. Amelia looked from Adam to her father and back again, and her heart clenched. "I don't want to leave you," she said. "I won't know whether I can return until Julian or I actually manage it again."

"This is not the place for you," Adam said.

Papa nodded. "Go back to your life, Amelia. I'm so very glad to have seen you, but if Richard says you shouldn't stay, then you shouldn't."

Adam and Amelia stepped out of the tent to find Richard, Miranda, and Julian waiting.

"Adam." Julian stared at his friend. He opened his mouth as though to say more but shut it abruptly. A slow, shaky smile curved his mouth.

Adam's grin wasn't steady either. The two men embraced.

"It's so good to see you," Julian said, drawing back to study him.

"You as well." Adam glanced at Richard. "You and Amelia should go, but please return. I would—the chance to talk to you—"

"I want that," Julian answered. "I'll come for a visit as soon as I can."

Adam drew a deep breath and nodded. He stepped back into the tent with his father.

Julian hooked his arm around Amelia's shoulders, and she leaned into him. After a moment, they started walking.

Richard added, "We'll help you return, Amelia. You will see them again."

If French wizards didn't destroy him. "Have you learned anything more about the plotters who want to come through?"

"I found the other fellow who made the crossing," Richard said. "Apparently, the wraiths chased him away. He and his comrades, who're based at Arles, won't try again until they can determine what to do about them."

"So we have breathing space," Miranda commented.

"A little. They're recruiting more wizards, possibly to see what greater numbers can do against the wraiths. If they could drive me away as that wizard did, they can drive off the wraiths. Once they realize that, they're ready to put their plan into effect. We also have a problem if one can successfully cross and bring more than one or two along. That would cut down on the number who must master the crossing."

"Do you know when they mean to act against the navy?" Amelia asked.

Julian answered, "When Bonaparte moves against the Allies, if they can master the crossing by then. They don't think he'll march out until after the big ceremony on the first of June. Unless that's a blind, of course."

Aysgarth Hall came into view, its lines blurred as though by a veil. "How do we return?" Amelia asked Richard.

"Imagine the chamber you want. For some reason, the shift from place to place is easier if you walk a few steps, but you should stay close to us until you can shield yourselves. Envision your destination, and we'll walk with you."

Amelia summoned the mental image of Julian's bedchamber. The altered ward there would let the ghosts enter. Gradually, the foggy veil over the house rolled back. As though the wall opened before them, they saw Julian's chamber. Then they were all standing in it.

Julian glanced at Miranda. "What do we do to pass through?"

"Hold your anchor in one hand and form a portal the same way you do to come here."

Amelia complied. "What next?"

Richard said, "Reach for that world as you reached for your grand-mother, envision yourself there, and step through. Miranda's planning to make a round of visits among our kin here, but I'll keep an eye out so as to be here when you're ready to return."

Focusing on the room's center, Amelia created a portal aligned with the walls and ceiling. She and Julian joined hands. Nodding readiness to each other, they stepped through. A moment of intense cold and dense air, and then they were standing in their chamber.

Grinning, Julian turned to her. Amelia flung herself at him, and his arms closed around her. "We did it," she said into his neck.

"We did indeed." His lips brushed her hairline. When she tipped her face up, his mouth caught hers in a long, deep, exultant kiss.

It broke, and they smiled at each other.

Julian's smile abruptly vanished. A thoughtful look rolled over his face.

"What is it?" Amelia asked.

"Richard also said we could penetrate wards from there. Perhaps we can sneak through that realm to Paris and steal Joan's armor in time to avoid a battle."

~

Intending to go on to Brussels as well, they packed a portmanteau with nightclothes and a single change of clothing for each of them. They also took a selection of Amelia's jewelry and some money, as well as Julian's pistols. Julian left an open letter on his bed telling Robin to meet them in Brussels. Robin would scry it and set out. Later in the day, before Dare departed for Scotland, he would burn the letter.

When all that was arranged, night was falling. They bade Dare a hasty farewell, and he promised to inform them of anything useful he learned.

Rafe Henshaw and their other men would take their baggage to Brussels on a friend's borrowed yacht. Two of the outriders would glamour themselves as Julian and Amelia until they left port.

"Your mother won't appreciate being awakened if we arrive in the middle of the night," Amelia pointed out.

"She keeps a busy social schedule. I'll be astounded if she's in bed before dawn. She'll be delighted to see us."

Amelia gave him a doubtful look. "Well, she's your mother, so I defer to you."

"Besides, if we arrive in the dead of night, there's at least a chance we can keep our arrival secret for a few days. I think we should remove ourselves from any plans Wyndon may be hatching in Yorkshire, but I'll feel better once we have Robin and our outriders to watch our backs."

Rejoining Richard in the afterworld went smoothly this time. As they crossed the cold threshold, his power enveloped them in a silver aura.

"Well done," he told them.

"I still need practice," Julian commented. "Amelia brought us here."

"You'll catch on," Richard assured him.

"We want to locate Joan's armor," Amelia said.

Richard nodded. "I'll accompany you, of course. If you can steal it before there's any prospect of battle, so much the better."

"Why?" Julian asked.

"Something Cabot told me. Once a battle looms, a sailor—or a soldier —cares far less about fighting for the man in command than he does about the man to his left and the one to his right. As battle approaches, events gain a certain momentum. You mustn't wait too late."

285

"That makes sense," Julian admitted.

They would locate the armor and see how securely it was guarded before going to Brussels. There were also other things they needed to do here.

"We must return to see Adam," Julian said.

"Of course." Richard paused. "You've heavy burdens to bear, though, and you must be at your best. So a brief foray into France in search of this armor, and then you should largely stay out of here aside from seeing him."

Amelia and Julian glanced at each other. "That seems wise," Julian replied. "If we can obtain the armor quickly."

"First," Richard said, "you must learn to shield yourselves. If our enemies gain a foothold here, their magic will overpower mine. You must know how to protect yourselves. Julian, you can set down that bag. The fog won't damage it. The two of you might move a bit apart."

He waited until they'd complied. "First, feel the magic around you, the power in this place."

"It's a tingling on my skin," Amelia said, "even through my clothes."

"Yes. Julian?"

"I feel it too."

"Good. Now draw the power to you. Envision it enveloping you, then settling around you like transparent armor."

Amelia tried to pull the power. "I cannot— Nothing's happening."

"I see it around you," Richard said. "Julian?"

"I feel it surrounding me, but I can't seem to draw it in."

Richard nodded. "Each of you take one of my hands. I'll build new shields around you. Feel what I do. It's much like the reverse of sending power into flame to scry or into a wall to ward it. You're taking back what has been deposited here. Drawing it to yourselves. Like this."

He repeated the process several times.

On the fifth try, Julian said, "I think I have it."

"Let me see you do it," Richard told him. "Amelia, keep an eye out for wraiths."

Julian clenched his fists and frowned. The purple-gray fog swirled around him, drawing closer and turning brighter. It gradually spread around him until he had an aura.

"I should test it," he said.

Amelia bit back a cry of protest.

"The sooner, the better," Richard responded. "Walk a few feet away, Julian. I'll stand ready if the wraiths attack."

"Once I move outside your protection, won't they do so? The only way to see if I've done this properly is to let them."

He was right. To keep from objecting, Amelia clenched her fists until her nails dug into her palms.

Richard replied, "Yes, that's true. Walk a few feet away. If they pierce your shield, I'll step in."

Amelia's heart pounded as Julian walked. About a dozen feet away, he said, "I don't feel your power anymore. Only my own."

"Then let's see," Richard said.

Julian took a few more steps. Gleeful shrieks split the eerie quiet, and wraiths surged out of the fog in a great, ghastly wave. He set his feet and his jaw and waited.

Amelia's throat tightened. She couldn't draw a decent breath as the skeletal shapes surrounded Julian. She couldn't bear to lose him.

Understanding struck like a hammer blow. This was why Julian held himself apart, kept some of himself back. He'd lost one wife. He didn't want to feel this dread again, and she couldn't blame him.

"All right?" Richard called.

"Thus far." Julian laughed. "I believe I've done it."

"Indeed. Now, holding the shield around you, shoot power at them and drive them away."

Silver with a tint of purple flared around Julian. The shrieks sounded angry now. The wraiths wheeled toward Amelia and Richard. She took a step closer to her grandfather as silver-purple light flared from his hand to beat them back.

Richard and Julian grinned at each other. "Well done, my lad," Richard said. "Very well done."

Amelia swallowed hard. At last, her heart rate slowed.

Concern shadowed Julian's eyes. "Amelia, are you well?"

"Yes. I was frightened. But it's all right now because you are."

"Thank you, sweet." His expression softened. "I'm sure I'll feel the same when you test your shielding."

"I'm ready." And she was. No matter how much she feared the wraiths, she would far rather face them herself than watch Julian face danger alone.

∽

A short time later, guided by Amelia's remembered vision of the armor and its chest, the trio watched a city appear. Moving through this realm grew easier with every step she took.

"Paris," Julian said as they walked toward it.

Through the gauzy barrier between worlds, a building of pale stone surrounding a courtyard came into view.

"The Elysée Palace," Julian announced. "Bonaparte moved here from the Tuileries last month." When Amelia gave him a startled look, he shrugged. "I've been here before. Though not inside, unfortunately."

"Someday, you must tell me more of what you've done for the Merlin Club."

Her vision of the armor tugged at her. She moved toward the building, into the second floor, with Julian at her side.

"It's warded." Richard sounded resigned. "I cannot follow you. Leave the valise with me."

Julian backtracked to set the bag at Richard's feet. Rejoining her, he asked, "How do you know where to go?"

"It's as though something is tugging me. If I turn the wrong way, I don't feel it as strongly. Do you want to try?"

"You have matters in hand, so carry on."

They walked a few more paces, passing through an ornate chamber with gilded fleur-de-lys medallions on the plaster ceiling. Armchairs with upholstered seats and backs and padded armrests were scattered around the chamber.

"These could be the royal apartments," Julian said. "Though I've heard this entire building is rather elaborate."

They entered a long corridor with tall windows spaced along one side. Candles in crystal chandeliers cast glittering light over thick carpet patterned in blue and red squares with gold rosettes at each corner. On the inner wall, a series of paintings of stuffy-looking men, sometimes with their families, hung at intervals.

Amelia nodded to them. "Who are they?"

"The portly one at the end is Louis XVIII. I suspect the others are recreations of other Bourbon kings' portraits."

"Recreations? Because the originals were destroyed in the Revolution?"

"Indeed. If you'll guillotine one king, you won't balk at burning pictures of others."

At the end of the hallway, flanking gilt-embellished double doors, stood a pair of guards in blue cutaway uniform coats with white facing at the lapels, red on the cuffs and epaulets, and white belts crossed over their chests. They also wore white vests, breeches, and gaiters. Their tall, black shakos each bore a short, red plume on the left side. They were emblazoned with a brass medallion in the front and draped with gold braid. Each man wore a saber at his left hip and held a musket with a bayonet.

"Ah, yes," Julian said. "They're Imperial Guard, the elite of Bonaparte's troops and those most fiercely loyal to him."

"They were in my scrying of his departure from Elba."

"We may well find Bonaparte himself behind that door. In fact…"

"In fact what?"

He halted and turned to her, his face grim. "We could dispose of Bonaparte and solve this problem before he causes more bloodshed."

"Assassinate him, you mean." Her stomach gave an uneasy lurch, but she forced it down. So many of the families she knew had lost sons in the twenty years of war with France. Why should there be more?

"What would change if we did that?"

"Not *we*. Me. Your hands are bloodless, sweetheart. I want them to stay that way."

While he killed to protect her. He'd killed the man in the lane and one in London. He might also have had to kill for the Merlin Club. Yet he wanted to spare her that.

"Thank you." She rose on tiptoe and kissed him.

With a groan, he kissed her back. His arms tightened around her.

The kiss broke, and he pressed his face into her hair.

Leaning into him, she asked, "What about Bonaparte? What happens if you kill him?"

Julian said nothing for a few minutes. At last, he said, "Civil unrest. The army will likely look for assassins in all corners. Louis XVIII would attempt to return, and they would resist. Paris loves the Corsican. The rest of the populace might be as glad to see him go, but the army would pose a serious danger. The same if we simply took him. Although he's no longer in fighting trim, that wouldn't be easy. Especially with the Imperial Guard lurking about."

"A double assassination led to my family curse. The one we're considering could set in motion events we cannot anticipate. It could make matters worse."

"It could. At the very least, the army would want a war to avenge him, and I doubt there's anyone who could stop them."

"So it's better to let matters play out?"

He sighed. "Much as I hate to say it, I think so. If we can steal that armor, though, it should eliminate some of his appeal, in turn eroding the loyalty to him."

"Then let's resume our search."

Holding hands, they followed the armor's pull through an ornate audience chamber. On a dais sat a gilt armchair with padding on the seat, back, and armrests under a blue canopy embroidered in Bonaparte's eagles. The canopy's front bore an elaborate coat of arms, a gold eagle on a blue shield clutching a thunderbolt in its talons. Around the shield hung a red mantle embroidered with, of all things, bees.

"His coat of arms," Julian commented. "He made fast work of having that restored."

They passed through the audience chamber into a smaller room, apparently a parlor, and then into the imperial bedchamber. The gilded bed bore deep red hangings rising to a peak surmounted by a crown topped with plumes.

"Rather fond of gilt," Amelia muttered.

The armor drew her beyond the bedchamber, through a dressing room, and into a small, windowless chamber. Two men in civilian clothes played cards at a small table with a lantern for light. Under the table between them stood the chest from her vision at the pool.

"That's it," Amelia whispered.

"They can't hear us," Julian reminded her. "They do seem to be fairly alert, though."

"If they're not wizards…"

"Let's listen, see if we can figure that out. With the fog between us, I can't tell whether I should have that sense of recognition or not." He glanced at her. "Do you speak French?"

"Fluently. I suppose you also do."

"Of course."

They watched the two men play for several minutes. Finally, one threw down his cards.

"Sacred heart, I'm bored," he announced. "I'd rather stand guard for hours outdoors than sit here with this chest any longer."

"Patience. When the time is right, the Emperor will march, and he'll take it with him. Meanwhile, we must keep it warded. If the English determine its secret, they'll try to steal it."

"Obviously," Julian muttered, "they're Gifted."

"The Emperor will crush the British and the Prussians before his enemies can unite. By then, our fellow wizards will have cleared the way to England."

"We can hope. Nothing will placate the royalist rebels in the west." The man took a long drink of something in a mug. "The Emperor should crush them."

"He would if we had enough men."

A third man walked into the room. The first frowned at him. "You took your time using the necessary."

The newcomer shrugged. "If we could use the Emperor's, it would be faster."

"We should go," Amelia told Julian. "It's difficult to keep track of time here, but I think we've been in this realm quite a while."

"You're right." He ran his palm gently down her back. "We'll go to Mama's house in Brussels, establish ourselves there, and come back here to see if they ever put fewer guards on this. You and I cannot take three together, not quickly enough."

"Or even two, most likely. I've no experience battling wizards other than you and Dare."

"I wish you would never have it, but I likely cannot steal that armor alone." Resting his forehead on hers, he sighed. "Since Richard says we shouldn't stay here overlong, we probably should go to Brussels now. But we'll return soon. Drawing magic is easier here, which could help us master Dare's lessons. If we can do that, we might have a chance against three guards."

CHAPTER 28

Julian drew on the memory of his mother's face as a guide, and they set off through the stinking fog. Although he kept his mind on her, part of it brooded about what they'd seen. There must be a way to snatch that chest. If they could do so before Napoleon marched out, erosion of his support at home could defeat him before he truly began.

"You know," Richard said, "they may actually have a lighter guard on that chest at times. The number of French wizards who've broken the Compact is limited, and they may need them to work with the army."

"A lighter guard would delight me," Julian admitted. "But if the French Gifted take the field, it makes everything worse, including what to do about them."

"It does." Richard shook his head. "The Merlin Club walks a line as it is."

"A razor-thin one sometimes," Julian replied. "So we'll focus on Joan's armor for now. Even if Amelia and I become adept at drawing magic from our surroundings and using it as a bludgeon, we may not be able to take three in close quarters. At least, not before they retaliate."

"Yes, distance is your friend when you're outnumbered."

They walked a few more steps, and a city appeared through the mists. Buildings were about the width of London townhouses, with tall, narrow windows across the fronts and ornate pediments around a single or double window on the topmost, narrower parts of the façades. Gilt panels adorned the stonework above the lower-story windows on many of the buildings.

"Brussels," Julian said. "Mama's house is near the park."

Amelia glanced at him. "Are you certain she isn't angry about the wedding?"

He squeezed her hand. "She's disappointed, but her delight that I've finally remarried outweighs that. Besides, she understands about the circumstances. When we settle this business, she can host a breakfast or a ball for us if she wishes."

Richard said, "We've meant to tell you, Julian, that you've done well with the Merlin Club. It's in good hands under your care. Cabot and Jeremy would be proud of you."

"Thank you, Richard." The unexpected compliment meant a great deal, all the more so because he'd included Julian's great-uncles. "I do my best."

"If you didn't, Miranda and I would have advised Amelia not to wed you. Lazy idlers make poor husbands."

Not sure what to say to that, Julian settled for replying, "I suppose so."

The image in his mind drew them toward a tall house of pale stone. Richard stopped outside the window. "Wards," he explained. "I'll follow you as best I can from out here."

Amelia and Julian passed into an upper floor and down a corridor—with more gilt trim on the white woodwork. Ghosting through a wall, they entered a darkened bedchamber. "This can't be right," Julian said. "There are two people in that bed, one of whom likely owns these uniform bits strewn about."

Gifted eyesight could make out the colors of the debris on the floor. Boots, a sheathed saber, blue overalls with a gold stripe down the leg, and a blue, waist-length jacket heavy with gold braid lay scattered across the carpet. Mixed in among the uniform pieces were a petticoat, stays, and a woman's drawers and stockings. The blue uniform jacket, with scarlet facings and gold frogging, looked like that of a hussar from the King's German Legion.

"This must be a guest chamber," Julian said, "or else we're in the wrong house."

"We followed your vision," Amelia pointed out. "Is it pulling you onward?"

"No, but...this can't be right." Shaking his head, he walked to the side of the bed. And froze. There were, indeed, two people in the bed, and one of them was his mother. Judging by the bare arm and shoulder outside the covers, lying over the muscular arm of the dark-haired man cuddling her, she was naked.

Aghast, he stared.

"Julian?" Amelia joined him. "Is anything wrong?"

"Damned right it is. That's my mother. But she can't be."

"I only met her a few times, and that was back in my first Season. This woman does resemble her."

"No, no." He waved that away. "She's my mother, but what the devil is she doing in bed with a hussar?"

"Sleeping," Amelia replied as he struggled to comprehend the scene in front of them.

Mama, in bed with a German officer. Had she married him? If so, word would've taken a while to reach England. Given his own hasty marriage, Julian couldn't reproach her.

But what if she wasn't married? What if...?

No. She wouldn't. She simply wouldn't.

Amelia touched his arm. "My dear, your mother has been widowed since you were small. It isn't unheard of for widows to seek, ah, casual companionship." He narrowed his eyes at her, but she finished, "Occasionally."

"She never did."

"So far as you know," Amelia gently responded.

He stared at her. What she was saying made sense. Scandalous sense, but sense.

On the heels of that realization came another. Amelia had been a widow for three years.

"Did you?" he blurted. "Seek companionship?"

Behind him, Richard muttered, "God's feet."

Julian scarcely noticed. The hurt look on Amelia's face smacked him with the realization he'd blundered horribly.

"I beg your pardon," he said quickly. "I've no right to ask you that."

"No, you truly haven't." She raised her chin and looked away from him. "Since we've established that this is your mother, perhaps we should present ourselves at the front door and let her know we've arrived."

"Amelia, I..." What could he say? He'd put his foot in it again. "As you wish."

They made their way easily to the front stoop.

"Wait." Richard embraced Amelia. Holding her close, he said, "Miranda isn't the only one who's wished she could touch you."

Amelia pressed her face into his shoulder. "I'm glad I had the chance to be with you, too. I'll see you again."

He released her and drew Julian into a quick, surprising embrace. "Be good to her," Richard said softly. Julian had the sense to recognize a warning when he heard it. What a ghost could do to punish him, he didn't know, but perhaps he didn't want to know.

~

The sky showed faint light in the east when Julian pounded on his mother's front door.

Finally, the door swung open. A middle-aged man wearing a brown robe over his nondescript breeches and shirt held a candle high. Graying brown stubble shadowed his jaw. Behind him stood three sturdy young men, probably footmen summoned in case this pre-dawn visit brought trouble.

"Good morning," Julian said in French. "I'm Aysgarth. We apologize for disturbing you so early, but my wife and I have only just arrived in Brussels and have no hotel."

"This is no hotel," the apparent butler responded, scowling. The sense of familiarity around him implied he was Gifted.

"I know that. As I said, I am Aysgarth. Your lady's son. Please be so good as to inform her of our arrival."

"Milady's abed yet, as decent folk ought to be," the man replied.

"Regardless, she will not be pleased if you turn her son and daughter-in-law away."

The man scowled but said nothing.

Julian sighed. "My good fellow, I have known my mother all my life. I can assure you she will not fly up into the boughs if you awaken her with this news. Which I must insist you do—at once."

Still scowling, the man stepped aside. "You may sit in the parlor to your left, sir. I will have her ladyship informed." To the group of footmen, he said, "Oskar, light the parlor candles. Frederik, stay with these folk until I return."

Frederik also bore the aura of the Gifted. The butler was taking no chances. A thin, brown-haired man hurried ahead, and the glow of candlelight appeared in a chamber on the left.

Julian bowed. "I'm glad my mother has a staff so dedicated to her safety."

Julian and Amelia walked through an entry hall with a gray-tiled floor and entered the room the man indicated. The delicate furniture covered in yellows and greens stood out against gray silk wall coverings with a floral pattern woven into them. A gray and green carpet woven in a medallion pattern covered the floor. Yet more gilt highlighted the furniture's white trim. Whoever owned this house either had money for ostentation or wanted to be seen as having it.

Julian sat beside Amelia on the yellow sofa. With Frederik hovering outside the door, however, this was not the place for him to mend fences.

They sat in silence. The ornate clock on the mantel ticked off the minutes a second at a time. Amelia's shoulders drooped, and he felt tired in his bones.

Light, rapid footsteps sounded in the corridor with a familiar cadence. Julian rose, and Amelia followed suit.

A moment later, his mother swept into the room wearing a yellow silk chamber robe embroidered in white. Gathered back in a white ribbon, her light brown hair showed signs of hasty combing. Her gaze met his, and her cool expression instantly warmed. "Julian! It is you."

She launched herself at him, and he caught her close in a long hug.

"I missed you, my boy." She planted a quick, firm kiss on his cheek. "Welcome."

"I missed you as well, Mama." Despite nagging him to go about in society more, she'd always supported and encouraged him. Behind the gray eyes so like his lurked a wickedly clever mind, and she'd used it to his advantage all his life.

She drew back to smile at Amelia. "Welcome to you also, my new daughter."

They embraced and kissed each other's cheeks. His mother slid an arm around Amelia's shoulders. "You look weary, the both of you. You can explain all later in the morning, but let us settle you in now."

She led them into the entry hall. "Do you want something to eat? I can have Cook send up a light repast."

Julian was famished, but he hadn't realized it until she asked. "I hate to disturb your cook at this hour. I can slice bread and cheese. Amelia?"

"I wouldn't mind something," she said, "but we don't want to overset your household."

"They start their day soon anyway. Frederik, you may go along to bed for a bit longer. First, though, ask Cook to send something light to the pink bedchamber."

"Yes, my lady." He hurried to the door under the stairs.

"We keep bedchambers ready for guests," Julian's mother continued, steering Amelia onto the ornate staircase. She paused to retrieve a single lit candle from a table by the stairs. "Is that all your luggage?"

"For the moment," Julian answered. "The rest is coming."

She made a tutting sound. "Amelia must go to my modiste. We'll do that tomorrow. Brussels has no shortage of tailors and modistes."

"Mama, we'd like to keep news of our arrival quiet for a while. Will your staff assist us?"

"Now, that, I do wish to hear about. We can rely on the staff, and I believe I know a modiste who would come here and be discreet about it."

Julian thanked her. "We have a couple of friends coming. I explained all in a letter, but we've arrived before it."

"You can tell me more when you've rested, but that won't pose any problem. As I said, bedchambers are always ready." Her lips quirked up in a smile.

They let her guide them up the steps and onto the first-floor corridor, which bore thick carpets. The candles in the wall sconces were not lit, so Julian created a ball of green witchlight to help see the way.

"My suite lies at the far end of the corridor." With a quick grin, Mama added, "It's the largest, of course, all done up in pale blue and yellow. Aside from being overly fond of gilt, the family who own this house have superb taste."

She stopped beside an open door. "I hope this will do."

Pale pink wallpaper with silvery leaf designs printed on it adorned the walls. Draperies striped with cream and a deeper pink hung at the windows and around the four-poster bed.

"It's lovely," Amelia said.

"Well, then. Sleep as long as you wish. We keep London hours here, with a very busy social schedule, so the days start late. There's a bell pull beside the bed if you need anything." She kissed them each on the cheek. "Again, welcome, my dears. Sleep well."

With that she bustled down the dimly lit corridor.

Julian escorted Amelia in and set down their valise. After he closed the door, he found her sitting on the edge of the bed, weariness etched in her face.

He sat beside her. "I truly am sorry, Amelia. Very sorry."

"I'm sure you are."

But that obviously didn't make her feel any better. Lord, he'd been an ass.

She sighed. "Julian, I have been intimate with exactly two men in my life."

His heart leaped. If she was confiding, perhaps she had forgiven tonight's slip.

"If that were not the case, though, would you disapprove? Judge me?"

"I…would try not to." Because the hope in her eyes faded, he quickly said, "I would resent any man you'd so honored. Bloody hell, I resent Buckton for having the sense to see your worth before I did." Was that relief on her face? Doggedly, he plowed on. "But no matter how I felt, I wouldn't hold anything against you that you did before we wed. It wouldn't be right."

Yet he still unfairly reacted as though she were Charlotte. She didn't say it, however.

"As for my mother," he said, "she's my *mother*. I don't see her as a dashing, attractive widow, though I suppose she is one. She's only forty-six." He rubbed a hand over his face. "I'd like to think I could've handled discovering her in bed with that hussar if I'd had a little warning. If we should encounter him—God forbid!—I'll behave as you and she would wish."

Amelia finally smiled at that. It was a tiny smile, an exhausted one, but a relief to see.

She stroked his jawline lightly. "Let's go to bed, Julian. Everything will look better after we've rested."

Perhaps so, but he'd made another marital misstep. Amelia didn't want to pay for Charlotte's sins. That was fair. Nor did he wish to have his first wife's ghost at his shoulder any longer.

There were other worries as well. Leaving Yorkshire in secret had been wise, but until Robin and the outriders arrived, Julian and Amelia had no one to watch their backs. Amelia had Seen that Wyndon would arrive tomorrow. Once he knew they were here, he would make mischief for them if he could.

Mama would understand why they chose to stay in the house until their reinforcements arrived. If her staff cooperated in keeping their presence secret, all would be well. If not, staying in the house would certainly stir curiosity, which would breed gossip that would, in turn, make them conspicuous when they needed to blend into society.

They couldn't worry about that now, though. The most important thing was to figure out how they could take that armor away from Bonaparte.

~

Death rode the battlefield. Amelia had seen this clash before. Wellington's infantry stood in squares four ranks deep. The front ranks, with bayonets fixed, either knelt or held their muskets low to form a bristling barrier of steel while the other two ranks fired. They'd stood firm against wave after wave of French cavalry.

This time, though, the French cavalry broke through the squares, slashing with sabers, cutting down the British soldiers. Some tried to block with their rifles, to stab with their bayonets, but nothing saved them.

The cavalry rode through the square, wheeled to re-form, and charged from the other side. Another slaughter. Amelia cried out in the dream. The scene shifted to a ridge, French infantry charging up it under thundering bombardment from British cannons.

A young officer in a red coat galloped his lathered mount up to a group of other officers, all mounted. "Wellington—they've killed the duke. Where's Uxbridge?"

"The surgeon's tent. He's had his leg shot off."

"Christ! Who's in command, then? We're crumbling. It'll become a rout if we can't bring the men back into order."

A scowling older man in a red coat and a tall shako replied, "Blücher and the Prussians are bogged down near Lasne, our left flank is too thin, and I wouldn't trust that idiot Prince of Orange to fight his way out of Vauxhall Gardens. Ompteda's Fifth Line Battalion were slaughtered after the prince ordered them into a foolish attack in the face of French cavalry."

The scene shifted again, to Westminster and the parade she'd Seen before. Napoleon Bonaparte rode down Whitehall to the Palace of Westminster. Amelia caught a flash of the chest holding Joan's armor inside the coach following him.

It wasn't helping him much here. Although people jammed the sidewalks, the French guardsmen lining the route were the only ones cheering. Perhaps Joan's armor didn't hold any charm for anyone not French.

She jolted awake with tears running down her face. Turned on his side to face her, Julian still slept, so she wiped her face quietly on the sheet.

Visions of the future never promised what would happen, only what could. Before she and Julian had come to Brussels, the battle visions had always shown the British and their allies doing well. Now they showed disaster.

Would something she and Julian did here doom the Allied cause?

CHAPTER 29

Y our mother's very kind," Amelia said to Julian a few days later. "She's also clever, telling the staff we wanted privacy because we're newlyweds. I don't think anyone other than the servants has guessed we're here."

"She's a strategist," he replied. "Taught me chess. After Papa died, she managed the estates. I was only a tot then. She had help from our steward, but she made the decisions and kept track of the money until I came of age."

They were using the gallery at his mother's house to practice offensive magic. An easel at one end held a four-foot plank about a foot wide and an inch thick. The servants had been told to keep clear, and Frederik, the Gifted footman, was posted at the staircase to ensure they did.

Amelia seemed to have forgotten the spat the night they'd arrived, but he couldn't assume she would entirely forget it until he brought his suspicions under control.

"Besides," he added, "she loves hosting balls and whatnot. The idea of putting one on for us more than makes up for missing those few minutes in St. George's."

Amelia sighed. "I hope matters come to that, with Bonaparte's threat ended and England at peace again."

"So do I. Do you want to go, or shall I?"

Amelia gathered the power around her hand and flung it at the easel eight feet away. The bolt of argent slapped the easel but didn't damage it.

"That's better," Julian said. He'd nicked the corner of it earlier. Lowering his voice so Frederik's Gifted ears wouldn't hear, he added, "Sensing and gathering the magic is easier in the afterworld, but the lessons seem to carry over here."

"Perhaps we should go back there. You haven't had a chance to talk to Adam yet, and we could practice."

"That's a good idea, but I would like Miranda or Richard to be standing by to shield us from the wraiths in case we're not as adept at that as we think we are."

Julian walked down the gallery to Frederik's post by the stairs. "Give me a hand with this, would you? We're taking it to our bedchamber." Earlier in the morning, they'd woven Amelia's magic into the warding there so the Mainwaring ghosts would be able to enter.

The young man frowned. "Your lordship needn't trouble yourself. I can manage."

"Yes, but in two trips. You take the easel while I take the plank, and it's done."

They returned to the bedchamber, and Frederik departed hastily.

Amelia said, "I think he isn't used to earls shifting tools for themselves."

"I think not. Let's see if anyone's here, shall we?"

Amelia reached for his hand. "Grandmother? Grandfather?"

In a ripple of argent, Miranda's translucent form appeared. "Good morning, my dears."

Amelia explained what they needed, and Miranda said, "Of course. Julian, let us see if you can guide the transition this time."

Using the open dressing room door as a reference, he formed a portal easily enough. The trick, however, would be traveling through it.

Hand in hand, he and Amelia walked up to the portal. "Ready?" he asked her.

She nodded. "I'll form the shield as we pass through."

Optimistic of her, but perhaps this time...

They stepped forward together. The familiar icy cold enveloped them, resisting their passage. Julian pushed his magic against the opposing force and stepped forward with Amelia.

The churning, purple-gray mists of the afterworld surrounded them.

His skin tingled as she drew power around them both, forming magical armor.

His wife grinned at him. "Well done, my lord husband."

"Thank you, my lady. I can't have you stealing a march on me, after all." He formed his own shield, and hers around him faded.

The wraiths rushed forward, screaming. Miranda emerged from the fog near Amelia and Julian but did nothing.

With a glance at Amelia, Julian drew power into his hand. She did the same. Together, they shot silver magic at the wraiths. "Begone," Julian shouted.

Shrieking in frustration, the ghastly spirits wheeled away. Amelia and Julian shared a triumphant glance.

"Well done," Miranda said. "If you link your hands and share your magic, you'll have more power."

"That's amazing," Amelia said.

Miranda smiled. "It's also useful. Before you begin your practice, would you like to walk with Adam? We encourage him to do that to become accustomed to this place."

She continued, "Amelia, it occurs to me that practicing here might also amplify your ability to send a summoning avatar."

Delight washed over Amelia's face. "That would be marvelous. Perhaps you and I could practice that and give Julian some time alone with Adam."

When she glanced at him, Julian responded, "I would enjoy that. I wish I'd had time to spend with him earlier."

"Julian," Miranda said, "let us see if you can guide us to Adam in 1813. Envision him and start walking. We'll come with you."

He did as she had said. Perhaps a dozen or so steps later, a blue tent came into view in the mists.

"You did it!" Amelia squeezed his hand.

"You can find us again the same way," Miranda said. "We'll return to 1815 in case Richard needs our help with the French Gifted." She and Amelia walked into the fog.

Julian stepped up to the tent's entry flap. "Adam?"

His friend flung the flap aside. Grinning, he embraced Julian. "It's so good to see you again. Papa is out exploring, or he would greet you as well."

"I'm content to have you." Julian's throat tightened. Adam looked the same, felt solid and alive. It would be so easy to forget he wasn't. "Let's walk," Julian suggested.

Together, they set out through the fog.

"You'd best be good to my sister," Adam warned, "or I'll haunt you."

"I'm doing my best." Carefully, Julian replied, "I want to make her happy."

"That's good then. What else have you been doing? How are the horses?"

"Getting along well, though Bonaparte has ensured I can't spend as much time with them as I would like." With a sidelong glance, he said, "I've a sweet mare for Amelia. Bought her at Tattersall's just before we left London, but I haven't told Amelia about her yet. When we're confined to the house for security's sake, presenting her with a mare she can't ride seems unkind."

Adam shook his head. "It's a shame you can't go riding, as both of you enjoy it so."

"Soon enough. We must deal with Boney first—and settle his account for good this time." Assuming he and Amelia didn't do something that defeated the Allies' efforts. She had shared her worries after her recent unsettling dream.

"I suppose the Merlin Club is helping?"

"Where we can." Julian detailed the agents he'd deployed and the current situation. "What we most need to do, however, they cannot."

"You mean stealing the armor?" When Julian nodded, Adam sighed. "Amelia told me about that. I wish I could help. There isn't a great deal to do here, as you might imagine."

"That's part of your difficulty, isn't it? You're bored."

"Utterly. The wraiths no longer terrify me, and I'm learning how to deal with this place, but above all, Julian, it's damned lonely. Except for Richard, Miranda, and Edmund, who can move through time to all of us, the only Mainwarings I have for company are Father and Grandpapa, and only in the years our lives overlapped."

"That seems odd."

"Edmund says time is a spiral, that we're all bound to the part of it we occupied in life." With a grimace, he added, "We're so isolated, it's a wonder we're not all mad. We don't see much of Edmund. Papa isn't precisely fond of him."

"Well, he did start the whole business. I can see why he isn't a prime favorite."

Adam snorted. "Far from that. But let's talk of happier things. How is Robin?"

"He's betrothed. Did Amelia tell you?"

"She mentioned it, but she doesn't know his lady."

"They haven't yet met. Barbara—Lady Barbara Gordon, eldest daughter of the Earl of Grampian, and Robin's utterly besotted—is as independent-minded as Amelia. From what Robin says, she's awake on every suit. I'll be astonished if she and Amelia don't get on famously."

Adam grinned. "He's besotted, eh? I hope it works out for him."

"I'm confident it will. When his father was gravely ill last year, Barbara and her aunt came down from Scotland to help out. Robin said he didn't know how he would've made it through without her. She and Sophie are fast friends as well."

They walked a few more steps. "Is she a ginger?" Adam asked.

"Oh, yes. Hair a deep, rich red, and eyes of brilliant blue." Not surprising, as Robin had always had a weakness for redheads.

The mists thinned, and there she was, on a wharf with porters bustling to and fro. Clad in a bronze traveling suit with a blue straw bonnet, Barbara looked around her with undisguised curiosity. An older woman stood beside her, facing away from Julian and Adam. Wagons on other wharves loaded or unloaded cargo.

Julian blinked. He hadn't expected the thought to take them to her, but perhaps he should've. "There she is, with that other woman."

The place was familiar, but he couldn't identify it.

"That's a stubborn set to her chin," Adam observed. "She'll lead Robin a merry dance."

"They clash now and again, but they both seem to enjoy it."

A hackney coach pulled up beside her. Robin stepped out of it. But how could that be? Julian had come to 1813 to see Adam. Robin and Barbara hadn't met then.

Julian walked closer. A porter strolled through him. His stomach pitched, but he strained to hear what Robin said.

"We'll need to stop on the road," Robin advised Barbara. The older woman with her turned around, revealing that she was Julian's Aunt Augusta.

But she'd never visited the Continent.

Robin continued, "We should reach Brussels tomorrow."

Brussels? Then that port was most likely Antwerp? And this was happening now?

How could that be? How could he see that from 1813? Or have Adam with him in 1815? And why was Aunt Augusta in Antwerp?

Barbara laid a hand on Robin's arm. "They'll be careful, my dear. Julian is aware of the threat, and he'll take precautions."

"I know. I know, but there's no one watching their backs." Robin blew out a hard breath. "You'll like Amelia."

Barbara replied, "Sophie speaks very—"

"What?" Adam turned a baffled look on Julian. "They came to Brussels in 1813? I thought Robin had never visited Brussels."

"He hadn't. Until now. My 'now,' I mean..." Julian took a slow breath and blew it out. "We must consult Richard or Miranda, but...it's possible this is today. My today, in May 1815."

"If it is..." Adam swallowed hard. "If you've taken me forward in time..."

The dawning hope in his face made Julian's throat tighten.

"If it is," Adam repeated, "we needn't be so alone."

Gripping his friend's arm, Julian added, "Whether I'm right about this or not, Adam, you know Amelia and I will come to see you. You'll have us both."

Adam nodded, but his expression remained hopeful. "I could observe your life, yours and Amelia's. That would mean so much."

"To us as well." It might also mean they had a solution to another problem.

If he was right.

~

Amelia sat with Miranda in the tent she and Richard used as their home. Here, too, the furnishings were simple, a low bed and a settle.

"I'll need to go soon," Amelia said. "I'm hungry, alas."

"And alas that I've no food for you. You did well, my dear. When Julian returns, you must show him how well you can form an avatar."

"I may need that skill." Amelia sighed. "If only I knew whether I would use it to help defeat Bonaparte or to bring about disaster."

"That's the frustrating part of the seer Gift. It rarely shows you all you wish to see—sometimes even need to see. It seems to show you what you should see."

"But not often does it show me what I should do. We came to Brussels because my dreams and visions about the ball and the battle after were so powerful. But if Julian and I do the wrong thing, we could ruin all."

Miranda nodded. "Choice is the bane of this Gift. Richard and I—and Edmund, little though you care for his opinion—are confident you and Julian will do the right thing. You're both clever and brave. And determined. We believe in you."

"I'm glad someone does."

Miranda cocked her head. "You seem a bit...not sad, precisely, but not happy either. Is it only Bonaparte who worries you? Or has Julian done something to distress you?"

Amelia hesitated. Confiding in Miranda would be a relief, but it could also turn her grandparents against Julian. She didn't want that.

At last, she said, "His prior marriage was not all it ought to have been. I've gathered his wife was not faithful, and that influences his outlook. More than he wants it to."

"Ah. Those who've been deeply hurt generally are slow to trust. He looks at you with great warmth, so don't give up hope."

"I find myself comparing him to Crispin, and that isn't fair. Julian and I come to each other by a different route, and I—I'm very fond of him."

"And perhaps more than fond," Miranda said gently.

If Amelia ever admitted to loving him, she should say that first to Julian. "He runs risks for the Merlin Club, and I worry about him."

"Ah. You also have been hurt, my dear. Crispin never betrayed you, but the loss of him was a deep wound. Protecting your heart is natural. As you and Julian go into this, he may take risks against your wishes. Remember, though, that you care for him because of who he is, even the parts of him that feel compelled to take those risks."

"He tries to do what's right."

"The Merlin Club would not be so effective otherwise, and his willingness to face danger as every other agent does earns him their respect." Miranda patted Amelia's knee. "No matter how difficult you find it, you must accept his choices, just as he must respect your feelings. Any other course breeds resentment, and that's poison."

"You sound as though you speak from experience."

"Richard took risks I opposed, and I worried. There were times when I could have stopped him, but the price we would have paid was too high."

"I'll remember that. Do you think—"

"Amelia! Miranda!" Julian called out. A moment later, he and Adam ducked into the tent.

Adam was smiling. He looked so happy that Amelia's throat tightened.

"Look who I've brought to 1815," Julian announced.

~

A short time later, after Edmund relieved Richard on watch in France, Julian and Adam told everyone what'd happened. Even Julian had difficulty believing the words he was saying. As he talked, Richard's face grew ever more thoughtful.

Julian concluded, "I have an idea, and I'd like to know whether you have the same one, Richard."

Richard replied, "I tried to bring Adam forward, but I couldn't do it. You, however, are a living wizard. The rules here are different for you."

"And if I can do it again, bringing more than Adam?"

"It could give us greater numbers to face any French Gifted crossing over. Improve our chances to defeat them."

"My thought exactly." Julian grinned at him. "Where do you suggest we begin?"

"With Sir Miles Mainwaring. He was born at Hawkstowe in 1545 and died there in 1621. It was he who had our titles restored by Queen Elizabeth, thanks to his performance against the Spanish Armada as the captain of the *Queen's Honor*. I've often talked to him since we first met, and he has an eager, curious mind. Besides, if you can convey someone forward nearly two hundred years, more recent members of our unfortunate little club should pose no problem. Come with me."

"I'm coming along," Amelia announced.

"As am I," Adam said.

Miranda cocked her head, regret on her face. Before she could speak, Adam did. "It will be a good test of Julian's ability to bring us through time. If I can't pass 1791, my birth year, we'll know his skill only works going forward. Which should still help us all."

"If I can bring someone forward to the present day, conveying someone backwards ought to work," Julian suggested.

"Unfortunately," Richard said in a dry voice, "*ought to* has little relevance here, where the rules of magic are so different from those of the living world. So let us see about this. Unless you can envision Miles's face, Miranda or I must lead you backward, but you hold onto Adam and see if you can bring him with us."

They set off through the mist. Julian hooked his arm through Adam's.

"I cannot bear this suspense," Amelia said. "Julian, tell me about Robin and Lady Barbara."

"Better not," Richard advised. "Any distraction could divert us from our path toward Miles. We must avoid that, as you've been here for some time now and should return to the living world soon."

They walked on in silence. Julian would've held Amelia's hand, but touching someone other than Adam might affect his ability to convey his friend through time. If that was, in fact, happening.

At last, the mists thinned to reveal a man. He wore the short doublet, ruff, puffy breeches and high boots of an Elizabethan captain. His strong features, dark hair, and blue eyes could've graced any Mainwaring portrait Julian had ever seen.

Julian's heart kicked hard. He exchanged an excited look with Amelia and then with Adam.

Richard raised a hand in greeting. "Well met, Miles."

"Well met, grandson." The two men embraced quickly, and Miles kissed Miranda's cheek.

"Who are your crew?" Miles asked.

Watching him carefully, Richard said, "The two on the right are your several-times-great-grandchildren Adam and Amelia Mainwaring, though Amelia is now Amelia Winfield, Lady Aysgarth. The other fellow is her husband, Julian Winfield, Lord Aysgarth."

"Odd to see a woman here," Miles noted, eyes narrowing. "Aside from your lovely wife, of course."

"She and Julian are not here in the sense the rest of us are." Richard explained about the time travel experiment.

Miles frowned. Once or twice, he shook his head.

When Richard finished, Miles rubbed a hand over his chin. "I'd ask if you were daft, but you seem well enough. Since no one dreams here, I must assume you at least believe what you've said."

"Is that any stranger than having a distant grandson turn up in 1588 Plymouth, not knowing where he'd gone?"

Miles grinned. The exchange obviously had some meaning to the two, but neither explained it.

"So what do you want of me?" the sea captain asked.

"We want to bring you forward with us, to 1815."

"If that can be done," Miles replied slowly, "can I return here if I wish? It's familiar, after all."

Richard looked to Julian, who answered, "I don't know. All this is new to me. Since I was able to bring Adam here from 1813, I should be able to bring you back if you cannot come on your own."

"One of those advantages of the living," Miles grumbled. "Very well, lads. And ladies. Let us see what we can do."

Miranda said, "Julian, Amelia, think of your bedchamber in Brussels as you left it. That should be a sufficient beacon. Julian, were you touching Adam when you traveled forward?" When he shook his head, she said, "Then do not do so now. Let us see whether Adam and Miles can accompany us forward in time without touching either of you. Adam likely could since he has done so before. His natural place is between 1791 and 1813, but that didn't matter last time."

"The target we stored in the bedroom before we left would do well," Julian suggested to Amelia. "It wasn't there yesterday."

"Very well." She nodded. Together, they walked into the mist. The others fell in behind them. She and Julian had also altered these bedchamber wards, so their companions should be able to enter.

There was no certainty bringing Miles and the other doomed Mainwarings forward in time would provide sufficient numbers to defeat any Frenchmen who crossed into this realm. It would, however, help them all feel less isolated. Companionship would also ease the difficulty of newly deceased, doomed souls in adjusting to this ghastly place.

Of course, finding Lady Eleanor's affidavit could free them all, though that was by no means a certainty. Amelia couldn't pursue that actively while the war took priority.

The mists rolled back, and there was the target, leaning against the wall behind the desk.

Julian glanced back. All their companions stood behind him and Amelia, grinning.

Her face echoed his delight. Laughing, he pulled her into a tight embrace.

"I take it that's the bedchamber in question," Miles remarked. "Well done, the two of you. I think I shall enjoy visiting the future and seeing its marvels."

Julian and Amelia looked to Richard, who seemed to know Miles best.

He raised an eyebrow. "While we'll all be delighted to show you the England of this era, Miles, we're hoping you and others who come forward might help us with a little problem. It involves fighting French Gifted."

"That's almost as much fun as sinking Spanish ships. Tell me about it."

CHAPTER 30

Three evenings later, at Julian's mother's insistence, Amelia and Julian accompanied her to a ball. Doing so seemed frivolous, but her warm welcome and obvious pride in her son and his new wife made refusing difficult. Besides, Amelia figured, cooperating in this was a small way to repay her for being so gracious about missing the wedding.

Robin, Barbara, and Aunt Augusta had arrived the day after Amelia and Julian's trip to the past. A day behind them came Julian and Amelia's outriders and luggage. Now that they had clothing, along with their outriders to provide security, the Dowager Lady Aysgarth, or Catherine, as she'd insisted Amelia call her, had refused to accept any excuses for not going about in society.

"You simply must," she'd decreed. "Otherwise, people will ask questions. Far better to stop that before it begins."

Now here they were, in a line of carriages waiting to let their passengers out at the party. Amelia had managed to forget how tedious such rituals were.

They'd told Catherine earlier about their experiences in the afterworld. "That is indeed marvelous," she said, "and yet you cannot tell anyone." With a wry smile, she added, "That must plague you, Julian, having knowledge you cannot share."

"It's irritating," he admitted. "At least I can share it with my family, and with Robin and Barbara since they've sworn never to reveal the truth. Via the afterworld, I can retrace many of Wyndon's movements and learn how deeply he's involved with the French. Travel in the afterworld may hold the key to all. At least we've more allies there to handle any French incursion. I hope they're enough."

They had brought all the surviving and sane Mainwaring souls forward in time. Only two had become so deranged in the past three centuries that bringing them would have no point.

But there still remained the question of how many ghosts were needed to overpower a single living intruder.

At last, the coach drew up in front of the house. The footman let down the steps, and their party walked into the entry hall. There, they inched forward until they finally reached the ballroom.

"Christ, it's hot." Robin tugged surreptitiously at his cravat.

Barbara said, "I dare say it's more pleasant on the terrace. Why don't we see?"

"With pleasure." He gave her his arm and led her away.

Catherine patted Julian on the shoulder. "Mingle, the pair of you. Show everyone what a delightful son and daughter-in-law I have."

A tall, dark-haired man with sculpted features and brown eyes shouldered out of the crowd. He wore the blue regimentals of a hussar in the King's German Legion. The ballroom lights glinted on scanty threads of gray in his hair and his neatly trimmed mustache, and fine lines marked the corners of his hazel eyes. The combination made him look older than he'd appeared in semidarkness. He did not have the familiar feeling of a Gifted, but he and Catherine smiled at each other with just that bit of something extra that marked them as intimates.

Julian stiffened, and Amelia held her breath. The cavalry officer bowed over Catherine's hand. Smiling, she introduced Major Ludwig Biedermann of the First Hussars to her companions.

"A pleasure," Julian said, exchanging bows with the major. If his voice was not quite so welcoming as usual, only those who knew him well would notice.

Catherine relaxed and turned an approving look on him. She had no reason to suspect Julian had seen her and Major Biedermann in bed, but she must know her son well enough to realize he might have qualms about her involvement in an affair.

"I understand you're a horseman, Lord Aysgarth," Biedermann told him. "You may be interested in watching the cavalry drills Lord Uxbridge conducts three times a week out at Grammont. We have race meetings there as well."

Julian's eyes lit with interest. "I would like that. Please call me Julian."

At that, his mother's smile widened, and pride in him swelled in Amelia's chest.

The orchestra struck up a tune full of sweeping crescendos. "The waltz," Julian said. "I learned it when I visited Vienna last year. Do you know it, Amelia?"

She shook her head. "I haven't had time to learn. When I had my Season, the waltz wasn't commonly danced. Nor was it yet accepted by the patronesses of Almack's."

"Bloody Almack's." Julian frowned.

Biedermann said, "Catherine, will you honor me?"

"Gladly." She laid her hand on his arm, and he led her away.

Julian watched them go. "You don't think they're serious, do you?" he asked quietly.

"I don't," Amelia assured him. "There's no harm in it, though, and you pleased your mother in the way you greeted the major."

"I tried. Let's go stand by the terrace doors and wait for the next set. It must be cooler over there."

He led the way, shouldering through the crush of people. Luckily, there was no one either Amelia or Julian knew, so no one impeded their progress.

They had almost reached the doors when Julian stopped. "Stand aside," he said in a low, lethal voice.

Amelia peeked over his shoulder and almost choked. Lord Wyndon stood directly in their path, smirking.

She checked the impulse to slide her hand into Julian's. Wyndon was the sort who would take any show of concern as an opening.

"I'm simply standing here," Wyndon said. "You and your countess may choose another path." Raising an eyebrow, he added, "Unless you wish to call me out over it. Although dueling me didn't go so well for you the last time you tried it."

Julian was stronger now. More adept. Would he give in to temptation?

His voice level, he said, "Yet, of the two of us, only I can safely return to England. I hope you're keeping a weather eye out for Council agents. One never knows where they'll turn up."

Reaching back for Amelia's hand, he steered her around their nemesis, the bloody rotter. She tightened her grip, but Julian showed no sign of prolonging the confrontation.

When they reached the terrace doors, he found a space for them a bit apart from others watching the dancing. "I gave you my word I wouldn't challenge him," he said softly. "I will keep it."

"I know that, but he'll make all manner of mischief if he gets the chance. I feared he might offer you provocation that would be difficult to resist."

"I wouldn't put that past him."

"Perhaps we shouldn't go about in society anymore. I don't care a fig for it, Julian, truly."

"Nor do I, but now we must venture out. Otherwise, Wyndon will tell all the local *ton* how he trounced me, and they'll conclude I'm afraid to show my face."

"He could still do that."

"But it won't carry as much weight if I'm unperturbed." He studied her briefly. "I dislike his being in the same room with you, however. Perhaps you should stay home."

"Under guard? No, thank you. I've had rather enough of that. You and Robin and our outriders provide security enough. Given the bad blood between you and Wyndon, he must know he would be the first suspect if anything happened to either of us. If all else failed, Robin would see to it."

"Yes, he would." Julian smiled.

"You're happy?" Amelia asked under cover of the music. "Why?"

"I'm fairly certain I know more than he does. And can shortly learn all I wish to know about his recent activities via the afterworld."

"But you can't tell the Council how you gathered this information."

"Once one knows what someone has done, finding ways to prove the truth becomes easier. I don't need to prove everything."

"You only need to prove enough," she said.

"Precisely. With a little luck, I'll be able to convince the Council to deal with Wyndon's mischief once and for all."

Robin and Barbara emerged from the crowd in time to overhear the exchange. Robin grinned widely. "I may be able to help you there."

"What have you done?" Julian asked.

Robin drew a square of white lawn from his pocket. "I lifted his handkerchief." As they gaped, he continued, "Amelia, do you think that might help raise a vision about Wyndon, perhaps even show us what he's been up to?"

"It might." Scrying was all very well, but a vision was stronger. Perhaps they could learn whatever it was Wyndon didn't want her to See. Then, once they'd stopped Bonaparte, they could set about finding the proof of whatever her vision showed her.

If they stopped him.

The next afternoon during tea, Julian's mother's efficient butler presented him with a stack of paper packets on a silver salver. "The post, Lord Aysgarth."

Julian accepted the stack and thanked him. Paging through, he paused. "I've a letter from Henry Talbot, cousin to Shrewsbury," he told Amelia. "Harris must've forwarded it from London."

"Lady Eleanor?" Amelia clenched her fists on her knees.

Julian broke the seal and unfolded the packet. "He has her prayer book. We're welcome to come and see it at our convenience."

"Oh, my." Her smile trembled at the edges. "I want to hope, and yet..."

"You fear to," his mother said quietly.

Amelia nodded.

"Regardless of how this turns out," Julian reminded her gently, "it's progress."

He resumed sorting the letters. When he reached the last one, his insides chilled.

He broke the seal and glanced over the contents. "It's an invitation. The Duke and Duchess of Richmond request the pleasure of our company at a ball on fifteenth June."

They looked at each other for a long moment. "Despite the date, there's always a chance it isn't the same ball," Julian said.

"I'll know for certain when I see the decorations." Amelia swallowed hard. "Even though that's a month away, I don't feel ready."

"Nor do I," he said. "We'll use the time until then to prepare. Then we'll simply have to do the best we can to muddle through."

Amelia and Julian sat in the sunlight in their bedchamber. Amelia held Wyndon's handkerchief in both hands. Catherine hadn't appeared yet this morning. Neither Amelia nor Julian remarked on the fact that Ludwig was usually with her when she took breakfast in her rooms. The house was quiet, which also meant interruptions were unlikely.

Summoning a vision was easier now. Softly, she murmured, "Wyndon... France... rifles... Bonaparte..."

The stinking fog rolled around her. When it thinned, she saw Wyndon seated by the hearth in his library. His aunt sat opposite him. This must've happened before he fled.

"It seems a very thin chance," the woman said. "They surely can't conquer the Highlands with a force of only a thousand men."

"That isn't the point, Aunt Sarah. There are no French soldiers to spare for the Highlands, at least not yet. The Scots simply must wait. They should be used to it. Meanwhile, they'll help eliminate the Royal Navy, not only in Scotland but in the Channel, and snare Mad George and Prinny."

"Yes, but why?"

He grinned, and it was a very unpleasant expression. "So we can open the south coast for invasion. Their failures to breach the dead realm thus far may force us to our contingency plan. I'm building caches of military supplies for French agents. If Bonaparte can defeat the allied armies, I'll help him roll into England."

His aunt shook her head. "You've no love for the French. Why would you do this?"

"For all of us, of course. We Gifted live in the shadows when we should rule. The unGifted are to us as chickens are to lions, and yet we let them control everything. If France wins, I'll have the Isle of Man as my domain. I'll build up an army of Gifted there and train them in magical combat. After a few years of rule by the hated French, the unGifted will be so grateful to us for overthrowing the Frogs that they won't care if we do it magically. We can live in the sunshine."

Reluctant admiration shone in her eyes. "Knowing you, Silas, you'll soon own that sunshine."

"And England as well. We all will."

That was what Amelia needed to know, at least for now. She let the vision fade.

When she looked at Julian, he said, "You found something." He must've read the satisfaction in her eyes.

When she explained, he grinned. "My dear, that's astounding. You've done brilliantly. This secondary plot must be what he feared you might discover."

"I can try again, perhaps gain more details."

"That can wait. We should see how matters are going with the French Gifted who want to cross over. Before we return to the afterworld, though, let's go up to the gallery and practice, shall we?"

~

T hat evening, they returned to the afterworld. Although Miranda stood by, they didn't need her help. Amelia created the portal and managed the crossing, to her great satisfaction, with Julian shielding them as soon as they passed through. Quickly, they explained the latest developments to Miranda.

"Richard is watching the French wizards who are trying to come here," she told them. "They hope to move immediately before Bonaparte attacks the Allies. Unfortunately for us, they don't know when that will be. Unfortunately for them, no more of them have mastered the knack of crossing over."

"If anyone learns," Julian replied, "you'll tell us?"

"Of course. If you've come to practice, you might as well join the others. We've a small village of Mainwaring men nowadays. They're all so happy to have the companionship that they don't seem concerned about going into battle. Richard is insisting they practice, though."

Rolling her eyes, she added, "I insisted, too, but they readily dismissed my womanly opinion. All but Adam and Charles. And Richard and my son Rob."

"Papa knows better, and he taught Adam better," Amelia noted. They'd met all the others earlier. Watching the easy camaraderie and affection between Rob and his parents had made them realize how much her ghostly kinsmen missed while they were trapped in different eras.

"Besides," Julian said, "they're only behaving as they would've in their lifetimes. They'll learn."

"They'd better," Miranda responded. "You know, since they couldn't move through time without help, we wondered whether they would be able to progress past the day you brought them. Yet here they are. You've changed the rules, and it's such a pleasure to have them with us."

After a few minutes' walk, they saw a clump of men in various styles of clothing that likely reflected whatever they'd worn in life. Some shot magic streams at each other or shielded against them while others watched.

"They're not using their full power," Miranda said. "They're reserving that for the enemy." Smiling, she added, "One of the great joys in this for Richard is being with his father, who's beginning to overcome his guilt about not lifting the curse himself."

Julian had counted noses when they brought the men forward. There were eighteen of them, not even half a military company's worth. "How many Gifted do the French have trying to learn how to cross over?"

Miranda frowned. "Still a dozen that Richard counted. However many of them cross over, they'll eventually learn how to pull magic in and punch it out as a weapon. Perhaps worse, the Lord Wyndon of our day somehow learned how to draw on the magic of this place to shape-shift. When we fought him, he became a dragon. We very nearly did not win that battle."

"He became a dragon?" Julian asked. "Or he formed one around him? I've heard of the latter, though it's rare, but not of the former."

"I'm not sure, but it did seem as though he had actually become the dragon. Richard stabbed its tail, and it bled."

Julian and Amelia exchanged a grim glance. "Let's hope the French cannot do that," she muttered.

Julian said, "Miranda, if you would let us teach one other person how to come here, you would have a living ally against these rebels. Richard couldn't best the one wizard he fought, despite having spent more than a century learning the magic of this place. You won't even have two-to-one odds. Let us bring you a living ally."

Although she frowned, she had too much sense not to see the advantage.

"He's a Grayson," Julian added, "the great-great-grandson of your friend Kit. He's also my second at the Merlin Club. You can trust him if you can trust anyone."

"We'll consider it," she said slowly.

"Amelia, Julian! Welcome." Adam broke away from the group of men and hurried toward them.

He embraced Julian and Amelia in turn. "Join us, Julian."

"You know," Amelia drawled, "I've also learned to draw magic in and punch it out. Since I may be going into a battle, perhaps I also should practice."

"Well...the others won't like it." Adam looked to Julian, who lifted his hands, palms out.

Julian replied, "She can practice with you and me if no one else can bring themselves to smite her, but she does need to practice."

"You could start," Amelia suggested, "while I show Miranda how much I've learned of summoning." They could also see how closely guarded Joan's armor now was.

They walked through the mist, away from the men.

"This is far enough," Miranda said. "Can you form an avatar?"

"Yes." With a grin, Amelia explained. "I've developed a special fondness for dragons, and it occurs to me a dragon flying over a battlefield would provide an excellent distraction for the French Gifted. It's a pity no one else could see. Watch."

She closed her eyes and concentrated on a spot about ten feet away. Drawing magic to her, she formed a mental image of a tall, green dragon. When she could almost feel the image, she fed magic into it. The image slowly developed a glow.

Amelia fed it power, imagining it standing at that nearby spot, until it glowed brightly in her mind. That was enough.

"Be," she said softly.

Miranda drew in a sharp, audible breath, and Amelia opened her eyes. A green dragon nine feet tall with scales that glistened in the eerie light stood exactly where she'd imagined it.

"Fly," she ordered.

Great wings rose, swept downward, and lifted the dragon from the shadowy ground. It rose in a spiral until Amelia called the magic back to herself. The power returned in a rush, energizing her and making her feel as though she also could fly. Fortunately, she knew better.

Miranda smiled broadly. "I knew you could do it." She drew Amelia into an embrace. "You've surpassed me as a falcon outflies a seagull. I'm so proud of you."

"I'm rather proud of myself, in truth."

"As you should be. Now let's see what the situation is with this armor."

Finding the Elysée Palace took only a few minutes. Miranda couldn't enter, but Amelia had no difficulty. Now that she knew where the armor rested, she needed only a few moments to reach that inner chamber. Soldiers still stood at their posts outside the audience room. In the small inner room, the chest holding the armor still sat under the table. One man paced the small space while another dozed in his chair.

Only two of them to deal with. Amelia waited, but no one else arrived. Perhaps they kept a lesser watch so late at night. Amelia hurried back to Miranda with her heart pounding. "I need Julian here as quickly as we can bring him. This could be our chance."

CHAPTER 31

A short time later, Amelia and Julian stood in the doorway of the armor's chamber, the scene veiled by the misty barrier between the afterworld and reality. One of the guards still slept while the other idly played with dice.

Her heart hammered as though it would explode. Surprisingly, Julian didn't seem to hear it. His face set in grim lines, and he stared hard at their target.

When he turned to her, though, his expression softened. "Are you ready, my dear?"

"As I'll ever be." She took a deep breath that did little to steady her.

"I'll take the one who's awake. We knock them out, shatter the ward on the chest, verify that the armor is in it, and bring it back here. Destroying the ward will alert the wizard who cast it, so we cannot delay."

"I know."

He smiled. "I always review before launching an attack. It's a habit. The entire business should require little more than a minute. Time may seem to drag, but that's only a perception. In truth, we'll be moving quickly."

Swallowing against nerves, she nodded. They'd resolved to steal the armor because they thought depriving Bonaparte of it was the right thing to do. Still, she worried that taking it would somehow lead to the catastrophic defeat she'd Seen.

With a glance at her, Julian formed a portal. The awake guard looked up at it. Frowning, he came to his feet as his comrade stirred. Julian and Amelia stepped into the living world, drew magic, and blasted the duo with crackling bolts of power. The force of it knocked them down and out.

No one came to investigate the sound. One problem dealt with.

They knelt by the chest. "Don't touch it until I break the ward," he said.

He extended his hand, palm down, over the chest. Silver magic flowed downward. The chest took on a reddish glow. Setting his jaw, he added more power.

With a loud *crack*, the ward flared brilliant red. A moment later, it vanished.

Amelia used magic to shatter the lock on the chest. She and Julian grasped the lid.

When they raised it, magic roared into the air around them. It seared her skin and pressed hard on her chest. She could barely breathe and couldn't move.

Judging by the alarm in Julian's eyes, he also was trapped.

"Stay back," a man's voice roared in the corridor. A *bang*, like a door slamming open, sounded in the outer room. Running footsteps approached.

Julian's lips tightened. Conveyed through the trap's magic, the strain of his effort to break free thrummed inside her. Her own struggle to do so knotted her muscles and burned along her nerves.

A tall, light-haired man who looked to be in his fifties paused in the doorway. His gaze traveled from her and Julian to the unconscious guards and back again. His lips curved in a slow smile.

In French, he said, "The trap has caught rats. I shall enjoy making you tell me how you did this."

He turned to the outer room and ordered, "Bring Monsieur Maravant immediately."

Perhaps breaking free wasn't the answer. Amelia turned her senses inward, sinking them into the magic searing her and enveloping the chest. As she'd done in the afterworld, she drew it to her.

Julian's gaze lit as he saw what she was doing. The next moment, his similar effort reverberated in the magic connecting them.

Scowling, the French wizard stepped into the other room. He snapped something in an angry tone, but Amelia had no attention to spare for that.

Abruptly, the glow around the boxed armor died. Power surged into her like a blow to the chest, but now she controlled it.

The Frenchman stalked toward them with guards behind him. Amelia's eyes met Julian's. He nodded.

Together, they blasted all the power they had absorbed at their would-be captors. The French wizard disintegrated. Amelia's stomach surged. The men behind him flew backward, likely protected from the brunt of the blast by his body.

Amelia leaped to her feet and formed a portal while Julian hefted the chest.

In her mind, she envisioned her favorite green dragon outside the window. The image grew. Spun. Time seemed to stretch. Footsteps sounded outside, coming nearer, while she fed magic into the image.

"Be," she breathed, "and fly." She opened her eyes in time to see the great creature leap into the air.

"Distraction," she told Julian.

"Let's hope this does what we need," he said. "Richard said he and Miranda will keep the armor safe until we can decide what to do with it."

Together, they rushed into the reeking fog.

~

By the time the date of the Duchess of Richmond's ball arrived, Amelia and Julian's sense of triumph had turned to despair. "It didn't matter," she told him as they dressed for the ball. "No one has abandoned Bonaparte."

She'd Seen him lead the Army of the North out of Paris at full strength three days ago. This morning, they'd crossed the border into the Netherlands and battled the Prussians at a place called Charleroi, as she had Seen weeks ago.

Julian shrugged. "Perhaps we should have moved sooner. Or perhaps Napoleon had enough charisma on his own and didn't need the armor. I'm still trying to determine how we might use it." He kissed her swiftly. "As long as you aren't certain we've opened the door to defeat, we must hope for the best. And look for a chance to intervene. You're certain the battle this morning wasn't the decisive one?"

"Yes. The terrain was wrong, and there were not enough soldiers." Amelia sighed. "We should go to this ball. Perhaps matters will come clear while we're there."

They rode to the ball with Robin, Barbara, and Catherine. Augusta had decided to stay home. Worried over what was to come, none of them felt like making idle conversation.

At last, they reached the Richmonds' estate. When they walked into the carriage house where the ball would be held, a chill rippled down Amelia's back.

"It's the same. The decorations are the same ones I Saw."

Their group stood together and surveyed the ballroom. The rose-trellis wallpaper, the floral garlands twined around the pillars, and the draping on the comparatively low ceiling of the Richmonds' carriage house precisely matched her visions. What happened here and after would determine all. She knew it, as only a seer could know.

"I suppose we must be social," she said. "I would rather be watching the armies, trying to figure out what we should do—or avoid doing—so we don't cause an Allied defeat."

Julian ran a gloved hand lightly down her arm. "Our only course," he said quietly, "is to do what we think is right."

He turned to the rest of their group. "Let's mingle. If you hear anything pertinent, or if the Prince of Orange is called out of the ball-room to meet a military messenger, find me."

Thanks to their time in Brussels, they now knew all the commanding officers' faces.

"Meanwhile," Julian added, "the minuet's ending, and I would like to dance whatever comes next with my wife."

When he held out his hand, Amelia laid hers in it. He was right. They had no choice other than letting matters play out and dealing with them as best they could.

The music began, and Julian smiled. "Now we see how well your lessons prepared you for the waltz."

Amelia returned his smile. They had engaged a dancing master a couple of weeks earlier. Actually waltzing in a ballroom should be fun.

Julian set his right hand at her waist and held her right hand in his left. If he drew her a bit closer than was strictly proper, who would care? They were married, after all.

She needed a few measures to find her rhythm. Once she did, she and Julian whirled with the music.

The dance swept her away from her cares. There was only the man holding her with tenderness warming his gray eyes.

When the music ended, he asked, "Have I told you how beautiful you are tonight?"

"No, but thank you." Amelia smoothed the skirt of her mulberry silk gown. When she moved, it shimmered with undertones of blue. At Julian's insistence, she still carried the Mainwaring dagger in a thigh sheath hidden by her skirts, even though Wyndon was not invited tonight.

"You're rather handsome yourself," she told him. The black evening dress set off his brown hair and contrasted with the snowy muslin shirt and white-on-white silk, embroidered waistcoat. A sapphire stick pin anchored the folds of his cravat.

"We make a fine pair, then, my lady." He glanced over the ballroom. "My mother is a veritable repository of gossip. She says she has a face people like to confide in. Let's find her and see what she has heard."

As they walked through the crowd, he softly commented, "If only we knew what time things will become interesting."

Amelia mentally reviewed the different visions she'd had of this evening. "I think...possibly around suppertime." That would be midnight. Hours to wait yet.

Hours to worry about what they should or shouldn't do.

Immediately after supper, a footman approached the Hereditary Prince of Orange, a general in the British army. The slender young prince followed him out of the ballroom. His scarlet uniform matched the one he'd worn in Amelia's visions.

Robin was closer to the door. Julian caught his eye and nodded.

Robin and Barbara slipped through the crowd to a position by the door. They smiled and chatted, apparently flirting, but Julian had no doubt they heard the discussion outside. Barbara had taken all of this in stride. She might make a good agent for the Merlin Club, though Robin would likely erupt at the idea. Not that Julian would blame him. He didn't want Amelia running such risks either.

Meanwhile, chatting with her about their social calendar, Julian watched Wellington. The duke had arrived late, possibly because of the battle at Charleroi.

Another footman approached the duke and spoke softly to him. He followed the messenger from the ballroom. Julian's heart beat faster.

Judging by the tension around Amelia's eyes, she had noticed the same things he did, but she continued smiling and chatting with him.

A few minutes later, the same footman found their host, the Duke of Richmond. He, too, left the ballroom. Robin and Barbara were well positioned to overhear, but waiting for their report was agonizing.

Finally, Wellington and his host returned. Both men smiled, but the smiles didn't reach their eyes.

Robin and Barbara worked their way through the crowd, heading for Julian and Amelia.

"Let's go meet them," Julian suggested.

Threading a path through the crowd took a few minutes. At last, the two couples stood together.

By tacit consent, they moved away from the dance floor. "It's as Amelia Saw," Robin said softly. "Based on the way they talked, they're facing a serious battle."

Amelia shifted closer to Julian. He dropped his hand between their bodies to grip hers, the handclasp hidden by her skirts.

Robin continued, "Wellington sent the Prince of Orange back to the army. He'll follow after a bit so as to give any French sympathizers the impression he's not concerned. And so as not to start a general panic among the guests."

Though panic would inevitably arise once officers began making their farewells and departing.

"The fighting will be terrible," Amelia said. "I know it. The dreadful battle I Saw occurred very soon after this ball."

Julian shook his head. "If we knew the military situation, we might know what action to take. Or whether we should act at all."

Richard appeared behind Robin, visible to Julian because he and Amelia were touching. Julian held up a hand to silence Robin, who looked perplexed when Julian stared past him.

"I have Edmund watching the French Gifted," Richard said. "I overheard the dukes and the messenger just now and went to the battlefield to investigate. Bonaparte is not on the field, but the armies are moving on a crossroads town called Quatre Bras. The Prussians are at a place called Ligny." He paused. "I'll keep watch on the armies. If I see a chance for you to help, I'll alert you."

Meanwhile, all they could do was wait.

~

The day after the ball, there were battles at Quatre Bras and Ligny. According to Richard, Quatre Bras had been roughly a draw, but the French had prevailed against the Prussians at Ligny. Then had come a downpour, as Amelia had Seen so long ago, that delayed any further action. By scrying, Amelia had learned neither of these was the sprawling, decisive battle she and Julian dreaded.

The Anglo-Dutch army had withdrawn from Quatre Bras early today and taken positions on a ridge called Mont Saint Jean, south of the village of Waterloo. Their long battle line eerily echoed what Amelia had Seen weeks ago.

Now rain poured down, as it had since afternoon. It precluded the possibility of any further fighting tonight.

Julian tried to watch Amelia without letting her know he was doing so. She'd confided earlier that seeing the Allied deployment made her cold with certainty that this was the battle that mattered.

He had found a map, but he couldn't help thinking they should watch from the afterworld. From there, they could move swiftly once they knew what they should do.

"Your visions emphasized the importance of the Prussians," he remembered. "I speak enough German to manage. We can find the Prussian commanders through the afterworld and learn their battle plans. Once we know what they intend, we can watch over them."

"I'll try, of course, but if the French Gifted intervene in the actual battle, what will we do? You said this agreement they broke by helping Napoleon forbade action against them directly. Didn't the head of the Council say that?"

He still wanted to curse about that. The events of March seemed eons ago, and yet they were only now coming to the crisis point. "It's best if they never know of it, of course, but there's an exception for actions in defense of others. If matters come to that, we'll be acting in defense of the Allied army, whether or not the Council would agree. We should go through the afterworld and see what the French Gifted plan. Our task here may be to stop them, nothing to do with the Prussians at all."

"Perhaps we're about to receive guidance." Amelia held out her hand to Julian.

He crossed the room to take it and saw Miranda standing by the hearth.

"My grandmother's here," Amelia told Barbara.

The other woman smiled. "Good day, Lady Hawkstowe. It's really too bad I can't see you."

"For me as well," Miranda said, and Amelia relayed the message.

"I have news," Miranda continued. "The armies are deployed, as you may know if you've been scrying or evoked a vision. Richard says Wellington has garrisoned the farm on his right flank, Chateau de Hougoumont, and the one in front of his center, La Haye Sainte. The Prussians gathered at a place called Wavre to the northeast."

"How are the numbers?" Julian asked.

"So many units are in motion that it's hard to know. Much will depend on who arrives where, and when. Bonaparte has dispatched a cavalry corps to keep the Prussians from joining with Wellington. He intends to hit the allied line before the Prussians can reinforce it. If he can break through the center, his forces can divide the battle line and roll toward each end. Then he'll see to the Prussians."

Julian and Amelia exchanged a look, and he knew she thought as he did. He nodded to her. "Perhaps," she said, "we should see what the Prussians plan. In my vision, Wellington needed them to arrive. Then we should probably sleep if we're to be up early."

CHAPTER 32

The battle commenced with French bombardment of the Anglo-Dutch lines in late morning. The thunder of the guns some dozen miles distant put everyone in Brussels on edge.

For the next several hours, Amelia and Julian alternated between the French cavalry at Gembloux and the Prussians marching from Wavre, one corps to join the Allied left flank and two corps to attack the French rear. Richard, Robin, and the Mainwaring heirs watched the French Gifted who wanted to enter the afterworld. So far, they'd all failed.

Vicious fighting around the farm on the Allied right flank filled the morning. So did attacks on the farm in front of the Allied center, La Haye Sainte. The carnage of battle didn't bother Amelia as she had expected it would, perhaps because she'd Seen so much of it. At least the smells of gunpowder and death couldn't penetrate this eerie place.

After several hours of going back and forth to see what was happening, hoping to learn what they should do, Amelia and Julian returned to his mother's house for luncheon and a brief rest.

"Why were the British soldiers lying down behind the ridge?" Amelia asked over the soup.

"The slope protects them from musket fire and, to some degree, artillery," Julian replied. "It's why Wellington likes to deploy on a ridge with a reverse slope."

Miranda, who had volunteered to keep an eye on the Gifted with

Napoleon, appeared to Amelia. Her grim expression had Amelia clutching Julian's hand so he could see too.

"Yes, Grandmother?"

"The Gifted with the French army are scrying, and whatever they've seen has them agitated. Unfortunately, I don't speak French. My dears, I know you're weary from all the traveling you've done today, but—"

Julian said, "I'll come at once. Amelia should finish her luncheon."

"If you're going," she told him, "so am I."

One look at her face, and he seemed to realize arguing was futile. Miranda led them to the French wizard and a young French soldier.

"The soldier is an aide-de camp, and the Gifted is a secretary," Amelia translated for Miranda. "They scried. Saw the future, two Prussian corps crossing the Lasne Brook near the town of that name. If the French can stop them on the east side of the river, they cannot help Wellington."

"That's likely II and IV Corps," Julian said. "Headed for the French rear with Blücher, based on what we overheard last night. The Allied line on the ridge has taken a brutal pounding. It's thin, and they need the reinforcements the Prussian I Corps will provide."

Amelia's heart kicked. "The French are sending two cavalry divisions to block their crossing. Apparently the French Gifted will not overtly join battle lest their doing so cause any Gifted on our side to use their magic."

"That's one good thing," Julian said. "Wait here, and I'll see where the Prussians are now." He walked into the churning mists, the glow of his silver shielding aura visible long after they could no longer discern his shape.

Minutes crawled by. Amelia listened to the French but heard nothing else useful.

At last Julian emerged, grim-faced, from the fog. "One Corps is headed for Papelotte and Wellington's left flank. Three Corps is pinned down at Wavre. The other two have reached Chapelle-Saint-Lambert, beyond the town of Lasne, and halted. They're waiting for trailing units to catch up."

"Meanwhile," Amelia said, "two French cavalry divisions are headed that way. If only stealing the armor had averted this." Still resting in Miranda and Richard's tent, the armor apparently hadn't inspired anyone to follow Bonaparte. That didn't mean it had no power, though. It reverberated with magic, and Frenchmen had followed the French girl who wore it, even though she had no military experience or claim to leadership.

"Julian?" Amelia asked. "How many men in such a division?"

"Around a thousand. What are you thinking?"

"That's about two thousand riders, a much smaller group than an entire army. Or even a corps."

Julian's eyes narrowed. "That isn't a *small* group, but—"

Richard strode out of the mist. "Two French Gifted came through earlier today. They drove off some of our men, but the wraiths killed one of them. The other fled back to the living world."

"Are any of you hurt?" Julian asked.

"They can send us far away, but they can't kill us. We're already dead." Richard shook his head. "They're now discussing what to do next."

"Meanwhile," Julian said, "our Prussian allies are about to come under attack."

"Perhaps there is a way to avoid that," Amelia said. "I can wear the armor. Pretend to be Joan of Arc. Frenchmen followed her in defiance of all the customs of their age. If two divisions—or even just their leaders— are a small enough group to influence, if the French cavalry will follow me, we can lead them to the southeast, away from all parts of the battle. By the time they realize I'm not Joan—"

"No," Julian responded. "There are musket balls flying out there. It's a good idea, but if anyone is to carry it out, I will."

"A ball can kill you as easily as it can me. Besides, the armor's much too small for you. It's too small for me, too, but I can likely manage if we let the straps out all the way. I can possibly wear the gauntlets. I'll need clothes to wear underneath, though. This dress won't do."

He shook his head.

"We've worked so hard," she reminded him. "Worried so much. Staged a theft that should've been impossible. Yet it wasn't enough. Soldiers are dying by the thousands. Horses too. If we can stop that, we should."

Again, he shook his head.

Richard put an arm around his shoulders. "Excuse us, my dears." He steered Julian into the fog.

"While we wait for them," Amelia suggested, "let's see how the battle is going."

They walked to a point near the Allied left flank. Smoke from artillery and muskets hung in the air, obscuring the scene, but they were close enough to see French infantry reach the Allied lines on the crest of the ridge and tear into the ranks. British cavalry responded, riding down the infantry and charging across the field toward the French battery.

A pair of riders rode through the two women's spectral forms. Amelia gaped. The sensation was strange, but only in her mind. She'd actually felt nothing.

"One grows accustomed," Miranda said, patting her arm.

Amelia glanced the way Julian and Richard had gone. If she had accompanied Crispin to India, her Gift might've warned of trouble ahead. That or her healing skills, if she been there to treat his illness early, might have saved him. Or they might not, but at least she would know whether there was anything she might've done. She would not stand by now while Julian ran a risk better suited to her.

"I will do this," Amelia stated. "No matter what he says."

~

At the same time, some distance away, Julian directed a hard look at Richard. "If you brought me over here to change my mind, you're wasting your time. Under no circumstances will I permit her to do that."

"Under what circumstances do you imagine you can stop her?" One corner of Richard's mouth crooked up.

"I would hope common sense would." Julian glared at him. "We don't know whether a magical shield stops a ball. It's only prudent to assume that if they fire upon her, they can kill her."

"If she's willing to take that chance, you cannot gainsay her."

"Bloody hell, I can't. She's my wife. She'll do as I say."

Richard's eyebrows rose. "Do you truly think so?"

No. Though he outweighed her substantially. "I'll sit on her if I must."

"Indeed? What happens to your marriage then?"

Nothing good. Julian scowled into the churning fog. Physically restraining Amelia would shatter his chances of winning her heart anytime soon.

"In my experience," Richard said, "love is the path to persuading a woman."

Julian shrugged. Amelia didn't want him to love her, or so he'd thought. Yet sometimes, she looked at him... If she meant to go into danger, if he couldn't stop her, perhaps she should know how he felt.

"The French," he said slowly, "will not fire on St. Joan. They may also hesitate to fire on any unarmed woman."

A plan took shape in his mind. "I'll talk to her."

~

A short time later, Julian and Amelia stood together and watched a British cavalry charge overrun the French artillery battery. The view was gauzy because they still stood in the afterworld and because of heavy smoke still hanging in the air. Several horsemen rode through them, but Miranda had been right. One did grow accustomed.

Sabers slashing, the horsemen surged into the gun crews.

Julian's lips tightened.

"What is it?" Amelia asked. For her, the slaughter of the British charge outweighed the beauty of the synchronized movements. She was selfishly glad Julian had not gone into the army.

"Those horses are blown," he said. "When they need to retreat—oh, God."

French cavalry and lancers charged the British riders. As Julian must've expected, the British horses could not summon speed to escape. The French overtook them. With their bright breastplates gleaming in the sunlight, they slashed and speared the British riders.

Riderless horses galloped through the lines. The bodies of men and horses littered the ground, and wounded mounts thrashed in agony. The entire scene was heartbreaking.

Amelia fought nausea. Julian turned her into his body.

"Don't look," he said. "Let's find those two Prussian corps and do our part."

She let him steer her away to the southeast, toward the Lasne valley and across to the east side of the river. They passed a large forest, which he said was the Forest of Blois.

"The French are just south of there, across the brook," he said. "I hope they haven't yet spotted the Prussians. The Gifted said they had scouts out. We'll need their horses."

The French cavalry were trotting, in no apparent hurry. If they'd seen the enemy, they would charge. Good. Leading them away should allow the Prussians to join the main battle.

If this succeeded.

Amelia wore the chest and back plates of Joan's armor, along with the vambraces on her arms and the gauntlets. She and Julian had made the pieces that were designed for a smaller woman mostly fit by bridging the straps with cord. The bits were tied together around her. She also wore the cuisses and greaves, upper and lower leg pieces. Under it all she wore a pair of Julian's old breeches and a shirt hastily retrieved from Aysgarth.

The helm, however, was simply too small. She would have to make do without it, so she'd braided her hair and tucked the braid into her shirt to look more like Joan's cropped style.

"This feel strange," she told him. "It's like…wearing magic." The sensation unsettled her, but if she admitted that, he might try again to stop her.

"I wish you wouldn't do this," he said, his face grim.

"To be honest, I would rather not." His eyes lit, but she continued, "My stomach's churning, and I'm so cold. But Julian, this could be it. This could be the thing that turns the tide, that determines which vision comes true."

"Then how can we be sure you should do it, not avoid it?"

"I feel that I should. If it leads to defeat, perhaps that's meant to be."

He looked aghast.

She cupped his cheek in her armored palm. "You said a seer's hunches are always to be respected. Besides, how can anything that reinforces Wellington's lines be other than good?"

His lips tightened. Grimly, he nodded.

"You must come back to me, Amelia. You must." The intensity in his gaze was new, and it made her already fluttery pulse kick.

"I plan to. I wish you wouldn't come along. I can manage."

"You'll not go without someone to cover your back." He would glamour himself invisible, seize a riderless horse, a pistol, and ammunition, and ride beside her. Anyone who fired upon her would do so only once.

"Perhaps I should've told you before. I don't want you to go out there not knowing." He took a deep breath. "I love you, Amelia. I know what I said, and I won't let this become a problem, but—"

"I love you," she blurted on a rush of joy.

"What?" He looked stunned.

"I love you. I've been afraid to say so because I thought you didn't want that from me."

"That was an idiotic notion of mine." Julian kissed her hard, then more deeply. Gradually, the passion in the kiss eased to tenderness.

Their tight embrace made the edges of the chest and back plates dig into her sides and waist. Amelia didn't care.

He buried his face in her neck and repeated, "You must come back to me."

She stroked his hair. "As you must return to me. I couldn't bear it if we lost the chance to build the life we want. The family we Saw at the pool. But first we must do this."

With a sigh, he released her. "They're cavalry. They live in their saddles. Staying ahead of them will be difficult, but if they overtake you, they'll see the ruse."

"You're a superb horseman, and you claim I'm fairly decent. If we must, we can interpose icy ground as a barrier. Though that won't last long in June."

"There is that. Are you ready?"

"The sooner, the better."

"Then let's get our horses," he said. "This may be too large a group for the armor's influence. If the French won't follow you, we'll glamour ourselves invisible and ride away. Agreed?"

That was only common sense. Amelia nodded.

They located the French scouts in the woods east of the brook. They were well ahead of the main body of cavalry. Julian opened a portal. Glamoured to be invisible, he and Amelia stepped into the living world. Two brief blasts of magic knocked the scouts unconscious. Magic held the frightened horses in place. Julian gave Amelia a leg up and mounted before they released the beasts. Having weight in their saddles seemed to calm them.

Amelia and Julian rode at an angle to intercept the French cavalry but didn't draw too near. Julian expanded his invisibility glamour to cover his horse. The magical shield around Amelia gave her a spectral glow and gleamed off the battered armor.

"Riding astride is easy," she commented. "Perhaps I'll do so henceforth."

"If scandal delights you," he replied, his voice dry, "I expect I can weather it."

Thanks to the armor, Amelia was already sweating in the day's heat, but there was no help for it. She could bathe in cool water when this was done.

They rode out of the trees and across the column's path. Amelia rose in the stirrups and held up one hand.

"*Mes frères*," she shouted over the din of the main battle, "the Emperor needs us. Follow me! Let us aid him."

The lead riders turned to look. For a moment, they simply stared.

"*Avec moi*," she cried, waving. "With me. *Pour le gloire de la France*."

"Sainte Jeanne," someone shouted. "Jeanne d'Arc!"

"For the glory of France," someone else cried in French, echoing her.

With one last *avec moi!*, she galloped to the southeast, away from the battle. A stream of Frenchmen followed her. As word spread through the ranks, more and more followed.

For the next hour, Amelia and Julian rode southeast. Staying off the roads slowed them down but also delayed the cavalry. When a convenient hill or clump of trees offered the opportunity, Amelia glamoured herself invisible and changed course. A few moments later, she reappeared and called to the soldiers. These tactics and occasionally creating icy patches of ground in front of their pursuers helped them stay ahead. Yet the horsemen inexorably gained. Ice lasted only a short time in the June heat.

Miranda appeared beside Amelia's mount. "The Prussians will complete their crossing before these men can reach them. Come back, my dear ones."

When Amelia relayed that to Julian, he said, "That copse of trees should hide us if we move quickly."

They rode into the trees, briefly losing sight of their pursuers.

Julian leaped from his saddle and formed a portal a short distance away. His mount neighed and fled. Amelia drew rein and rose in her stirrups to dismount. As she swung her right leg over, her horse shied from the portal. With both legs on the horse's left and only one foot in a stirrup, Amelia lost her balance and fell, landing hard on her back. Above her, the horse wheeled. Something glanced off her head.

Julian's cry of horror seemed to come from a great distance. As his dear, terrified face appeared above her, the world went dark.

CHAPTER 33

Julian took Amelia back to his mother's house. None of his allies in the afterworld had healed anyone in about a hundred years, and Mama was an adept healer. She and Barbara helped put Amelia to bed and checked her injuries.

While they examined her, terror drummed in Julian's veins. The horse's hoof had glanced off her temple. When he'd been hit in the head, he'd been damned lucky to recover. Now Amelia didn't awaken, and her left arm hung at an odd angle.

He set his jaw. He couldn't lose her now. He wouldn't.

Barbara turned from the bed and laid a hand on his shoulder. "The horse's hoof must have made only glancing contact. There's very little swelling. Catherine is tending to that now."

The words offered hope. If he grasped it, and she was wrong...

Barbara smiled. "We don't want her to awaken until we've fixed her shoulder. She dislocated it in that fall and wrenched her hip. She has some bruising too." Studying him, she added, "She will be in fine fettle by tomorrow, Julian. I promise you."

"So do I," his mother said, smoothing the sheet over Amelia. "Her shoulder will be sore. I'm not healing all the pain because I want her to be careful. Pain is a reminder to do that. Anyway, I don't want to give her laudanum until her head's clear for a while."

She also patted him on the shoulder. "Call me if you need me."

"Let me know how Ludwig fares." When he had arrived with Amelia, his mother had been in her chamber scrying the battle and watching him.

Despite the warm day, Julian lit a fire in the hearth. His limited skills sufficed for scrying a battle currently happening not far away. Watching, he sat by Amelia's bed and held her hand.

She awoke about half an hour later. Blinking, she stared up at him. "Julian? Did we do it?"

He kissed her swiftly. She was talking. Her eyes tracked. Relief threatened to choke him. Fetching her some water and supporting her while she drank gave him time to compose himself.

"What's happened?" she demanded.

He grinned at her. "The lead Prussian units emerged from the forest near the town of Plancenoit around half past three. They didn't wait for their comrades to arrive but immediately began bombarding the French lines. As reinforcements reached them, they launched an attack on the town, behind the French right flank. That drew off the French reserves."

"That's good, isn't it?"

"It is. The Prussians also reinforced the Allied left, which let our cavalry reinforce the battered center. But the farm below our center, La Haye Sainte, has fallen."

Amelia tugged on his hand. "The hearth is too far away. I can't see."

"You're supposed to stay in bed. Besides, the day is warm already. It'll be hot by the fire."

"We can make a nest on the floor. Please, Julian. I must know how this goes."

He used pillows and the coverlet from the bed to make a seating area at its foot. Leaning against the footboard, he drew Amelia back against his chest. With his arms locked around her waist, he had all he could want in the world.

Bonaparte was leading a column of men, a huge mass of blue-clad infantry, down to the valley.

"That's the Imperial Guard," Julian said. "They've never been defeated."

"The line on the ridge looks thin," she muttered. She laced her fingers through his.

"It is. Dangerously thin."

The French column stopped short of La Haye Sainte and split into two.

Bearing left, both columns of the Guard strode up the hill. It was rough going because of all the bodies in the way and the churned-up soil.

Artillery shells and musket fire assailed them. Yet on they went, aiming at that weakened line of red coats.

Amelia's grip on his hand tightened.

"We needn't watch this," he told her.

"I want to know." Twisting to look up at him, she asked, "Don't you?"

He nodded, and they turned back to the flickering images in the fire. Julian shifted the view closer so they could see better.

The French right column, moving slightly ahead of the left, neared the crest of the ridge. The Duke of Wellington said something to the officer next to him. That officer spoke over his shoulder.

From behind the ridge, a wall of red-coated soldiers rose.

Julian's jaw dropped in amazement and sudden hope.

"I forgot they were there," Amelia exclaimed.

The French advance stopped, likely out of shock.

The redcoats opened fire. The front ranks of the Guard fell. Those behind them returned fire, only to be met with another British fusillade. One of the four red-clad ranks reloaded while the next moved ahead of it to fire. Then that rank dropped back, and so on.

Meanwhile the redcoats to the right of those firing deployed in a line and wheeled to face the Guard's left flank. They opened fire, and Frenchmen dropped. The Guard turned to face them, firing, but couldn't withstand the combined musketry of their enemies. They buckled, forming squares and attempting to retreat.

On the ridge, the Duke of Wellington rose in his stirrups and waved his bicorn hat. The entire Allied line yelled and charged down the slope.

The French retreat became a rout.

The battle was won.

Julian pressed a kiss into Amelia's dark hair. "It's over. They'll likely be forced to chase Bonaparte back to Paris, but he's finished."

"We made the right choice." Nestling against him, she sighed.

Resettling her in the bed took only a few moments. Despite the warm day, he stretched out beside her. She snuggled against him, and contentment flooded him. Julian rested his cheek against her hair.

No one would ever know the role a bookish earl and a too-bold-for-her-own-good seer had played, and that was just as well. The Merlin Club liked the shadows.

~

The high cost of victory quickly became apparent. As Amelia had Seen, thousands of men and horses lay dead on the battlefield. Even those transported to field hospitals weren't sure to survive, and looters plundered those awaiting burial or transport. Wellington had come through unscathed but was said to be deeply saddened by his personal losses. About half the officers of his headquarters staff were killed, with almost as many wounded. Only two or three besides the duke were unhurt. Many of the dead and injured had been his friends.

Three days after the battle, Frederik knocked on the door of the upstairs parlor where Amelia sat reading. "Major Biedermann is here, my lady. The dowager countess is due back any time, but I thought you should know he's in the downstairs parlor."

"How does he seem?" Amelia asked, rising. Catherine had said he'd been shot in the left shoulder. The wound obviously had been severe enough to keep him from riding toward Paris with the army yesterday.

"His left arm is in a sling," Frederik replied, "and he moves stiffly."

"I'll go down at once. Thank you."

Amelia hurried down to the front parlor. She found the uniformed hussar staring out at the street. When he turned to greet her, she had to steel herself against shock. Grief lined his face and darkened his eyes.

"Amelia," he said, for they'd long since reached that level of friendship. "Good afternoon."

"Good afternoon. Catherine is out, but she's due back any moment. Would you care to come upstairs?"

He accompanied her and sat in the chair next to the sofa where she'd been reading. When she offered, he accepted a cup of tea. An awkward silence fell.

Unsure of her ground, Amelia asked, "How are you, Ludwig?"

"I am alive. Many of my friends..." His lips tightened, and he shook his head. "I've never been in a battle with such a high casualty count."

"I'm so very sorry."

He acknowledged that with a nod. "One expects...that is, soldiers know we may be killed." Anger slashed through the grief as he added, "But we hope we don't die for stupidity."

"What do you mean?"

He took a deep breath. "I have friends in our Fifth Line Battalion. Before the battle, I had more of them."

"This is a unit of the King's German Legion?"

"Yes." His hand shook. He set the tea down and clenched his fist on his knee. "I beg your pardon. This is not fit—"

"I would like you to tell me." She didn't want to hear it, but turning away from his obvious suffering was more than she could bear.

"The French had taken La Haye Sainte."

"The farm in the center of the line?"

"Yes." Dully, his eyes unfocused, he continued. "Lt. General Alten ordered Colonel Ompteda to retake the farm. The colonel pointed out that there were French cavalry around it and his men would stand no chance."

Amelia's Sight told her what was coming. Dreading to hear it, she braced herself.

"The Prince of Orange rode up and insisted the cavalry were Dutch, not French. He would not listen to the colonel's objections and ordered Ompteda to attack. So the colonel led out the Fifth, and as he had foreseen, the French cut them to pieces. He died with them."

"I'm so sorry." The words were completely inadequate. She reached over to squeeze his hand.

At that moment, Julian walked through the door.

Amelia froze, but she would not withdraw her hand. Ludwig was suffering.

Please don't let this be like last time. But the circumstances were all too similar.

Her eyes met Julian's, and she couldn't read his face. Her heart pounded painfully.

Julian sat beside her. "I've seen the casualty lists," he said. "Ludwig, I'm deeply sorry for all your losses."

"You are too kind." His throat worked. He blinked rapidly. "Both of you."

Catherine hurried into the room. She knelt by Ludwig's chair and put her arms around him. "My dear, I'm so dreadfully sorry."

Hooking his good arm around her, he buried his face in her neck.

Amelia looked at Julian, intending to nod toward the door, but he was already moving. Quietly, they left the parlor and closed the door.

Julian said nothing about finding her with Ludwig. Should she mention it? Or the fact that the looks on Catherine's face as she entered and on Ludwig's when he saw her implied theirs was no casual affair after all? Perhaps it was best not to raise that possibility. It was Catherine's concern, after all, not theirs to pry into.

When they reached their chamber, Amelia told Julian of the attack Ludwig had described. "What he said explains why the soldiers in the vision of disaster had so little regard for the Prince of Orange."

"He's brave but arrogant and inexperienced." Julian put his arms around her. "I heard about that stupid attack. I'm glad Ludwig was not caught up in it."

"You are?" She searched his face, hardly daring to hope.

"I am." He looked directly at her. "And I'm glad you comforted him when he needed it. I cannot imagine what he must be feeling."

"Then you're not..."

"Jealous? Suspicious?" He smiled. "No, I'm truly not. Knowing you love me, doing all we've done together, has burned away the wariness you never deserved. So I'm asking you to forgive me for the times I behaved so badly. It won't happen again."

Amelia's joy bubbled up into a smile. "I believe you. I forgive you. I love you."

"I can't ask for more than that," he said, and he kissed her.

CHAPTER 34

Amelia and Julian and their friends returned to London in late
June, after Bonaparte abdicated for the second time. Traveling
via the afterworld, they stashed Joan's armor in the safest place
in Britain, the vault of the Merlin Club. Julian would seek a way to strip
the armor of its magic so they could return it to its rightful owner. With
the armor safe for now, they could turn to other concerns.

Henry Talbot sold them Lady Eleanor Butler's prayer book. As they
had hoped, her affidavit was concealed in it, under the back endpaper.

Julian and Amelia had taken it to a friend of his at the Society of Antiquaries to have it authenticated. Now, after only two weeks, his unGifted
but—according to Julian—brilliant friend, Augustus Lacey, had sent for
him. He and Amelia took a hackney to Somerset House, the site of the
Society's offices and library. A clerk ushered them into a book-lined
room.

Amelia's heart pounded. If they could prove this was authentic, would
it free her family's souls?

A few minutes later, Lacey, a short man in his sixties with a cherubic
face and thinning gray hair, strolled into the room. He carried the prayer
book and Lady Eleanor's affidavit along with a sheaf of papers.

"Most interesting," he said, laying it all on the table in front of Julian.
"This was most interesting. Fortunately, Lady Eleanor Butler gave a
manor to her sister in 1468, and we were able to use that deed for signa-

ture comparison. That would ordinarily take much longer, but I know people who can be very helpful."

"So it's authentic," Amelia said.

"Yes." He studied her for a moment. "That does not, however, mean it's probative. At least, not for what you said you wanted. It goes to King Richard's motives toward his nephews, but it doesn't prove he didn't do away with them, you know."

"I know, but perhaps it will change some minds." If it changed enough, it would lift the curse, but she hadn't been able to See that happen. She could still hope, though.

He continued, "I have supplied affidavits to support the authentication. Unfortunately, too many of our fellow Britons believe Master Shakespeare was an historian, not a dramatist. So they forget he, like all dramatists, made things up for a living. I do wish you luck."

Amelia and Julian walked into the sunshine with the book and papers in a satchel. "Now what?" Amelia asked as they strolled past the shops along the Strand.

"Now we see if I can muster any support in Parliament. If I can't, we'll publish it and hope for the best."

With Parliament out of session, gauging support was difficult, but everyone Julian consulted refused to accept Lady Eleanor's affidavit as proof of Richard III's right to the throne. Or of his innocence in his nephews' deaths.

"After all," one elderly man said, "even a king with an ironclad right to the throne may see the need to eliminate rivals."

That was what Amelia's latest use of her Gift had warned them would happen, but they couldn't give up until they'd tried to reach a wider audience. They found a small historical journal to publish the affidavit and an article by Lacey arguing in King Richard's favor.

The fates of the Mainwaring ghosts, however, remained unchanged. The affidavit was not enough to satisfy the terms of the curse.

In mid-July, Amelia went to the afterworld to tell Adam. She wanted the news to come from her.

"It's all right," he assured her. He stood with his arm around her shoulders. "You did what you could, and you know who likely has Edmund's confession. Now the trick is to recover it."

"We won't give up. Sooner or later, I promise you, a Mainwaring will obtain it."

"I know. It's better here now that we've so much companionship.

Some return to their own times for a while, but they eventually rejoin us. Being together reminded us we're a family." His arm tightened. "Do me a favor, Amelia. Don't come here often."

"But I miss you!" She couldn't keep the hurt out of her voice.

"I miss you, too, but now I can see and talk to you. That's some consolation."

Now that they were in the same era, they could communicate as she did with Richard and Miranda. "It doesn't console me," Amelia argued.

"You have Julian and a life to build. The hope of a family. Live that life and know I revel in your happiness."

What he said made sense. Reluctantly, she nodded. "But I'm coming here every year on our birthday. I can't bear not to share it with you."

"Fair enough," he conceded. "I'll enjoy that."

"Where are Miranda and Richard?"

"Having an overdue chat with Cousin Gerald. He's now the direct heir. He should know what's in store for him."

"Poor Gerald," Amelia said. He was a staid, practical fellow. Thinking ghosts or curses had anything to do with him would unsettle him severely, and with good reason. "He won't readily believe them."

"No, he won't." Adam mock-frowned at her. "Now go home. Remind Julian I said he'd best be good to you, or I'll haunt him."

If Adam could joke, he truly was doing well. Amelia smoothed back his hair. "Miranda, Richard, and Edmund have agreed that someone in each generation must learn the secret of traveling here."

"That's wise. Now go. Celebrate your great accomplishment. And think of me sometimes."

"I will." Amelia kissed his cheek. Smiling at him, she stepped out of the afterworld and into her new life.

Apprehending Wyndon took time, as did tracking down evidence to prove what Amelia had Seen in visions. In due course, the Merlin Club found both him and the evidence they needed. The day after they returned him to London, Amelia and Julian sat in the basement of London's Green Bull tavern, which occupied the site of the former Roman Temple of Mithras. Julian had laid out all he'd learned about Wyndon's support of the Scots rebels and the French and his treachery toward Amelia.

When he finished, Alice Gresham turned to Wyndon. "You may offer rebuttal, Silas."

"The conversations Aysgarth claims to have overheard never took place. I conduct my business in warded structures, which are impervious to scrying. He cannot know what I did in these places and is inventing fictions to gain revenge for the thrashing I gave him."

Alice said, "Julian?"

"The evidence speaks for itself." He'd been adamant about not revealing Amelia's Gift to the Conclave and so had built his case without that. Wyndon couldn't mention it either. A seer's evidence would carry even more weight than the information Julian had offered.

Alice looked around the room. "Whether that is adequate is for the Conclave to decide. We will now vote."

"The hell you will," Wyndon snapped. "I demand my right to face my accuser in combat arcane."

A shocked gasp rippled through the long room. Amelia bit back a cry of protest.

Alice looked at Julian for a long moment. Was that regret in her eyes?

"Do you accept the challenge, Julian?" she asked.

He nodded. Amelia drew in a sharp breath and turned a pleading look on him. "I must do this," he told her quietly. Standing, he stripped off his coat, waistcoat, and cravat.

Other wizards cleared a space in the center of the tile floor. Julian and Wyndon, who had also removed his outer clothing and cravat, faced each other in the center.

Alice watched while the remainder of the Council warded the circle.

As soon as the last ward gleamed, Wyndon shot a bolt of argent power at Julian. Amelia's heart lurched.

Argent flared around Julian, deflecting Wyndon's bolt. Although the wizards in the path of the deflection shrank back, the bolt sizzled harmlessly against the wards. Julian advanced on Wyndon. The accused wizard launched another bolt. Delivered at closer range, it knocked Julian back a step, but only a step.

He blocked a right hook from Wyndon and drove his glowing right fist into the other wizard's face. Wyndon lashed out with his left, and Julian ducked. This time, his blow crashed into Wyndon's belly. Circling, they exchanged blows with their fists glowing.

Julian never lashed out with a bolt. Was he trying to lure Wyndon? No. He'd promised Dare he wouldn't reveal that secret. She and Julian had also agreed admitting he had this skill could make him a target. What the Conclave chose to make of Wyndon's actions was up to them.

Wyndon had experience fencing and sparring, but Julian trained horses. He had the strength, determination, and patience for that work. As the fight continued, his greater endurance drove Wyndon back.

Wyndon gripped Julian's shoulder. Julian stiffened, his head falling back, as magic flared around him. Wyndon drove his fist into Julian's belly and shoved him away.

Amelia found herself standing, clasped hands in front of her mouth.

"Easy," Robin whispered, sliding his arm around her shoulders. "Trust him."

The aura around Julian suddenly brightened. He had absorbed Wyndon's power.

Driving a blow past Wyndon's guard, he slammed his fist into the other man's chin. His absorbed power met Wyndon's magical shield in a blinding flash of light. Wyndon's head snapped back. He dropped to the floor and lay still.

Julian looked at Alice.

"Tobias?" she prompted. A wave of her hand dispelled the wards.

The Gifted doctor left his seat and knelt by Wyndon. He put his fingers to the fallen earl's throat and held them there.

After almost a minute, he looked up and shook his head. "He's dead."

Alice glanced left and right at her fellow Councilors.

"The verdict," she announced, "is decided. Lord Wyndon is guilty, and his crimes are punished with his death."

Julian's eyes met Amelia's. The Council would undoubtedly want to know how he countered Wyndon's magic, but he would simply say it had been instinct or luck. The shadow of Wyndon's threat was banished at last.

EPILOGUE

I n early September, Amelia stood beside Julian in the entry hall of Aysgarth House. Their mothers flanked them, both smiling broadly as they greeted the guests. Catherine was officially the host of this belated wedding breakfast. Amelia had been concerned about how Mama would take that, but she had been at her most charming. She'd even called Julian *darling boy*, so she must've reconciled herself to the marriage.

If she knew the secret Amelia and Julian were keeping, she would be speechless with delight. But they wanted time to enjoy the prospect of their coming child before the polite world butted in with anecdotes and advice. Amelia's lips curved in a smile, and she resisted the urge to place a hand on her belly.

The one shadow over the day was their inability to find Edmund's confession. Any wards Wyndon had set should've dropped with his death, but they still couldn't locate the document. They could only conclude that it must be hidden by some sort of magic they didn't understand.

There had been altogether too much of that lately for Julian's taste. At least the mystery of Amelia's ability to use magic at Pendragon and the effect of Morgan's pool on her powers was solved. Morgan's hand-maidens confirmed her seer abilities let her work magic, and using the pool had increased her power. After the baby was born—the gray-eyed, dark-haired girl they'd Seen in the pool?—Amelia would go there and use the pool to refine her Gift.

Newly returned from Devonshire, Sophie and Ned entered together. Sophie kissed Julian's cheek and embraced Amelia. "I cannot believe I missed all the fun. Next time you go on an adventure, you must be sure to include me."

Amelia smiled at Julian. "I hope there won't be any more adventures."

"Amen," he said.

But his gaze fell on his mother. Despite her bright smile today, she'd become quieter since Brussels.

Amelia squeezed his hand. When he'd told her he feared his mother missed Ludwig, Amelia had admitted the looks on their faces when they first met after Waterloo had made her wonder if their affair was more serious than it seemed. Given Catherine's cool demeanor, however, the idea of asking felt like a transgression.

After the last guests came through, Julian said, "We should start the meal."

He offered Amelia his arm. Followed by their mothers, they walked into the ballroom. Three long tables there were laid for their guests, who mingled in clumps around the room. Mama Bainbridge and her sons Lucian and Oliver were chatting with someone near the head table.

Just inside the door, Amelia and Julian met Crispin's father and youngest brother, Gabriel. Amelia smiled at them. "Come with us a moment?" she asked the two men.

She led them clear of the crowd before turning to her husband. "Julian?"

He drew a long piece of folded paper from his coat pocket and presented it to her with a slight bow. Amelia offered it to Gabriel. "From Crispin and me to you. It's the deed to Leyburn Manor."

Gabriel's jaw dropped as his father exclaimed, "My dear!"

"You—you cannot," Gabriel stammered. "Cris wanted you to have that —for your security."

"He also wanted me to remarry." Amelia smiled up at Julian. "Leyburn Manor belongs to a life that might have been. I have a new path to follow, and there's no sense in the manor standing empty while I do so. It needs life and joy within its walls. I've removed the few pieces of furniture I want. The rest is yours."

As the youngest of five boys, with all the family lands entailed, Gabriel had had few options. Now he had a new one. Amelia believed he would love the manor and would erase the taint of grief she'd left there. She had already sent the portrait of her and Crispin to his parents.

"My dear girl." Lord Bainbridge kissed her cheek. "You take care of her, Aysgarth."

Solemnly, Julian replied, "To my last breath."

"Take the deed, Gabe," his father said.

Gabriel thanked her with quiet dignity. "You are welcome anytime, of course."

"We are neighbors," Julian replied. "So you'll certainly see us."

Lord Bainbridge said, "We mustn't keep you, as your guests are waiting, but I want you to know, my dear…" His eyes misted, and he swallowed hard. "I promised Crispin I would urge you to wed again." Glancing at Julian, he added, "I hope it isn't presumptuous to say I believe he would agree you've made a fine choice. All of us wish you both a lifetime of happiness."

They thanked him and moved on. Guests noticed them heading for the high table and found their own seats.

At the high table sat both their mothers, Augusta, and Amelia's aunt and uncle. Amelia touched Julian's arm to stop him before they sat.

"Papa Bainbridge was right," she said. "I have made a fine choice. I love you, Julian."

"I love you, too." He kissed her quickly, and the guests who saw cheered and applauded.

Julian seated her at the center of the table but stayed on his feet. He picked up his glass of champagne.

"Welcome, everyone. We're deeply grateful to my mother for hosting this party and to my lady's mother for her assistance with the arrangements. Thanks also to all of you for sharing this day with us."

Smiling into Amelia's warm eyes, he hoisted his glass. He hadn't told her what he meant to say, but she would know how much this simple toast encompassed. "To a family—of blood and of the heart."

"To family," the smiling guests called back.

The End

ABOUT THE HISTORY

The Battle of Waterloo was the cataclysmic event of its age. Gathered together, the books written about that campaign would easily fill a library, possibly even requiring double shelving. I consulted enough of them to see that they were not consistent in their details. What one author found engaging, another ignored altogether. So I exercised the novelist's prerogative and chose the ones that best fit my story.

I also found considerable disagreement as to what action or actions turned the tide in favor of the Allied armies. Here too, I did what worked best for the book. It seemed to me that the battle might have gone very differently without the Prussian army. The Prussians spent the night before Waterloo in Wavre, to the northeast of the main battlefield. Leaving III Corps to protect their rear, I, II, and IV Corps went to Wellington's aid the next day. With Field Marshal Blücher, II and IV corps marched down the Lasne brook, crossing it at the town of Lasne so they were on the same side of it as the Waterloo battlefield.

Their I Corps reinforced the Allied left flank, allowing resources to shift in support of the battered center at a crucial time. Meanwhile, II and IV Corps emerged from the Bois de Paris and attacked the town of Plancenoit behind the French lines. This attack forced Bonaparte to use his scarce reserves in defense of the town, so he didn't have them to throw against the Allied battle line when they might have made all the difference.

While the Prussians were in transit, two French cavalry divisions were sent to reconnoiter but didn't go far enough along Lasne Brook to spot the approaching forces. This gave me the idea for Julian and Amelia's actions at the end of the battle.

If Waterloo is one of history's pivotal events, the fate of Edward IV's sons, the Princes in the Tower, is one of its greatest mysteries. The traditionalist (Shakespearean) view is that Richard III, their uncle, murdered them. Others beg to differ. I've been interested in this controversy most of my adult life. A college classmate gave me a copy of Josephine Tey's *The Daughter of Time*, and that book reminded me that getting one's history from a playwright, even one so well known as Master Shakespeare, isn't always wise.

Since then, I've read widely about King Richard and his nephews. Turning over what I read and playing "what if"—one of my favorite games —led me to write this book and its siblings in the trilogy.

I don't think the historical evidence supports the traditional view of Richard III as a power-mad, murderous hunchback. He actually was asked to take the throne by nobles and clergy, with oaths of allegiance from various leaders following. His right to rule was ratified by an act of Parliament in 1484. While I would never say that it's impossible for him to have murdered his nephews, I haven't seen convincing evidence that he did, and without that proof, I believe he's entitled to the benefit of the doubt.

No one knows for sure what happened to Edward IV's sons. I've always liked the theory that Richard III had the boys spirited out of the country as the threat of Henry Tudor's invasion loomed. I first read this in *The Mystery of the Princes* by Audrey Williamson, but there are many books proposing alternatives. For an excellent examination of the different theories regarding their fates, see Matthew Lewis's *The Survival of the Princes in the Tower: Murder, Mystery, and Myth*.

I chose to build this trilogy around the possibility the boys had been murdered, with the Duke of Buckingham as the culprit, because of the possibilities that story scenario offered. Buckingham rebelled against Richard III in the autumn of 1483, around the time the two boys were reportedly last seen at the Tower of London, and there was no parliamentary act declaring that the duke should sit on the throne. He arguably had more of a motive to do away with them than King Richard did.

An urn in Westminster Abbey contains bones that are purportedly those of Edward IV's sons. Whether this claim is true is debatable.

Modern scientists have taken issue with the forensic examination of the 1930s, but the Crown refuses permission for an examination with modern DNA techniques.

Lady Eleanor Butler did exist, and proof (now vanished, as Augusta notes in *The Steel Rose*) of her prior contract of marriage with Edward IV led Parliament to declare his marriage to his queen bigamous. Their children thus became bastards ineligible to inherit the throne. Lady Eleanor really did die in an abbey, and she did give a manor to her sister. Unfortunately, as is often the case with medieval women, records of her life are few. *Lady Eleanor: The Secret Queen* by the late Dr. John Ashdown-Hill, MBE, FSA, FRHA, offers a closer look at this relatively obscure but ultimately very important woman.

Modern historians range all along the spectrum of opinion from those who think Shakespeare had it right to those who think every wrong laid at Richard III's feet is bogus. That's part of the fun of reading about this and weighing the different arguments.

For more information, check the websites of the various Richard III Society branches around the world. You can also find an essay on my website, www.nancynorthcott.com.

I'll close with a detail note about Julian and Amelia's ride in Hyde Park. If you've visited Apsley House, the Duke of Wellington's London home, you may have noticed that it's faced in stone, not red brick. The original house, however, was red brick. Wellington had it expanded and given stone facing around 1828.

Thank you for reading!

AUTHOR'S NOTE

Thank you for reading *The Steel Rose.* I hope you enjoyed it. If you're inclined to leave a review on an online vendor site, I would appreciate it. Just be aware that any pop-up review option at the end of the book will not show up on the site.

If you'd like me to keep you posted about new releases, you can sign up for my newsletter on the right-hand sidebar of my homepage. Just go to www.nancynorthcott.com. I never share your email with anyone outside of my newsletter team. Newsletters come out only when I have a new release or other important news, so you'll hear from me just a few times a year.

Thanks again!

ACKNOWLEDGMENTS

The women of Avocat Noir, Jeanne Adams, Donna MacMeans, and Cassondra Murray, offered critical insights as I shaped this story. I later received valuable feedback from each of them and from Debbie Yutko, Amy Herring, Gerri Russell, Staley Nance, and Ann Wicker. Darin Kennedy and Jeanne Adams helped me work out a knotty problem.

When I first became interested in the controversy surrounding Richard III, I relied heavily on the Richard III Society's American Branch library to educate myself. Their website and that of the parent society, in the United Kingdom, also offer a great deal of helpful information.

Regency England, the era of the Napoleonic Wars, was one of elaborate and meticulously observed social customs. To a writer who enjoys reading Regency novels but has never studied the period, it looks a bit like a minefield. I'm grateful to Patricia Rice and Teresa DesJardien, authors of many Regency novels, for their help. Teresa DesJardien is also the author of the forthcoming comprehensive regency reference *Jane Austen Shopped Here*. I did skip some of the bowing and curtseying at social affairs for the sake of moving the story along. Any errors are my responsibility alone.

Anna Sugden and her husband, a/k/a Doc Cambridge, are always ready to help with research questions across the pond and to listen to me go on about Richard III or the various places I've visited. Jules Langley accompanied me through Apsley House and waited patiently while I explored the shop. It's not particularly large, but it still involves choices!

Rob Rundle went with me to Bath. Even though I didn't end up using it in the book, the visit was like walking through the Regency. He and my other friends in London, Jules Langley, Jules Clark, Hass Yusuf, Gary Hellen, and Will Morgan, have sat at many a dinner table while I blathered on about all the interesting (to me) things I saw that day.

Judy Horwell and the late Alan Rowley of Yorkshire's True Tours made it possible for me to explore Yorkshire and scout locations for my characters. They greeted every request with enthusiasm, and no spot was too obscure for a visit.

I'm grateful to Falstaff Books for giving this trilogy a home and to my editor, Lucy Blue, for helping me make the story the best it could be.

My agent, Beth Miller, has always supported this project and every other. She never fails to step up when I need assistance or advice.

Lyndsey Lewellen created the gorgeous cover for this book and its siblings in the trilogy.

My husband, Mark, always stands ready to check out story locations, haul books home, be a sounding board, and help me with my research in any way he can. He has always encouraged me to pursue a writing career, even when I had my doubts. His support and that of our son are invaluable in this and so much else.

FALSTAFF BOOKS

**Want to know what's new & coming soon from
Falstaff Books?**

**Join our Newsletter List
& Get this Free Ebook Sampler
with work from:
John G. Hartness
A.G. Carpenter
Bobby Nash
Emily Lavin Leverett
Jaym Gates
Darin Kennedy
Natania Barron
Edmund R. Schubert
& More!**

http://www.subscribepage.com/q0j0p3

ABOUT THE AUTHOR

Nancy Northcott's childhood ambition was to grow up and become Wonder Woman. Around fourth grade, she realized it was too late to acquire Amazon genes, but she still loved comic books, science fiction, fantasy, history and YA romance. A sucker for fast action and wrenching emotion, she combines the magic and high stakes she loves in the books she writes.

A highlight of Nancy's college years was the summer she spent studying Tudor and Stuart Britain at the University of Oxford. She has written freelance articles and taught at the college level. Her most popular course was on science fiction, fantasy, and society. She has given presentations on Richard III and the Wars of the Roses to college classes studying Shakespeare's *Richard III*.

Married since 1987, Nancy and her husband have one son, a bossy dog, and a house full of books.

For more information about Nancy and her books, check out http://www.nancynorthcott.com.

You can also connect with Nancy on social media.

facebook.com/nancynorthcottauthor
twitter.com/NancyNorthcott
goodreads.com/Nancy_Northcott
pinterest.com/nancynorthcott

ALSO BY NANCY NORTHCOTT

FANTASY

The Boar King's Honor Trilogy:

The Herald of Day

The Steel Rose

The King's Champion (forthcoming)

SCIENCE FICTION

The New Badge, a novella in the *Welcome to Outcast Station* anthology

Scorpions for Christmas, a novella in the *Christmas on Outcast Station* anthology

"Justice for Tillie," a short story in the *Predators in Petticoats* anthology

The Speaker for All, an Outcast Station novel (forthcoming)

ROMANTIC SUSPENSE

Danger's Edge, an Arachnid Files novella

Worth the Wait, an Arachnid Files novella

The Last Favor, an Arachnid Files novella in the

Christmas at Caynham Castle anthology

Mr. Never Again, an Arachnid Files novella in the

Trick or Treat at Caynham Castle anthology

ROMANTIC SPY ADVENTURE

The Deathbrew Affair, a Lethal Webs novel

www.ingramcontent.com/pod-product-compliance
Lightning Source LLC
Chambersburg PA
CBHW050616110726
47899CB00001B/127